About the autl

Uri Geller is the world's most investigated and celebrated paranormalist. A vegetarian and fervent promoter of peace, he has used his psychic gifts to track serial killers and work for the FBI and the CIA. He is the Mind-Power coach to Premier League footballers, industrialists, Formula One drivers and racing cyclists. As a columnist, he writes for *The Times* and *GQ*, as well as being syndicated in newspapers and magazines around the globe. The Honorary Vice-President of the Royal Hospital for Children in Bristol, and of the Royal Berkshire Hospital, close to his Thames-side mansion, Uri is the father of two teenagers and the author of eight bestsellers, including the novel, *Ella*.

Some of his books and lots of other incredible information and pictures are available on his Internet website at **www.tcom.co.uk/hpnet/** where you will find Uri's biography plus facts about him and his work. You can e-mail Uri at **urigeller@compuserve.com** or write to Headline Book Publishing, 338 Euston Road, London NW1 3BH England

Other books by Uri Geller

My Story, Praeger/Robson/Warner Books
Shawn, Goodyer Associates
The Geller Effect, Henry Holt/Jonathan Cape/Grafton
Uri Geller's Fortune Secrets, Sphere
Change Your Life In One Day, Marshall Cavendish
Uri Geller's Mind-Power Kit, Penguin/Virgin
Uri Geller's Little Book Of MindPower, Robson
Ella, Headline Feature
Uri Geller's Parascience Pack, Van der Meer
Mind Medicine, Element

Some books about Uri Geller

Uri, Andrija Puharich, Doubleday/Robson
The Amazing Uri Geller, Martin Ebon, New American Library
Uri Geller: Fup Eller Fakta? Leo Leslie, Samlerens Piccoloboger
The Strange Story Of Uri Geller, Jim Colin, Raintree (for children)
In Search Of Superman, John Wilhelm, Pocket Books
The Geller Papers, Charles Panati, Houghton Mifflin
The Geller Phenomenon, Colin Wilson, Aldus Books
Superminds, John G Taylor, Macmillan/Picador
The Metal Benders, John Hasted, Routledge and Kegan Paul
Mysterious Powers, Orbis Books
Uri Geller El Descubierto, Ramos Perera, Sedmay Ediciones
Uri Geller, Magician Or Mystic? Jonathan Margolis, Orion

DEAD COLD

Uri Geller

HEADLINE
FEATURE

First published in Great Britain in 1999
by HEADLINE BOOK PUBLISHING

A HEADLINE FEATURE hardback and softback

10 9 8 7 6 5 4 3 2 1

British Library Cataloguing in Publication Data

Geller, Uri
Dead cold
1. Suspense fiction
I.Title
823.9'14 [F]

ISBN 0 7472 2128 6 (hardback)
ISBN 0 7472 7644 7 (softback)

Typeset by Palimpsest Book Production Limited,
Polmont, Stirlingshire
Printed and bound in Great Britain by
Mackays of Chatham PLC, Chatham, Kent

HEADLINE BOOK PUBLISHING
A division of Hodder Headline PLC
338 Euston Road
London NW1 3BH

Dedicated to the memory of the Chairman of the Board,
Frank Sinatra,
who died during the writing of this book.

Panagiotis Michalakopoulos

One thing leads to another,
Too late to run for cover,
She's much too close for comfort now!

Frank Sinatra: Too Close for Comfort
Bock/Holofcener/Weiss – Carlin Music Corp/Memory Lane Music Ltd, 1959

CHAPTER ONE

The first thing I want you to understand is I could never survive without Mimi.

The second thing is, I talk a lot. A lot a lot. So if this veers off the point from time to time, bear with me. I do radio, you've got to fill the gaps. The worst thing with radio is long silences. The second worst is short silences. Any kind of a silence is bad.

My publisher says books aren't like this. I got to stop and pick my words. But I tell him – I stop, I dry. I'll just let it flow. I'm doing this in one take, and if I use the wrong word now and then – who's noticing?

OK, from the top, because that's the only way to tell a story. From start to finish. You want flashbacks, dream sequences, whatever, this is the wrong book. I try to do flashbacks, I get lost. Believe me, keep it simple. You want flashbacks, read Proust.

So it starts on a Thursday. Definitely a Thursday. I wouldn't normally remember what I said on which show, largely because I'm making it up as I go along, but this show is fixed in my mind. Because of the very bad things that happened to me the next day.

I was sitting where I always sit, across the desk from Kerry. Mimi was beaming at me through the window, signalling thumbs-up, 'Everything's going to be great!' And suddenly I got this bad, bad feeling. Everything was not going to be great.

God knows why. It isn't as if I'm psychic.

I guess you thought I was, if you ever heard my radio show. If you're the kind who listens to radio psychics, you probably believe in your horoscope, and lucky lottery numbers, and spooky coincidences, headless nuns on the stairs, magic crystals, all that stuff. Maybe you're pretty shocked to hear the truth. I know, I put on a good act. Sometimes I believe it myself. So I guess I've got some explaining to do.

The first thing is Mimi. She sits in the engineer's booth, with the

1

producer, and she takes the calls. She screens out the screwballs, and she quizzes the rest of them.

Anyone who phones in is hoping to get on the radio. That's the whole point. If they wanted a serious consultation, they'd write and ask for a personal one-to-one. It happens, once in a while. Mainly in the fall, for some reason. I charge £35 an hour and let the client do all the talking.

Radio's different. I have to get the ball rolling. I have to be psychic. That's what it's all about. But because the callers want to be on radio, they don't mind telling Mimi a few personal things. She starts off nice and simple – name ('Is that your real name, the one you were born with?') and address ('Are you calling from home?') and age ('Have you been a fan of Mikki's for long, then?')

After that it's, 'And what did you want to talk to Mikki about?' Usually they go coy then, they say, 'Well, he's psychic, he can tell *me* what it's about.' So Mimi agrees and she checks helpfully on a couple of facts ('It could be five or ten minutes before he gets to you, you don't mind waiting? You're not too busy? You know it's a Freefone number, don't you? So do you listen often?')

All the time she's tapping notes and comments into the terminal at her end of the mixing desk. And what she types comes up on the studio VDU.

She's very good at her job, my little Mimi. She looks after me.

I'd trust her judgement without question. So why, before that show, on that Thursday, when her happiness was shining in her funny round face and her excited thumbs were waggling at me, was I getting such a bad feeling?

I glanced at the monitor. Only two lines of type, and I had to lean over a little to read it. Thin black letters on a blue background – maybe these computer people have shares in Optrex.

'Sarah Whelan, Mrs. Age 47. Lives Evans Grove, Hounslow. Wants to know if animals pass over to the other side. PS thinks you're lovely. I let her keep believing it.'

I managed to grin at Mimi. She grinned back, which made her slanting eyes disappear altogether. Her face reminded me of a happy little apple, with spots of red on her yellow cheeks. The fringe of her hair was very straight, very severe, like a black plastic helmet – something out of a Samurai movie. Not that she was Japanese. I offended her once with that assumption. She was a Londoner, and her parents were South Korean.

She forgave me the offence. Mimi liked forgiving me.

2

I slipped the cans over my head. One ear on, one ear off – otherwise you can't hear yourself think over the echo when you start talking.

They were playing my song. One of my songs, anyhow. 'New York New York'. Sinatra. Anything by Sinatra rates as one of my songs. I claim them as my own.

That uneasy feeling melted away, and the music must have been making me look happy, because Kerry flashed one of her looks at me. Some smile that girl had. Wasted on radio. Bright blue eyes. And blonde hair, brushed straight back from her forehead and behind her little pink ears. Everybody was expecting her to head into television any day now, and they'd been expecting it for three years. Maybe when Kerry Allison said she liked radio, she meant it.

She pressed the fader on Frankie and said: 'That's "New York New York" which can only mean our very own Boy from Hoboken, ol' brown eyes is back – hello, Mikki.'

Now I don't know where Kerry got the idea I come from Hoboken like Sinatra, because the fact is I come from across the river in Brooklyn. But she always says it, and maybe it's because I told her it was true. These things happen. So I don't correct her.

I said, 'Hi, Kerry, nice to be here. My senses are telling me something and I don't believe the listeners are picking up on it.'

'Tell us then?' She looked at me and fiddled with her hair-grip. I sometimes teased her on air, and she didn't know quite how to deal with it. She liked it, but she tried not to get drawn in.

'You've bought something new to keep the hair out of your eyes. Kind of got tiger stripes on it. See, I never said this was my psychic sense. It's just everyone listening in, they can't see you. Kerry has long golden hair, if you don't know, but without a hairslide her face disappears. The curtain comes down.'

'I had a boyfriend once who told me when that happened I looked like I had a lampshade on my head.'

'I'm glad he's in the past tense. Never go out with a man who compares you to an item of furniture.'

I glanced up at Mimi. She wasn't smiling. She couldn't stand me flirting with Kerry. I winked at her, and she forgave me. I think I told you already, she liked forgiving me.

That bit of banter, it serves a purpose. Maybe you thought it was the radio equivalent of tooth fillings, plugging the gaps. It's more than that. The listeners need to settle. A new voice stirs them up – who's this, what's he talking about, sorry where were we? So I chat

3

a bit, let them get used to my voice, mention the words 'psychic' and 'energy' once or twice.

OK, on with the show. Let's go to the phones. 'Hi, who's this?'

'This is Sarah. Hello, Mikki.'

A friendly voice. Thank you, Mimi. Sometimes they can be very aggressive, and I have to admit aggressive is something I find hard to handle. I don't mind a good debate, I can even handle an argument. But aggressive is when they snarl out a word or two and then go silent on me. 'You think you know it all.' That's one. 'If you're psychic why aren't you a millionaire?' That's another. Most radio hosts would just snap something aggressive back, but that isn't my style. I tried to sound wise and pitying a few times, but it just came over all nervous. So I figure it's best to pretend I heard nothing, close the line and go to the next caller. After all, who's in control here?

Conversation not confrontation, that's my motto.

'Hello, Sarah, I seem to sense a sadness in your voice.'

'Well, yes . . .'

'In fact it's something deeper-lying than your voice, because maybe you feel this is a sadness that's hard to express.'

'Mikki, that's so right.'

Of course it's right. She already told Mimi why she's calling – do animals have an afterlife, she wants to know. And the only reason for that is she's just lost a pet. So she's sad. Only people aren't supposed to take it so hard when it's just a pet that died. It's kind of like saying your pet meant more to you than most people.

So be honest. Of course your pet meant more. You loved it. It loved you. You find a human being means that much to you, you marry them.

I'd say this to Sarah, but I'm not an agony uncle. The show has one of those already. I'm the psychic.

'Are you sad about an animal? Because if that's the case, I don't think you have to be.'

'Why? Why? Do you . . .'

'I sense a presence.'

'Oh! Is it—?'

Well, come on, Sarah! Is it *what*? Do I have to guess what kind of animal it was? Give me a name at least! But she's too choked up to get the words out. This is a little tricky. I don't want to sound like I'm fishing for hints. But I'm used to this. It's what I do for a living.

'Now I'm going on impressions here. I'd like to emphasise I

don't know anything about Sarah. I don't even know your second name, do I?'

'No, no, we've never spoken before. But you can sense—?'

God, she's crying again.

'Sarah, please. I sense much warmth, much love here.'

'Yes, she was a very loving little thing.'

Thing! *Thing!* Is that any way to talk of a dear departed pet? It tells me nothing.

'Very faithful,' Sarah adds.

Faithful! So dogs are faithful . . . 'That type always are.'

'Well, the word is variety. To a breeder.'

Variety! What comes in varieties? Apart from Heinz tinned foods? Fish – but when are fish loving and faithful?

Mimi is at the window, flapping her arms. This is studio lingo for, 'We've got a crisis on here,' but the producer is staring remotely at the ceiling. Some crisis.

Flap! Flap!

Got it! I want to stand up and shout, 'Bird! Bird!' But I don't.

'I feel this little spirit, fluttering around the studio. And I get an impression of vivid colour . . .'

'Edna was an Amazon macaw, the most gorgeous parrot you've ever seen.'

A dead parrot. What was this, Monty Python?

'And I can assure you, Sarah, that beyond the veil Edna still is.'

'Thank you, Mikki, thank you so much.'

Well, not at all. That's what it's all about. Doesn't hurt anyone, cheers a few people up every day, provides some general entertainment. Everything in life should be like this.

CHAPTER TWO

The spidery letters on the blue screen read: 'Eric Vasey, 61, lives Shooter's Hill. Says he's got a worry about his future. Bit nervy about taking psi-power seriously.'

No problem.

'Eric, before you say a word, I'm getting a very strong impression of you. I know you've told my production assistant your name and address, but that's all – and yet, this is uncanny, I'm finding it pretty spooky but I feel like I know you better than your best friend.

'You are no fool. That's very strong. And you prefer the company of people who are also intelligent – but if they aren't up to your mark, you exercise patience. In fact, basically your temperament is self-contained, you can cope without people and you might even get on better, but you have this talent for working and socialising with others. Your sense of humour helps a lot there, even though it tends to mask a serious and thoughtful person. I know you try not to show it, but there are great wells of sensitivity in your personality, Eric. I think you feel things very deeply. That's under the surface. People see a confident, outgoing man, someone who can be a perfectionist and at the same time you don't like to be snowed under with irrelevant detail. That adds up to a pretty complex guy, Eric – but shall I tell you why I can read it so exactly? Because you're focused. You can home in on your objective. And that strength of mind is like a beam of energy hitting me right now.'

'Mikki, that's . . . that's pretty good. Amazing.'

'You made it easy, Eric.'

I didn't tell him the tough part was making it sound different from what I always tell everyone. That was a perfect Cold Reading. How much of it was he going to disagree with? Who wants to hear they are stupid, impatient, arrogant, a sheep, friendless, humourless, frivolous, thoughtless, insensitive, introverted, careless, an anorak, a simpleton and a dilettante?

Plus, that stuff is so vague. Now it's up to Eric to paint in the detail, which he duly does, assuming that I know him inside-out so why hide anything?

He was worried about money, and I told him not to expect a big windfall but stick to his budget, and that way his guardian angel would make certain there was always just enough to survive on.

It would be irresponsible of me to say, 'I see a giant lottery win, so stop worrying and start spending.' That wasn't even what he wanted to hear. He just wanted to know he would cope. And without wanting to go in detail into his finances, I knew he would cope. He'd coped for sixty-one years, after all. The future always looks scary if you try to take big bites out of it. Just go for one day at a time – that's all you'll ever be asked to manage.

Damn, I took a wrong career turn somewhere. I really should have been an agony uncle. Or a priest.

Most agony preachers are ex-doctors, obviously. Failed doctors, sometimes, but at least they got as far as failing their exams. I got as far as being kicked off the second year of my American Commerce college course. And my religion, very nominally, is Greek Orthodox. I never thought I'd look too good with a beard like a tea-tray.

Of course, you wouldn't know. You've only seen me on the radio.

There's a black pane of glass next to Mimi's window. This is the Privileged Guests Area, where the station directors take anyone they want to impress. Reclining leather seats, opaque Pyrex coffee tables. You can smoke, but cigars only. And because of the way it's lit, with big bright lighting in the studio and a kind of join-the-conspirators'-club dusk in the suite, they can see us and we can't see them. All we can see is our reflections. To be accurate, I can see myself but Kerry would have to turn round.

If one of these Privileged types tells me, 'I was watching you through the one-way glass,' of course I answer mysteriously, 'I was perfectly aware when your eyes were on me – and when they were elsewhere.' Guilty conscience, everybody's got one. It takes a psychic to spot it.

So I find I'm looking at my reflection from time to time. I'd be lying if I said I hated what I saw. I'm an OK-looking guy. It's the Mediterranean blood. We're Greeks. Third generation Americans, but very racially pure. One hundred per cent Greek peninsula. No European contamination. My father used to say, 'I'd sooner have cut my dick off than marry a girl from Macedonia.' Which didn't stop

7

the old goat chasing the women from the pretzel bakery at the back of our tenements, but then I don't believe he ever went closer to our ancient homeland than Dimitris Taverna in Queens. He was always too scared to fly.

Which doesn't tell you anything about my reflection. Or maybe it does. I look like my name – Panagiotis Michalakopoulos. Call me Mikki. My curls are almost black, my eyes are so brown they're almost black, and if I don't shave in the afternoon, I eat dinner with a very black and piratical stubble. My looks are on the romantic side. Mimi wanted me to wear gold hoops in my ears, but that would be too much tinsel on the Christmas tree. Plus, if my brothers ever saw me, they'd think I had gone gay. I said to Mimi, 'You want to tie up my head in a red bandanna too.' You could see she thought it might be rather fetching.

That's the truth why I'm a psychic. With looks like mine you've got to do something unorthodox. People expect it. And when you start telling their fortunes, they believe you.

You want to try an experiment? Get your hair cut, wear a three-piece suit with blue braces and a big tie, stand in Covent Garden market and offer to do astrological readings. It's inappropriate behaviour. You'll get no takers. But put a dark-eyed rascal in the same place, with tight denims and a leather jacket, and there'll be two dozen eager folks thronging him inside a minute. Believe me. I've tried it.

That's how I got thrown out of college, for doing astrology readings. Plus, I shouldn't have been generating them on one of the faculty's Apple Macs. And particularly I shouldn't have taken the Mac home with me for the purpose. I appreciated that, when it was explained to me. I tried to be very contrite about it, but there's only so far you can get with being contrite.

Anyhow, that episode launched me on my career, and not everyone on my course can say the New Jersey Institute of Business and Commercial Studies did so much for them.

What I learned from astrology was this: People like to hear good things about themselves. You don't need a psychic to tell you that. They also like to hear bad things. In moderation. And especially, bad things about people close to them.

'You're mother's going to suffer an illness – you'll be intensely worried, but she'll recover.' That always goes down well. I mean, analyse it. You've got the relief of knowing that where your stars portend serious illness, it isn't for you directly. And then maybe your mother deserves a bit of a going-over from your celestial aspects. You come out of it well, glowing colours – you're worried about her. Intensely worried. Going to look good, right? And there's no guilt trip at the end, because everyone lives happily ever after.

I use that one a lot.

My first programme was the basic package by Silver Starways Inc, a Californian company who sell divination software and nothing else. Maybe they're sincere. Maybe they truly believe a computer can paranormally take on the attributes of its user. Maybe they've got an eye for a fast buck.

No complaints about the software. It came with a fonts package that let me print out an entire alphabet of mystic symbols. It generated skymaps for any night this century. It calculated conjunctions, squares, sextiles, trines and oppositions with one push of a button. And all it asked in return was a date of birth. It didn't even demand those irritating specifics, like precise time of day, or latitude and longitude. This software was smart. It could fudge the pedantic stuff.

Then one day it let me down.

I could be fashionable and accept the responsibility, like counsellors say you've got to. But let's be honest – this was a software limitation. I was advertising, in all innocence, 'Hand-drawn star charts, personally compiled readings, attractive presentation – only $20.' And a guy claimed his reading contained 35 per cent identical phrases to his room-mate's reading.

What was worse, his room-mate wasn't even one of my customers. He'd answered some tacky ad in the *Weekly World News*.

The guy was threatening to sue me, and he didn't just want his twenty back. He wanted a personal reading. And not from me either. I ended up forking out $250 to a bona fide, genuine, Romany-blood-and-second-sight psychic operating out of Vermont for a hand-written analysis of this guy's inner self. And I swear there weren't two sentences that meant a thing in plain English.

I learnt an important lesson. Don't be afraid to make this stuff up yourself. And don't be afraid to charge for it.

All of which has nothing to do with me, sitting in London PrimeTime's Studio No 1 with the very blonde and blushing Kerry Allison. Except to explain how I got here. And maybe to help you understand that for certain reasons, which I'll expand on later, I might be required to leave in a hurry.

9

CHAPTER THREE

The blue screen said simply, 'Lucas Willens. Age 34. Lives on Southampton Row. Another guy who thinks you're the Second Coming.'

Oh Christ. I was expecting this. It was probably why I felt uneasy before the show began. We'd had weirdos phoning in every day for a week from this loonytoon church looking for a saviour.

Dumb cults.

The Evangelists of Superhuman Perfection – they called themselves ESP-people. Don't ask me what was supposed to be superhuman about them. Or perfect. I can't stand it when people have these half-stewed ideas and can't be happy until they're dragging you along with them. It's like they won't be so insane if they can find other airheads to say, 'Yes! Yes! I have seen the Light too.'

Not this airhead, thank you. I have no grand conception of the universal scheme, and I'm keeping it that way. If God had a plan, I didn't ever want to know about it.

I'll come clean, when we got the first call I was amused. That had been about ten days earlier, and it was an earnest girl offering me the chance to be Jesus Christ II. The Deity, Part Deux. These ESP-people had some venerable guru with a long white beard and a neat line in prophecy, and since he was at death's door they were canvassing for a replacement. Job specs: Must be charismatic, psychic and in good health. Good candidates were apparently hard to find. I couldn't think why, till I asked about the pay. 'We are dedicated to poverty,' the girl said solemnly.

'Maybe I should apply anyhow,' I said after the show. 'I always thought it would be fun to be worshipped.'

'It can't be a very good cult,' Kerry said. 'Not if their guru is dying. If you're going to be a saviour, you should at least choose a religion that lets you be immortal.'

So when another cultee called in the next morning, I told her so. 'Eternal life or nothing,' I said, 'it's non-negotiable.' Which got the

10

Christians stirred up. Did I realise that eternal life was exactly what Our Blessed Lord was offering? They rang up in scores. And too late I remembered one cardinal rule of paranormal radio – keep religion out of it.

That begged the question: what in hell was Mimi playing at today? Were we at the barrel's bottom? Was Lucas Willens the only person in south-east England who wanted to talk to me? I tried to look angry and bewildered at my faithful assistant. I guess I just looked anxious. She made 'keep calm, don't panic' gestures. So I took the call.

Lucas Willens was very nice. He didn't have any questions, he just wanted me to send healing energy to his guru. Madox Bligh was the guru's name, and he'd suffered a paralysing stroke.

I sidestepped: 'There's a terrible number of sick people in London. Of course I hope your guru gets better. But I'm sure he'd be the first to admit, he's an old man. And there are children who need every scrap of healing energy we've got to offer. So everybody listening, join with me to pray for the children. They're the ones who need it most of all.'

I always let my voice go quiet and low when I'm doing this. Insistent, intense, understated. Some people get worked up in a frenzy, but that isn't me. I concentrate on sincerity. And I am sincere – God knows, I'd like to help sick children if I could. It can't be hurtful to say prayers over the radio. I've seen statistics, scientific experiments into helping people heal with prayer-power. It seems to have a beneficial effect.

I never quite understood it, because you'd think prayer would either work 100 per cent or not at all. I mean, is God up there sifting the quality of prayers? Or the volume? Do you have to score a certain number of really heartfelt pleas before he zaps the sickness away? Or does it depend on whether he likes you? Because some people get prayed for very volubly, and they die anyway. Is God being personal there? Makes me wonder.

People like to join in, so it makes good radio, whatever. The interactive element.

At the end of the prayer, I thought this guy Lucas Willens had gone, but he was still there. Persistent little cult. 'Thanks for putting your whole soul into those inspirational words,' he said. 'And I think you already know, Mikki – you have many true admirers among the Evangelists of Superhuman Perfection. Why don't you come and see us one day? Soon?'

'I'll take a raincheck,' I said, tugging my forefinger across my throat vigorously. The producer wasn't looking. Mimi gave him a nudge. He got the picture. Lucas Willens disappeared off the screen.

I guess my face was thunderclouds, because Kerry bounced in, and she doesn't usually interrupt. 'Mikki's segment this morning is very uplifting. As it always is. And I sense he needs a moment to recharge his psychic batteries here. So let's play some music. You know we always have plenty of Frank Sinatra in the CD players when Mikki's about. And maybe Sinatra is listening in, somewhere up there. Who knows? Ring us if you happen to know any psychic anecdotes about Ol' Blue Eyes – we'd love to hear them. Meanwhile, here's "Stardust".'

Mimi was concentrating on a call. Her head was bowed, and I could only see the crown of her head. A pale line of scalp shone between the two black sweeps of her hair.

I took a couple of long, deep breaths. Sometimes people think I must be meditating when I do this. Actually it means I want a cigarette. That's another reason why I remember it was a Thursday, the day before this nightmare stuff started – it was exactly four weeks and two days since I quit smoking. That type of milestone sticks in your mind.

On the screen Mimi's typing was scrolling up. 'Serious caller. Kris Ingman. Psychology professor. Wants you to participate in an experiment.'

I stared at her, but she was still totally involved in this call. Her left hand was typing, but she wasn't looking at it. Mimi was full of clever tricks like that. I couldn't even type, at least not on the studio terminal. There was no keyboard.

What was she doing to me today? Religious nuts, women with dead parrots, now psychology experiments. Didn't people want Tarot readings any more? What was she telling me, there was no future in being a psychic? (OK, so that's an old joke. But it's one of my favourites.)

I didn't like serious calls. This was live radio. You could make a mistake, take a wrong decision, and 440,000 independently audited listeners across the Greater London region heard you do it. No alibi.

At last Mimi looked up. I held out my hands to her, imploring her. Please Mimi, find me a nice caller. But she just grinned and gave me the double thumbs-up.

I felt such a beast, scowling back. Like I was an ungrateful child. Mimi kept grinning and grinning. She couldn't believe I was ever really cross with her. This must have been some kind of game.

I took the call. I should have pulled out the jack and dropped the headphones in a bucket of water. But I took the call.

CHAPTER FOUR

A deep, precise voice said: 'My name is Professor Johannes-Kristian Ingman.' His accent was European – I mean he didn't sound American or English. Maybe Russian. 'Is that true or false?'

'Who cares?' I said. 'I thought you were a serious caller. My mistake. Let's go to the next line.'

But there wasn't a next line.

'Forgive me,' Ingman said. His voice was slow, smooth and powerful. Like coffee dregs. 'I gave way to the temptation to set a little trap.'

'Listen, Prof, this airtime isn't for people to show off their big brains. It's about helping people. You want to set little traps, play some checkers or whatever it is you intellectuals do.'

'Touché,' said Ingman. I stared up at Mimi. She was looking aghast at me. She knew she'd fouled up. There was no big grin now.

She started and grabbed at the phone. Before she'd spoken half a dozen words, I was nodding at her, waving my arms. My gestures said, 'I don't care who it is – put them on. I want that caller!'

But Mimi was shaking her head.

And during all this pantomime I had to keep talking.

'You professors must be short of things to do, you have to ring up radio shows to make clever remarks. What's wrong with your lectures? Don't any students turn up?'

'I must say, you startle me, Mikki. I have not heard you angered before.'

'Well, maybe I've taken a sudden dislike to you.' I was imploring Mimi with my eyes. Begging. I *wanted* that caller.

But she put down the receiver.

I was stuck with the intellectual.

'Do you often dislike people?'

'Almost never. I like everybody. Except you.'

'Remarkable. I wonder what kind of energy I emit that troubles you.'

'Soundwaves,' I said. 'It's called words. I don't like the ones you use.'

'Such a great pity that is. Because I was about to use words which I am quite certain you would like.'

'So shoot.'

'I want to pay you £5,000. For two hours' work.'

Professor Ingman could have no idea how much I would like £5,000. No exaggeration to say £5,000 was the sum I wanted most in the whole world, £5,000 was the missing link between me and a massive alteration to my mode of living not to mention dying. £5,000 translated to maybe 8,000 bucks, which made it sound even better. £5,000 I would do a lot for. A lot a lot.

And, incidentally, it was about £4,999.98 more than I could expect to be laying my hands on, in the foreseeable future. The foreseeable future, obviously, being my speciality.

None of which would it do to admit on air. I said, 'Forget it.'

'You surprise me. Again.'

'Money doesn't interest me.'

'But we all need it.'

'Now that isn't a clever, intellectual thing to say, Professor. To me that sounds like a cliché. If anyone's got an interesting psychic question, right now would be a good time to call – 0800 611 0110. It's a free call. Pick up that phone and make the connection.'

Psychology – if he was serious about his £5,000, he'd come back at me. If he wasn't I didn't lose anything. Psychology. He was a professor of it, so it ought to work on him.

'I shall make my point clearly and concisely, as I should have done at first, and I apologise for wasting your time. I am in charge of the parapsychology unit at University College London, and having been convinced of the genuineness of your psychical abilities, by listening to your broadcasts for some weeks past, I am inviting you, in return for suitable remuneration at the sum stated, to participate in some controlled investigations into telepathy, clairvoyance and prediction – that is to say, extra-sensory perception – to provide our experimenters with a benchmark, a high-water mark if you like, which demonstrates the results which can be expected from a subject possessing highly developed paranormal powers.'

Mimi was grinning again. She was waving the receiver in her hand. There was nothing on my screen but, whoever it was on the line, they were about to make me very happy. A superficial, shallow, cheap happiness, but none the less satisfying for that.

15

I let the professor steam to his appointed destination, and said: 'I'll think about it. Now who's this calling?'

'Ooh, Mikki,' an old lady chirruped, 'I'm Veronica and I think your attitude to money is just lovely. That silly man, offering you £5,000. As if that could matter to you.'

As if.

Dan Nally, the producer, got up and walked out of the room when I came in. I don't imagine it was personal. Dan never wasted time on social chit-chat – you know, stuff like answering basic questions or saying 'Hi'.

I don't think he'd even acknowledge my existence, unless I was standing over the desk and threatening to pull out a handful of his little red plugs. Maybe not then. But he was like that to everyone.

He could sit and stare out the window when Mimi was talking to him. And when she finished, he'd say nothing. Just let the silence go on and on. That's so rude. It bothered me at first, I like everyone to like me. Mimi says I don't understand why anyone could dislike me, which has the ring of truth. But I think Dan couldn't afford to like people, because he hated himself. It certainly seemed that way. He didn't take pleasure in any damn thing.

If a show went well, he got up and banged out of the room the second it was over – just the same as he did if it went indifferently, or disastrously. He hated his job, and he hated himself for doing it. I couldn't see why, and I didn't waste much time wondering. Most media people would love to have a crack at producing a radio programme. I know I would. But that was his problem. I don't know why I bothered mentioning it.

Mimi was doodling on her notepad, a mass of spirals and mazey lines. She was wearing an orange jacket. It was one of my favourites – we'd bought it together at Kookai in Knightsbridge, after a pizza lunch. Orange looked good on her – the contrast with her black hair.

'That could have been worse,' she said.

'I could have been abducted by sex-crazed aliens,' I agreed.

'They'd get more than they bargained for with you.' Mimi didn't have an accent – at least she sounded like all the other Londoners I knew, and I hadn't ever learned to tell if they came from north or south of the river. But she had a sing-song way of talking, which sounded Chinesey. What I mean is, Koreany.

I used to tell her she should smoke, because then she'd sound husky and sing-songy, and the combination would be devastating.

'Why'd you dump that professor in my face? Do you secretly hate me now?'

She looked guilty. 'I'm sorry. You should have heard him off air. He couldn't be nice enough about you. Saying how he listened every day, how you were the only totally genuine psychic he ever heard of, this was his specialist field and he wanted to pay you a lot of money to do his experiments and make you famous.'

'And you thought, "He says he's a professor, he must be telling the truth"?'

'I thought, "He can go on air and say all these lovely things about Mikki".'

'And I could go to his university and be very psychic and earn lots of money?'

'Of course.'

I watched her, still doodling on the pad. I'd never come straight out and said, 'Mimi, you know I'm not honestly psychic – I'm just what you'd call a good guesser.' She was always so impressed when I tickled the truth out of a caller and made it look like I'd known all along. But she must have realised how much help her little hints gave me. And sometimes, like the business with the dead parrot, she was better at guessing than me.

'These tests. Do you think I have to pass them before I get paid?'

Mimi shrugged. 'He said he'd pay you to take them, not pass them. But the idea was you'd be top-of-the-scale. The target for everyone else. Which you would.'

'Your confidence touches me.'

'So you aren't cross?'

'Mimi, Americans don't get cross. Only the English get cross. We get mad.'

'Are you mad?'

'To work here, I must be.'

'Boom boom.'

'What?'

'Boom boom. When I was little there was a fox that said . . . forget it.'

'A fox that said, a talking fox?'

'Forget it.'

'Mimi, you've been very unbalanced today. I want you to get your head looked at. Take the doodles. They probably mean something.

17

So you've got the professor's phone number? He wrecks my show, the least he can do is pay me five juicy ones.'

She looked at her pad, and held it out. 'I think he was on there. Somewhere.'

I stared at the dark, scrawling mass. 'Now,' I said, 'I am mad.'

CHAPTER FIVE

I may have talked too much about Mimi. I don't want to give the impression there was anything going on.

That was all over.

She'd been very understanding about it. She knew I didn't hang around in relationships. She'd known me for long enough before we started dating. Dating is the wrong word – we started screwing.

I'd been in England about eight months, I'd been at the station most of that time, and Mimi was assigned to me on Day One. I got through three or four girls in the first three or four months, and I talked to her about them – not that Mimi was my special confidante, but I just enjoyed talking about my relationships. They were casual, they didn't hurt too much – OK, I think sometimes some people got hurt, but those people didn't turn out to be me.

You probably don't like me very much for saying that, but I feel I should be honest with you. There's no point in showing my hand, telling you I'm a bit of a trickster in the brainwaves department, then lying about my relationships.

But hell, I think you know me well enough already. I'm not the kind of guy to promise a girl the stars and the moon. Or if I do inadvertently get carried away, it's obvious to anyone I don't mean what I'm saying. Nobody seriously regarded me as marriage material.

Mimi and I flirted for the first few months. She made it fairly clear that we could get together if I liked. She was never heavy. She just liked me, and let me see it. I liked her. She had a lovely round face. It was sometimes all I could do to stop myself leaning down and kissing her on her small, scarlet lips. But I worked with Mimi. It didn't seem clever to risk messing up a very useful working partnership.

And one night it was her birthday – she was thirty, she's a few years older than me – and we all went over the road to the David Copperfield, which was named after the boy from Dickens and not the magician from Metuchen, New Jersey. And Mimi and me, we ended up in bed. I accused her the next day of getting me drunk on cherry brandy and taking advantage. But it was too late. The dirty deeds were done. So we started going together.

Naturally we talked of nothing else but work. Well, not nothing, not 100 per cent – but it hung over all our conversation. Work even hung over the bed. We were sleeping partners for about two months, which is quite long enough, and I think we were getting a bit sick of it. I say, 'I think'. What I mean is, I know I was.

And then something happened, not connected with Mimi except it had the effect of breaking us up. She was fine about it. Like I said, she enjoyed forgiving me. She'd had two months of coddling me day and night, and that's probably the maximum limit for any woman on earth. You can have too much of a good thing. She still got to take care of me five mornings a week.

What Mimi didn't currently know, and what she might not have forgiven so easily, was that I'd been sleeping with Kerry for the past week.

Now this was stupid. It was dumb enough to risk a good working relationship with my production assistant. To do it with the show's host was a kamikaze sex mission. Plus, it hadn't been easy. There was no getting giggly and falling into bed with Kerry. She had to be pursued.

All I can say is there was provocation. First, she was decidedly a looker, and totally unattached. She'd dumped her last boyfriend about a month after I went to London PrimeTime. She had eyes like blue paint swirled in glass. Second, she never showed the slightest interest in me, and she didn't know how to flirt. A very serious girl. Which obviously is a challenge. Third, I was going through a very tough stage in my life, and what I needed was the distraction of an ill-advised affair.

How ill-advised it would be, if Mimi ever caught on to what we were doing, I never liked to think. Kerry wasn't going to tell anyone. She was ashamed of how unprofessional she was being. Inside the station building, there was no hint in her manner to me. No in-jokes, no secret glances, no hidden touches. Outside the building was just the same. It was only in her flat, with the doors locked, that she let herself rip.

Rip was the word. But I've got more self-respect than to start telling you the details.

I didn't hear her walk into the production room. I was too busy trying to read Mimi's doodle-pad with X-ray eyes.

Kerry said, 'Well? You going to do it?'

'Kill Mimi? I should. Will you go alibi for me?'

She laughed, because it was obviously a joke and she knew that's what you did with jokes. But sense of humour wasn't Kerry's zone. 'I mean the experiment. That professor.' She stopped behind me and breathed, 'Hey,' like a revelation had come down upon her. 'You could do it live on air.'

'I could be blindfolded,' I said. 'That would make such dramatic radio.'

'We could make it work.'

'No. We couldn't. Because Mimi has done a big black Rorschach all over the prof's number.'

'He'll call back,' said Mimi hopefully.

'Sure he will. I was so nice to him.'

'You really went for the guy,' Kerry said. 'Not your usual self.'

'Yeah, well, I've got worries.'

'Don't bring them into the studio,' she said primly.

'That reminds me,' Mimi piped.

'Reminds you what?'

'Anyway, if he doesn't call, you can ring him at London University,' she said, switching back.

'If I remembered his name.'

'Ingman. I know that much. I had to make him spell it.'

'Maybe,' I said.

'Ring him now.' Mimi lifted the receiver. 'I'll ask 192, they'll know the university numbers.' She really wanted me to do those tests and prove my psychic wonderpowers, beyond doubt, to the whole world.

'Maybe,' I said again. 'You said something reminded you.'

'Oh yeah.' She put the phone down, leaned forward and whispered. Not that there was anyone in the room but her, me and Kerry, and Kerry knew my problems. But Mimi whispered.

'Your wife called.'

CHAPTER SIX

I sat across the cold, marble-topped table from my wife, watching her feed a piece of stringy pasta into her face, and I thought there weren't enough words to describe her. She was one of those women who, just when you believe you've got them pinned down, turn out to have one more major personality flaw which you haven't begun to explore.

Living with Jane had been a revelation. I never realised anyone could be so heavy about everything. Every little thing. And not only sometimes, but she could keep it up too. We'd been married six weeks, and already I was at the point where just watching her eat pasta was enough to make death by strangulation an almost irresistible prospect. *Her* death, preferably, but failing that, mine.

She kept saying, 'Mmm.'

Not, 'Mmm, this is good pasta,' but 'Mmm, I'm about to say something and I can't because this stuff is stuck to my false teeth.'

Her tongue kept searching around the molars, and she kept thrusting more and more pieces between the twin wedges of lipstick, but in the end she had to poke one red-tipped finger into the corner of her mouth and scrape off the gunk with a nail.

'What do you see when you look at me?' she asked.

I didn't like to tell her.

'I'll tell you what you see. A gilt-edged British work permit. That's all I am to you. And I truly believe the money is secondary. I'm just the chance for you to keep doing your job.'

She didn't sound self-pitying. The note in her voice was triumphal, a points-scoring joy at being right as usual. With a little bit of hauteur on top. Haughty was one of the many good words for Jane. She could be like a headmistress from one of those old-fashioned British movies.

She had the looks for it. Her curls were grey with a sheen of royal blue. The hair colour had been added – so had the curls. The silver-chased emeralds in her ears were the size of squashed grapes.

She had a lined face, especially around the mouth, with jowls that could use a more constructive approach to make-up. Like surgery.

OK, I'm being unkind. I'm entitled to be. But you've a right to hear me tell the truth, and the truth is Jane was an attractive woman. I mean sexually; we're not talking about personality.

She expected to be obeyed. She always had been. If you were required to find her desirable, you dropped everything and fell into her arms. That was part of the attraction. But most of it was more basic than that. She had a ravening appetite for love. Not to say rapacious. Not to say plain randy. And that transmits itself to any man.

First time she told me her life story, she was forty-nine. I didn't argue, but I must have looked a bit shocked, because she added: 'To tell you the truth, I've been forty-nine for a little while now.' Coquettish. That was another of those good words that didn't come near the whole picture.

Just before we married, she whispered in my ear: 'Jane's been a naughty girl, Mikki. Guess what? She's been lying about her age.'

'I know. You're trying to mother me. I refuse to believe you're a day over forty.'

'You are a flatterer,' she told me, approvingly. 'But you really ought to know. I was fifty-three last birthday.'

I realise, glancing back over the weeks, that you, if you are a sensitive reader, might think that in the days before my wedding, my gallantry to Jane was a little nauseating. It could make you puke. It makes me want to puke, but for different reasons. So what can I do? Change the facts? As if.

Just don't try to eat and read at the same time.

She said she was fifty-three but I noticed in the register office she kept her hand over that part of the paperwork.

Let's fix this straight. I needed to marry Jane Lyons. I mean, I could doll it up in romance, like I had to get hitched to a senior citizen before I could inherit my eccentric Uncle Brewster's billions. Or maybe Cupid's dart had flown on wings of love across the generation gap. But the fact was I needed to fix my wedding day on June 13 latest, because June 14 my work permit ran out.

I was an American. I could have tried telling the immigration men I was a Euro national, but frankly my accent is none too Frenchified. The permit should have run a year but, owing to a slight miscalculation and a severe fit of optimism, I acquired the permit about four months before I could afford the airfare from

JFK. So I arrived at London's golden sidewalks with one-third of my work potential gone.

This was not a major source of anxiety. Eight months was plenty of time for something to turn up. Eight months was a lifetime – and, if I stayed in NY, it was likely to be a lot more than a lifetime. My lifetime, anyhow. I won't go into that. But it was time I got to see England.

Six months later, and I was eating, sleeping and working with Mimi, and I hadn't been elevated to the status of national icon, and I hadn't won any lotteries, and there had been a phone call the night before that I really don't want to talk about, and I suddenly woke up to a short-term future. Literally woke up – I was in Mimi's bed, which was only a single and that meant I had to dangle one shoulder-blade off the mattress. I'm a slender guy and Mimi's a lightweight but in a single bed, unless you're on top of each other, you're both falling out.

So it was quarter to six and light of course and at least half an hour before Mimi would agree to get up and make me coffee. And I was staring at the ceiling. Thinking life wasn't too bad, except I could do with a change of ceilings.

When it occurred to me that what I'd get, I'd get a change of continents, was what I'd get.

To go back to sleep after a jolt like that is not easy. I lay and added up all the best chances I had to stay in the country.

I could do a disappearing act. But that wasn't simple, given my name was on 200,000 radios every morning.

I could apply for British citizenship. But a minor conviction for an infringement of financial regulations, which written in single letters spelt F-R-A-U-D, might complicate that. It just looked so bad – past record, dishonestly selling 'psychic' character readings; current status, psychic radio presenter. People could draw unfair inferences.

I could pretend there wasn't a problem, which would be fine until the police came in the middle of a show to drag me away. Or I could beg the directors of London PrimeTime to pay me in cash and let me broadcast from a secret hideway. I seriously considered that one for a few minutes. Demonstrates the level of panic I was suffering when I hit on the brilliant solution.

I could marry.

As the husband of an Englishwoman, I'd be immune. No police were going to drag me away, no snidey civil servants were going to write 'unsuitable applicant' across my nationality papers. Love conquers all, even immigration officials. So who could I find to love me?

Mimi was the obvious choice, and the wrong one. She would have done it, no question – sacrificed herself on the altar of good radio. But she owned too much of me already. I didn't want her fixing my breakfast, sorting my show, and then taking me sofa shopping at Ikea after lunch. God, I'd feel like I was married to her.

That was not what I required. Genuine wives need not apply. What I wanted was some helpful female, currently unencumbered, who'd enjoy the scam of marrying Mikki simply for its own sake. No complications. When a decent interval had elapsed, I could pocket a British passport. Then an amicable separation.

No hard feelings. That was the idea.

None of the emotional tangle that was spoiling my relationship with Mimi. I was thinking about marriage. Naturally that meant sex, but whoever said it had to involve love?

Plus, there had been that phone call the night before. Very unexpected. On the other hand, I'd been waiting for it ever since I landed in England. I really don't want to go into details, but a name and a sum of money were mentioned. The name was Solomon's Child, and the debt was enough money that if I was ever going to enjoy a sense of long-term security – say, expecting to live till Christmas – I would need to find an extra source of income. Marriage might meet it.

I began to imagine an eligible Englishwoman. Maybe a more mature lady, since her well-lined bank account was more important than her innocent smile. She might be a widow, why not? Widows and older divorcées have very special charms. I should know. We psychics are irresistible to ladies of a certain vintage.

And when I started to think about it, this imaginary marriage would have another side-effect. This business with Mimi would get stopped, before it went too far. She was a strange girl in some ways. You don't want me to go into details, but she was intense about me, and she wanted me to do some intense things to her. She said she wanted to find extreme ways of proving she loved me. I told her, 'I'm red-blooded, but I draw the line at drawing blood.' I managed to pretend some of her weirder suggestions were just jokes, but frankly, we did a few things that I wouldn't want my mother to know about.

This was the plan, then: I had to get married to someone English, someone rich, and someone who wasn't Mimi.

I've sold this to you frankly. I haven't pulled punches. So surely you've got some sympathy. You don't have to adore me – but don't you agree I was a tiny bit unlucky to wind up with Jane Lyons?

CHAPTER SEVEN

I'd explain to you what Mimi thought of the whole idea, but I get the impression I've filled too much airtime about her already. So we'll say she got used to it, and come back to the details another time.

I was trying to tell you about Jane, but the pasta distracted me. We'll fast-forward a few minutes. This is the scene: she's finished eating, there's a couple of waiters leaning on a pillar who aren't collecting our plates, there's a few people eating at tables but not too near ours. We can talk. Over by the window a guy is eating fettucine. Bear him in mind – he matters later.

Jane said: 'You know very well you aren't properly married to me.'

'Oh yes I am.'

'You can't be. You've no right to be here at all. You're probably married to women all over the world. Nothing would surprise me now. I could have you thrown out of the country in a minute. That man by the window. He could be a policeman.'

'The porky guy with his tie showing under his collar? He's badly dressed enough.'

'I could snap my fingers and you'd be deported.'

'Jane. Darling. I'm your husband. They don't deport over a lovers' tiff.'

'Ah! Exactly! Let's count what you can be deported for. Lying on your visa application. Lying on the radio for a living. Being a member of the Mafia.'

'For God's sake, how could I be in the Mafia? I'm Greek.'

'I'm sure hoodlums don't split hairs.'

'You've got this insane thing about me being a gangster, and you know very well I'm nothing like that.'

'You're a criminal.'

'You don't have to yell it to all Kensington High Street. I have one tiny black mark against me. Hardly any worse than a parking violation.'

'It's what they haven't caught you for that counts.'

'Jane, I've said I'm sorry. I had some problems, and I should have told you earlier. I was embarrassed.'

'You were not embarrassed. You knew perfectly well there wasn't one girl in the country who would have married you under those circumstances.'

She was wrong there. But then, I had never mentioned anything to Jane about Mimi.

I said: 'Perhaps my status here was dubious. But luckily you married me. And no one can deny that.'

'Mikki, darling, you married my chequebook, my passport and my thighs. Did you imagine you could ignore the rest?'

'How could I ever ignore any part of you?'

'We'll have to find out. It appears to me that marrying your Englishwoman has left you free to fuck everything in a mini-dress between here and Islington.'

The two waiters still weren't collecting our plates but they were facing towards us now, with their ears flapping so hard that napkins were twitching in the breeze.

Strange what a load of bullshit is talked about the English being ruled by embarrassment. Jane Lyons was the queen of embarrassment. And this native New Yorker was curled up cringeing. I would have called for the bill and scuttled right out, but I was financially embarrassed as well.

I said: 'You'll be surprising me next with the news you're seeing your lawyers.'

'I see my lawyers all the time. Thank God.'

'Thousands of happy marriages aren't always . . .'

'The word is faithful.'

'Yes. Thank you.' I was trying to instil some reason into this row. 'You and I aren't dewey-eyed teenagers, Jane. We've loved before. We know the innermost secrets of the heart. That's a rare wisdom, granted to few before their time is all but over.'

I stared deeply into her contact lenses. Hypnotist's hint for you: don't look for the soul, just fix on the surface of the eyeball. And keep your voice ringing and even. It's hard to sound spiritual in a pasta parlour, but I was trying.

'Picture a film star's deathbed scene. The bride, garlanded with white blossoms, translucent with illness, faded almost to a shadow but suddenly, for the last few happy minutes of her life, made brilliant by joy.'

Jane went for this sort of thing. Usually. I wasn't sure it was clicking now. I pushed on: 'All because – the man she has doubted so painfully in their brief marriage is pledging himself to her. For eternity. Hers for all time. What does it matter then, if her earthly life is over within a few hours? He and she endure for ever. And it is a love beyond the urges of the flesh.'

Jane sat back in her seat and eyed me beadily. 'Are you promising to love me throughout time?'

'Of course,' I said weakly.

'And are you going to confess you've been sleeping around?'

'Of course not.'

'Isn't Ambrose's love going to endure throughout time as well?'

Ambrose was her first husband. He'd brought us together. I resented him for that, although he had been dead for seven years.

'I'll share you with Ambrose.'

'Well.' She kept eyeing me. I was starting to think I was over the worst. 'You married me for love, eh?'

'And not merely for lust.'

'Now there, I believe you're telling the truth.'

'I never lie, Jane.'

'Your life is a lie.'

And I began to suspect the worst hadn't happened yet.

'You married me for love, and you weren't desperate to extend your visa, and you really didn't want my money to save your skin, and you were telling the truth about everything Ambrose communicated to you.'

'Yes, yes, yes.'

'And there's been no one else?'

'Jane, how could you?' I really wrung the words. The waiters were popping their buttons to tune in and I think I sounded so sincere, one of them was weeping.

My wife made a jerky wave with one thickly ringed finger. 'Oh, Mr Marsh. Do you have those pictures?'

The fat man with the fettucine and the badly knotted necktie by the window shoved back his chair. He picked a cardboard folder from the floor beside him. Jane watched him approach. She showed her distaste with a grimace. And a dollop of smugness.

'Mr Marsh has been watching you, Mikki.'

I nodded and gave my best impression of a smile. It wouldn't have topped any talent parades. 'Most people don't watch, they listen to me,' I said.

29

'Hardly anyone listens to you, Mikki.'

That cut.

'Mr Marsh is a private eye. You Americans invented them, so you mustn't be appalled that I've been paying him to snoop and take pictures.'

'You used to appall me, Jane – now it's fading down to mild nausea.'

I shouldn't have said that. The situation was probably salvageable, up to that point. Messy, but within bounds. That little bubble of acid really burned her. Her eyes spat like flints. The remark was never going to be forgotten or forgiven.

This situation, the whole thing, the marriage, lurched into freefall.

'Show him the pictures, Mr Marsh.'

The whole restaurant were craning their necks. Mr Marsh pulled his face back into his chins and then jutted it importantly. He looked like a policeman, and I was his suspect. I recognised the relationship. If he'd had his way, he would have massaged my kidneys with a lead-weighted blackjack before opening his folder.

'These pictures were taken on July 29, the first of them at six eleven p.m., when the subject claimed to my client he was unavoidably detained at a meeting in his workplace,' said Mr Marsh.

'Talk normally. We're not in court. Yet,' snapped Jane.

I picked up the first snap, a Polaroid taken from about forty yards away. It was me – the image wasn't too clear, but it was like enough to corroborate Mr Marsh's assertion that he'd seen me. I was walking up the steps to Kerry's house, an eleven-roomed Victorian pile in Fulham divided into five flats. Kerry had the basement, which was nice when the sun shone and damp when it didn't – I'll tell you about it some other time.

I held the pic for half a second and tossed it onto the table. Mr Marsh proffered another, and I glanced without taking it. 'So?' I said.

'You were not where you claimed to be,' admonished the detective.

'So?'

'Mikki, if you're simply going to say "so", I'm going to become angry.'

'You'll become angry. You hire a dick to spy on me going to my boss's house, you confront me in a restaurant, and then you think you have the right to become angry?'

I sat back, trying to look elegantly contemptuous.

Jane's eyes studied the look. Doubt flickered in them, just for a moment. But she was still fiery with hate for what I'd said about nausea.

'All right,' she said. 'Justify yourself, young man.'

'I had a meeting. With the woman who runs my radio show. She needed to talk work-stuff, and she didn't want to do it where we were going to get overheard. Or noticed. This is media politics, it's a bit subtle for Kojak here.'

Mr Marsh tried to take it squarely, but I saw him flinch. He wasn't bald, but maybe he would be when he took off his hairpiece.

'So I went to Kerry's house.'

'How long did this meeting last?'

'Couple of hours.'

'You came in after one a.m.'

'I went for a walk, had a drink. Thought about what I'd been told.'

'Which was?'

'Classified information.'

Jane's searching look intensified, which was what I'd been aiming for. I was in control now. Guiding conversations was my job. What I wanted was to give Jane the chance to win, without losing anything myself. If I let her, she'd ferret out the secret content of my meeting. The office politics. The classified information. And maybe she'd be satisfied.

Mr Marsh dropped his third snap in front of me. 'This is the subject leaving the same residence at twelve fifteen a.m., a period of approximately six hours subsequent to his arrival.'

'So I stayed a little longer.' I shrugged. 'Do you expect me to remember everything?'

'We're talking about last night, Mikki.'

'Last night, last year, it's all the same to me. I'm a psychic. My mind lives in the future. Jane, there are certain facts about my mental make-up that you'll have to get used to – it's the price of my gift. This is part of what I was explaining to my boss.' I was trying to regain that element of control. Jane might have handed it over, but Mr Marsh didn't give her the chance. I was getting the idea he'd taken a dislike to me.

'And,' he said, 'this is the tape.'

'Tape?' I asked, like it was something we didn't come across in radio.

'Metallised audio cassette, duration two hours, subject the alleged office meeting between my client's husband and one Kerry Allison, twenty-seven, blonde, unmarried, a radio hostess and collegue of the subject.'

I made to snatch it. I failed.

'That's very illegal.'

'Of dubious value as a piece of legal evidence,' said Mr Marsh airily. 'But very useful in indicating a small matter of the truth to my client.'

'Jane, have you heard it?' I demanded.

'No. But I'm going to. Please play it, Mr Marsh.'

Mr Marsh took a Sony Walkman with a butterfly-thin pair of speakers from his jacket pocket.

'And don't play it too quietly, Mr Marsh. I'm suffering rather from my tinnitus today.'

CHAPTER EIGHT

Tinnitus was what gave my wife a headache when she was stressed. She didn't look stressed. She looked like she was licking blood from her gums. And loving it.

I said, 'How do I know this isn't faked?'

Mr Marsh held up a hand. The Walkman was balanced discreetly on his lap. The sound on the tape was almost inaudible. It could have been someone breathing.

'That's a blank,' I said.

Mr Marsh ignored me. Jane was straining to hear. The breathing became louder. It became panting – the kind of noise you get from a throat mike on a jogger.

'That's tape hiss,' I said.

Somebody moaned.

'What is this, a haunted house?' I said.

Somebody shrieked. I knew it was Kerry's shriek. And I knew exactly what caused it. I'd put enough effort in, finding out.

'It's meaningless,' I said.

Somebody screamed, 'Jesus-Jesus-Christ-Almighty!'

I squirmed and glanced at Jane. She was half out of her seat, her lips parted and her eyes glistening. She was turned on.

Mr Marsh was impassive. His face twitched a little – it could have been a smile – when the voice on the tape shrieked, 'MIKKI!'

Then I could hear my own grunts. Anyone's voice on tape sounds weird, even when they're used to it. I hear myself on headphones every working day, but my external voice is always different from the one I hear in my head. My external voice grunting on a snoop's Walkman was a lot weirder.

The tape wasn't faked. Nothing about it was faked.

I said, 'You can turn it off.'

Jane was biting a pink, wrinkled knuckle. The other hand was pressed on the thigh of her shining blue trouser suit. She couldn't trust herself to speak. She didn't have to.

'Quite a meeting,' said the snoop.

'I bet you liked typing up the minutes.'

'Play it again,' said Jane.

'Jane, I'm confessing, it's me, we don't have to . . .'

'Put it on the table this time, Mr Marsh. And turn the volume right up.'

Mr Marsh kept his hand on the player as it rewound, in case I had an idea about sweeping it off the table and mashing it down with my foot. As if.

I'd thought the restaurant was half empty, but suddenly every seat around us was filled and every neck was made of rubber. Maybe the manager was out there in Kensington High Street, advertising it to passers-by. Live Sex Show! Hot Tapes!

I pushed back my chair and grinned around the room. When the tape reached the bit where Kerry started yelling, a redhead with a glass of Chianti grinned back. I glanced up at the ceiling and opened my hand. I didn't know exactly what the gesture was supposed to mean. She could read it as she liked. Maybe, 'I've never understood why women do that in bed with me.'

The redhead said something to the guy with her. His back was to me, but he swivelled round. Then he faced back and they both laughed.

The guy at the next table was dining alone. He had grey hair, slicked back in rigid lines, with white curls like wings above each ear. He acted like he wasn't listening, but I knew he was, because his mouth was still. It's easier to hear when you're not chewing.

I remember all this because I was focusing on it. Like I said, Jane didn't know what embarrassment was, but she knew how to inflict it.

By the time the tape got to my grunting, there was a big man in a suit next to me. When I didn't look up, he bent down.

'You want to buy a copy?' I asked.

'Turn it off, please, sir. You are disturbing our other diners.'

'Don't look at me. It's her tape.'

'I don't care who owns it, sir, I'm asking you to comply with a reasonable request.'

'Keep your shirt on, pal,' said Mr Marsh, who didn't appear to waste his evidence-in-court style on the lower classes. The Walkman dropped into his pocket.

'We are leaving,' announced Jane. 'Kindly bring the bill to my husband.'

I just shrugged. She knew I didn't have any money. If she wanted to humiliate me about that too, then fine. She'd been doing it for six weeks.

Usually she said something grandly self-pitying, like: 'Am I expected to pay every bill? What will people think of you?'

This time she didn't.

This time, she reached over to the table on her right and, with a brittle 'Excuse me,' lifted a steaming cup of cappuccino from its saucer, dipped a fingertip into the froth, winced at the heat, and slopped the whole drink into my lap.

The scalding didn't start for a few seconds. I was on my feet, cursing, flicking the boiling suds off my jeans, when it soaked through to my skin. I let out a couple of shrieks and hopped around. Half the customers were staring silently and the other half were laughing, but I guess every one of them was watching. I don't know, I wasn't too concerned with them. I was trying to pull the wet denim away from my crotch, which wasn't easy because these were expensive jeans with a good fit.

I was close to unzipping and dropping my pants when the nerve endings started letting my brain know a reaction was setting in. The heat had gone out. Pretty soon I was going to be walking round in cold, clammy denims.

Jane was at the door. I was waddling after her when a fat hand clapped me on the shoulder. The guy in the manager's suit had looked big when I was sitting down. Now I was on my feet, he wasn't looking any smaller.

'Don't forget your bill. Sir.'

The door closed behind Jane. Mr Marsh was three paces ahead of her. Maybe he was searching for a taxi, or maybe he was just sweeping the sidewalk with palm leaves.

'She's taken my wallet,' I lied.

He glanced at me. I was wearing a PrimeTime T-shirt and a pair of jeans that were partway through the shrink-to-fit process. If I had any money on me, it would be folded up square and taped between my toes.

'Office,' he said, jerking in the direction with his thumb.

I wasn't anxious to be strip-searched. Or worked over. If there had been £50 notes between my toes, I would have unwrapped them.

'If you're going to humiliate me,' I said, 'do it at this table. These people are used to it.'

35

The suit took my left arm and twisted it up. He was squinting at the watch, and I knew he wasn't wondering about the time.

'Hey!' I jerked my hand free. I didn't expect him to break any bones in public, but there was no point in leaving opportunities open like that. 'You want the watch for collateral, have it.'

'Your watch wouldn't buy a bowl of doughballs. Sir.'

'Listen, I'll leave my address.'

'It's not as simple as that. Sir.'

That 'Sir' got nastier every time. I kept expecting him to forget himself and say 'Shit' instead, because that was the meaning.

'The gentleman may leave his name and address with me.'

I looked around, and stared in the face of the grey-haired diner with the winglike white curls. It seemed reasonable – everyone else in the place was getting involved with my private difficulties, so why shouldn't he?

'I shall pay his bill, and I know he will repay me once his wife returns his wallet.'

I grinned at him happily. Maybe those white wings marked him down as an angel. My guardian angel.

But as it turned out, he wasn't.

CHAPTER NINE

Kerry asked, 'So who was he?'
    'I don't know. He gave me his card. It's in the other room. In my trousers.'
    'You don't even remember his name?'
    Kerry had taken the whole story harder than I expected. In fact, I was glad she didn't have the whole story. I'd kind of omitted to explain what Jane and I were arguing about. And Mr Marsh hadn't entered the narrative at all.
    It seemed better if my sweet co-presenter didn't know a private detective had been sat outside the door with a tape recorder the full six hours I'd been with her. Or that he was probably out there now.
    She didn't have much of a sense of perspective about those things.
    She also hated to imagine what it was like being in a restaurant with no way to pay. To me, that wasn't the worst part of the experience. Hot coffee in my underwear was the killer. Kerry seemed to think physical pain was meaningless beside the horror of being forced to accept money from strangers.
    Maybe that's the true meaning of Englishness.
    But more likely, she just didn't understand that my favoured route to unimagined wealth would be repeatedly accepting money from strangers.
    We were in her bathroom. I'd taken a shower and was wearing a towel. She was fully dressed, and it looked like she'd stay that way.
    She hadn't been expecting me, and when I'd walked for ninety minutes to reach her flat – the stranger's largesse didn't extend to Tube fare – I was concerned she'd be out. Or, worse, she'd be in and not receiving visitors, specifically not this visitor. That's to say, we hadn't signed exclusivity contracts.
    She wasn't the girl to put it around. But your mind generates worst-case scenarios after a scene like I'd just lived through. I was almost surprised when she opened the door.

She was in, she was alone, she didn't seem terribly pleased to see me. Being a refuge to lovers in the aftermath of marital rows was already one stage of commitment too far for Kerry. She was a professional woman being very unprofessional about a love affair, and she knew it, and this was one more piece of evidence that she'd stepped onto a slippery slope. She could either apply the brakes now or she could rocket all the way to the bottom. Next stop media oblivion. I guess she'd already nearly made her mind up on this, and when I staggered haggard and coffee-crotched onto her doorstep, it just gave her the little push she needed.

Now I'd freshened up, and she'd had a few minutes to think. She said, 'Mikki, this can't go on.'

'I know. I know.' I held up my hands in defence. 'I'm not here as a lover. I'm here as a colleague.'

'None of my other colleagues get dumped by their wives and want to come and live in my sitting room.'

'I don't want to live here. I'm not moving in on you, Kerry.'

'Good.'

'I swear it.'

'Because I won't let you.'

'Kerry. I'm a grown-up.'

'No you're not, Mikki.'

'OK, I'm an overgrown kid, but all I'm asking is, the sofa for one night. Because I don't have any cash for a hotel. From tomorrow, it's the Sheik's Suite at the Ritz. Soon as I get my wallet.'

'I thought Madam had confiscated your credit cards?'

This was true, essentially. And I was lying about only needing Kerry's hospitality for one night. If I didn't go back to Jane, I couldn't afford hotels. I couldn't afford youth hostels even. But I'd deal with tomorrow night when I got there.

I have to explain a little about me and money. It's kind of difficult. It's the one subject I don't like talking about. Not in an English, 'Ooh filthy lucre,' way – I just think it's better to be mysterious about cashflow.

If I need to ask you for payment, I'll ask. If I want a loan, I'll come straight to the point. About these things I'm not squeamish.

But there's no advantage to me if you know the exact state of my bank balance. You might be thinking, 'That Mikki, on the radio every day, bet he earns packets. He must be loaded. Dripping with dough.' Or you could think, 'He's such a nice guy,' – because I am, I really am, I wouldn't harm a hair on a fly's head, there's not one drop of malice in one ounce of my flesh, I'm the original nice guy. You might be thinking, 'He's so nice, I wouldn't be surprised if he gives half his salary to some charity for orphaned puppies.' And I really don't want to spoil your ideas by getting down to specifics.

However. If I don't explain, you won't get the story. Because most of what has been happening in my life up to this point, and a fat portion of everything I'm going to tell you, is on account of the financial situation.

In brief: Jane had dough. This was one of the logical requirements for the future Mrs Michalakopoulos. On the other hand, if I made this obvious, the bride-to-be might get the wrong idea. No one likes to admit they're being married for money. Even the obscene octogenarians who get wheeled down the aisle with six feet six inches of sculpted silicone – they kid themselves it's for their fascinating personalities.

So this was my pitch. I needed a work permit, so a rapid courtship had to be part of the deal. As soon as Jane accepted my proposal, I delicately explained this to her. But note – she accepted me first. I didn't bully her with tales of cruel immigration men and the terrifying ordeal that awaited deportees. It was her choice.

Jane agreed to marry me for her own reasons. One, I was a cute guy who needed mothering, and the rest. Two, I was a media personality and pretty useful at making her friends envious. Three, and most important, I was getting messages about her dear departed husband, Ambrose. Reassuring messages from the beyond. And in fact, the spirit world was pretty hot on the idea of Jane getting hitched with me. So obviously that weighs on a woman, when her dead hubbie is enjoying the hereafter, and his ghostly guardians are recommending a successor.

Shortly before the nuptuals – like about four hours before we were due at the register office – I broached the subject of money with Jane.

We were in Selfridges, at the warpaint counter, and the woman who was almost my wife was hovering between two shades of vermilion lipliner, and she asked me to get both of them.

She said, 'Mikki, darling, I simply can't decide, and it will ruin my day if I buy one and it's the wrong one. Just get them both, won't you?'

And this was my ideal opportunity. I couldn't buy anything, because that morning I had been requested by my last remaining credit card company to snip their property into small pieces and post the remains back to them.

I laid my fingertips gently on her woolly orange sleeve and whispered, 'There's nothing I'd like better than to treat you, but I'm going to have to be honest with you about a certain subject which, to be frank, I've avoided . . .'

Jane looked squarely at me. 'I wondered when we'd come to this.'

'I suppose it's obvious I'm not wealthy.'

'It's obvious you spend a jolly sight more than you can possibly be earning.'

I tried a joke: 'I have tastes above my station.'

She looked at my clothes. New leather jacket, shades hooked over my head, gleaming Cuban heels. I wore black because it suited my mystique and my complexion, and I never wore anything black once it started to fade. Effective, but not cheap.

'You do dress most impressively. And I must be honest, since you are being honest – although of course, Mikki, darling, I know you are never anything but – I'll say this, that I like you to look so romantic and dashing. It reflects well upon me. But you needn't think you're about to marry an open chequebook.'

'Jane,' I declared emotionally, 'I've never uttered one peep about your finances, and if I ever did I'd hope my gift would be snatched away from me by the spirits. If there is one thing in the world that is not compatible with psychic energy, it's money.'

'I didn't intend a slur on your talents, darling boy. Just so long as we understand one another. Do you have debts?'

'A few credit cards.'

'More than £2,000?'

'Maybe.'

'More than £3,000, then?'

'Possibly.'

'So in excess of £4,000?'

'I haven't checked precisely.'

'Dear me. And all at 25 per cent I dare say. Well, I was not unprepared. My lawyer had suggested, delicately of course, that this situation might arise.'

'You've been talking to your lawyer?'

'Naturally. Mikki, a girl doesn't embark upon a romantic adventure like ours, for the third time in her life, without checking the weak points very carefully. Experience must count for something.'

A stray word there had me sidetracked, and I forgot to be indignant. 'Third?'

'What was that?'

'You said, "the third time". Third marriage.'

'Ah, yes. Well, a girl must have some secrets.'

'Of course.'

'And you don't want to rake up every unpleasantness through which I have been forced to prevail.'

'Obviously not.'

'So we'll just say that the dear love of my life, before you, was Ambrose, and leave it at that.'

'Not mention the third,' I agreed.

'He doesn't count.'

'But experience does,' I steered her back.

'Which is why I asked my lawyers to put an arrangement in place. You see, your debts will be paid by my bank.'

'Oh, Jane . . .'

'And then your salary will be paid into one of my accounts.'

'Hey?'

'Until such time as I feel you have become responsible.'

'Until I've paid you back.'

'Possibly. We shall measure your progress.'

'Jane, that isn't very manly of me. To hand over every cent, without a whimper.'

'No one need know. I certainly shan't tell anyone.'

'And neither will I, but how am I supposed to live?'

'You may have whatever you wish, within reason.'

'All I have to do,' I said dryly, 'is ask?'

'Precisely.'

'I don't think it will suit me, to be always cap-in-hand.'

'And I don't think it will suit me, to be married to a bankrupt. Much better and more civilised, to do it the lawyers' way. And as an incentive,' she added, 'when that necessary attainment of responsibility has been achieved . . .'

'When I'm to be trusted with my own money?'

'If you put it like that, yes – then I shall make you a gift of £30,000, to enjoy as you wish. And though I am certain that you will be prudent with the bulk of it, it will be only proper if you have yourself a bit of a wing-ding with the rest.'

I was staring at her with dreamy eyes. It must have looked like heart-zinging adoration. A bit of a wing-ding – I could do more than that with £30,000. Thirty thousand pounds sterling came out at fifty thousand US dollars. And with $50,000 I could save my neck.

CHAPTER TEN

A t this stage, I didn't tell her how useful $50,000 could be to me. No point in alarming a respectable, law-abiding woman. Particularly a woman with all those solicitors. But this bout of negotiations did confirm to me something I'd been assuming optimistically all along – Jane Lyons had dough. Enough to bake a mountain of doughballs.

And if she wasn't going to deliver the whole platterful straight away, well, what would anyone expect? The only chance of an instant jackpot would be finding an ultra-rich widow who was senile. And I didn't think I could stay amorous in the face of senility. Jane was older than she admitted, but she wasn't a wreck.

I didn't like my end of the bargain, handing over my earnings. I'd known a few families back home where the wife demanded the pay packet, sealed, in her hand, every Friday, but alcoholism was usually involved. Or gambling. I'm not a heavy drinker, and where gambling is concerned I'm an all-or-nothing, headlong romantic of a guy – my life on the line. In the case of the Benji brothers, my life, literally. My life or $50,000 – whichever I was able to pay.

I'll explain, but not yet. Let's keep this narrative in some kind of order. When I married Jane, I hadn't explained about the Benji brothers to anyone, not even Mimi.

Without access to my salary I'd be asking Jane for money pretty nearly every day but, after all, I was used to asking women for money. They kind of expected it. If Jane wanted to put this on a legal basis – that I had to hand all the bills to her, because she held both the purse-strings – so much the easier for me.

And if she was in a position to hand out £30,000 for pocket money, then I was in a position to go along with the show for a while.

God, I had it all worked out that day.

I wasn't even phased when she jumped me with a surprise of her own.

'Now that we're talking frankly,' she said, twining an arm into

42

mine as she shunted me out of Selfridges' big doors into Oxford Street, packed and shuffling, 'let me talk about a subject I've been avoiding. I don't want to be Mrs Mikki.'

I stopped dead. She was going to jilt me, before lunch on my wedding day? How could any woman be this heartless?

'Oh, don't choke, darling boy. I'm still going to marry you. You won't be lonely tonight. Feel how my heart beats for you.' And she pushed my hand onto one of her big, woolly, orange breasts.

'We really do have to get married today,' I said.

'Darling boy, you're so passionate. I love you for it.' She gave my hand a bearhug. 'And I know you're not going to be difficult about this one little thing. It's your name.'

'My name isn't a little thing,' I said, surprised.

'Of course it's not.' She was being all bunny-wunnyish now, and if I hadn't been a bit distracted that day, with the wedding and everything, not to mention the thought of a £30,000 cash bonus, I might have started to feel sick at the sound of her voice before I married her, instead of later.

'Your name,' Jane explained, 'is so dreadfully foreign. I mean, it's all Greek to my friends.'

'Michalakopoulos.'

'Such a mouthful.'

'Easy when you know how.'

'But no one ever takes the trouble to learn. And it would just be so awkward for me. I mean, I'm not embarrassed by you having Greek relatives or anything.'

'Thanks.'

'I mean, everyone can see you're American basically, and not Continental at all. But I can't tell my friends to call me Mrs Michaelmoussawhatsis, now can I?'

'Michalakopoulos.'

'Oh, darling boy, don't be huffy now, not on our wonderful wedding day. You can see why I was so anxious about bringing this up.'

'So you can just be Mrs Mikki.'

'Darling child! I'd sound like the wife of a fish-and-chip man!'

'And what's your suggestion?'

'You become Mr Lyons.'

I said nothing. Jane took this to be a good sign.

'I'm certain Ambrose's spirit guardians would say, "Do it," if you asked them. Oh you can still be Mikki – Mikki Lyons. It's like you're gaining an extra name, not giving anything up. And everyone knows me as Mrs Lyons, and nobody knows you as anything but Mikki.'

I still said nothing.

'Don't forget I'm going to give you £30,000.'

I hadn't forgotten that. I said, 'Let's sleep on it.'

'Oh, Mikki, you are wicked!'

To recap: I have no credit cards, my wife gets all my salary, I am no longer on easy terms with my wife and certainly not easy enough to bill her for my hotel rooms. Plus, I have not to date seen anything that looks like $50,000.

And Kerry is clearly unhappy to let me stay one night, never mind longer.

So where do I go?

There's Mimi. But that would be total capitulation. 'Sorry, Mimms, you were the girl all along. How can I ever apologise for breaking your heart, and can I slum on your sofa tonight? Oh, and here are my balls on a platter.'

Or there's Jane. 'Darling, I have returned. I slink. I cower. I am unworthy of your fine and generous nature. Never shall I transgress again, and feel free to treat me as your exclusive sex toy from now on. Oh, and can I have 50p for a coffee, please?'

Choices, choices.

The cardboard-box option was starting to look attractive.

There was one ray of light. I refuse to believe in a world without one ray of light. That night, I was pinning my hopes on an arrogant professor with £5,000 he didn't know what to do with.

CHAPTER ELEVEN

Afternoon of the following day, which was a Friday, I'd had a good show. There were no premonitions of the nightmares about to come whirling down on me. No little voice whispering, 'Go back to bed! Go back to bed!' Except, now I come to think of it, there was one thing . . .

One of those nice people from the Evangelists of Superhuman Perfection called in to say how all their enemies would soon be consumed in flames. I told him I'd had enough calls from his cult, thank you so much, and he rang off. They'd be back. They were kind of the spiritual equivalent of double-glazing salesmen.

Apart from that, a good show. And now I was on my way to see the prof. Mimi fixed it, like she fixed everything.

Yes, she'd remembered his name. Yes, she knew where he worked. Yes, directories had been happy to give out the university number, and yes, the switchboard had put her straight through.

Professor Ingman had taken her call personally. Apparently he had £5,000 to splash but no secretary.

She got the details, she fixed the appointment and, before I even showed up for broadcast, Mimi had got me a line on more dough than I'd seen since my bachelor days. Also, she set off a chain of events as surely as if she'd found a grenade and pulled out the pin to pick her teeth with. And until the first big bang, I never had a clue.

Ingman was offering the money if I would only do him the honour of sitting down to his dumb tests.

And I knew just how to spend it.

Downpayment to the Benji brothers, $5,000, which came out at £3,000. That left £2,000. Maybe technically some of this should be tax, but I was never any good at technical stuff. Jane could pay my tax when the time came. I hoped I lived that long. £2,000 would give me some freedom. Freedom from asking Jane every time I wanted 20p for the men's room. Freedom to get some phone vouchers without

45

itemising every call. Freedom from the fear that if Jane was really going to kick me out, I'd be sleeping in the studio. But most of all, freedom from the nagging anxiety that any day the Benji brothers could turn up with a circular saw and rubber gloves, to extract their pound of flesh.

When I thought about which pound of me they intended to collect, I had to sit with my legs crossed.

I'd done this sum days ago, before I had any notion that £5,000 was in the offing. At least, my conscious mind was unaware of the impending moulah. Maybe my subconscious was psychically attuned to the coming change of fortune. Maybe my astrological conjunctions were powerfully sympathetic to financial aspects.

Maybe it was a big coincidence. Who gives a toot?

And suddenly, it was more than just a fantasy. I was walking up to the portals of Alfred Russel Wallace House in Queensberry Place, SW7, a tall lump of sandstone in a terrace across the road from the Natural History Museum. Inside there was a man with a conceited voice and some idiotic card tricks and a nice cheque for Mikki. My hand almost trembled as I pressed the middle button on the brass plaque.

Ground floor at Queensberry Place was the Department of Infant Neurodevelopmental Studies, with two names crammed onto the bellpush – a Prof. Stanley and a Prof. Laurel. This I remember for obvious reasons. There was every reason to expect my professor would turn out to be a comedian too.

The top button, for the top floor, belonged to the Neurasthenic Psychological Disorder Unit, headed by a Prof. Wurt. And in the middle, with the name label inscribed in italics, was the Department of Parapsychology, presided over by Prof. Ingman.

Italics. That was just right. The moron spoke in italics. Even when he took a dump, it would have to be in italics.

I pushed the button.

A girl with short red curls and a jaw that could take a punch came up the steps behind me. She pushed a key into the Yale lock and held the door open.

'Do you want to come in?'

'I'd best stay here and announce myself. Professor Ingman might want to send a delegation of secretaries down to greet me.'

'If you're waiting for an answer on his entryphone, you'll have to wait till I get upstairs,' she said. She sounded serious.

'You're the secretarial entourage?'

'No, I'm the department's research assistant.'

Something in my sense of humour was pissing her off. Good start.

'My name's Mikki, I'm a radio presenter.'

She looked unimpressed. I noticed she had nice eyes, green eyes, and a big nose between them.

'And I'm here at the prof's invitation.'

'You're the psychic. And you thought I was a secretary. Impressive.'

'Sorry, did I poison your cat in a previous life or something? We don't seem to be hitting it off.'

I followed her into the hallway, which was strip-lit, always a disaster in these big Victorian houses. They built their entrances to be filled with candlelight and flickering gas burners, with holders in dozens down the walls. So how clever was it to stick one blinding tube of phosphorous on the ceiling and call it lighting?

The place felt like an aquarium, with the water level way above our heads.

As we climbed the stairs, the tube-light was suddenly on eye level, scorching my retinas for an instant. The rest of the stairwell was dim and my feet stumbled till we reached the first floor. Another strip lit the landing, and again it felt like someone was shining a torch down through water.

I must have been edgy. University houses are not fishtanks. Edgy makes me talkative, and probably I was gassing the whole way up, I don't remember. Definitely the redhead didn't say anything back. She reached the prof's door without speaking again.

I stepped past her into a room that could give conscientious librarians a nervous breakdown. Every surface was hidden by books, journals, papers, texts, catalogues, cuttings. It wasn't strewn – everything was carefully piled and arranged. The papers weren't dripping off the desks or fluttering in the breeze from the doorway. They were orderly and distributed with meaning.

It was just that you couldn't move without treading on them.

A stack of yellow pamphlets with an occult-type logo, which had some meaning I couldn't decipher upside-down, was propped up the cushions of one armchair. The other armchair had dog-tagged A4 files where your auntie would have hung doilies and antimacassars. This was not a good room for sitting around.

I picked my way towards the far doorway, past the desk with a word processor and piles of hardcover books high enough to fill a shelf if you turned it end on. All the corners were neatly aligned.

These books had been stacked by a book-stacking pro. The spines were mostly black with faded silver lettering that spelled out titles like *Supernormal Faculties In Man* and *Lucidity And Intuition*, but if you'd reached out for one the whole tower would have toppled.

A Bakelite triangle was embossed with a name: Louisa Simons. I looked over my shoulder.

'Nice filing system, Louisa.'

The redhead looked straight through me.

At the other end of her gaze, the door to the next room opened. A man stepped out.

He had grey hair, combed back in grooves like a toupee made from lead wire. Above his ears were white curls, like wings.

After everything that happened, this seems painfully trivial, but the first thought in my head was, out of my £5,000 I'm going to have to pay him back for a pasta dinner.

Chapter Twelve

Professor Ingman came through the door and said to me: 'Ah! I was expecting someone else! But it's very good of you, I must say I hardly expected to see you again. You quite restore one's jaded faith in human nature.

'Louisa,' he added, 'this is the young man of whom I spoke, who was found to be at a financial impasse in a pasta restaurant following a contretemps with his mother. £42.60, if memory serves.'

I had held out my hand across the desk when he entered, but he managed to ignore it.

I didn't turn round when Louisa said: 'This is the radio man about the Zener tests.'

'Good Lord! But I'm not mistaken? You are the fellow whose tab I collected yesterday?'

There was no denying it. 'That was me.'

'Or "that was I" in fact. But I notice from your accent you are not English. Not English, though English is your first language. Whereas I am not English, neither is it my first language, which engenders a sometimes overfussy yearning for grammatical precision.'

It was time to push back. 'Sorry, you do or you don't talk English?' I asked.

'I do, of course.'

'So talk it.'

There was a pause. 'I see,' said Professor Ingman at last, without letting on what it was he saw.

'I believe my assistant made arrangements for some psychic experiments?'

'I made the arrangements,' retorted Ingman. 'Your assistant merely made notes in a diary. You see the difference?'

'But not the point you're trying to make.'

'My point is, precision. Imprecise use of language creates vagueness, obfuscation and confusion, three factors which render accurate scientific observation impossible – in any science, in any discipline, but especially parapsychology. There are enough immeasurables and imponderables in my field without clouding the issue with weak grammar.'

Ingman clipped every word. He was probably afraid imprecise pronunciation might let him down. The tone was snappish and guttural, like a stage Nazi, but the accent wasn't really German. It was weirder than that. I found out later he was a Finn.

'So where's the laboratory?'

'Eager to start, that's good,' noted the professor. He'd already needled me good and deep, and this added burst of condescension jabbed it deeper.

'Eager to get it finished,' I said.

'And yet it is so extraordinary – that I should speak to you for the first time yesterday, on air, by telephone, and have a long conversation without, naturally, either of us guessing the other's appearance. And then that I should, all unwitting, assist in that embarrassing débâcle in the restaurant. And we neither of us recognise the other's voice. Remote contexts, of course.'

He wound a finger into one white wing and tugged pensively. 'And now you're here. No, it is more than coincidence.'

'Synchronicity,' I said.

'Naturally, you are familiar with the term, in your line of entertainment. But I suspect you use it simply as a synonym for coincidence.'

'There are no coincidences,' I intoned. It seemed important to stand up to casual accusations, like the suggestion that what I did was just for entertainment. As if.

'Nonsense,' snorted the prof.

He was getting to really cheese me off. There was no way he'd ever get his downpayment on that pasta back.

'Of course there are coincidences. Can every little accident be part of some ludicrous cosmic design? Are we to see grand meaning in the bleatings of every half-cooked astrologer?'

'Half-baked,' I corrected him. 'We'd better be precise about it.'

'Jung's synchronicity is a scientific concept of the utmost beauty – a sublime, causeless process by which one event affects another irrespective of time, regardless of distance. Now I hope you will never again confuse such a thrilling concept with the everyday coincidence.'

He was getting quite cranky about it.

'So what you're saying is, when you paid my bill in Bella Pasta last night, that wasn't coincidence.'

'Absolutely.'

'That was something sublime and causeless, right?'

You could have measured the sudden chill with a thermometer.

'You know,' he said, 'I never have quite been certain of your name.'

'Just Mikki is fine.'

'Do be sure to write down any unusual spellings, just for the sake of precision. You see, in this environment, even your correct name matters.'

I tried to think if there was any remark of mine he hadn't yet managed to turn into an insult. Nothing came to mind.

'See Louisa about that,' he added.

I'd forgotten she was there, and she was ignoring us. She was sitting on the rim of one chair's arm, reading a journal which she'd folded round on itself. She didn't look comfortable, but she did look brainy.

Her attitude told me something useful – Professor Ingman was like this with everyone. It was nothing personal. If he was singling me out for special sarcasm, she would be listening, or trying to shut him up. But she wasn't interested. So she must have heard it a million times before.

That needn't have made me feel better, but it did.

'The experiments will be conducted in my office.'

I followed him out of the librarian's nightmare, into a room like a hypnotist's daydream.

I know something about hypnotism. It's one of the tricks of my trade. I'll give you some tips later on, next time I get a chance.

And I recognise when someone else is pulling the technique.

First, the room was quiet. Louisa closed the door behind us with a heavy click, and the three of us stood in an arena so instantly silent you could hear our different breathing patterns. The sash window was triple glazed, and the deep brown carpet continued up the walls to the dado rail. A single clock was ticking, but either time moved slowly in Professor Ingman's chambers or the pendulum was set to swing only 45 times in a minute. The beat seemed to linger interminably. My heartrate ticks below average, but this was way slower. You could go into a trance just telling the time.

All the furnishings were built to absorb sound. It wasn't just the way shoe leather got sucked into the shag-pile – the massive wooden desk was as solid as stone, and the high-backed chairs were upholstered in enough horse-hair to fill a mattress.

Curious treasures were placed around the room. A buffalo horn tipped in silver stood on a cradle of metal lace. It looked expensive. So did the oak dresser facing the window, with three books in pristine jackets displayed on the top. I didn't have to inspect the covers to guess their author was a certain Johannes-Kristian Ingman.

The electric chandeliers hung above either end of his desk – this was one room which had escaped the strip-lights. Ingman walked round to his chair, one hand hovering above the polished desktop but never quite touching it. I knew that gesture. It signifies a man who hesitates before he begins.

He turned his head and looked at me sideways, and at last he said, 'Ah.'

I tipped a chair back and stretched my boots across the carpet. I wanted to look in control. 'Look,' I said, 'you probably know I'm not going to summon spirits for you or levitate the desk. What I can do is offer you a reading. If you've got a tarot pack, that's fine – otherwise, I can work from telepathy. Subliminal telepathy. Your assistant can record my predictions, and you'll be able to measure up their accuracy.'

'Mmm.'

'I usually like to start with a question. To establish the link. So let's say, what do you see as the most challenging area of your work?'

'Actually, Mikki, greatly though I admire your cold reading subterfuges . . .'

'Whoa, boy, whoa!'

'. . . for subterfuges they are . . .'

'You're way off line, prof.'

'In fact, psychic predictions were not what I had in mind.'

'Then we're wasting each other's time.' I made to get up and leave, but not too vigorously, because there was no way I was going anywhere without a £5,000 cheque in my hand.

'I have a hearty respect for your ingenuity, and having heard your little programme on several occasions I don't doubt you could spin a most plausible monologue about my future adventures. But parapsychology, being a science, demands something more concrete.'

'You're implying I make stuff up. That's a slur on my professional self-respect.'

'As to self-respect, Mikki, I make no comment, particularly with regard to last evening's farce. Now I shall outline . . .'

'Let's get this straight. The readings I do for callers, I'm making nothing up. I tell them strictly what I know to be true.'

'By sometimes rather subtle deduction. I assure you, I admire your techniques, but I am not about to propose you practise them upon me.'

'Deduction is for Sherlock Holmes. I'm just a psychic.'

'Which assertion we shall endeavour to test.' He pulled a pack of cards from his desk drawer and slapped them down. 'This is not a Tarot. You are familiar with the Rhine theorem?'

'Geography was my weak subject.'

'Not your only one, surely.'

He fanned the deck. 'There are five, as you see, patterns. Three wavy lines, a square, a cross, a star and a circle. With twenty-five cards in the pack, each symbol occurs five times.'

'So what do we play, snap?'

'These are Rhine cards, sometimes called Zener cards, after their inventors: Joseph Rhine and Karl Zener.'

'Oh-ho.'

'I shuffle the pack. What are the chances that the topmost card, shall we say, is a circle? In fact –' he turned it over – 'so it is. A circle.'

'Not impressive. I've seen people make the card rise out of the pack on its own.'

'This is not a conjuring trick, Mikki.' His unruffled pedantry was like a challenge to me. He was in deep under my skin – I was going to jab the needle right back. 'So now you predict the next card.'

'Ace of clubs.'

'Is your own time so worthless that you must waste it with every breath?'

'So I'm being paid to watch bad card tricks.' I shrugged.

'These are not tricks,' he snapped.

'Parlour games, call them what you like. My powers are about helping people in the real world.'

'The real world, Mikki, includes a scientist's laboratory.'

'That's a pack of cards.' I was right where I'd aimed, under his skin. 'That isn't science.'

'It is mathematics. It is as simple as numbers. And like numbers, it possesses infinite variety. Your variety act, on the other hand, I confess to finding a little irritating.'

'Glad to hear it.'

'Then let us proceed, without more ado.'

But ado, as it turned out, was the one thing the prof couldn't do without. Before he laid his cards on the table, he had to give me chapter and verse. I had practically begged him to can the explanation, but I got it anyway.

'In 1934 a monograph based on experiments conducted at Duke University in North Carolina was published. Its title was Extra-Sensory Perception, which as it happens is a term originally coined by the man who first translated the Kama Sutra into English. He was also the first European to set foot in Islam's Forbidden City, Mecca. I penned his biography which you see there. His name was Sir Richard Burton.'

'That makes me Elizabeth Taylor.'

Ingman was ignoring me and lecturing me at the same time. 'The monograph demonstrated that in stringently observed tests, some subjects were able to descry the hidden symbol on one of Rhine's cards. Not once, but repeatedly. Not all subjects tested possessed this ability. But one, Hubert Pearce, scored so accurately that the possibility he was simply guessing has been calculated at ten thousand million, multiplied by a million, remultiplied by a million, to one, against.'

'So that's very lucky.'

'Luck is a meaningless concept at those esoteric levels. To illustrate – making nine correct predictions in a row is around 2,000,000 to one. I believe it is Koestler who comments, in his Roots Of Coincidence, on the peculiar reliability of chance. When applied to a large sample, chance becomes an immutable, a certainty.'

'So consider me blinded by science.'

'There is a 20 per cent chance, for example, that a computer programme could accurately predict the turn of the next card. With one test, the machine will be either 100 per cent right or 100 per cent wrong. It cannot be 20 per cent right. But if I conduct a hundred tests, or a thousand, then 20 per cent is exactly what it will achieve. Put another way: once in two million tests, the computer will achieve nine correct predictions consecutively. The inflexibility of chance, you see. One of the rational conundrums of mathematics.'

'So what does a genuine psychic prove about mathematics?'

'A genuine psychic,' Ingman replied seriously, 'would explode the inflexibility of chance. And most of what we call conventional science would simply – unravel.'

CHAPTER THIRTEEN

I felt a prickling on the back of my neck. When I twisted round, the professor's silent redhead was staring at me. 'So have you found any genuine psychics?' I asked. 'Anyone to compare to Mr Genius?'

'Hubert Pearce? His abilities evaporated before tests could be repeated. All this was long ago, of course. Parapsychology has moved on. Rhine's tests are little used. But it occurred to me that if a subject exhibiting psychic longevity could be identified, the simplest tests might once again prove the most effective. Presumably, Mikki, your talent has not simply mushroomed overnight?'

'Been this way all my life.'

'And though you exercise your talent daily, yet it does not diminish?'

'Stronger than ever.'

'Synchronicity! I have daydreamed for years that a candidate with your prescience would be sent to me. It is almost as though my dreams have willed you into existence.'

This was suddenly more like home territory for me. 'The universe is not only stranger than we imagine,' I quoted at him, 'it is stranger than we can imagine.'

'Yes, yes, the physicist JBS Haldane,' he enthused. 'And now you are about to create psychic history.'

Just a bit too enthusiastic. I didn't understand why he'd been so eager to insult me, if he thought I was the original Greek superhero.

'Didn't you say I was just a cold-reading pundit?'

'That's the window-dressing, Mikki. The goods on display are the real thing. I would recommend you to read a paper by Professor Marcello Truzzi, Reflections on the Sociology and Social Psychology of Conjurers. He posits that any illusionist may unwittingly employ psi ability in his act. In other words, it might look like a trick, but sometimes it can be real magic. Even Houdini, for instance, was powerless to explain how he achieved some of his effects. He simply willed them – and they happened. With you, I am convinced, psi is a crucial element. You think you are using a cold-reader's trickery . . . but sometimes your immense unconscious talents are at the fore. I'm certain of it. Now to prove it!'

I didn't give a Harlem shuffle what was going on in this egomaniac's head. He ran me down like I was a fairground fake, and then he got keyed up to take the credit for a defining instant in human evolution. For me, the defining instant would be when he wrote that cheque.

I was all ready to demonstrate powers which I didn't possess in the smallest scrap of my body. I might as well have been inviting the prof to scoop me up and hang me out to dry.

'Blindfold, Louisa.'

It was not unpleasant, having Louisa's warm, dry hands press two circles of black velvet over my eyes and secure them with a ribbon knotted behind my head. 'You've got an expert's touch,' I remarked. 'Do you do handcuffs too?'

She yanked a tuft of hair above one ear and said: 'Knot slipped. Sorry.'

'The format is perfectly simple, Mikki. You are blindfolded and facing away from me. A video camera positioned within the dresser is already recording this session. A full visual record of these experiments is naturally essential. Other than this, the room is devoid of hidden mechanisms. There are no mirrors, and cheating, even accidental cheating, is not possible.' His clipped voice was making an effort to be treacly. More hypnosis signals. The clock ticked slowly.

'When I say "Card" tell me the impression you receive. It will be one of those five symbols – cross, waves, circle, square, star. Are you ready?'

I felt a surge of self-confidence. Maybe I could be the first subject ever to score 100 per cent. In one quick experiment, I'd become a monument of parascience. An icon.

I've always had this optimistic outlook.

'Card!'

My chances dipped instantly when I realised I'd forgotten one of the cards. Cross, waves, square, circle, cross . . . or had I counted cross already? What was the fifth one?

'Remind me,' I said, 'what were those five again?'

Louisa's voice said, 'The professor is not permitted to say any word other than "card".'

'So you tell me – what are the five.'

'Just rely on your psychic senses. Repeat what comes into your mind.'

'That would be vulgar,' I said.

'Card!'

'OK, triangle.'

'There is no triangle,' said Louisa.

'Shit. I mean circle.'

'I'm afraid we have to record that as a miss.'

'There goes 100 per cent. What if I get every one wrong – isn't that as impressive as getting them all right?'

'It happens. The chances are lower, but it's still rare. One theory suggests it occurs where the subject is deliberately blocking psi-power.'

Now that Ingman could say nothing but 'card', Louisa was coming out of her shell.

'The professor's waiting.'

'Do I have to answer immediately?'

'No, but first impressions tend to be the most accurate.' Her voice was low and smart. 'Thinking about it doesn't help.'

'OK, so circle.'

And I went through the pack, shooting with the four symbols I could remember. I figured there was still a good chance I'd hit maybe ten – enough to look better than a guesser. If I got lucky.

I said, 'Square,' 'Square,' 'Circle,' 'What's the other one, waves,' 'Circle,' 'Waves,' 'Cross,' with no particular pattern. I didn't get any sense of what the cards were, I didn't go warm or cold according to hits and misses – I just shot, and figured I'd strike lucky because I usually did.

At the end of the pack, Ingman said: 'That was telepathy.'

'You mean I did good?'

'I mean, that was the test for telepathy. I looked at each card before turning it. A high proportion of hits might indicate an ability to see through my eyes, or register my brain signals. In the next test, I shall shuffle the pack and not turn over the cards. You will predict their order, all twenty-five.'

'So how do we know if I get it right?'

'When your predictions have been recorded, we reveal the pack. This is a test of clairvoyance – seeing something which exists in our own dimension of time, but which is unknown to any human mind.'

'You still going to say "card"?'

'If you find it efficacious.'

'Effing right.'

'Card!'

And I realised I'd forgotten to ask about that fifth symbol.

I had to wait till the third test before they'd clue me in. It was a star, a five-pointed star. Obvious. I should have got that.

The last test was precognition. I had to predict the order of the twenty-five cards before they even got shuffled. At this point we were in the realm of serious BS. Ingman claimed some subjects scored higher with precog than in either of the other tests. I could only assume some people got very lucky.

'Card!'

And away we went. This time I threw in a few stars. If I was very bright, I'd have given him five of each symbol, but my mental arithmetic isn't that sharp.

By three p.m. Ingman was slotting my results into a drawer that slid on silent runnings from the back of his desk. When he stood all the polished wooden surfaces were as bare and clean as before. No computers, no journals, no scrap – his office was like a display case after someone had removed the crown jewels.

He reached out to shake my hand, and turned it into a gesture towards the door. Maybe someone told him New Yorkers don't shake hands.

I said, 'So is that a cheque or do you pay cash?'

'Ah, but payment is already in hand, yes. Already in hand.'

'Not in my hand.'

'Your assistant informed Mrs Simons where to remit the remuneration.'

'She did what?'

'A cheque will be sent shortly.'

'Thanks, but I don't mind waiting. I'll take it with me. Banknotes would be appreciated.'

'Of course, I was forgetting your delicate pecuniary situation. But in fact the department machine may even now have authorised and submitted the payment. It would be too late to stop a cheque at this stage.'

'I was expecting to be paid now.'

'Mikki, £5,000 is rather a lot of money. I'm sure you didn't expect me to produce it from my wallet.'

'Most of London heard you promise to pay. It would be kind of embarrassing for the university if I don't get the money.'

'Absolutely no question, Mikki. My assurances. The great money machine has been set in motion, and can be neither interrupted nor prevented in its task.'

'You mean the cheque's in the post.'

'Once again, thank you so much for your efforts this afternoon.'

I took this to be my exit cue. I looked at the professor, staring down his hooked nose at me. I looked at his assistant, holding open the door to the roomful of papers. I shrugged and walked out. It didn't seem likely we'd ever run across each other again in our lives.

In this I was half right.

Chapter Fourteen

What a lot I never knew about my wife before. Most people get married thinking they'll discover their spouse's character, and it'll be a great adventure. I got married caring nothing about who my wife was. So I guess the trouble I got I deserved.

With Jane Lyons I did what I do with everyone – I sized her up and dropped her in a box marked 'First Impressions'. For me, this is usually enough. My first impressions are shrewd enough. I don't leap to any instant judgements, and I know those questions that bring the real personality to the fore.

Look a stranger in the eye and ask about her hopes and fears, her true opinion of herself, and she'll give you an honest answer. If she believes you truly want to know – that you're intrigued and excited by her – then she'll tell you things you might never have learned in ten years of conventional conversation. And she'll be grateful to you for it.

It's a technique that comes naturally to me. I never really noticed I was doing it – I just noticed other people don't do it. No one has ever stared straight into me and said: 'I want to know how you feel doing your work. What is it about your job that really affects you? The hard part?' If anyone asked, I'd be powerless to stay silent. When a question goes right to your heart, you have to answer. But though I've put it to many people, no one ever yet threw it back at me.

When the stranger has spilled out her secrets for two or three minutes, and said the things she thought she would never say to anyone, I've got a pretty clear first impression. I know this woman.

After that, I'm not too interested. I want to move on, dissect the next one.

This first-impression method doesn't work on people with more than one personality. And Jane Lyons could walk into a room twenty times, and be someone different in every case.

She could be a teenage innocent, all flirty eyelashes and fillings in her teeth. She could be a soupy-eyed romantic, who stared at couples in the park and sighed for her lost loves. She could be intelligent about radio – she said to me one time, 'I despise Classic FM. They just give you the orgasm without any of the foreplay.' I don't know if she read that someplace or made it up, but I liked it.

And then she could turn right round and be a brain-dead snob who was proud to read Barbara Cartland because she was somehow related to Princess Diana. She could be sweetness and light, salt and vinegar, fire and brimstone, fine and dandy.

She could be all these women in the space of half an hour, and carry on changing her character all day without repeating herself. Whether she had an audience or not didn't seem to matter. She was well-read, a TV junkie, placid, impatient, jealous, long-suffering . . . Every time I figured her out, that was the way she wasn't anymore. By three weeks into the marriage, I'd given up keeping up. I just let her flow over me.

She kept coming back to certain themes. My name, her money, our sex-life. Whatever the mood of the moment, these were obsessions for her. It was just the arguments kept changing.

'I didn't say that,' she would insist when I accused her of rewriting her lines. 'I couldn't have, I wouldn't have, because it would have been totally out of character for me.'

Naturally there was no hint of this the first time I spoke to her. How could I see it coming? And she did seem to get worse after the honeymoon had collapsed, as if there had been one dominant strain in her character that had prevailed right up to the marriage, trying to maintain everything on a steady course – and when that keeled over, everything else spilled out.

So I'm playing psychologists again. But Dr Freud would have drooled with excitement at the thought of my wife.

The initial Jane Lyons, the one in my first-impression box, was middle-aged and lonely. She had a hankering for spiritual balm, and a yawning gap in her life. To me it looked like a husband-sized gap. This was a reasonable assumption, since she made it clear the hole had opened up when she got widowed.

She rang in one Tuesday and talked to Mimi. This, it happened to work out, was the Tuesday when I woke Mimms up and said, 'I think I've got to get married.'

Mimi was bright, she picked up on nuances. She heard what I said, and she didn't mistake it for, 'I think *we've* got to get married.' To her credit, most girls wouldn't be so sharp.

She didn't understand at first why there was suddenly this terrible urgency, and I guess she figured it was just a novel way of getting myself off the hook. But maybe she'd been expecting it for longer than I realised. Maybe she just accepted all good things come to an end, and I'd been one of them.

Anyhow, it didn't look like she was going to sulk. She didn't talk much as we rode the Tube to PrimeTime. But she didn't spit in my face either.

And later, fielding the calls, she tapped in this helpful suggestion: 'Jane Lyons. 49 Kensington Church Street. Widowed and hoping for information about late husband, also future romance. Could be just your type. Why don't you chat her up?'

Mimi was grinning through the glass, and if her expression was a shade forced, I couldn't see it.

Jane had the kind of voice to make a prospective suitor hopeful. Well-educated, probably came from a nice family where girls were taught not to ask tricky questions about money. Not noticeably neurotic.

That depends on your viewpoint, of course. Maybe you think anyone who trusts a flake like me qualifies straight away for the funny farm, but you probably don't have any idea how desperation can take a sane person and rip out all their preconceived notions. You imagine you don't believe in psychics, and survival beyond the veil, and premonitions. So wait till life snaps your anchor chain and you go flailing out into the measureless, directionless sea. What will you cling to then?

I see myself as a lone rock in the wild waters. Something to hold on to. Not a harbour, but maybe the first landfall of a new country.

And nobody is compelled to use me. I don't lure unwary sailors aground. No siren voices.

So this is getting too poetic.

Jane phoned me. That was always my point. I didn't ring her. I didn't approach a rich stranger and say, 'Pardon me, but your late husband would like you to marry me.' So how could I have been plotting to snare her money-pots? I said this to her, after the honeymoon, over and over again.

What she said to me, that first Tuesday morning, was: 'Mikki, I'm a very sad and troubled soul, and I wonder whether it's in your power to assist me.'

'Tell me, Jane, what's at the heart of your sadness? Not the peripheral stuff, not the flotsam and jetsam of misfortune, but the real aching core?'

'Oh, I knew you would focus on the real thing. You've got such . . . such a laser beam. You won't be distracted. I mustn't be distracted either. I must follow your example. Now, I have lost my husband.'

'And this is – not a recent loss.' Not such a hazard. It takes time for distractions to accumulate round grief. For the first few weeks, grief is usually something that stands alone, repelling other problems and not attracting them.

'Recent? The wound burns so, it feels like yesterday.'

I thought, Oh really? That doesn't sound very convincing, Mrs Lyons. It sounds a little affected, if you don't mind me speaking my mind. But you want people to think you're grieving, or maybe you want to believe it yourself. Is that because you're ready to marry again? You're a little concerned what people might think, maybe?

This I thought. But what I said was, 'Time doesn't heal, Jane. It merely dulls the pain.'

'That is so perceptive. It has been six years since . . . since . . .'

'I understand.'

No, I don't! I've been doing this for years, and still I make these basic screw-ups. She was going to tell me Hubbie's name – there was no way to end that statement without it. And now I have to ask. Looks bad. Or at least, sounds bad. This is radio.

'What was your husband's name, Jane?'

'Oh, it was really very unusual.'

'I sensed that.'

'What with me being a plain Jane. People laughed when we got married. The wedding invitations might as well have read, "Chalk and Cheese". But we weren't, oh we were Ham and Eggs. Fish and Chips.'

Still haven't said his name. And I can't ask twice.

'I know you believe in the hereafter, Mikki.'

'It's not a question of belief, just a simple fact. I know it's true, like you know you're holding a telephone.'

'Ambrose was a believer too.'

Bull's-eye! And I would never have guessed 'Ambrose'.

'A believer, that will have greatly assisted his transition. I think sometimes a soul that's less prepared fights the change, and expends a lot of energy denying what is really happening. I'm glad Ambrose had an inkling of what to expect. Did you and he have an arrangement?'

'I'm sorry?'

'Sometimes a husband and wife agree that whichever of them

63

crosses the bar first, they will try to return and make contact. A predetermined word, a signal. Perhaps a pet name.'

'We never imagined he would die so young.'

That should have been an alarm bell. Beware of widows whose husbands died young. At least find out what the last one died of, before you become the next.

'Jane, I have a friend on the other side.'

'I've heard her speak on your show.'

'Her name is Leaping Deer. I know a lot of people have difficulty with this, but it's one of those facts you just can't change.'

'Oh no. Quite.'

'Leaping Deer was a granddaughter of Geronimo, the Apache chief, and she lived – not very long ago. In this century. But she died when she was barely more than a girl, in a car crash.'

'That's very tragic.'

'She was prepared, you see. That's why she made the transition so – well – I guess gracefully. Tragic in one way, but you ought to envy her too, she's very happy and she knows her work with me amounts to a mission. Serving the whole of humanity.'

Or at least, I thought, that portion of humanity that tunes in to Psychic Mikki on PrimeTime.

'Can you reach Leaping Deer for me?'

'I can try. But it involves a trance state, as you may know. Now I realise that long silences are supposed to be very bad radio, but you'll have to bear with me, folks. There's no way round this. I need to channel Leaping Deer, and she can't get in if I keep chattering. So for a few seconds, all you're going to hear is my breathing. I'm emptying my mind and opening the doors. Opening up wide to the heavens. Leaping Deer . . . Leaping Deer . . .'

Dan Nally, our producer, slammed my mike up high so every breath sounded like a tungsten file on sheet iron. But I never let this ride for more than three seconds anyhow. Talkless radio is genuinely bad radio.

And then Leaping Deer began to speak.

Chapter Fifteen

I do Leaping Deer without trying. It's a falsetto voice, fluttering and flutey, birdlike. I don't know where the name came from – like an Indian mother, I just picked the first thing that came into my head. I don't exactly know when Leaping Deer turned up, either. I guess I was at college, maybe fooling with the Ouija board or something.

Though fact to tell, I don't remember I ever did kid round with stuff like that. The point was, taking it seriously. I pulled a grave face when people suggested paranormal party tricks, like spoonbending. Too weighty a matter for frivolities, I'd say. Only the initiated may enter these realms in safety. And initiation itself is hard and dangerous. I have endured . . . I have triumphed. And for twenty-five bucks I can do you a hand-tooled astrological reading.

So when did Leaping Deer make the scene? Maybe I should tell you it's as if she's always been there. But even now, you might believe me. So, she crept up on me. Sometime, I don't know when. And I guess she came to England with me.

Dammit, I'm even talking about her like she has some separate existence. Like she's real. She's just a voice I do, OK? Easy as that. I scrunch my balls up and do a high, whistley voice, and that's Leaping Deer. I make it known she's my spirit guide, a guest in my entranced body, but that's strictly for the customers. For you, the beloved readers, I affirm Leaping Deer is purely a piece of voicebox gymnastics.

Leaping Deer said, 'I am here.'

And Jane said, 'Ah, Leaping Deer, it is good of you to find time to assist me.'

Her tone was more than just motherly – it was the voice middle-aged English ladies use to the hired help. I realised much later that Jane regarded Leaping Deer as a foreigner, which to her meant one notch below working class. Leaping Deer should count herself privileged to be talking to Mrs Jane Lyons, and damn fortunate to be asked to help.

Leaping Deer said, 'In my realm time has no meaning.'

'My husband died six years ago. Is it worth giving you facts like that? If time has no meaning?'

'Ambrose has progressed far on this plain.'

'Really? Well, he always was ambitious.'

'We do not know the meaning of that concept.'

'He wanted to better himself.'

'No one is here who does not desire that for themselves and their loved ones.'

Jane sniffed. 'Well, I'm sure you know best, Leaping Deer, but I can think of a good many people who have never shown the slightest inclination for self-improvement.'

'They do not reside here. They return to your plane, to try again.'

'Indeed – as animals of the lower order, I believe?'

'As humans. You yourself have made many returns. You are a soul of much experience.'

'Well, I must say I've often felt I'd been here before.'

'But you will learn. Eventually,' promised Leaping Deer.

A chilly silence followed. I was about to have Leaping Deer start throwing a few predictions around, when my caller said: 'So. Does Ambrose have any message for me?'

'Ambrose . . . Ambrose is far from you . . . do not cling to him . . . he wishes you to progress. Jane, do you wish to remarry?'

'Why – no! That is, I cannot say the thought ever has crossed my mind.'

I know when someone is lying. So does Leaping Deer. And that statement couldn't be true, coming from anyone. Every widow under ninety thinks about marrying again.

'Jane, honesty is everything. There can be no hope of progress when we bear the dead weight of a lie across our shoulders.'

'Well really!' Jane burst out. 'I dare say you're terribly wise now, but it might be as well for you to remember – I've lived a good deal longer than you did, and I've always found it best to tell the truth.'

'Search your heart,' urged Leaping Deer gently. 'I do not accuse you of encouraging suitors. I am asking, do you wish, wish in your romantic soul, to find a man you love and marry him?'

Hard to say No to that one. Jane swallowed her pride and said, 'Yes.'

'Because,' said Leaping Deer, with the splendour of a spirit guide who is revealing an immense and eternal truth, 'that is what Ambrose desires for you.'

Jane's 'Oh!' was a little gasp, nothing more.

'You're English, of course?'

'Naturally!'

'And Ambrose has not left you in – difficult straits?' That's the way to ask the question: sound concerned, sound delicate. For Christ's sake, never ask a woman, 'So, you've got a pile of dough?'

'He was always good about taking my advice. I warned him often that one day I might have need to call on prudent provisions, and we arranged some life insurance, yes. Which I have handled with due care. But I expect Ambrose can see all these things.'

'Ambrose's spirit is content,' Leaping Deer said reassuringly. 'Except he desires romantic fulfilment also for you. A soul mate. He wishes your spiritual being to have its earthly compliment.'

'He never was a jealous man,' murmured Jane sadly.

'Jealousy has no meaning on this plane. He is glad you anticipated his death so wisely.'

'But I never guessed at all!'

'The financial anticipation,' prompted Leaping Deer.

'Oh well, that. But we never suspected he was going to die so suddenly. Or so young. I don't suppose the insurance company would have covered him, if they'd known. About his heart. In fact, he only took out the policy in the middle of May, and by July he was dead. Less than six weeks.'

'How tragic,' whispered Leaping Deer. 'One so young. I myself died so young . . . I was only . . .'

Jane wasn't listening: 'They made a lot of trouble, the insurance people, it was so unpleasant. Of course, it went right over me, I was so much lost in my grief. They kept asking why he'd insured himself for such a large amount.'

'I suppose he thought a million was necessary,' agreed Leaping Deer.

Now the great thing about being a psychic, especially a psychic with a spirit guide on board, is you can afford to be wrong once in a while. It adds authenticity. So for the big questions, you can take a stab and wait to be corrected.

But all Jane said was, 'Oh Leaping Deer, I suppose money is another meaningless concept on your spiritual level.'

My own voice, my Mikki voice, cut back in. Doing the falsetto could be a strain. Sometimes I forgot myself and slipped up an octave, but that could be passed off as a momentary possession. A rip in the veil, a spark across the chasm . . . give the listeners some visual images, it helps them cope.

I said, 'Leaping Deer? Leaping Deer? I'm never going to get used to that, the suddenness, the wrench when she vanishes. Talk about down to earth with a bump!'

'Mikki,' Jane said warmly, 'you are such a different personality. It's hard to believe those two voices can speak from one mouth.'

I got the feeling Jane Lyons didn't like Leaping Deer too much. Feminine rivalry.

'I don't recall too much,' I said, 'but am I right in feeling there could be much more guidance Leaping Deer would like to impart? You seem such a complex person, such spiritual depths . . . I don't know, I just sense they're there.'

So what's she going to say? 'No Mikki, I'm a very superficial type of woman.'

She said, pitifully, 'I am weak, I feel vulnerable, yes – I need guidance urgently.'

'Jane,' I ordered masterfully, 'stay on the line and we can talk some more after the show.'

Which is the formula I use for, 'Can I have a date?' I just never thought I'd use it on a victim old enough to be my mother's big sister.

CHAPTER SIXTEEN

I borrowed £50 from Mimi to give me some elbowroom on my MasterCard, and I took Jane to dinner at Graceland. This took some arranging, but the rock'n'roll wrinkly who ran it owed me a favour. Basically I energised some crystals for him to ward off sciatica on his last world tour.

Either the crystals worked, or a bottle-and-a-half of Jack Daniels every afternoon is good for lower back pain. Whichever, he was grateful and I was in possession of a backstage pass inscribed, 'This intitles the barer to the best table in the house, signed The Prezzident.' It was a tug to see it go, but I delivered it to the maitre d' and three days later I got a table. By the big window, spotlights and candles, everything. Some going.

Jane Lyons was impressed. She ought to be. Cheeseburgers were £21.60, and the cheese was an optional extra.

I did Leaping Deer for her, right there in Graceland. Leaping Deer had taken the trouble to talk with Ambrose's spirit guides, and the guides were kind of specific about the guy Jane ought to be marrying. No Limeys. American was best. Had to be dark. ('Oh, but not black!' exclaimed Jane, who hadn't caught Leaping Deer's drift yet.)

Age was specified, psychic ability was a must, media type preferred. Leaping Deer even had some suggestions about clothes sense. Guess what? She recommended a guy who wore black.

'Oh,' twittered Leaping Deer, 'isn't it almost as though they know about Mikki? But of course they can't.'

I didn't propose over coffee – I had to drop some hints about the permit situation first. But by the time we were sharing a minicab I had grabbed her hand and was murmuring heartbreakingly about the loneliness of celebrity life. How I longed for a sensitive soul to share my burdens and wistful dreams. Someone who would be undazzled by the media glitter.

Before Baker Street station Jane was saying, 'Oh, Mikki, I've been searching and you've been searching . . .'

I didn't give her the chance to rethink the rest for herself. I just seized her other hand, took advantage of a jolt in the road to lurch into her lap, and gasped: 'We've found each other!'

Surprising – it's so much easier to make the adoration sound genuine if it's all synthetic. I guess emotion gets in the way during these big scenes.

So look where it got me. A wife, a work permit, a blank space where my credit rating used to be and a private detective under the window.

After riding back from the university in South Kensington to Jane's flat, I let myself in with the key Jane left taped under the letters flap for the daily help. I hadn't much idea what I was walking into. Silence was what I was hoping for. Some women deal with tension by clamming up. That had never been Jane, but it couldn't hurt to hope.

She was in the bath.

She sang out, 'Is that you, you naughty boy?'

Didn't sound terminal. I called back, 'I hope you weren't expecting just anyone at bathtime,' because sullen is never my style.

'Come in here and scrub my back, you wicked wicked child.'

That was OK. Jane was apparently expecting me to ravish her in the tub, which meant she didn't have two goons waiting behind the door to break my legs.

The bath was brimming over with froth. If I'd sprinkled chocolate powder on it she'd have looked like she was sitting in a monster cappuccino. Her hair was sealed inside a yellow rubber cap, tight enough to pull the lines out of her chins.

'Loofah glove,' she said. 'And very very gently. I have sensitive skin.'

I began massaging between her shoulders. Her skin was the texture of that very thin toast you used to get in fancy hotels. Maybe it had been freckled, before she set about grilling it with the very exclusive brand of UV rays that shine on the Côte d'Azur.

'Tell me about your day,' she ordered. And while I was wondering whether we were pretending the night before had never happened, she added: 'You needn't include anything before eight a.m., because Mr Marsh has already told me.'

Kerry and I had arrived at the studios just before eight. So our sleuth had been keeping tabs right up to the PrimeTime security barrier.

'Your Mr Marsh had a very boring night, I'm afraid,' I sympathised.

'He can't expect your cheap friends to perform for him every time,' Jane said. Her voice was dripping so much acid, it made the bathwater steam.

'So I went to work. I did the show.'

'I heard it.'

'My most loyal listener. And then I met a professor.'

'The great experiment,' she commented.

'He claimed it would rewrite history.'

'That's enough back, thank you. Would you pass the Vitamin E cream please?'

Jane seemed genuinely content in her domestic wallow. An attentive husband, a hot tub, a catty gossip about the day's doings. She was forgetting the sex tapes and the fact she hadn't seen me since pouring coffee over my crotch in a pasta parlour – but hell! All women have selective memories.

'What did you think of Professor Ingman?'

'Pompous,' I said. 'Droner, self-obsessed, humourless, treated his researcher like a temp. Behaved like the whole world could be boiled down to five little drawings on playing cards. But I didn't go there expecting to like him.'

'Why did you go there at all?'

'I'm always proud to participate in the march of science.'

'Now you're talking through your bum-hole, Mikki.'

'That's crude, darling.'

'I thought Americans were always crude.'

There was something odd about her tonight. Something uninhibited, like she was laughing at a joke only she could hear. I knew she didn't drink – or at least, if she did drink, it was something I didn't know about. She might have swallowed some pills.

'Have you been at the happy tablets?' I asked.

'In a man's world, every woman with a sense of humour must be either drunk or drugged,' said Jane. 'And I don't believe in your high scientific ideals, so why did you go to the university to see Kris?'

'Who? Mr Telepathy? You know, I'm a winner both ways with that geek. I score high, it confirms what we already know: I'm psychic. I score some misses, it's not my fault – the bozo and me didn't click. Good telepathy relies on rapport, strong mutual vibes. I can't just turn it on like a telephone system.'

'I hope you told him so.'

'He ought to know. He's the specialist.'

71

'But his tests must have some counterbalance built in, to take account of that vibes thing. Otherwise they'd all be meaningless.'

'Maybe they are.'

'Which is why I asked – what did you do it for?'

Jane was hot on this point. She wanted me to spell it out.

'He asked me.'

'But as I remember, you said "no".'

'I changed my mind.'

'Mikki, you're being very contrary and you know perfectly well you did it for the money.'

'So, maybe. What if?'

'We have an agreement about money.'

'I'd hand it over, but he never gave it to me.'

'Now, don't tell me lies. I can accept any amount of trouble from my friends, but no lies. That's betrayal, simple and straight.'

'Simple and straight is what I'm giving you. The cheque's in the post.'

'You honestly and truly walked out without getting paid?'

'I had to. He said it was handled by some other department.' A void was opening up where my stomach had been. Jane was right – had I really walked out of that dump without my dough? And I really thought it was going to turn up in the next pile of junk mail?

'You will have to consult your natal charts, Mikki,' she reproved me. 'I think the stars are going to say you were born yesterday.'

'It's an institution,' I said. I tried to sound confident.

'Don't whine. You know what British institutions are. Licensed dens of vagabonds and thieves. I don't suppose that university has put a cheque in the post to anyone since we went decimal.'

'Easy come,' I said, 'easy go.'

'And what were you plotting to do with your secret horde? I believe £5,000 was the proffered carrot?'

'I never believed in it anyhow.'

'I expect Kris will write something like, "The subject did not score highly and failed to *foresee* that payment would be withheld".' She cackled.

'So what's to gloat for?'

'You must grant, it is terribly amusing from my point of view. You were probably planning to disappear with some silly girl. With the professor's £5,000 to underwrite the great dirty weekend. Am I right?'

'You read my mind.'

'Or perhaps it was for something more serious. To pay off your gangster friends. Or do you imagine you can get a divorce lawyer to act for £5,000? Get a juicy settlement out of me, and pay all those debts with it? Well, if you ever try that lark, Mikki, my boy, you'll soon find out the truth. You can't look up the word "divorce" in a dictionary for £5,000.'

I stood up to leave the room. Suddenly it was time to watch some TV. Maybe start smoking again. Just a couple of packs.

Jane's voice cut me dead.

'I'll tell you something for free, Mikki,' she said. 'You can forget about divorce and you can forget about eloping. And if you ever think of pulling a fast one on your clever darling wife, just remember she's got a scientific report that says you're about as psychic as this rubber duck.'

It was a yellow plastic toy, and when she squeezed it round the neck, it squealed.

CHAPTER SEVENTEEN

I had been stitched up. Like I'd been fitted for a suit – no holes for the arms, no holes for the legs, no holes at all.

I really wigged out.

Jane had fixed it, and now that darling Mikki was sewn into his snug straitjacket, she was too pleased with herself to keep her mouth quiet.

Jane and this professor cooked up the Rhine card trick between them. She knew him – she didn't say how and I was in no frame of mind to be asking coherent questions. Details didn't matter at the time. My point is, she knew this prof from some episode in her dark and distasteful past. And now she had the motive, he had the scam and I was a prime mug.

It was her £5,000 on the table, though she smartly figured it didn't ever need to pass through my hands. She knew why I wanted the dough, and exactly how much I was needing, and exactly how far I'd go to get it.

That £5,000 was one gigantic joke at my expense. Like holding a Big Mac out to a starving man. And then feeding him a slab of concrete.

This was a lot to take in, as she sat smirking at me in her tub of bubbles. The money didn't exist, the tests had been fixed, the prof had been doubled over with laughing at me from the minute he stood up to pay my pasta bill. From before that, even – he was winding me up on air. Now there was nothing to stop him phoning Kerry's show, or at any rate some rival show, and bragging about how dumb I'd been.

He must've been on the phone to Jane the minute I walked out of his office. He and the redheaded female who did all the reading, they had calculated my grade in nought-point-eight seconds and it was clear Mikki wasn't a high scorer.

The professor had told her, Jane claimed, I was the kind of subject who made paranormal powers look about as probable as fairies at the bottom of Aunt Lucy's garden. Jane had been informed I used every conceivable trick to cheat, and had still failed. Which was not true. I had failed, but I hadn't been given the opportunity of trying to pull a fast one. They missed a finesse there.

So I would have liked to score high. I thought it might be good for business to luck out with a perfect twenty-five. But the fact was I thought it couldn't matter one damn red rouble how I scored – until now, after I'd found out who was setting the exam.

I couldn't exactly work out where Jane got her hooks into this professor, who genuinely seemed to be a genuine paid-up university geek doing some genuine research.

What I had worked out was how deep Jane had her hooks into me.

She could do a real job on me. Say, give the results to the *Daily Mail*, with a gaudy version of how I wooed her. Spill the beans about Leaping Deer, and the messages from beyond the veil, and the size of her bank balance. Spice it up with a frank disclosure about our sex-life.

I'd be finished. Wealthy Widow's Saucy Seance With Fake Radio Psychic. Medium Mikki's Lies From The Next World. Boffin's Card Trick Trumps Cheating Seer.

Then they'd rake up the problems in America – the astrology scam and the college exclusion and the thing with the personal ads, and if I was really lucky they'd find out about the Benji brothers and the horses. The Benjis would be so happy when they read their names in the British papers, they'd want to honour me in a special way. Like using my skin for a car-seat cover.

How to prevent this? How to save my neck? By doing everything Jane ever asked of me, ever. That simple. I could make myself her slave, and she would protect me from my own crime. She'd let me carry on earning, providing I carried on giving her all my money. She wanted my whole attention, all of the time, with no added girlfriends and unquestioning sexual obedience thrown in.

'Why?' I said.

'Mikki, don't whine. You sound like a twelve-year-old who can't stay up to watch the late film. "Wh-hy-yy?"' She was enjoying herself. She was tooting her horn. I was fighting off an urge to push her head under the suds.

'Why do you suddenly want to prove I'm not a real psychic?'

'So you admit it, then!'

'I'm not admitting, I'm asking a question.'

'Read my mind and tell me the answer.'

'Boy, you're down on me. Is it all because I slept with Kerry? Really? I'm sorry, OK? I have a libido thing, you knew that. You benefit on that score too.'

'Dear boy, I've lived long enough to take sexual indiscretion in my stride. For your transgression, ordinarily you would get your bottom smacked. But not today. What I said just now is the truth: I don't like liars. And you have been lying to me.'

'It's not like that.'

'Of course it is. Right up to our wedding day, you were full of predictions, and your little spirit-guide voices, and psychic vibrations. But you haven't bothered to keep it up, have you, Mikki? When was the last time we had a message from beyond the Great Divide?'

'I can't live that way,' I said, 'not every minute of our married lives. It's exhausting.' But she'd nailed me. I had let the mask slip after the wedding. I was like a bridegroom who forgets ever to tell his bride he loves her after the first night. Only in my case, I should have been telling her the spirits loved her.

'I don't expect you to perform seances at breakfast,' she said, 'but I'm afraid you have been a little over-confident. I started to suspect you had been embellishing your performances to beguile me. And then I started to wonder if you'd made up every word of it. And then I got a private detective, to see what else you might be lying about . . .'

'I never said I was in contact with Ambrose.' This was my justification – I'd never claimed to bring her messages from her dead husband. That would be too callous, even for a guy who was aiming to wed a widow for her cash and her passport. (And also – let's be a little bit fair to me in all this – I enjoyed how active she was when we made love, and she knew it.)

'You said you were getting messages from Ambrose's spirit guides, and that he wanted me to marry a boy like you.'

'Did you ever do what Ambrose wanted when he was alive?'

'Not always, no,' she admitted.

'So you weren't obliged to listen to anything I said that his guides said he said.'

'Don't hide behind words. You're a selfish child, Mikki. You don't care how anyone else feels or what happens to them, so long as things work out well for you. But do they work out well? Answer me that – do they?'

'So what do you want me to say?'

76

She stared at me. I wanted to know what she was thinking – I would have given a lot right then to be psychic. And then she nodded and said, 'Give it up, Mikki. Throw it in. Or at least, stop doing all your stuff on the radio. Just keep it for private occasions. Parties and when we have friends round, when we're abroad and meeting new people. I shall keep you in luxury, my dearest boy.'

'I'll be your psychic pet. Is that it?'

'You'll be my full-time husband. After all, you always intended to make a lot of money from me. It might as well be your proper job. And you can still be psychic, but save it for when I'm showing you off.'

'No.'

'I can always force you.'

'By stopping my pocket money?'

'By exposing you. Kris has a very precise measurement of your real psychic ability, and I'm quite sure you won't have a job left by the time a few newspaper editors have seen your results. So you'll just have to withdraw gracefully, before you get kicked out.'

'Kick me out,' I said. 'If you're giving me the choice between quitting to be your overfed lapdog, and being dumped in the street like a mongrel, I'll be a mongrel. Because I'm nobody's damn poodle.'

And I walked out.

'Next time you come crawling back,' she screamed after me, 'You'd better be prepared to suffer.'

The people across the landing were hanging out of their doorways as I walked down to the lifts. I was too mad to make a joke of it, and not quite mad enough to start a fight with them. So I ignored their goggling faces and stared at the walls.

I don't know exactly what time this was. The police were hot on that question later, but I wasn't wearing a watch. There was no clock in the bathroom. What am I expected to do, take a cab to Big Ben? I didn't know the time. Big deal.

The police made it a big deal, anyhow.

The people across the landing, they seemed to think I left around seven p.m. I don't see how it can have been that early, I'd say eight or nine, but like I told you, I didn't have a watch on.

So sometime between the start and the end of Friday evening, I went to a phone box and rang Kerry. She wasn't there. Or if she was, she was letting the answering machine field her calls. I left my message and the number of my call box, but I didn't expect her to dial straight back. My message wasn't exactly what would make her

77

laugh and sing – 'Hi, any problem if I crash down on your sofa again? Just one more night? Please?'

She had a mobile, but I didn't know the number by heart. I'd had a mobile once too, with her mobile number programmed in. Jane took it. And hid it.

When your wife destroys your personal possessions, this is a sign there are problems in the marriage.

The phone booth was on the embankment. I'd kind of wandered over there, through Kensington Gardens and over the Serpentine, along Constitution Hill and past the Palace, down to the Houses of Parliament. These ancient institutions were all having a big laugh at my expense, but I thought they were romantic anyhow. And some genuine romance was something I could use.

It was a hot night and the coolest places were by the water. So I stood beside a phone that was not going to ring, looking at Westminster Bridge and thinking I might be sleeping on its steps pretty soon if my life continued on its current giggle-a-minute flightpath.

There were flat barges floating under the arches. People don't know this, the Thames is still a working river. Some of those big boats, they can load whole skyscrapers onto them. The men running and jumping across the stacks of wood and concrete and boxes look like ghosts from the British Empire. Out of Dickens. Makes you feel adventurous.

I swung a leg over the wall and measured my dive into the river – how far down to the water, how deep it would be at the edge, how long I'd be swimming before I reached the first barge. How hard it might be to haul myself silently aboard and stowaway.

Stowaway to where? Amsterdam would be fine, Rotterdam I could live with. But say it was Tilbury and no further. I would have got wet for not very much advantage. And which way to the sea? The nearest barge was going right to left, and I was on the north embankment . . . therefore . . . damn it, I never could do maps in my head.

Face facts. I wasn't going to escape anything by stowing away on a barge.

The phone, incredibly, still wasn't ringing. So I took positive action.

I rang Mimi.

She wasn't answering either. And she didn't have an answering machine.

Mimi wasn't in. This was outrageous. Supposing I needed her?

I did need her. How was I supposed to get hold of her? Had she thought of this, before she started hitting the town?

Selfishness, that's what it boiled down to.

I was angry for quite a while. I stood and glowered at those barges, which were going places I couldn't go. The light started fading. Someone came over and asked me the time, and I snarled. Then I started to feel bad. I shouldn't let my personal problems get so great that I was rude to strangers in the street. After all, I was still an American abroad, and we have standards to keep up.

It was a hot night. So what if I slept in the park? Was it raining, was it snowing? The grass was dry and the sky was clear. People paid good money to sleep in the open, they called it camping.

I started walking.

Maybe I could do some sort of competition on air in the morning. Win a psychic on your sofa for the night! My listeners would be ringing up in teams. Begging for the chance to meet me and give me breakfast.

It was an idea.

In fact, this was Friday, so there was no show in the morning.

I told myself, Be practical. Stop trying to kid around the issue. There's a disaster looming here. Your wife is about to expose you as a fraud. She's already kicked you onto the streets, penniless. Ex-girlfriends are short in supply, to the point of non-existence. You can't go back to Brooklyn, because the Benji brothers have pledged themselves in blood to serve up your heart in a Lender's bagel, and it's hard to be sure they were joking about this.

What are you going to do?

If I was giving myself psychic advice, what would I say? If I was consulting Leaping Deer . . .

I couldn't help it. I put on the high, flutey voice and I said out loud, 'Destroy the evidence.'

There it was. A message from the beyond. And a message that made sense.

If I could just get hold of my test results and shred them, Jane would lose her handhold on my balls. And he'd said there was a video running – was that true? And who had the tape? Was it still in the camera, locked inside that oversized cupboard?

I wanted the papers, and I wanted the tape, and without them the professor could claim what he liked. Without the evidence to back himself up, he'd be open wide to a libel case. And I'd be urging him on. English courts are weird about libel. Someone says something hurtful about you, and they have to pay more money than you can earn in a lifetime.

At the very least, without the test results we were all back to status quo levels. I was needing £5,000 and Jane was having me trailed by a private eye and Kerry was looking for the excuse to close down our affair. At least we'd all shown our hands now.

I discovered I had walked back past the abbey and barracks, across Green Park and onto Piccadilly. I knew how to get to South Kensington from there. Back up Piccadilly, round Hyde Park Corner, past Harrods and onto Cromwell Road

I knew there was a Tube station right outside the Natural History Museum, but I didn't have £1.20. I didn't have 12p, to be frank. So I could walk. It'd do me good.

I wasn't going to see the dinosaurs. It's just something of great importance to me was in a drawer across the road from the museum. My future.

CHAPTER EIGHTEEN

There was a bum on the steps of one of the big houses in Queensberry Place, a couple of doors down from Alfred Russel Wallace House. In England, they're frightfully polite and say, 'members of the homeless fraternity'. Like it's a club. In England everything is a club.

If I didn't find those results and make confetti of them, I'd be hammering on the doors of the club pretty soon.

If on the other hand I struck lucky, and the results could be located and maybe even doctored to show I had a perfect 100 per cent score in every test . . .

But there's such a thing as being too smart. And I was forgetting the video.

I stared at the bum, like I could somehow keep myself out of the club by Facing My Fear. The bum buried his face; he didn't like being looked at.

I went on to No. 16. The plan was simple: I wait till no one is looking and I break in. It was kind of a surprise to discover all the windows were barred. What were they expecting? Hot-headed spiritualists would force an entry and levitate all their tables?

I was loitering on the doorstep when the portals swung back and out stepped the redhead. Louisa Simons. She was arm in arm with some other woman, an older female with her hair up in a massive loop. They were laughing. In fact, they were falling about. I wondered if they'd been splitting a pint of sherry.

'The idea of it! As if Jung would ever have confessed to that!' the other woman was shrieking. And the redhead was laughing too, not so hard, but hard enough that it didn't register with her when I held the door for them.

She even said, 'Oh, thank you.'

And then they were laughing off towards the museum. And I was in the hallway.

I know it sounds childish, and it's probably trivial, but I was glad they were laughing about that guy Jung and not my test results.

They'd turned off the lights as they went. I was in the dark, and I wasn't going to try to do anything about it. The first switch I found could be the strip-lights, or it could be the alarm. I'd got this far, and it was up to me to be grateful.

I felt my way upstairs.

The prof's door was second on the right. This I remembered. I got there by touch, though there was some moonlight and my eyes were getting used to it. The floor was silent under my feet, big heavy boards covered with cheap acrylic carpeting, but the building was emitting hums and clicks like I was being monitored. As if the house was feeling where I was.

That was my over-sensitive ears. What I could hear was the lights cooling off, the electricity meters whirring slowly and the water pipes vibrating. There were no spy cameras, because a place like this didn't need them.

And the idea of ghosts – just because this was a parapsychology unit, didn't mean the staircase was haunted.

Be reasonable. I could hear a humming noise. I wasn't seeing headless grey ladies marching across the landing.

The door to the prof's outer office was locked. I turned the handle and nothing yielded. I stood back, and tried again. I turned it both ways and leant on the door. As if that would do anything. The door was solid oak, you could crush bricks in the hinges.

There had to be keys somewhere.

I felt all along the top of the frame, under the edges of the carpet, under the door. No key.

I hadn't come this far just to take a nap on the landing. The house was deserted, it couldn't be later than midnight and I wasn't booked to go any place. Somewhere there was a bunch of keys, and I was intending to find them.

I edged back down the passage, waving my hands in front of my face like a blind man conducting the New York Philharmonic because I was becoming genuinely a little edgy about walking into a ghost. The fact the door was locked gave me the creeps. Which wasn't logical, because professors probably always lock their doors. To keep prying colleagues out.

I stood at the top of the stairs and breathed in deeply. I needed to calm myself. I needed to focus my thoughts. I needed a cigarette.

There was a smoky odour in the air, and it wasn't tobacco. It hadn't registered till that moment. I inhaled again. It smelt like a burnt pork dinner. Maybe the professor ate in his rooms.

I turned and felt my way back up the passage, to the locked door, sniffing the air all the way. The smell was stronger. It could have been something was on fire at the end of the passage, but I couldn't see any glow. I edged further along the wall.

There was another door. It was no more than ten feet along from the first one, and it had to open onto Ingman's private office. I didn't remember noticing it, but there wasn't any reason why I should have. When I went into Ingman's room I was looking for tricks and hidden mirrors, not emergency exits.

I turned the handle. This door wasn't locked. As I pushed it open the burnt meat smell got a lot stronger.

It was pretty much of a stench. A bad reek. It wasn't normal. This couldn't be the way Professor Ingman wanted his nice office to stink.

Except Professor Ingman was way, way past caring.

CHAPTER NINETEEN

His body lay on the rug like a shadow. Black and charred and stinking. The shoes had toes stuck up at angles, and the tips drooped like they were half melted. Which is what they were.

In the yellow streetlight from the window, his legs were sticks of dark ash, shiny and bubbled. The pelvis had crumbled into flakes of carbon, with the scorched and twisted metal of his trouser-flies coiled in the centre. The brass buttons of his blazer had fallen through the ribcage and lay against the black smudge of charcoal that was Professor Ingman's backbone.

The skin had peeled off the skull, and the white wings of hair were melted into beady globules. There were no eyes and the nose had collapsed, but the head retained its roundness, like blown glass.

I'm telling you this in detail because that's how I saw it. In sharp-focus detail. I took everything in with a single look. Maybe I should have rushed to the window and puked, but it was simply like my brain was downloading a big data file. Machine-like. All that information, down to how the ashes rested on the fibres of the rug.

Afterwards, I was sick. At Louisa's flat. I brought up breakfast, lunch and dinner. But that's getting ahead of the story.

From the ankles and wrists down, and the neck up, the professor was just dead. All the rest of him was plain obliterated. The shoes and the big opal ring on his left hand would be enough for police identification. I had no doubts this was Johannes-Kristian Ingman and none other.

I didn't touch him. He was on his back, arms at his sides, legs apart, palms down as far as I could make out. Weird position to die in. Not as if he'd fallen.

His pipe was on his desk. The bowl had been scraped out, and there was no tobacco nearby. I couldn't see matches either. He could have set light to his clothes accidentally – only how did he wind up on the rug?

I guess I stared for ten seconds or so. The professor's body looked

84

like a scientific exhibit. Like a mummy that has been unwrapped, and then rotted.

I made a decision to ignore it all. Ingman was dead and it was the last problem I needed. I couldn't help him. It was too late for a bucket of water. Or an ambulance. And if I called the cops they'd be curious about what Mikki was doing in the late professor's rooms after midnight.

But give me some credit. I ditched the plan to steal back my tests. I'm not that cold-blooded. Plus, it would be the act of an imbecile, to rifle the drawers of a mysteriously dead man.

No one was going to be interested in my Rhine results now. The prof was going to get all the attention to himself.

I started to back out of the room and closed the door on his corpse.

This was Friday night. Who'd be the next person to find Professor Ingman? Maybe the parapsychology department employed cleaners on a weekend. But it didn't look that way. Most likely the discovery would be waiting for the redheaded researcher when she came in on Monday morning.

She'd gone out of the building laughing. I didn't want her to turn up for work to this. I wouldn't want any woman to see the blackened thing on the rug.

So who did I tell? Not the emergency services – they taped every call. I didn't want to be tied up with this in any way. What I wanted to do was pass the discovery on to someone else.

Not the PrimeTime newsdesk – they might recognise my voice. Maybe a newspaper. The *Sun* – they must have journalists on duty all night. Just do the anonymous call, tell them something interesting awaits their attention in SW7.

What if they ignored me? And was I going to leave all the doors open so the press could let themselves in? And what if they ever did trace that call to me, what if an incriminating shoeprint was pressed into the ashes or the air-con had extracted strands of DNA from my breath? You couldn't tell how much these forensics people could work out from one stale breath.

What it boiled down to was, I had a superstitious fear that because I'd been in the room, someone would work it out. So why say anything to anyone? Why not just go?

I turned and stepped out into the pitch-black passage. I started to close the door. I was leaving – this was none of my business, and it didn't have to be my problem unless I made it.

I stood there, with my hand on the handle, and my brain replayed the words Jane had hurled at me earlier that night. 'You're a selfish child, Mikki. You don't care how anyone else feels or what happens to them, so long as things work out well for you. But do they work out well? Answer me that – do they?'

I wasn't admitting for one second that she'd been right. But I had found a body, and if I didn't report it someone else would go through the nastiness of finding it too, and that someone was probably the redhead with the book collection. That wouldn't be fair. So who should I tell?

Someone who knew Ingman – but not Jane. That was a hostage fortune could live without.

It would be easiest, I thought, to ring someone neutral, someone I didn't know, and use a false voice – maybe I could get my Leaping Deer voice to make the call for me. I'd simply say that Ingman's body was in his room, and then hang up. And leave.

I pushed back into Ingman's room, stepped over the body and went through the inner door to the redhead's office.

If anything, her room was in a worse state than it had been that afternoon. The stack of books on her desk had gone over. So had the pile on her chair. I was ankle-deep in obscure psychology texts. The phone was balanced on a pillar of A4 reports, and the LEDs of a small stand-up digital clock were glowing redly. It was 12:38 a.m.

Who could I call? Was Ingman married? What was his home address? Who did he work with, apart from the redhead? Who would be looking for him now? If I found an address book and rang a number at random, how did I know I wouldn't be calling the killer?

I had to make a decision. I couldn't stay in that outer office all night. Apart from anything, there was the smell, seeping under the door and infecting my lungs. Probably stinking out my clothes too. I wanted to be away. I didn't have the nerve to start playing guessing games with the phone book.

It didn't occur to me to inform the cops. Simply did not occur. For a person with my upbringing, dialling for the cops is like reciting the Lord's Prayer backwards to summon the powers of darkness. You just don't.

I had to compromise. I could ring Louisa Simons and warn her, without exposing her to the full horror of her boss's corpse. That was OK. If I knew her number.

It was easy enough. She'd scrawled all her useful numbers on a page torn from a notebook and taped them to the side of her word processor. I liked this girl. She knew the best way to store text on a computer is with a Biro, a sheet of paper and some Sellotape.

Ingman's number was there, just listed as J-K-I. No hint of his marital status. I guessed unmarried, because that opal wasn't a betrothal band.

A couple of women's names were listed – Irene, 267, and Jo, 271. They looked like extensions. Sure enough, Louisa Simons's phone was 264. Then there was the Rudolf Steiner School GG, and Jodie (babysitter), which suggested the redhead had kids. As if I cared. Except I didn't want to start ringing numbers in the dead of night and scare her children.

So what am I supposed to do, ring her babysitter?

I could have walked out and left the call till morning, but I'd made my decision to be noble now. If I left it, maybe the cleaners would find him, maybe the redhead would come in, maybe I wouldn't sleep for worrying about the call I had to make. So get it over and done with.

I picked up the receiver in a folded piece of A4, to keep my prints off it, and I pushed the buttons with my knuckle. My hands were shaking suddenly.

A woman's voice said, 'Yes, professor.'

My hand was hovering, poised to cut off the call.

'This is a friend,' I said.

The temperature at the other end of the line dropped about 20 degrees.

'I'm on a mobile. It says you're using my phone – who are you?'

'I have something to tell you, it's . . . upsetting . . .'

'Who are you, what are you doing in my office?'

'I . . . I . . . the professor's dead,' I blurted. Sensitive approach, but what else is there?

'Why are you calling me?'

She didn't seem to be getting it.

'Listen, I'm in your office, I've just found Ingman in his study and he's dead. I thought you'd better know.'

'You're the radio man, the American. The one he tested today.'

I dropped the receiver back on the cradle. Then I picked it up and redialled. If I had wanted to place an anonymous call, I should have gone to a box and imitated an English accent. So maybe I wanted her to guess who was speaking. Maybe I needed to talk.

There was a long pause between her picking it up and saying, 'Yes?'

'Your name's Louisa, right? I'm Mikki. You let me into the building tonight, but you didn't realise it.'

'I certainly didn't.'

'You were with a woman and her hair was tied up. And you hadn't been in your office for quite a while, right?'

At least, I hoped to Christ she hadn't. What if these women had been busy doing the murder? In fact, what else could they have been doing in the building at midnight on a Friday? It wasn't standard working hours.

'Did you say Professor Ingman is dead?' She said it like it was news to her. I had to believe she wasn't fooling me. Louisa didn't strike me as a murderer. I don't mean I was picking up her psychic vibes or her aura, but from a first impression, cold-reading take, she wasn't a girl who would set fire to a corpse and then walk into the street laughing.

'He's a kind of gruesome sight,' I said. 'I didn't want you to find him yourself. But I thought you ought to call the police. Only I'd like you to leave me out of it, OK?'

'Why?'

'Just tell them this was just an anonymous call.'

'God, he's dead? You're certain? God. My God.' She left a long pause. I wanted to put the phone down, and I was about to when she said: 'What were you doing in our offices?'

Honesty is the best policy, the truth will out, I cannot tell a lie, etc. 'I'd come to collect my results.'

'From this afternoon? Why? If that isn't a stupid question . . .'

Well, she certainly wasn't being too quick. As if I was.

'I wanted to rip up my records, OK?'

'You were wasting your time. I've brought them home with me.'

'OK. I wish I'd known. I'm going to go now.'

'You're not psychic, I suppose you realise that.'

'I don't think it matters. Have you got what I told you?'

'I'm not ringing the police,' she said.

'Ah. Louisa, can you swear you knew nothing about this already?'

'I don't understand you.'

'I'm asking, you didn't kill the professor yourself?'

'What? Do you mean – Ingman's been killed? Is it murder?'

I hadn't been making myself too clear. 'What did you think I was saying?'

'I thought – he had a heart attack last year, I assumed – it's not natural causes? Why? What makes you think that?'

'I just know. It's obvious, OK?'

'Has he been shot?'

'Shot? Who'd shoot him? Did you hear shots?' We were talking in circles, almost like we were using different languages and our meanings kept missing each other. And then, she barely sounded like she was listening to me. I wondered if maybe she'd just fallen asleep before her phone rang.

'I think, before I call the police, you'd better come and tell me exactly what's happened.'

'Louisa, really, I'm not part of this, I don't want to get involved. I have enough trouble already.'

'I don't think – you don't have any choice.'

'I'm going to go now,' I said again.

'Go where, where are you going?'

'It doesn't matter.' But it was a fair question. Where the hell did I think I was going to go?

'Look, just come over and tell me what you've seen and what's happened to Ingman. I need to know.'

'And then you'll call the police?'

'Then I'll call the police.'

'And leave me out of it.'

'If that's what you want. If you really only found the body and that's all. Just come and – tell me. All right? I need you to tell me everything about it.'

'Where are you?'

'Don't you know? I'm opposite you – right opposite. Look out of the window.'

Across Queensberry Place a light shone in a third-floor window. Curtains gave the room a bell shape, and a table with flowers in a big water jug stood in the centre. A figure came and leant on the table, peering at the dark windows of Alfred Russel Wallace house.

'Push the button labelled "Simons",' she said. 'Number Three.'

I guess I felt protected by my innocence. If I'd topped the prof myself, I wouldn't have gone to talk to her. Then, I wouldn't have phoned her. I was hardly to guess I'd be leaving her apartment in a patrol car come Saturday morning.

CHAPTER TWENTY

S he let me in with a buzzer, and gave me a thorough inspection through a spyhole before opening the door to her apartment.

Her short red curls were bristling like they were alive. The first thought that hit me was, maybe this woman is so intelligent she generates electricity with her brain. She wore a blue pullover that was torn full of holes and loose threads. She had pulled it over a nightie that reached halfway down her calves. Her legs were strong, shaved and slender at the ankle. She had long feet too. That always turns me on.

She shut the door behind me, tugging the hem of the jumper down in front of her and pointing me towards a sofa. 'Ingman's really dead?' she said. 'I can't take it in.'

'It must've come as a shock to him too.'

'You woke me up,' she said. 'Sorry if I don't make much sense, I'm useless at this time of night.'

'Do you take something to help you sleep?' It was in the back of my mind, she might not remember much about this the next day. But she shook her head.

'I boiled a kettle,' she added, reaching into the kitchenette and grabbing two cups. The one she handed me was cracked and full of hot coffee. I could hear the fissure fizzing three feet away. I held it well to one side. My underwear didn't need another boil-wash.

I looked around, and took in a small apartment. The kitchen was a cupboard with a sink and a microwave. The room we were in was 15 feet square, no more, and the wall to my right looked like a piece of emulsioned chipboard with a door cut into it.

'I thought you might have kids,' I said.

'One. A boy. Dani, he's six.'

'Short for Daniel?' I hazarded.

'Of course. Because we're Jewish.'

Obviously. With her red hair and the skin that was ivory rather than white, and the strong nose and wide lips. My God, I found

90

Jewish girls sexy, it was a weakness I inherited from my father. Her university manner had stopped me seeing her properly. I'd been looking at her feet, and her jumper, and the brutal way she cropped her curls, when if I'd looked at her face—

She had green eyes. I stared at them.

She stared back. 'Are you trying to hypnotise me or something?'

I was on known territory now. An attractive woman who needed to be able to trust me – my personality is honed for these situations.

'You have eyes like a certain kind of crystal,' I said.

'Oh.'

But I knew she'd have to ask.

'What kind is that, then?'

'Malachite. It's green, but a kind of cloudy, misty, swirling colour. Very good for healing a broken heart.'

'You're an expert, are you?'

'I've never broken one deliberately. A few by accident.'

'I was referring to crystals.'

'Crystals have many paranormal qualities, of great assistance to a psychic.'

'If your tests are anything to go by, you'd need a crystal the size of a bus before you qualified as psychic.'

'It's a good thing,' I said firmly, 'that you're going to bin those results. In return for me being 100 per cent honest with you. You know that card-symbol crap was meaningless.'

'It could be.' She shrugged.

'Seriously? So why do it?'

'What I mean is, Ingman wanted you to fail. So you met his expectations. Sometimes, a real psychic will pick up on those preconceptions and perform accordingly.'

'So this proves I am psychic?'

'It proves nothing. But I know you're not.'

'How come you're so clever?'

'Because I'm psychic.'

She was sitting back, smiling at me, and she had that English sense of humour that Americans can never decide about.

'Nah,' I said. 'Being psychic is a state of mind, it's a way of living. Being open-minded. For instance, a psychic wouldn't laugh about crystal energies.'

His hand dipped into the neck of the blue pullover and fished out a long gold thread. Swinging on the end was a chip of clear quartz with a perfect azure flame inside. For a moment I thought she had a lump

91

of diamond dangling in her nightdress. Then I realised the stone was drawing in the blue of her jumper and refracting it in twenty glittering fragments.

'Do you wear that all the time?'

'Even in the shower.'

'It looks highly charged. With personal energy,' I said.

'Sometimes,' she answered, 'it's almost too hot to wear. It leaves a mark.'

And she pulled down the lip of the jumper and there, at the V of her collarbone, was a dark red triangle.

I usually made the right noises about crystals, I could recite their healing properties on air, but to me they were basically small, pretty chips of stone. Apparently I'd been underestimating them.

'Are we getting off the point?' I said.

'You started it, flattering my eyes.'

So that had gone home. One compliment can do a lot of good work. I hadn't taken much to this woman on the phone, and she was asking a hundred and one too many questions, but I could forgive that because she was a researcher and it probably comes naturally. Plus, she had a sofa which I was intending to sleep on, and at some point she would have to be told this. Plus, I want all good-looking women to like me. It's an ego thing, I freely admit it.

On the other hand, there was something we had to clear up before I started flirting in earnest.

'I think the police have to be told about Professor Ingman,' I insisted.

'You want me to say I found him? Why can't you state the facts yourself?'

'Because of who I am.'

'Mikki – are you connected in any way with his death?'

'No! Would I have phoned you? From there?'

'I don't know. I'm not a detective. Motives can be complex.'

'So ask your psychic senses.'

'I have,' she sighed. 'I don't think you're any sort of a murderer.'

That was the first time I started to take her seriously about paranormal powers.

'I'm just a radio presenter. And if I go to the cops, one of those enterprising characters is going to see an opportunity for an easy buck, and he'll ring his friends on the *Daily Post* or wherever, and he'll say, "Hey boys, guess who we got in the cells? Helping us with our murder inquiries?" So before you can say Page Five Babes, I'm a front-page suspect. They get to be judge and jury, rake up all my history, make up a whole lot more, and way before the cops decide I'm innocent, my image is trashed and my career is colder than a dead penguin.'

'You've given this some thought.'

'It's a nightmare haunting me,' I said earnestly, 'every day of my life.'

'If I'm going to claim I found the body, I can't call the police now. Why would I be in the office at 1:30 in the morning?'

'You were there at midnight.'

'Judith and I went over there for two minutes to collect her bag. She'd been here for dinner – she's the receptionist, and she's divorced and I'm not married and we're both Jewish, so sometimes on a Friday night we eat together. She left her handbag in the hallway, and when Dani was asleep we went to fetch it.'

'You didn't see anything? No one hanging round?'

'I didn't even notice you, and you say we let you in.'

'OK. Why did she need you to go with her? Didn't she have her own key?'

'Sometimes you get weirdos hanging round the unit. Judith didn't like to go in there on her own. At the moment I've got a good alibi, if anyone ever asks me what I was doing all the evening.'

'They will.'

'But if I start inventing reasons to go over to Ingman's office now, and just happen to find his body, what's that going to do to my honesty profile? The police might think I'm lying about everything. No, if it has to be me that finds him, then we've just got to be cool and leave it for tonight. I have to go in tomorrow, a little earlier than ordinary, and make the discovery normally.'

'There's no cleaners? None of his colleagues are going to wander in by accident?'

'Is it a problem if they do?'

'Only if they're of a nervous disposition.'

'He died horribly? Did he bleed much?'

'He burned.' And, since she was going to have to stick her head around Ingman's door, if only for a second, I gave her a sanitised version of what to expect.

Her skin was white to start with. When I'd told her what was spoiling the decor in her boss's office, she was paler than the white rabbit's ghost.

Then she started asking her questions again. The first one was weird. I hadn't thought of her as so callous. 'Was the rug badly burned?' she said.

'I didn't check. It can't have been too much. In fact, I can't remember it was even singed. It was that valuable?'

'Nothing else in the office had caught light?'

'No. I guess not.'

'Was anything melted in the room?'

'Maybe. Yeah, the shoes, I noticed they were softened up.'

'The head, hands and feet were much less badly burned than the rest?'

'The torso was ashes,' I answered. 'You couldn't recognise the head, but the hands were not too bad and the feet were like I said.'

'Was there a foul smell?'

'What do you think? It stank. I can smell it on me now.'

'Mikki.' She leant forward and fixed her malachite eyes on me. 'It may be the professor wasn't murdered.'

I stared back. 'If it was suicide, he must have really hated himself.'

Louisa pulled a book from a pile stacked by a radiator. I took it and glanced at the spine – there was a little chessboard symbol, which meant the publisher was EarthAir. I had some of their books myself – easy-to-read mumbo-jumbo with plenty of pictures. Not the kind of stuff I'd expected this intellectual to be reading.

I looked at the title – *Devouring Flame: An investigation into the phenomena and psychology of spontaneous human combustion.*

The picture on the cover was of a charred corpse. Not at all unlike the professor's, except this one was wearing high heels at the ends of its embers.

'Right,' I said, and made to pass the book back. 'Spontaneous human combustion. Professor Ingman just went up in a puff of smoke. That's bound to be the first idea the detectives get too.'

'I know the book's a bit lurid. There are serious books on the subject, it's just I don't have them here. I bought this one at a jumble sale for 10p. Take a look, look here.' And she held open a full-page panel headlined The Candle Effect.

'Yeah, nice.'

'Read it. Do you think this is what could have happened to the professor?'

I tried to ignore the disembodied feet sticking out of a fireplace in the black-and-white plate, and read the panel: 'Simple physics provides an answer to the human combustion enigma.

'When horror-stricken Amanda Thomas discovered her mother's fire-ravaged corpse, there was little to suggest spontaneous human combustion. Mrs Elsie Mallett, 83, a frail widow who lived alone in a two-roomed Macclesfield house, appeared to have slipped while tending the grate. Her head rested at a sickening angle in the fireplace. Her feet trailed away from the hearth. The rest of her body had burned to cinders.

'But how could the tiny fire which was Elsie's only source of warmth have consumed her so utterly – while leaving the rest of the room untouched? For while the walls and windows were darkened with a thick layer of yellow grease, and plastic ornaments on the mantel over the grate had softened and twisted in the heat, other furnishings in the room were undamaged.

'The carpet was not scorched, except for a few fibres where Elsie's blazing body had lain. The wool-worsted chair-covers were not even singed. Yet the corpse had burned with an intensity to devour all but the extremities. To achieve such complete destruction, a crematorium chamber must be heated to at least 1650 degrees Centigrade. At lower temperatures, the human body, which is 90 per cent water, will not burn.

'Elsie's death was a mystifying paradox – until forensic investigator Dr Timothy Poniard stepped forward. He suggested the old lady could have suffered a stroke as she tended the grate, or perhaps tripped and knocked herself unconscious. "As she lay in the flames, she was helpless to move. And her clothes caught light."

'The doctor explained: "Mrs Mallett was a large woman, with plenty of body fat. Human fat tissue melts at a much lower temperature than could cause it to ignite. If the melting fat dripped onto burning cloth, it would create a gruesome candle of cloth wick and human wax. The wick would keep burning, just as an ordinary candle does, until all the wax was burned out. In this case, only fat-free parts of the corpse survived – the fingers of one hand, the feet which were protected in shoes, and the cranium. The rest was gradually reduced to ashes – over a period of at least twelve hours, I should estimate.

' "The evaporating tissue would emit greasy smoke – hence the thick, oily deposit on the walls and around the corpse. But the candle would never burn hot enough to set light to furnishings. In fact, the conflagration would be quite unspectacular, since oxygen in the room would be quickly used up and the flames would be maintained as a low, insistent flicker. The comfort for Elsie's family is that she could not have been conscious when the accident occurred, or she would have dragged herself clear from the grate. In fact, she may even have been dead before the candle effect commenced."'

I couldn't help scrutinising the photo, trying to make out the remains of the head in the chimney and searching for the unburnt fingers. A wave of sickness broke suddenly over me. There was no struggling against it. I could either try to reach the kitchen, or vomit over the book.

I made for the kitchen.

I almost got there.

I was mopping the floor with a dishcloth when Louisa said behind me, 'I'm sorry. I wasn't thinking. You're hardly likely to view Professor Ingman's death with my professional interest.'

'Is that all you feel about it? Interest? You worked with the man.'

'I couldn't stand him.'

'Did he do anything to you?'

'It wasn't what he did, it was what he said. And the way he said it. But I shouldn't speak ill of the dead.'

'I don't see why not. Unless as a parapsychologist you're worried he'll come back and haunt you.'

'Ingman didn't believe in ghosts. He ought to refuse to be one, on principle. But I don't think his principles ever got in the way of any advantageous career moves. There I go, speaking ill. There's not many in the faculty who'll mourn him, though. Not any, I should think.'

'Anyone who'd go to the trouble of cremating him in his office?'

'That's for the police. But I think when they see the evidence they'll opt for the forensics expert's explanation. Candle effect.'

'You think he set himself alight and forgot to put the flames out?'

'He probably couldn't. He must have fallen – maybe it was a heart attack after all, or he could have slipped and cracked his head – and his pipe set his jacket on fire.'

'He wasn't smoking. I checked.'

'There could have been a burning match.'

'Maybe. But he wasn't lying like he'd fallen. More like someone had laid him out. Like a corpse in a funeral parlour. And there was no grease on the walls and windows. Plus, when did you leave your office?'

96

'Sevenish. Bit later.'

'You'll have to decide on that before the cops get a hold of you. And I was in there round midnight, a few minutes after. Is that long enough for a full Candle Effect, plus the time it takes the heat to dissipate and the embers to die out? Your book figured at least twelve hours.'

'Was it not hot in the office at all?' Louisa shrugged. 'Spontaneous human combustion was one of the professor's pet hates. He reckoned it gave serious paranormal phenomena a bad name. Every time a book was published he'd buy it, gnash his teeth over it, denounce it at the next department meeting, and give it away, usually to me. Hence my collection. Now that's synchronicity. I hope his last act was to disprove one of his own theories.'

'You didn't like him very much, did you?'

She looked at me seriously. 'No one did. If it actually is a murder, there'll be no shortage of suspects. Judith in reception. Annette in admin. Carla, who is his other researcher. Me. The police will be mobbed by people with motives. There'll be a queue round the churchyard to dance on his grave.'

'In America people might think you were a callous young woman. But we Yankees are sentimental. Just don't go boasting to the homicide men how glad you are he's dead. They could be tempted to make something of it. Low on imagination, those guys.'

'I'm just saying it so you don't feel bad. There's lots of people with motives better than yours.'

'I don't have a motive! Do I have a motive?'

'I suppose you'd found out the test was a trap. Isn't that why you wanted your results?'

'How do you know it was rigged?'

She looked at me wide-eyed. 'It wasn't rigged. But I realised Ingman had an ulterior motive in testing you. Obviously.'

I sighed. 'I don't know whether I like you or not.'

'Ah, but I think you're the kind who tries to like everyone. Providing they're prepared to like you back.'

'Perceptive. Very smart. But most people with degrees and doc-torates think they're too clever to believe in anything hocus-pocus. How come it isn't beneath you, looking for things that go bump?'

'Anyone with real intelligence,' she said, 'anyone who can think, is going to have to admit that the universe is very big and very strange. To me, the paranormal is self-evident. Of course it exists. It's there to be explored. Think of a magic number,' she suddenly challenged.

'Seven,' I said. 'Or no, eleven. Eleven is better.'

'Exactly. Both prime numbers. Not divisible by any other number. The other ones people often say are thirteen and three. But all primes have a weird aura. Seventeen, twenty-three, seventy-one, a hundred and thirty-one. The bigger they are, the stranger it seems that they can't divide into any of the other numbers. And the strangest thing is no one has discovered the limit. Prime numbers go on infinitely. When the numbers are millions and millions of digits long, you still get primes. So if eleven is a psychic's number, how weird is an eleven million figure prime number? That's how paranormal the world can be.'

'I love it,' I said. 'I'm using that on Monday's show. But you did real psychology before you got into the spirit world thing?'

'Of course. I did my degree at Manchester and my MSc at Edinburgh, in the Koestler unit.'

'Why Manchester?' I wanted to get her talking about something else except human candles. Also, I wanted to be certain we had enough rapport that I could sleep on her sofa.

I didn't think there was any chance of doing better than the sofa, and I didn't feel equal to trying it anyhow. I wouldn't feel irresistible again till I'd had a hot shower and a scrape with a blunt loofah.

'My family's from Manchester. Well, my mum had gone by that time, she left my dad when I was twelve or thirteen.'

'I sense you weren't too traumatised.'

'Accurate. How did you deduce that?'

'Telepathy, I guess.'

'Cobblers. You're as telepathic as a house brick.'

'Very nice. All right, it's a talent. Why should I reveal it to you?'

'Because you need me to like you, remember?'

She was grinning. I thought she did already like me. Unless she was laughing at me, of course, in that ironic English way no one has ever been able to explain so it made sense to me.

'If you were really chewed up,' I said, 'you'd know when she left. You'd say, "When I was thirteen years old," or, "Four weeks after my thirteenth birthday". The date would be intensely meaningful. You said something vague, "twelve or thirteen".'

'Elementary, Watson.'

'If you want to know – you're a parapsychologist, you should want to know – there's no such thing as telepathy. What there is, is mentalism. Real mentalists can read every twitch on your face. Slight tension over one eyebrow, the way you twist your mouth, they use all that and read your mind like a book. They can work out what number your house is, and what you had for breakfast, just by the way you hold your face. And most of them waste it in tacky stage acts, where everybody knows it's a trick, but just can't see how it's done. Because in the end, what's the point of being able to deduce someone's phone number from the way they comb their hair? What I do, it's less skilled. More intuitive, almost. I let people ask their questions, then I get them to supply their own answers.'

'What you do isn't tacky?'

'I don't think it is.'

'Make much money?'

'What is this, who's asking the questions? You were telling me about your parents. Why'd your ma leave?'

'Dad was sick.'

'That's a nice reason.'

'He was very depressed, I think he'd been down for a long time. Of course, he was just my dad to me. Children take things like depression for granted. He was in the police, and something happened to stress him out, or maybe it was a succession of things, and he took a lot of time off, and when I was eleven he got early retirement.'

'By which time his relationship with your mother was already weakened?'

'That's an understatement. She treated him like something the cat threw up.'

'So she went off with another man? And you stayed with your dad?'

'Someone had to. Both my sisters, I had one older and one younger, they went with mum. As a matter of fact, I think her new stud refused to take more than two extra kids. He had two of his own, from when his wife left him, or died, or something.'

'So you weren't too close.'

'They wanted to leave me and dad – stuff them. That's always been my attitude.'

'When Dani's father left, did you say "Stuff him" too?'

'Yup. Did I tell you Dani's dad left?'

'Cold reading again.'

'You're good.'

'Want me to do your astrology chart?'

'I want to go to bed. Aren't you ever leaving?'

'Ah-ha. I was coming to that.'

She was good about it. She dumped a pillow on me and pulled a blanket off Dani's bed. 'It doesn't matter how hot it is,' she said

99

proudly, 'even if he was sleeping in a sauna he wouldn't go to bed without two blankets and his woolly scarecrow.'

'It's OK, I don't need the scarecrow. I can get by just sucking my thumb.'

'It goes without saying,' was the last thing she said before shutting her bedroom door on me, 'that I can deal with strangers who don't know where their luck runs out. In case you had any obvious ideas.'

'You didn't need to say that.'

'But I've said it anyway.'

In the eight or ten seconds I spent trying to get to sleep on her short, lumpy sofa, I tried to puzzle Louisa Simons out. Very bright, and earning nothing at all, by the look of this flat. Good-looking, and didn't give a damn about it. Loving, but there was no man I could discern on the scene. Honest, but pretty suspicious of me. Spiritual, but scathing about parapsychology, which was bread and butter to her. Cool enough to ignore her own boss's body in her offices, but jumpy enough to be rude before she switched out the light.

Confusing. Just like a woman. Maybe one day I'd meet a nice, straightforward girl. Not like Mimi, not like Jane, not like my temporary landlady, Louisa.

And what would a nice, straightforward girl make of me?

Like I said, I worried about this for about as long as it took to scratch my backside. Then I blanked out. It had been a long day.

When the police started ringing the doorbell forty-five minutes later, I really didn't feel I'd had enough sleep.

Chapter Twenty-One

The interview room was smaller than you'd guess from detective shows, maybe because they didn't have to cram a TV crew into this one. It was five feet across – I could have stretched out and touched both walls at the same time. There was a door at my back, and when that opened it banged into my chair. There was a table, longways, facing me, and two chairs tucked tightly on its corners. The chair-backs leant against the other wall, below the only window.

It was getting light outside, and the window was ajar. We were on the first floor, but I could have stood on a chair, hauled myself up, wriggled through the window and dropped to the ground easily enough. I'm fit.

In case I tried it, there was a plainclothes officer in each of the chairs. Cops are smart like that. They think of everything.

One of the cops was a big guy with a square jaw and a thin mouth, and short fair hair brushed forward. He had blue eyes and he used them to make a lot of contact. Someone at interview school had drummed it into him, 'Look them in the eyes. Makes them trust you.'

This hadn't been explained properly to cop number two. He was staring at his hands, on the table. Maybe he was wondering why he bit his nails so bad. Maybe he was wondering how his fingers got so stained with nicotine, when his cigarette stayed in his face all the time.

We'd been in that little room about forty minutes, and the smoke was going in and out of his lungs a lot faster than it was going out of the window. I was suffering from that. I was thinking how it was now four weeks and four days since I quit smoking. There was a pack of Sovereigns on the table. I didn't see how I was going to make it to four weeks and five days.

The cop hadn't offered them. If he did, I was going to say No. But I was scared he'd leave them there long enough, and I'd ask. Or I'd just reach out and take one. They were within easy distance. They were intended to be.

That would signal I'd cracked. I was willing to beg a cigarette, I was ready to beg for mercy.

Life can be strange. I was being questioned on suspicion of murder, and what was worrying me was whether to start smoking again.

I knew it was murder, and I knew I was a suspect, because this had been explained to me. Kind of at length. When I pulled myself off Louisa's sofa and staggered round her dark sitting room, trying to work out where I was and what that thing was going buzz-buzz, I was acting dopey. I wasn't much better when Louisa had opened the door and sworn at them for waking her little boy, and they were apologising without even trying to look like they meant it, and flapping cards that identified them as Detective Inspector Nicholas Tripp and Detective Constable Niall Bowen.

They said they were investigating a suspicious death at the university, and I went dopily to the window and stared out and saw an ambulance and two patrol cars and uniformed police standing across the entrance to Alfred Russel Wallace House. Then I wasn't dopey anymore.

I went quietly, because it wouldn't do any good to keep disturbing young Dani. As they took me down the stairs we passed a woman police constable. She looked as though three a.m. on a Saturday morning was her very least favourite time of the week. I didn't think she was going to offer to babysit.

Bowen lit a cigarette before he even turned the ignition key. Tripp sat next to me on the back seat. I asked if he thought I should be handcuffed, but he just said evenly that I wasn't under arrest, not at this stage. He exuded this calmness, mildly superior but not enough to rile you, which was also a kind of deference. I made a jibe or two, and he kept his replies very bland. Like he was saying, 'Insult me if you feel you need to – it's all part of my job.' Unrufflable. Like a good waiter.

But it was Tripp who kept me waiting thirty minutes in that tiny room, while Bowen kept his lips tightly shut round a filter-tip. When Tripp turned up, banging the door into my chair, he apologised. Sorry for knocking into you, sorry for the delay. Just like a good waiter ought.

'I don't think much of the service in this dive,' I warned him.

'Haven't you had a coffee? I can get you one. From a machine, though, I wouldn't want to drink it myself.'

'Forget it, it's too early for breakfast.'

'Right, maybe we can get this all over with and you can get a decent coffee at the end of it. You Americans like coffee, don't you?'

'And blueberry pie.'

'You're – pardon me if I say this wrong – Panagiotis Michalakopoulos.'

'Who told you that?'

'Is that your name?'

'People call me Mikki.'

Bowen looked up for the first time. Without removing the Sovereign, he said, 'Fucking Mikki Mouse.'

I got it. Good waiter, surly waiter. I'd been in plenty of restaurants where they pulled this trick.

'And you reside at 110c Conan Doyle House, Kensington Church Street? The property of Jane Lyons?'

'My wife. It's OK with you boys if I live with her?'

'And you were seen entering this evening at a few minutes after midnight the premises of 16 Queensberry Place, where at two fourteen a.m. today the body of a Professor J.K. Ingman was discovered. Yes?'

'Listen,' I said, 'you want me to tell you how it happened?'

'Mikki,' said Tripp, 'that would save all of us a great deal of trouble.'

Bowen leaned forward. 'Smoke?'

Thank Christ for that. 'No thanks.' My resolution lived to fight another day. The rest of this murder crap would be easy.

I told them everything I could think of. I figured that as I was innocent, and I had no clue who killed the prof, and I didn't give a damn who got hanged for it so long as it wasn't me, it couldn't do me anything but good to co-operate. I told them about Ingman's call to the show, about how he'd paid my restaurant bill, about Jane and the plan to paint me as a fraud – naturally I explained Ingman was going to falsify the results, masking my psychic gifts deliberately to discredit me. I told them about rowing with Jane, I told them about my lonely walk to Westminster Bridge and back, I told them about sneaking into Ingman's offices and finding the corpse.

I talked for ten minutes, maybe more, fast. I didn't wait for questions. At the end I apologised nicely for not calling them as soon as I found the body, on account of being a bit surprised and needing a coffee. And when Louisa showed me the human combustion stuff, it was obvious Ingman had probably set fire to himself, and so we didn't want to cause the police any trouble in the middle of the night.

'I realise now,' I finished off on a humbly penitent note, 'I should have come straight to you. I've made a lot of trouble for you and your colleagues.'

That was a line. I was inviting them to rap my knuckles. I was even giving them some easy repartee – nasty waiter could growl, 'You've made a lot of trouble for yourself,' and nice waiter could collect up the plates and sweep off the crumbs and say, 'Thanks very much for being so frank, I'm sure we'll be in touch if we need anything more, I wish all our suspects were as helpful as you.'

I sat and looked at them expectantly.

Bowen said, 'That is. A crock. Of shit.'

Tripp said, 'What he's trying to say is, there's some aspects of your story that don't add up.'

'It's all true.'

'It's a crock.'

So this is what you get in England for being articulate and compliant. It makes the police suspicious.

'OK, you think it's too glib.'

'A little.'

'So insert burning splinters under my fingernails and beat the confession out of me word by word.'

Nasty waiter eyed me like I was trying to send a plate of lasagne back to the kitchen. 'You reckon this is a big joke. You talk bullshit for a living and you think we like sitting here listening to you spouting it. But you are going to tell us the real facts and by the time you do you're going to wish you'd started explaining from the minute we kicked your arse out of that tart's bed.'

My blood rose. I knew that was what Bowen wanted, it was what both of them wanted because they were working this together. I managed not to give them the satisfaction of seeing it. But my blood rose.

'First fact, Ingman probably set his clothes alight and burned himself to death.'

'Don't fucking insult my intelligence! Fucking Mikki Mouse! You've got all those old slappers phoning you up because they go for your New Age bullshit – you can forget that in here! If you try to feed me any more of your bollocks I'm going to stuff my boot up your arse. You got me?'

Staying cool was getting hard now. Half of it was anger. Half of it was fear. I swallowed them both down, and said, 'I used to think British policemen were so wonderfully civilised.'

Bowen said, 'I'm going to bust his fucking balls.'

He started round the desk. I gripped the lip of the desk.

Tripp said, 'Wait a tick. I need a slash.' I looked at him – I thought my expression was blank but it probably had F-E-A-R etched into it an inch deep. Tripp saw I didn't know what he meant, and as threats were meaningless unless I understood them, he translated himself: 'I'm about to go to the toilet. Before I am forced to leave you alone with my colleague, is there anything about your statement you'd like to revise?'

'You can't beat me up. You haven't even charged me.'

'Listen, shitbag,' Bowen growled, 'we don't have to beat you up. We can leave you a couple of days with two or three gentlemen who like boys like you for their cell-mates. We can leave you as long as we want, nobody's going to write to their MP. You're a small-time American criminal who's working his cons on our patch. Added to that, your wife hates your guts so much she has you followed everywhere by a private detective. Even your girlfriend won't give you houseroom. Now if a few bones get broken while you're enjoying our hospitality, who's going to file complaints?'

'You bet I will.'

Bowen was still looming at my shoulder. 'Not if what gets broken is your neck.' He clamped his hand on my bicep and gripped the artery against the bone.

The pain in the muscle made me flinch, but he held me hard enough to keep the arm still. The top of my hand started to tingle. The fingers went numb, and the numbness spread past my wrist, up my forearm. The hand started to clench into a claw. Already it didn't feel like my hand.

'I didn't kill him, how could I kill him?'

'Unless you tell us, I don't think we'll ever know,' said Tripp.

'But you are going to tell us,' snarled Bowen. His face was at my ear, and his grip began to twist my arm out of its socket. The balljoint blazed. Below the elbow, my arm felt as swollen and lifeless as a balloon-ful of sand.

'I want to help you,' I yelled, 'I'm trying to help you!'

Tripp gestured at Bowen. The grip suddenly relaxed and Bowen spat, 'Fucking pathetic.'

I massaged the arm hard. As the blood flooded in, it felt like my skin was being scorched with wire brushes. 'You say he was murdered, I believe you. But all I know is I found the body. He was already dead.'

105

'Nobody's buying it, Mikki.'

I stared at them. What was I doing here? I'd seen a body and hadn't reported it. I hadn't even broken into the building, I'd been let in by the staff. It was a $50 fine, maximum. And here were the Met's mental crew, ripping my limbs off. Someone had fitted me for this.

It had to be my wife.

'Listen,' I gasped, 'you say I'm being followed. I met the guy yesterday, he's called Marsh or something. He'll tell you, I was only in that building thirty minutes, maximum. Talk to him.'

'We already did.'

'So that corpse was cremated. Ashes. If someone did that with a blowtorch, it's got to take a lot longer than thirty minutes.'

'Who mentioned a blowtorch?'

'How else are you going to get him to burn?'

Tripp pretended to be perplexed. 'But you said earlier, you thought he'd set his clothes alight with his pipe.'

'Now you're suggesting,' said Bowen, 'it would take a blowtorch to make him burn. You seem to know a lot about cremations suddenly.'

'Christ. You're twisting me.'

'We just want to know how you did it, Mikki.'

'I didn't, I didn't do it!'

'I'm really going to have to take a leak now,' sighed Tripp.

'Beating the shit out of me isn't going to change it! I didn't have time to murder anyone. Talk to Marsh.'

'As I told you, we did. And he doesn't know where you were before twelve eleven this morning. You gave him the slip, didn't you, Mikki? And he spent his evening traipsing round Kensington, hoping he'd see you on your way back to Mrs Lyons's home.'

'You know he's lying.'

'That's five hours he can't account for your actions. Shall I tell you what I think? I agree, you didn't kill the professor in his offices. You're right, you didn't have time. Also, there are no scorchmarks.'

'Thank you, Sherlock Holmes.'

Tripp carried on without blinking.

'Marsh saw you leave Mrs Lyons's home at seven fifteen p.m.'

'It was later than that. Much later. And it's not just her home, I live there too.'

'Marsh says seven fifteen. It's in his notebook. I'm sure Mrs Lyons will be able to settle the question. How come she isn't called Mrs Michalakopoulos, Mikki? Smart, good-looking boy like

106

you, I'm surprised you married a woman of – fifty-six years, I'm told.'

'He's a greedy little pervert, that's why,' snarled Bowen.

'Your account tallies with Marsh's notes till we reach Westminster Bridge. Then you suddenly grab a taxi and you lose your tail. Bit too easy, I should think, wasn't it? Marsh doesn't seem a proper pro.'

'I didn't get a taxi.'

'Next time Marsh sees you, you're walking up Cromwell Road with a body-bag. About midnight, a few minutes past. Right?'

'Yeah, I said that all along.'

'You never mentioned the body-bag Mikki.'

'I didn't have a body-bag.'

'Just said you did.'

'You said it.'

'You agreed.'

'I never had any body-bag.'

'For Chrissakes, Mikki, I'm trying, I'm doing my best to help you. You're just digging yourself deeper. Marsh says you had a suitcase, he saw it – now you admit it, and then you try to deny it. It's too late, you're just tying yourself in knots and that's going to make everything worse in the end.'

'So where's this body-bag, what did I do with it?'

'We'll find it. And when we do, there'll be charred ashes in it.'

'Tell me how I did it, then.'

'Correct me if I'm wrong. You take the cab to Ingman's flat. He opens the door, you knife him. In the chest. Probably you're wearing a jacket and gloves, so if there's blood you don't get it on your real clothes. But there isn't much blood. You know how to take a man with a knife, right, Mikki?'

'I get faint if I have to cut my nails.'

'You torch the body. Half-burn down the apartment while you're doing it. You set fire to the carpet, the furniture, the curtains. Tell me, have you got the psychic ability to breathe through smoke?'

'Yeah,' I said, flicking a hand at Bowen, 'I'm doing it now.'

'At eleven twenty-one p.m., you've actually got the nerve to call the fire brigade. Cool touch that. Because the apartment's on fire, and if it gets any worse it's quite likely to burn down the whole block. And you'd hate that to happen. Naturally, you don't hang round to see Blue Watch arrive. You take another cab, with your suitcase, into which you've packed the remains. Probably wrapped in plastic. Which gives you plenty of time to be strolling up Cromwell Road round midnight.'

'So I go to the prof's place. Even though I don't know where that is?'

'Yes.'

'I pull a knife I don't own from a bag I don't know I've got, and I stab him.'

'Yes.'

'Also from my bag, I produce a blowtorch. I cremate him. But I leave the hands and the feet, right? And I only give the head a light toasting. The rest is charcoal. Yes?'

'Yes.'

'Meantime I've accidentally set the apartment on fire. But I don't panic, I scoop up the prof, I wrap him in my bag and I dial 911.'

'Yes. Except you know it's 999.'

'Then I take a cab to Queensberry Place, arrange the prof neatly on the rug and call his researcher to tell her the glad news. When I'm sure my P.I. pal is watching, I saunter across the road and settle down to await my friends at the Met.'

'Yes.'

'Doesn't sound like the strongest case in history.'

'The fact is, Mikki, you've just described exactly how the professor was murdered. Now if it wasn't you – how do you account for that? Psychic powers?'

'You have got to be crazy. I never . . .'

I didn't get to finish.

Detective Inspector Tripp was suddenly on his feet, screaming at me. He was waving his fists so close to my face I jerked back and almost slid off my chair. He was lunging over the table, yelling, 'You're a fucking dirty little shitshagger! I've never been so disgusted by a piece of shit like you. You make me puke! I've seen corpses dragged out of burning houses that were charred to fucking crisps – and they weren't as bad as what you did to that poor bastard. You're fucking evil! They're going to bring back the fucking rope for you!'

Tripp slumped back in his chair.

I was shaking. I was really shaking. I could hear the feet of my chair rattling on the tiled floor.

Bowen said quietly, 'He gets like this. He's fine. Fine for days. For weeks. This very rarely happens. But when something upsets him – fuck me. And you've upset him, son. He started off liking you. But you've upset him now.'

'I get it,' I said shakily. 'Nice waiter and nasty waiter are swapping aprons.'

Tripp got up and lurched to the door. 'I give up. I'm going for a shit. I'm going to be at least a quarter of an hour. He's all yours, Niall.'

Bowen's face was a big grin with a stub glowing in the centre. He reached for his Zippo and, as Tripp slammed the door behind him, Bowen turned the wick up full and flicked the flint. A flame the height of my head roared out.

Bowen snapped shut the lid. Then he flipped the flame again. He laughed. It was the kind of laugh Vincent Price used to do so well. The act was good enough. It scared the living wits out of me.

'My name's Mikki,' said Bowen. 'And you're Professor Ingman.'

I don't know if I had already started screaming. But when the door swung open into my chair I was ready to faint.

Tripp stood behind me. He reached across the table and worldlessly handed a sheet of A4 to Bowen. The junior man glanced over it and said through his cigarette, without looking up, 'This just come in?'

He read it again. Then he lowered the paper and stared straight at me. His eyes were dark brown and raw-rimmed. A jerking spiral of smoke ran like a tic up his face.

He said to me, 'You're fucking dead meat now.'

CHAPTER TWENTY-TWO

'You are Panagiotis Michalakopoulos? Of 110c Conan Doyle House, Kensington Church Street?' asked Bowen.

'What are we doing, starting over?'

'And you are the husband of Jane Lyons, of that address?'

'Still yes.'

'Mr Michalakopoulos.' Bowen said my name with a face-screwing sneer. 'I regret to inform you that the body of your wife has been discovered at your home.'

He didn't sound like he regretted it. The only thing he was regretting was the need to postpone his entertainment with the Zippo and my eyebrows.

I should say I was staring, or I was dumbstruck, or I was gasping, 'My God! My God!' But all I did was turn my head slightly on one side. I felt the movement happening very slowly, like I was some immense piece of machinery.

'The body was found just after six a.m., when three crews of fire officers responded to an emergency call.'

'She took an overdose or something?'

'Fire crews, Mikki,' said Tripp behind me.

'My God!' I said it now. 'There's been a fire?'

'According to the report,' Bowen said, 'the officers did extinguish a small blaze. Smoke damage, nothing more.'

'I don't get it. Read me the report, let me see it. She died of smoke inhalation? Or what?'

Bowen deliberately folded the report and clasped his fists over it.

'What she died of was being cremated with a blowtorch.'

I couldn't say anything. I never in my life had this sensation before. I hope to Christ I never have it again. It was like the top slice of my brain died.

'Tell it to me again.'

'I think you heard.'

'What have they done with the body?'

'Forensics will clear it up. Eventually.'

'Was it – did she suffer?'

Bowen flicked open the report, scanned it and leered at me. 'It doesn't say here. Why don't you tell us?'

'No. No, no, no. The last time I saw Jane she was in the bath. I wouldn't hurt her. I'd cheat on her, but I wouldn't, not physically, not hurt her.' My head was swimming. 'I walked out last night and she was revelling in life, she was totally in control.'

'What time was that?'

'I'm the last person who saw her, so I killed her – is that what you're saying to me?'

'Is that what *you're* saying to *us*, Mikki?'

Oh Christ! It was like talking to an analyst. Every time I asked a question, it came back as an accusation.

'It doesn't make sense, does it?' I urged them. 'You're telling me there was a small fire at six a.m. And Marsh has said I wasn't in the apartment since last evening. So if I killed her before I left, how come the building didn't burn down?'

'According to Marsh,' intoned Tripp, 'you weren't the last guy with her. Because he was with her from half ten till midnight.'

'Why? What did Jane want with him for that long? He was debriefing her?'

'Call it what you like, son.'

I started swearing. I don't know exactly what I said, but my fluency came back. Bowen was almost blushing.

When I stopped, suddenly, and stared at the wall, Tripp asked, 'Has she two-timed you before?'

'Look, let's nail this one down – this doesn't offend my morals or anything. You know I had a girlfriend. Marsh has already told you. She threatened to kick me out for that.'

'How long has she been threatening?'

'Last night was the first real, open time.'

'So infidelity, the prospect of divorce, humiliation, and in addition to that, she's a very rich woman with a lot of money coming to her husband if she dies.' Bowen was loving this, and it showed. 'You've got a lot of motives there.'

'No opportunity,' I answered tersely. 'If Marsh left Jane at midnight, and ten minutes later he sees me, and he's got me in sight till you come to collect me – when have I got the matches out?'

'We'll work out a good answer to that one.'

111

But they were running low on gas now. I could not have killed Jane. They didn't admit it, but they knew it. And there was zilch to prove I'd been within a mile of Ingman's flat all night. It seemed I had plenty of motive for killing both of them. But at the very most, they could only suspect me of one.

And there's something so distinctive about being done to death with a blowtorch, even Scooby-Doo and Shaggy would wonder if these murders were connected.

Marsh could have done both of them. I tried suggesting this, a couple of times. Or more than a couple. Bowen snarled, 'Why would he wait till you were in here before cooking your old lady?'

Bowen wasn't what you'd call tactful, but his mind was logical. When it wasn't asking questions about me.

They took my evidence right through again. Then they started at the top and did it all a third time, increasing the detail and the depth with every version. Every time I offered up something I hadn't said before, they threw themselves on it – 'How come you didn't say that before? Bit strange you should suddenly remember vital evidence, isn't it? Or are you embellishing a good story? Do you know the difference between fact and fiction? Aren't you contradicting yourself now?'

This was one big advantage I got from telling them the truth first time round. I wasn't fighting to remember what I'd said. If they'd smelt that, Tripp and Bowen would have ripped my arms off and used them to beat my skull to pulp. But all I had to do was keep cool, and not try to tell them anything just because that seemed like what they wanted to hear.

It worked. But it took a long while. It was way past breakfast-time when they turfed me out.

There was a kind of conference, just outside the door, when they left me alone for ninety seconds or so. My brains were so fried, I would have grabbed the chance and left by the window, but trying to run away was probably the only thing that could guarantee I stayed with the cops for the rest of the weekend.

All my nerves were fried too, and my stomach was grilled and roasted and my eyeballs were baked and my balls were barbecued. I stared at the window like it was the moon, it looked so far away.

The door bounced off my chair again. Tripp said, 'You can go now, Mikki.'

Bowen said, 'Fuck off then, son.'

'We must do it again some time,' I said.

'You fucking bet we will.'

CHAPTER TWENTY-THREE

I didn't stop for that coffee. I just wanted out. When I got through the door, I didn't have an idea where I was supposed to be, and my pockets were as empty as they had been the night before.

The thought hit me, like a wave of the Saturday morning heat coming off the sidewalk, that Jane's will was going to leave me nowhere. She'd spelled out to me several times, before and after nuptials, that I was specifically written out of everything. Not that she was of a suspicious mind, she wanted me to understand, but it wouldn't have been the first time in history a younger man had wed an older woman in order to drop her over a cliff-edge.

There were days I would have dumped Jane off an Alp for free. I wouldn't have needed to be a beneficiary. But knowing she was dead, we were never going to see each other again, we were never going to make up for that week's tantrums – it upset me.

And financially, I was in freefall now. No house – that had been in Jane's name. No bequests. No income – that was all sequestered by her lawyers. And how long would it take to unsequester? What if her estate got to claim everything I earned for the rest of eternity?

Naturally, if I also got kicked out of the country, this would be less of a problem. Jane's estate would probably raise no objections if the Benji brothers cased me in concrete and took me boating on the Hudson.

I didn't know if my work permit would stay OK.

Either it would or it wouldn't. This was one thing to save worrying over till later.

I needed to eat. Also I needed to rest. Also I needed to talk to someone. And for all the reasons that applied on the Embankment the evening before, I didn't want to go shuffling on my knees to Mimi or Kerry.

I thought about my producer, Dan, for a moment, but it was one of those very short moments. Hummingbirds take longer to beat their wings. Dan and I had a professional relationship. Plus

I always got the feeling he would hate my guts, if he could be bothered.

Which left Louisa. Who lived conveniently the nearest of all my acquaintances. And who was inconveniently most likely out.

I'd been walking in the wrong direction for ten minutes when I worked out where I was and started retracing my path to Queensberry Place. Louisa didn't answer her buzzer. I stood and pressed it, and pressed it, and pressed it in fast little bursts, and pressed it for long long droning buzzes. I figured if she was asleep I was going to wake her up, and if she was ignoring me I wouldn't let her. But she didn't answer. She wasn't there.

I had given up, and was leaning with my forehead on her door, remembering the bum I'd seen on the steps opposite the night before, when the premonition struck me that maybe I'd be living in a box pretty soon, and I was just reflecting how psychic I must be to have spotted that one coming, when Louisa said behind me, 'Hi.'

'Oh – right!' I had a line prepared, and I fumbled for it. 'Listen, my father told me, never get involved with a woman who's got more problems than you. And I figured, right now that means I could be double-dating Fergie and Rosanne.'

'I don't know what you're talking about.' She reached over me to unlock the door.

'I mean, if you want to apply my Pop's rule, I won't get offended.'

She shrugged. Offending me wasn't a problem with her. 'They let you go?'

'I'm not on the run, if that's what you mean.'

'So they accept you didn't kill Ingman.'

'It's maybe half a degree more complex than that. Just half of half of one degree.'

I started laughing. The line isn't so funny, thinking back on it. But I started laughing till tears ran either side of my nose and dripped over my lip. They tasted hot.

Louisa grabbed my arm. 'Get in here. You're a wreck. Tell me about it. For God's sake.'

She gave me coffee and I calmed down and she told me what had happened to her.

The WPC had been asking questions for over an hour. Dani wouldn't go back to sleep, so at four in the morning Louisa had been explaining to a short-tempered sceptic in a checkered cap how Rhine cards worked, while her son watched Thomas the Tank Engine on video. At seven thirty they'd come back, banging on the door,

114

wanting to know if Louisa's story was still the same. It was easy to guess what was in their bright little brains – was she sure that evil, blowtorch-wielding Greek was really in her front room all through the small hours, and not back at Kensington Church Street flambéing his old lady?

'Thanks for telling them the truth,' I said. 'And thanks for letting me sleep on your sofa.'

'Not much sleep you got.'

'But if you'd sent me home, I'd be looking at life, no remission, and if I got to ninety, as a special treat they'd deport me in leg irons.'

'Once again, I don't know what you're talking about.'

So I told her.

When she knew more about my life than my mother ever had, it was past two in the afternoon and all I had eaten was toast and butter. I complained, 'A good Jewish girl like you should have bagels at least.'

'Sliced bread is cheaper. Anyway, you'd probably moan what rubbish bagels are in England.'

'You come from a fishing village, frozen fishfingers don't taste so good. With me it's bagels. You should go to Carmeli in Golders Green, they know what a bagel is. We had a kosher bakery behind our tenement. My ma bought all their bread, my pop seduced all their girls. I don't know what it was about the smell of fresh bagels but it made my pop very excitable. They used to boil the dough for eight hours before they baked it, and this warm sweet doughy smell comes floating up through the windows and the colour rises in Pop's face and he starts crossing and uncrossing his legs, and then he says he's got to go out. And three hours later, he's still stood round the back of the bakery, flirting with whichever of the girls has got time to waste.'

'What did your mother do in revenge?'

'Revenge? She's a Greek's girl, she knows you can't control rampant nature. Try shouting at a stallion, see what effect that has.'

'Oh, right.' She had that tone English feminists get – 'God, you're so sexist I can't even be bothered to argue with you.' I think it means secretly they admire an old-fashioned man.

'His exploits were bound to cause bad feeling between the girls. They went for revenge, now and again. One time my ma sliced a loaf and cut Pop's spectacles in two. He'd left them on some Jewish girl's bedside table. I guess that took some explaining.'

Louisa stared at me. Then she couldn't help herself. She started laughing.

115

'So where's your son?' I asked. 'I haven't met him yet.'

'With his father.'

'That's where you were when I was draining your buzzer batteries? Taking him for an access session.'

'Uh-huh.'

'When did you and his pop split up?'

She tried to grin, and it went all on one side. 'Just after I found his glasses in a loaf of bread.'

'Like that, eh?'

'Ish.'

'Long ago?'

'Just before Dani was born.'

'You were pregnant and you threw him out?'

She was facing the sink, refilling the kettle, and she didn't answer until she turned round. I could see in her face when she did, we'd gone way beyond where she normally stopped discussing this with strangers.

'I was ten weeks' pregnant.'

'He knew this?'

'No.'

'But you knew it?'

'Yeah.'

'You could have had an abortion.'

'I could go in Dani's bedroom and strangle him while he's sleeping,' she flashed angrily.

'Sorry.' There was a silence, and I didn't want to stop her from talking. I thought she needed to talk. So I did what I would do on the radio – I asked her to define something about her personality. It's cold reading, but it works.

I asked her: 'Did you know you were the sort who wouldn't have an abortion, before you got pregnant?'

'Not exactly.' She said it heavily, and the silence that followed was like lead. 'I thought that whatever was the opposite to what the rabbi said, that's what I believed in. I was an anti-Orthodox, anti-everything Jew. My father was devout. It didn't show so much when he was in the police, but even then he wore his tephillin under his uniform sometimes. He said the worst thing about the police was working on Shabbat.'

I could think of worse things, but I didn't say.

'When they retired him, he grew his beard, he started wearing his yarmulke always.'

'Did religion give him much comfort?'

'He said so. I could never see it.'

'And did he mind that you were agnostic?'

'He said I was like my mother. Which I hated.'

'Your mother wasn't devout?'

'She was a devout hypocrite. She said she embraced all the laws – what she was embracing was anything in a shirt and tie. It made my life simple. Do everything the rabbi says you mustn't, ignore everything he says is right and how can you screw up?'

She sounded tired and bitter. I reminded myself she'd had only a couple of hours' sleep more than me, and the shock about Ingman was just sinking in. Of course she didn't normally talk like this, but she seemed to want to now. I hoped it was doing less harm than good.

'How old were you when you got pregnant?'

'Eighteen.'

'Jesus,' I said.

'My dad killed himself the year before.'

'You married straight after?'

'I never got married. That's what the rabbi would have liked. I had some money from Dad, and I could afford to rent in Manchester. I'd just started at the university. Usually, as a local girl, I was expected to live with my parents – not take up valuable space at the halls of residence. Only in my case – no parents. So I was renting. First-year girl with her own flat, it's bound to attract interest. My big romance was a third-year biology student. Turned out he made a career of deflowering virgins.'

'Virgins with their own places to live?'

'Usually.'

I looked at my shoes. My shoes looked back. They recognised the description.

'He doesn't sound like a guy who'd demand access to his children. Particularly if he was off the scene before they got born.'

'Stuart knew about Dani. Remember, I threw him out. He wasn't begging to go. He spent a month sleeping in libraries and washing at the leisure centre.'

My shoes were still looking at me like, 'You listening to this, pal?'

'Dani was born just after Stuart took his finals. And Stuart had a job waiting for him in Edinburgh, and I was still talking to him in monosyllables, and that was on good days. Now he says he would have stayed in Manchester and helped if I'd wanted it. But I didn't.'

117

'What did he do to freak you out that badly? If,' I added lamely, 'you don't mind me asking?'

'You can ask. It's telling you that's awkward. I came back from the Student's Union one evening, early, eight o'clock-ish. And he was in my bed with another girl.'

'I guessed. First boyfriend, you're eighteen, it's tough.' Some women, I knew, felt strongly about that kind of behaviour.

'Stuart had planned it. He wanted a threesome. He thought the sight of him shagging someone else would turn me on.'

Bad psychology. In the ordinary run of things, psychology that bad deserved to finish a relationship. But there was an extra complication here.

'You knew you were pregnant at this time?'

'Oh yes. And Stuart didn't. And the other thing he didn't know, his new girlfriend was my sister.'

'Oh, that is bad. That is bad.' I really felt this one. It was one of those stories that make you want to curl up in a ball and wrap your elbows over your eyes. 'One of the sisters who went off with your mother, right? Older or younger?'

'Older. Does it matter?'

'And neither of them had any idea?'

'She had her stepfather's name. I suppose she hadn't asked mine. When I came into the bedroom, my sister screamed and hid under the pillow. Stuart thought she'd suddenly changed her mind, I suppose. He'd done this with her a couple of times before, so there was no reason for her to lose her nerve that Stuart could see. This was her bag. But he could see in my face he'd done the wrong thing. I went straight out of the room to the kitchen, and he said from my expression he thought I was fetching a knife. If I'd thought of it I would. What I got was a big bowl of water, and I dumped it on their clothes. There was this pile of knickers and jeans in my doorway. Then I threw the bowl at my sister, threw their wet clothes out of the window and threw the pair of them out of the door.'

It didn't sound too funny, told in her voice. I kept quiet for a long while – a long while for me. Then I said, 'You still decided to keep his child.'

Louisa gazed at me unblinkingly with her cloudy, malachite eyes. She said: 'Dani is my child. A piece of me.'

118

Chapter Twenty-Four

We walked over to Kensington Court Street, and I probed once or twice more, but Louisa had run dry. There was no emotion left in her. She was blank inside.

I guessed she'd been low on fuel before last night, even. She was living in one big room divided up by plasterboard, and bringing up a little boy there. If she had a car I hadn't seen it. If she had enough food to feed them both, there wasn't much sign of it. She was working for a pompous pinhead who spent his department budget on carpets. It would drain anyone.

She told me she didn't have a boyfriend, but that might have been just because she didn't have the energy to discuss it. She told me Ingman had never tried it on with her, and I believed her. I asked if she tried to do what the rabbis advised now, and she said, 'No.' That was all I got. No explanations.

I said, 'Tell me about Dani,' and most mothers would talk your ears off, but she just said, 'He's a nice boy.'

'You're not worried, leaving him with his father?'

'No.'

This girl needed a rest. And she needed some help. She didn't need a fake psychic with a dubious work permit, mixed up in murder, with debts that could be fatal and a wife who was newly toasted by a blowtorch maniac.

So I had to go back to the apartment, and I invited her along. She said, 'I could do with a walk.'

We stepped out of the lift on Floor 3 at Conan Doyle House and there was red-and-yellow tape across the passageway. The people from the apartment opposite were trying to get past a policeman, back to their door.

'We live here!' the husband was squeaking. He was a short guy, barely reached to his blubberbutt wife's shoulder, and his hair was dripping with a rose-scented oil that shone like tar. He had a thin moustache as well, so black he must have soaked it in ink every night.

'If you have any identification on you, sir,' the cop was repeating.

'Good God, officer, this isn't Nazi Germany, we don't have to carry papers!'

'Perhaps if I could make sure first that your key fits the lock?'

'Do you seriously expect me to hand over my keys to you?'

His wife, who was looking around for assistance, maybe from a passing ambassador or the chief commissioner of police, saw Louisa and me at the lift. She gave a low gasp. 'Anselm! Oh, Anselm!'

'My God!' He raised a quivering finger at me. 'Officer, you must arrest that man.'

I took a step towards them. I didn't mean it to be menacing, but they shrank back.

'He's the man. The man who did this awful – ohh!'

'Hi, my name's Michalakopoulos. I live here. This is a friend who's keeping me company. Can I go in and collect some things?'

'In ten minutes,' said the cop. He didn't slap irons on me, but he didn't call me 'sir' either. 'The forensics people have pretty much finished.'

'Aren't you going to demand identification from him?' squeaked Anselm.

'You've already done that for us, sir. He's the murderer.'

Which made me think, this copper was damn sure of his facts. He knew I'd been picked up and given a long hard look, or he'd be arresting me now. Ditto, he knew I'd been released legit. He knew I was not seriously suspected of killing my wife. And he knew I was low enough down the order of human slime that he could laugh in my face.

Someone must have told him to expect me. That was simple enough. I'd have to collect some stuff.

But all of it was giving me such a nice, warm feeling.

A face with a cigarette in it looked out from my doorway. 'Thought I recognised that cheery twang,' Detective Constable Bowen said. 'I've been sorting through your collection of dirty videos, son.'

My stomach turned to icy slush. They hadn't got me on the murder, so I was being presented with a gift set of Met porn tapes, just enough to make sure I went to a comfy remand wing where they could keep an eye on me.

Bowen smirked. 'My little joke. This time. Who's the tart, Mikki?'

'A policeman's daughter.'

'They're the worst. Don't get attached to Yankee Doodle Dandy, sweetheart,' he said to Louisa. 'He's going away for a long time.'

Louisa hissed at him, 'My father was proud of his job!'

'Yeah? Didn't stop him topping himself, though.'

I wrapped an arm around her arm and squeezed her hand as Bowen dodged back inside. I didn't like that Bowen knew so much about her history, but that was the short end of it. What I really didn't like was he had the manners of a hyena with its nose up the ass end of a zebra's corpse.

Bowen reappeared. 'Come on in, Mikki. Yeah, bring the copper's daughter. Tell me what this is.'

He opened his palm and revealed a gold band. It was undamaged, with a fleck or two of ash on the rim and a faint dusting of powder. 'Know about it?'

'It's the wedding ring I married Jane with.'

'Yeah, I thought that. It says, From Mikki to my darling Jane,' and it's dated about seven weeks ago from today. I knew it had to be you.'

'He's like Lieutenant Columbo,' I told Louisa.

'The thing that made it difficult was, it wasn't found on her hand.'

He waited for me to ask. I didn't. So he told me anyway.

'It was between her teeth.'

'Nice touch,' I said.

Bowen stood aside and I saw into my home.

The lights were on, though it was nearly one in the afternoon. The curtains were pulled. The front door opened straight into our main room, and it looked like a team of removals men had started on emptying the apartment and then got called away on urgent business. All the free-standing stuff, the bookcases and the dresser and the art deco lamps and the wooden elephant with the boy mahout, had been pulled away from the walls. On the bedroom side, the carpet was rolled back. Cushions were stacked upright beside chairs.

The walls, the ceiling, everything was darkened by smoke.

Tripp walked out of the bedroom.

I said to Louisa, 'Another friendly face.'

'Mikki, we've been expecting you. Maybe we should have offered you a lift over.'

'You can stick that.' With a woman beside me, I felt double the need to show no fear.

'Who's your friend?'

'None of your business.' But Louisa volunteered her name anyway.

121

He stood, barring the way to my own bedroom. I didn't particularly want to go in. But I knew I would have to.

'Your wife's body is still being examined. It's going to be a difficult job transporting her to the mortuary, I'm afraid. There'll be some deterioration. I'd prefer it if you identified her here. Though I don't think we'll be able to say with 100 per cent certainty, "This is Mrs Lyons," until the dentals are checked.'

'How was she killed?'

'No way to tell. We've found no trace of a weapon. I hope it wasn't with the blowtorch.'

'Yeah. I hope that too.'

There was no easy image of how to kill a woman with a miniature flamethrower while she is conscious. I didn't want to work too hard imagining it.

'No one heard any screams,' Tripp added. 'So we can hope she didn't suffer. I'd rather you didn't come in, Miss,' he said to Louisa.

I drew a long breath and pushed past him.

All I can say, no definition of 'She didn't suffer' applies to what was done to Jane.

Her corpse lay on its side on the scorched floor. The carpet, which was still white and fleecy in the corners, had been burnt away to the blackened boards all around her. Her arms were stretched behind her, with the remains of bonds at the wrists. Her legs were wide, both naked feet pointing to the door, like she had been hit by a fireball as she tried to leap into the sitting room.

The feet and the hands were red and shrivelled, as if they'd been held inside an oven. The rolls of fat around her ankles and wrists were literally melted away, and the bones were exposed. Further up the legs and arms, those bones turned to black powder.

Nothing remained of her torso. The chest, the stomach, the limbs to her elbows and knees, there was just ash. The ash didn't even lie thickly enough for the lines of the spine and the ribs and the pelvis to be seen, the way they had been carefully displayed in Ingman's corpse.

The bedroom was still murky with smoke. The smell of roasted flesh was thick and sweet, overlaid with a stinging odour of butane. And vomit. Beside Jane's bed was a red pool of vomit.

The window was open, and the black tatters of curtains flickered out into the Kensington air. I walked across and took a few deep breaths. I wasn't going to throw up. That thing on the floorboards

122

wasn't human, it had nothing to do with Jane. I was just going to keep breathing till I could face it again.

Tripp stood beside me. 'You were with us when this happened. From what neighbours can tell, it was about four fifteen, four thirty a.m. There was no noise. Just the smell. People started to notice it. It woke them up. Then about six a.m., when the fabrics in here had been smouldering for an hour or more, enough smoke seeped into the corridor to set off the alarms. You didn't have any alarms.'

'Yeah, that would have saved her life, right?'

'This isn't my fault, Mikki.'

He was obviously feeling the guilt, or he wouldn't have said it. Tripp was forgetting he didn't haul me out of my own bed. I was slumming on Louisa's sofa. I couldn't have protected Jane from the killer. And if I had been home, I might have got toasted myself.

'Bowen said my wedding ring was in her mouth.'

'That emphasises the personal nature of this, Mikki. Can you think of anyone who hated you and Mrs Lyons? Maybe someone with a connection to Professor Ingman too?'

I stared at him. What was he expecting? If I clasped my hand to my forehead and cried, 'My God! Why didn't I see it before? There is someone with a grudge against all three of us! And – he's a travelling blowtorch salesman!' would Tripp congratulate himself later on his shrewd questioning?

I was ready to turn around now. Ready to look at her face. Because she still had some face left.

There was hair, though it wasn't blue-rinse any longer. There were patches of skin under the scalp and above the eyes. The nose was bare cartilage and the teeth were exposed – I could see the bridgework on the right side and the gold fillings. We didn't need to wait for official dental reports. This had been Jane Lyons.

I looked away, across the room, to where Bowen was kneeling, scooping the red vomit into a dustpan with a rubber glove. So it must have been him who couldn't keep his breakfast down. I wasn't going to blame him.

'I want to get out of here.'

Tripp led me by the arm past her corpse. I didn't look down again. This wasn't anything like a goodbye. Goodbye was what I'd said when she was hurling abuse at me in the bathroom.

Tripp repeated his question in the sitting room, and he inverted it for Louisa's benefit – was there anything that linked Ingman with me and Jane, and all of us with murder?

123

I looked across at Louisa. For six hours this morning I had tried to be open and honest and frank with Tripp. What he'd done in return was place my balls between the jaws of his pet Rottweiler. I didn't want Louisa to start making the same mistakes with him. At least, I wanted to talk to her first.

I don't know what went into my look that gave her the message. I know I didn't shake my head, because Tripp was watching me. She opened her mouth and shut it again.

Tripp turned to me: 'Have you ever seen that suitcase?'

He pointed at a green bag the size of a sea-trunk, with a pair of rubber-tyred wheels at the base and a two-foot black steel handle. You could have packed a wardrobe in there. Or a corpse.

'Why does it matter?' I asked.

'Because Marsh says you were wheeling a suitcase when he spotted you in Cromwell Road just after midnight.'

'And he also says he saw me go into Ingman's building with this case. Presumably because I had the prof's body all parcelled up in there. But then he says he watched me leave the university and walk over the road. No mention of a suitcase then. So how am I supposed to have brought it here?'

'Did you bring it here? Or do you deny you ever saw it before?'

'Yes, I deny it. And I also deny that Marsh is telling the truth. I still say he killed Ingman and he killed Jane and if you take the initiative and open the suitcase, maybe you'll find he's sewn his nametag in there.'

'We've opened the suitcase. There's a couple of plastic suit covers in there, the big ones with zips all the way round. When you zip them up, they're airtight.'

'Nice. A serial killer who looks after his clothes.'

'They weren't used for clothes, Mikki. Inside both the bags there's a lot of smeared ash. We haven't tested it yet, but you know it's going to match Ingman's remains. That's how his corpse was carried intact from his apartment – zipped into plastic bags inside that suitcase.'

I said, 'Listen, I'm wasted. I can't think. I can't answer questions here.'

'We'll take you back to the station,' said Tripp considerately. 'Maybe you'll remember if you ever saw that suitcase before. Or you'll think of some other reason why it's in your apartment.'

'Christ, you know I couldn't have brought it here. It's obvious – whoever killed Ingman came here and killed Jane. And left the bag.'

124

'Why? Even if he doesn't want to transport your wife's body, why leave his suitcase? We're bound to be able to trace it, something so distinctive.'

'I don't know. Why ask me?'

'Because I think you know the answer.'

'Give me a break, yeah? You know I'll try to co-operate. I can't think straight, let me clear my head. I'm not under arrest or anything. We'll go out, take a walk, we'll ride a bus or something. OK?' I added to Louisa. 'Then we'll report to the station and try to tell you everything you need. Just – give me some space, will you? Some air?'

Tripp waited a long time. He didn't look at Bowen, or the two forensics men who walked into the apartment. One had a bodybag rolled under his arm.

'OK.' This was Tripp's guilt talking. The policeman in him wanted to shove me in another interview room and put my balls back in the dog's mouth. 'I want you to report to me by four, OK? Get something to eat, clear your heads, and report in by four.'

'I'll need some cash,' I said to Louisa. 'I've got to get some clothes.'

'Bowen can fetch things from your wardrobe,' Tripp suggested.

'Everything'll stink. Do you think I want to walk around smelling of my wife's murder? I've got to buy new stuff.'

'I'm afraid you can't take money out of this apartment, Mikki. It could be evidence.'

'I can't have my own money?' I stared at him wide-eyed and disbelieving. Tripp couldn't know I had no money. I didn't even have a clue where Jane hid it. Or if she hid it. 'How much have you found, anyway?'

'I can't tell you that, Mikki.'

'Oh come on! It can't have been above £500, anyhow.'

'Substantially more. You know I can't discuss evidence with you casually.'

Substantially more than £500? He was talking about thousands. So what was Jane doing with that shovel-load of dough indoors? Did she always have it? And I'd never known? Christ, I'd have been tempted to kill her myself.

'It's OK,' Louisa said, 'your credit cards are here.'

'Thanks.' I took Jane's card-wallet from her without even glancing at it. 'I can have my own cards, right?'

'They are your cards and not your wife's?'

I flipped the wallet open and held it out to him, like I had nothing to hide. Like even answering his question with words was too much effort. Everyone, even policemen, expects lies to be spoken, not said in a gesture.

And as I held out the cards, I let my hand drift a little, so the name on the cards would drift before his eyes. Those shiny letters are hard enough to see when they're lying still on a counter under your nose. Waving in the air, they're impossible.

Tripp could have taken the wallet out of my hand. But he'd caught me telling the truth so often today, maybe he was starting to believe me naturally.

I snapped the wallet shut.

'Don't do anything silly, Mikki. Don't start spending your inheritance. That's serious advice, OK? And stay in London. And be at Notting Hill Gate nick, four o'clock latest.'

I was already steering Louisa round the copper and the red-and-yellow tape, and into the lift.

CHAPTER TWENTY-FIVE

We went past the next set of tape and coppers, on the portico'd steps to the entrance of Conan Doyle House, without a sideways glance. I was saying nothing, just holding her elbow and keeping up some gentle pressure. We were halfway down Kensington Church Street, heading for the High Street, before I said, 'And I thought you were a nice Jewish girl.'

'Aren't they your cards?' she asked innocently.

'They're yours now.'

'What do you mean?'

'Can I sign as Mrs J Lyons? With this beard?' I jutted a chin at her that was bristling with eighteen hours' unhacked growth. I looked like George Michael with an ouzo hangover.

'I'm not signing for anything.'

'You want to eat, don't you?'

'We can eat at my flat.'

'So there's a Waitrose round the corner. You can stock up, get some cashback, put it on Jane's AmEx. For Christ's sake, she would have let me if I'd asked. She isn't going to mind now.'

'The police won't think it's funny that she was buying groceries after she died?'

'Who'll tell them?'

'Mikki, get real.' She stopped and pointed at me. 'The police are looking for reasons to charge you with Ingman's murder. Don't go round committing fraud too.'

'I won't. You will.'

She walked away. This was a girl with strong moral principles.

'So why give me the cards?' I asked.

'I thought they were yours.'

'Financially, I've been a non-person ever since Jane married me. I didn't even get to keep my second name.'

'Did she give you an allowance?'

127

'I got cash when I asked. Sometimes.'

'Well then, it probably wouldn't be fraud to use a cashpoint with one of her cards. You wouldn't have to sign for anything.'

'Great idea. I can use my psychic powers to guess the PIN.' I dug the thin gold folder out of my hip pocket and flipped through it. 'There's enough plastic to buy Harrods here. And –' I held up the wallet and kissed it – 'there's a theatre ticket with a four-digit number on the back.'

The dispenser wanted to know what language I was using. That part was easy. Then it wanted the personal identification number, and that was less easy. What Jane had written was 6–1–4–8 and the machine wasn't accepting it.

There are two ways to hack a cash dispenser. One is to know the PIN in advance. The other is to lose the card. You get three goes, and there are 9,999 possible combinations. The chances of a correct guess are 3,333 to one. You can try 1–2–3–4, 2–5–8–0 (down the middle of the pad) and 9–8–7–6. Then you wave bye-bye to the card.

I'd already failed with 6–1–4–8 and I didn't have Jane figured as a 1–2–3–4 woman. But she was the type to carry a note of the number. She couldn't remember what she'd said five minutes ago, how could she remember secret combinations?

So 6–1–4–8, if it wasn't the solution, must be the clue. I tried it backwards – 8–4–1–6.

'Welcome Mrs Jane Ingman,' displayed the machine. 'Please enter service required.'

'Thank you, thank you,' I murmured.

'Are you there?' asked Louisa, peering over my shoulder.

'Push button for sum desired.'

The highest on the display was £250, but I chose 'Other' and entered £1,000. This was a Gold Card, for pity's sake.

'Sorry, maximum withdrawal £250.'

'Okey-dokey, begrudge me even when you're dead. £250 will do for the aperitif.'

'Mikki, what did it say when I first looked?'

'You tell me.'

'Please wait for cash,' said the machine.

'I think something strange registered on my brain and I don't understand what it was.'

'Your head's spinning.'

'It was something definite.'

'Please take cash and wait for receipt,' the machine's faded green display said.

'Definitely not right.'

'Please take card,' it offered.

'Let me see the card,' Louisa asked.

'You never seen a gold AmEx? Ain't it purty?'

'Ingman!' she exclaimed. 'Mrs Jane Ingman.'

'Lyons,' I said automatically but it didn't sound like 'Lyons' because my jaw was dropping.

'She couldn't have been Mrs Ingman, you would have known.'

I stuffed the wad into my back pocket and the AmEx back into the folder. 'I didn't know anything about her,' I told Louisa seriously. 'Not a damn thing.'

We got on the Circle Line, because our thoughts were round and round, and the Underground seemed our best chance to catch up with them. Plus, we needed to sit down, and we needed to talk, and we didn't need to be inspected by passing policemen. The Tube is one place in London where policemen never go.

Every carriage has two pairs of seats at either end, and when we'd walked through the tiled passageways at Kensington High Street and boarded the squealing, hissing, foul-tempered armoured car that called itself public transport, we were jerked into the darkness. Blue sparks burst by the windows with explosions like lump hammers hitting twenty-foot sheets of aluminium.

I hate the Tube. Maybe that's why it seemed the right place to be talking about murder. And deception.

Also, no one could hear us. Between stations, the train made enough banging and rattling that we had to raise our voices to hear them ourselves. At stops, the rumbling of doors and the commotion of people boarding and scrambling off meant no one was paying any attention to our discussions.

Tube passengers don't eavesdrop, anyhow. And they'd rather stick their fingers in their eyes than look straight at you.

I said, 'I knew she was married a third time. There was Ambrose – she wanted me to contact Ambrose beyond the veil. But there was another husband she mentioned just once, on our wedding day.'

'Another dead one?'

'I guess not. She would have asked me to reach him too. She would have wanted to say to Ambrose, "Don't be too hard on the new guy".'

'Don't you ever . . . ?'

'What?'

'I mean, is nothing sacred? Don't you ever draw the line?'

'What I do for a living isn't bad. Doesn't hurt people, provides a lot of innocent entertainment. I never claimed to be in touch with her dearly departed. She wanted to believe there was life on the next level, and I let her believe it. That's all. And – I hope she's right. I hope Ambrose was there to meet her.'

'You only pretend to be heartless,' she said. 'When you were crying and laughing on my doorstep, I thought you were shaken up by the police. But now, I think it was more to do with your wife. You liked her, and you don't have to deny it to me.'

'Sure I liked her. I liked her enough to marry her. Even for a rat as shallow as me, that's got to mean something. Now can we discuss ethics another time? Let's keep this logical. Step by step. Before the man with the blowtorch decides to make a start on me.'

'There's a lot – a lot to think about.'

'So let's start with this gold AmEx. All the other cards say Mrs J Lyons. On this one she is Jane Ingman. Why?'

'You never asked about her third husband?'

'I told you, I know nothing about her. I was never interested. I thought it was all simple, what you see is what you get. I didn't imagine she had dark secrets. Especially nothing to get murdered for.'

'What was her name before you married her?'

'Lyons – same as after.'

'Are you sure? Did you see the certificate?'

'Matter of fact, no – she kept it covered. I thought she didn't want me to know her age.'

'Passport?'

'We honeymooned in Crete . . . I wasn't allowed to see the passport either.'

'So she could have been Jane Ingman? I'm assuming she married someone called Lyons – then, when he died, married Kris Ingman, got divorced, married you.'

'Or didn't get divorced. Maybe she was so desperate to marry me, she committed bigamy.'

'She really wanted to marry you that badly?'

'She was nuts about me.'

Louisa was shaking her head.

'Hey! What's so hard to believe about that? I was a trophy husband, all right? Media glamour, plus a psychic gift that knocks them dead at parties. Plus I've been told by a lot of women that I'm very good-looking.' There was something about Louisa that undermined my confidence. I didn't need undermining right now.

'Step by step, let's stay logical,' she reminded me. 'Why are we supposing your wife had been married to my department head? There are other Ingmans. Or perhaps it was her maiden name. Or they could have been brother and sister.'

'Come on, the prof was Swedish, right?'

'A Finn.'

'Reindeerland, anyhow. Jane was an English rose. It's too coincidental, his name on her card. And she knew him for certain. That's how she fixed up my tests.'

'He was doing a favour for someone on Friday,' Louisa agreed. 'He was all unctuous, strutting round in his I-have-your-boon-within-my-power mood.'

'Everyone hated him, right?'

'Hate is too strong a word.'

'But some people did? One of them must have. So what I need is a list of people who hated Ingman and a list of people who hated Jane, and where they overlap that's the killer.'

Louisa looked sceptical. 'Did anyone hate your wife?'

'She was very hateable. We'll find someone.'

'But no one springs to mind?'

'OK, no!' I was exasperated. 'But when it happens a lightbulb will go *ping* over my head. OK?'

CHAPTER TWENTY-SIX

A n electronic voice was reading out the stops. 'Your next station is
Farringdon . . . Farringdon your next station.' 'Your next station
is King's Cross . . .' It should have been a simple tape loop, but it
managed to sound like a computer was figuring it out syllable by
syllable. The noise refused to fade into the background. It kept
interrupting. One more reason to go by taxi.

'You thought Ingman was a bachelor, right? No live-in girlfriends?
What about casual romances?'

'If he had them he didn't talk about it.'

'Was he a faggot?'

'He never gave that impression.'

'Big circle of friends?'

'He talked about work to me. Nothing else. He ate at the Reform
Club sometimes, and he had relatives in Helsinki he visited.'

'How often?'

'In the two years I've worked with him, four times.'

'And I guess he was too aloof to go to the university dinners,
ceremonies, stuff like that?'

'He went, you have to. It would be unforgivable to treat the
institution with contempt. He wasn't the only eccentric academic,
remember. The place is crawling with them. If one is allowed to skip
the boring bits, they'll all want to.'

'Did other professors ring for chit-chat, play some poker, talk about
the ball game? OK, so if he's going dutifully to all the set pieces, and he
doesn't hang round with a clique, how come he gets everyone's back up?'

'You saw his manner.'

'And who had he pissed off lately?'

'There's another researcher in para, Carla Panetti. He upset her so
much on Monday I haven't seen her since.'

'She walked out?'

'Uh-huh. Big scene. And there's Judith in reception. He was rude
to her, always so rude. Treated her like a servant.'

132

'Anything lately?'

'Just constant. But I was with her last night, remember.'

'OK, I saw you and Judith leave. She's mid-fifties, grey hair and wide across the berth? So she didn't strike me as the kind of receptionist who could napalm a guy's intestines in between her manicures.'

'I can't imagine anyone who could do that. Quite literally no one. Yet someone did. And now that he's dead, I can think of people who won't be sorry. Annette in admin. She's one, for the same reason as Judith. He treated her like dirt. She's a nervy type of mouse, always in a fluster. Ingman would ring her first thing in the morning and if she hadn't finished all his filing from the night before, he was horrible with her. Vicious.'

'So his files mysteriously disappeared and all his letters had embarrassing typos – was he too dumb to learn?'

'We didn't dare do that. He had us knuckling under. If ever a file did get lost, Ingman would humiliate everyone for a week. Judith and Annette really lived in dread of him. I know he could make Judith weep, because I've seen it.'

'And you?'

'I dealt with him by ignoring him. He got the silent treatment. I suppose he just thought I was haughty. But things got done the way he wanted. It wasn't worth my while to make a stand.'

'And the other girl?'

'She flared up sometimes. I don't think Ingman ever really understood what was goading her. When he deliberately rubbed her nose in the dirt, she could take it with dignity. But the little asides, the twists in the tone of his voice, the needles turning under the skin – those things Ingman did unconsciously. He wasn't purposely setting out to aggravate people, it was just his manner. And precisely because he did it without thought, Carla got into some thundering rages.'

'What was the last row over?'

'Just trivial – the way she'd downloaded some data from one of the American universities. There's a very well-known investigator at the University of California, a man named Tart. Charles T. Tart. This isn't relevant, except you'll see why people could loathe Ingman. Tart has published several papers on connections between marijuana use and psi ability. And Ingman has criticised them, in print, for tending to strengthen the public association between drugs and parapsychology.'

'You're starting to talk shop.'

'Sorry. The point is, Ingman hated anything that made him look like a hippy. He got very sensitive when people said, "What's he on?" So Carla logged onto Tart's website, copied the paper Ingman had asked for, and saved it with the filename Tart had used. Ingman got ratty. All the students were hacking into his PC, according to him, and they'd see the word "marijuana-and-psi" and by tea-time the campus would be awash with rumours.'

'What rumours?'

Louisa shrugged her shoulders pompously. With a fair imitation of Ingman's clipped, precise intonation, she said: 'My colleagues will imagine I sniff ganja all morning, and inject weed all afternoon, in pursuit of mystical enlightenment.'

'So what was Carla supposed to do?'

'File it under "Tart, C: Irresponsible theorem" or some such.'

'And he bawled her out?'

'She could cope with his lectures. No, he got a little condescending and explained how he would have done it, and she accused him of looking at her like she was half-witted.'

'Didn't he look at everyone that way? That's the look I got.'

'You're – well, you're Mediterranean, like Carla.'

'So?'

'There's a kind of prejudiced mindset some Scandinavian men have . . .'

'Like how?'

Louisa tried to cover it with irony, but she was obviously embarrassed. 'Your hair's dark, he probably regarded you as one rung up from a chimpanzee.'

'Thanks a bunch.'

'I got it too. Because I'm Jewish.'

'You're saying he was an out-and-out racist?'

'Not in an aggressive way. That's what was so enraging about him. It was just his unconscious attitude – he was North European, so he was genetically superior.' She was shrugging it off, like she was used to it. She probably was – she must have run into anti-Semitism every week of her life.

I stared out of the black windows at the thick clusters of wires trailing through the tunnels, like electric ivy on the walls. We were getting deep into Johannes-Kristian Ingman's personal underground now.

'OK, Carla's on one list with a big tick. Annette, we'll talk to her in case she saw anyone Friday night with a big bag full of cooked Nazi. Anyone else in that place hate him?'

134

'I've been through all this with the police. There are always a lot of people drifting in and out of the building.'

'Students, I get you. Do you think we should be considering a student with a grudge? Some guy who fails his finals and reaches for the flame gun?'

'That wasn't what I meant. Professor Stanley on the upper floors works with the homeless. Charting the progression of mental illness in people with transitory home habitats.'

'Like cardboard boxes.'

'And hostels, B&B, that sort of thing. Drug users, alcoholics, abuse victims – he measures their deterioration against a control group in home or hospital surrounds.'

'You mean he watches people fall apart?'

'I suppose he thinks they'll fall apart, whether he watches or not. He has been arguing for a closed-circuit TV system in the corridors, in case they try to leave with any of his computer equipment.'

'God forbid they should flog a couple of screens and buy themselves medication. It could screw the whole research. So Stanley's ruthless enough to be a killer, at any rate.' Then I caught up with the obvious notion: 'You mean there are cameras running in the hall? The killer must be on video.'

'Ironically, no. Ingman wouldn't permit it. He vetoed the proposal on the grounds of personal privacy. I don't suppose he actually cared about being filmed while he went about the building. He just wanted to needle Professor Stanley.'

'Thus giving Stanley a motive. Maybe we should make a list of people who didn't want Ingman dead, it'll be shorter. What about Stanley's pal, Laurel?' The name was unforgettable.

'Never there. Had a nervous breakdown about a week after I arrived. I think I saw him twice. Enormous fat man, with stains on his tie. Hated Ingman's guts, apparently. Wouldn't sit at the same table with him. For a month or two when I first came here, Ingman would say things – "My ceiling has stopped sagging since our esteemed colleague took himself away." He was very smirky. After a while, he forgot to be so triumphant.'

'Do you think Laurel forgot about him?'

'How would I know?'

'It's a possible,' I said. 'Revenge with a long, long fuse. Another tick on your side of the list.'

'What about your side?'

'You know, Jane almost kept me at arms' length. I didn't get to *meet*

135

Jane's friends – I was *shown off* to them. She took me to parties and she talked on and on about who I was and how wonderful I was and she never let me speak. She never left me alone with her friends and especially she never let them establish any relationship with me.'

'Possessive?'

'Jane was very jealous. I don't mean she was scared I would start sleeping with all these appalling people, though maybe it was that as well – the real fear was, I would cease being hers exclusively and 100 per cent.'

'You're saying you don't know anything about her circle of acquaintances.'

'I'm not just making excuses.'

'But you never learned anything about the people round her.'

'Right.'

'Has it ever occurred to you that you're a completely self-centred man? You married this woman without a thought for her personality. You have no idea about other people. And you don't care that you're so ignorant.'

She really snapped the word. She was cross with me. I sat and let her say what she wanted. Maybe talking about Ingman had brought her anger to the surface. After all, she couldn't really mean it when she called me self-centred.

'You don't believe it,' she added, like she was reading my mind, 'but you are. Self-centred! And yet you're very sensitive about anything with a bearing on you. You lack empathy. You see a lot, but you can't put yourself in other people's bodies and feel what they feel.'

'You didn't become a psychologist by accident, did you? Talking horseshit is your big talent.'

'I think I'm right.'

'Shrinks always do.'

'You've been to a psychiatrist then?'

'Is that relevant?'

'Only if it transpires that you're a madman and I didn't know.'

'I haven't ever seen a shrink. And psychologists are not supposed to use language like "madman". It degrades people.'

'I'm a parapsychologist.'

'What does that mean, you analyse ghosts?'

'You're just a very classic case, that's all.'

'Case of what?'

'An egoist. Utterly self-focused. It's unusual to meet an egoist as pure as you.'

136

'You're wrong there. I'm not pure.'

'Mikki, Mikki, it's pure Mikki with you. I bet there isn't one person in the world you seriously give a damn about except yourself.'

'I – I – Well, I've been unlucky in the people I meet. I would give plenty of damns. If I found the right person.'

'And you start every sentence, "I". I, I, I. I this, I that.'

'I don't.'

'See?'

'I think we can move on now.'

'See again.'

'OK, I confess, I'm an egotist.'

'Egoist.'

'That too. You know, I don't think you're so pretty when you look smug.'

'We can't move on. We're stuck. You haven't taken the blindest bit of notice of your poor dead wife since the day you married her. You've got no idea about her past. There could be a busload of people all itching to murder her and you wouldn't know one of them. So what can we possibly discover that the police can't?'

'We already know she was married to Ingman.'

'And we should tell the inspector.'

'Before they get another word from me they'll have to rip out my fingernails. This morning they were going to do that anyhow, before they knew about Jane.'

'You can't withhold information.'

'No? I told you, I'm not pure. What I need to know is, what was the deal between Ingman and my wife? Do you know where he lived?'

'Obviously. I have his spare key.'

'Why are we sitting here? You have his key with you? Now? Jeez, Louisa! We could be round there, we could be opening drawers and finding the answers instead of beating our brains to Jell-O.'

'We're not going in his apartment.'

'Where is it? Are we near?'

'Baker Street. We're miles away.'

'Really miles?'

'The last stop was Blackfriars. It'll be half an hour to Baker Street.'

'Even if we get off and go back? Great.'

'It's not an issue. I'm not going into Ingman's flat.'

'Fine. I am. I'm a dynamic guy. You want I should sit here and go in circles for ever? I need to act.'

'You need your head examined.'

'You're the girl for the job.'

She let out a noise, one of those irritated English sounds, sort of, 'Pah!' and sat back with her arms folded.

I stared at her reflection in the black glass opposite. She stared back, but she wasn't seeing me. Pretty soon I stopped focusing too. The wires rushed past the window and swept my thoughts along.

Ingman and Jane. Marsh and Jane. Ingman's charred body. Bowen's blazing lighter. Jane's scorched head.

The coach shuddered and rolled, and people were hanging on the straps and the bars, and shoving through the sliding doors, and the coach shuddered and rolled away again. Over and over. Waiting for Baker Street to come round again.

I felt a light touch on my shoulder. It was Louisa's face. She was asleep.

CHAPTER TWENTY-SEVEN

Above ground, the air was hot. And close. The dust and fumes hung like thick tobacco smoke in front of our faces. Traffic was locked solid on Baker Street and we crossed the road between stationary cars on our way from the Tube to Ingman's apartment.

A guy in a cape and deerstalker handed me a yellow leaflet. 'You are now entering Sherlock Holmes country,' it read. They didn't know how true. There was a drawing of a murdered woman and an address for the Museum of Detection at 221b Baker Street. And a reminder – 'Be sure to visit Madame Tussaud's.'

Unless my luck changed soon they'd be installing me in Tussaud's Chamber of Horrors.

Ingman's pad was at 121 Baker Street. Not 121b – just Third Floor, 121. From the outside it was red-brick, four storeys of four sash windows, and every window criss-crossed into sixteen panes. Most of the Baker Street houses had been knocked about, had shop fronts punched into their ground floors, were hung with awnings or remoulded in concrete. Ingman's was one of the survivors. I guessed it was built some time in the last century, and it kind of reminded me of the tenement where I was raised.

Inside it was strictly nineties.

There was a desk of curving aluminium tubes for the concierge, and a carpet so red and velvety it should have been draped over the windows. Two chairs like African thrones were half-turned from the near wall, with crimson velour on everything and a smoked-glass circular table primly stacked with *Vogue* and *Arena*.

At the desk a flunkey in braid and buttons flicked us a glance from under his peaked cap. 'Mrs Simons.' No pause, no memory trawl – he knew her instantly. 'You've come in connection with the tragedy, of course.'

'Oh. Hello. Yes.'

I could see lying was not going to be one of Louisa's strengths.

'May I be of assistance?'

'The university has asked me to collect some of his papers. If they haven't already been too badly damaged, or lost by the police.' She said it mechanically. It was what I'd told her to say. I should have added to sound alive when she said it.

'I was on hand, all the time the forensics people were here, Mrs Simons,' Flunkey said gravely. He was late-fifties, ex-cop I guessed, with broad hands and nicotine-yellow fingertips. 'No papers were removed, I saw to that. I carry out my duties to the home-holders, even to the grave, if that's what is necessary.'

Great. A stickler. I couldn't see him turning his back and picking his teeth while I ripped pages out of the prof's address books. And what was 'home-holder'? Did he mean tenant? And they were too classy for a word like 'tenant' here?

'Good,' said Louisa. 'Good, good. Um, is it OK if I go up then?'

'And the gentleman with you?'

Flunkey tried not to sneer but he had one of those expressive faces.

'He's one of Professor Ingman's subjects. One of his most important.'

'I see. Naturally, Mrs Simons, if you're satisfied I'm satisfied.'

'I have a key.'

'No need, Mrs Simons. I shall unlock for you, and wait to lock up again. I take my duties seriously.'

'Were you on duty Friday night?' I asked.

'I left the desk and locked the front doors at eight p.m. precisely, as I always do. I expect you'll be aware, Mrs Simons, my colleague Andrews is on duty from six a.m. to one p.m. I relieve him and remain until lock-up. On Sundays a younger man named Ellis is here throughout the day. Home-holders are fully informed of the necessity of keeping the front entrance secure at all times between eight p.m. and six a.m. It is my experience that this precaution is properly kept.'

'So you didn't know if anyone was with the professor when you left the building on Friday?'

'There were no visitors for the professor, I can say that with complete certainty. What is more, all the people who were admitted after one p.m. were known to me as bona fide visitors for other home-holders. Mr Al-Aud on the second floor, his brother was here between three thirty and five, for instance. There was no one unaccountable. Naturally, had any suspicious person attempted to force an entrance, they would have been prevented. And with new

140

visitors I always insist on their credentials. This gentleman, as an example, would not be permitted to remain without your say-so, Mrs Simons.'

'That's very good,' I said.

'We will go up by the stairs if you are agreeable, Mrs Simons,' Flunkey wheezed. He looked like a thirty-a-day man, minimum. If he didn't chance a smoke at the shiny desk, there would be plenty of times when duty demanded he took a precautionary check of the back yard. Just to make certain no one had stolen the drainpipes. 'Avoiding the lifts is one tip for preventing laziness from creeping up on you. Laziness is the enemy of efficiency in this occupation, Mrs Simons. Can't afford to slacken for a minute.'

He was pompous, but there was something else besides. A little too much emphasis on his trustworthiness. I remembered what Louisa had said – the way Ingman could inspire the people who worked for him with dread – dread of being caught out in a mistake. Maybe Flunkey was scared of his home-holder even after the blowtorcher had come visiting.

Or maybe he knew he had slipped up and didn't want us guessing. Knew his job would be history if anyone found out. Dereliction of duty. Leaving the front door unlocked while he puffed on a Senior Service in the concierge's cloakroom. Because he couldn't lock up every time he had a smoke. Even if it was only two or three times a shift.

Suppose a home-holder was outside with no key and it was pouring with rain? That would never do.

So anyone could have walked in, if they judged their moment. And by the time they'd finished their cookery evening, Flunkey would have been long, long gone.

'I reported the incident with the tramp, of course.'

'A tramp came in?'

'Most definitely not, young lady.' Louisa forfeited the 'Mrs Simons' for that outrageous suggestion. 'No tramp will ever pass through that portal while I am on duty. But I observed this layabout, loitering around the pavement outside, and when he decided to sit down in our doorway, I decided to remove him with the toe of my boot. Which solved that little local difficulty fairly swiftly, I might tell you. Although I did observe he was hanging round some of the shops for the rest of the afternoon, and peering in at me like he had a very healthy respect for my boot. As well he might, Mrs Simons.'

The stairs were steep, and the ceilings were high, and I was wondering when we'd reach the top floor. 'I bet Professor Ingman took the elevator, right?'

'A very busy man, the professor,' said Flunkey. 'And a man of few words.'

To you, maybe, I thought.

Unless he was humiliating them with long words while he stripped braid off their uniforms and stamped on it, I didn't think Johannes-Kristian Ingman was the type to spare many words for the non-commissioned classes.

The top floor was deserted. I wasn't expecting to see Bowen and Tripp, but when a murder has been committed you expect the Great British institution to stick at least one of its bobbies on the door. This was Saturday night, so maybe they needed every man in the riot vans. Saturday night was obviously a good time to do some private investigations.

Flunkey turned the Yale lock and swung open the door on an apartment that stank like someone had wired 240 volts through the toilet seat and then taken a dump.

The room inside was black. Flunkey reached in and flicked the lights on. Now it wasn't black, just very, very dark grey.

Flunkey's fingertips were smeared with soot from the switch. Everything was coated in carbon powder and smoky ashes. The carpet was pitted with paths of lighter grey footprints, where soot had been trodden in.

The furnishings were blackened, but glancing around I couldn't see anything charred or reduced to flakes. The only thing that had really gone up in here was the professor's corpse. I'd seen how little was left of that.

The rest of him was all round us.

'The place'll have to be ripped out, of course,' remarked Flunkey. 'Gutted. Of course, if his executors want to try and salvage anything . . . but I don't see as how they could.'

The rug had been burned away to its fringes in a black oval. The ash in the middle had been swept away. I stared at it, biting my tongue so I didn't blurt out to Louisa that hey, look, right there was where the prof had been scraped up.

Grey foam hung from the curtains and puddled the rugs. An extinguisher had been squirted round, but not for long. When the firemen arrived Ingman's flat would have been smouldering quietly in places, that was all. No raging flames.

A long table stood to the right, with the window down onto the

142

courtyard beyond it. Four slender chairs, coated with greasy soot, were drawn up to it. The nearest had been rubbed, leaving a smeary circle front and back and a distorted view to the next room through its glass back. The chairs were all glass. The legs, when I looked closer, were stacks of thick, jagged panes, clamped together by an iron skewer.

They must have cost a fortune. For the set, $3,000 dollars minimum. Maybe, with a lot of scrubbing, they'd get clean. But Flunkey was right. No one was going to call in the restorers here. All Professor Ingman's worldly possessions were destined to be trashed.

The thought crossed my mind that maybe this was what someone had wanted.

Flunkey looked at Louisa. 'You all right, Mrs Simons?'

That was a question I should have asked. She looked sick and green. But she raised both hands to signal, I'm OK. Just don't ask me to speak.

'I wouldn't linger too long in here, Mrs Simons. The atmosphere's not healthy. If you need to collect anything, I won't stand looking over your shoulders. I know the professor trusted you to have a key, Mrs Simons, and his trust is good enough for me. I'd better be getting down to my duties. If I can insist, however, you'll be good enough to sign with me at the desk for anything you take out of this room? Papers and such for the college?'

'Oh yes,' Louisa said. Her voice sounded from the back of her gorge.

Flunkey left the door open. I could hear him wheezing down the stairs. He wasn't going back to his duties. He was going to have a contemplative Senior Service in the courtyard. And if anyone asked – yes, he'd had to leave his desk to accompany Mrs Simons to the top flat. Flunkey was a schemer, in little ways. I recognised the technique. It wasn't my own style, I always found you got further when you leapt first and looked later.

But then, how much did my situation have to recommend it?

'OK,' I said, 'detection time.'

'This soot. It's revolting. And we'll leave fingerprints.'

'It's no secret we're here. How come the bellhop knows you so well?'

'I've been here twice before.'

'So that's not exactly a close relationship. He called you "Mrs Simons" straight off.'

'The first time Ingman brought me here, the commissionaire

wanted to know my name. The second time, he stood very upright and barked out, "Professor Ingman! Mrs Simons! Good evening!" I suppose he has a memory for faces and he's proud of it.'

'What was Ingman's excuse for luring you back to his parlour?'

'Work. I told you, he never tried a pass on with me. He was always . . .'

'A gentleman?'

'Neutral. There was no sexual energy there at all.'

'Maybe that's why he didn't stay the course with Jane. That's what I want to find now – wedding picture, marriage certificate, something that ties them together. You know where he kept photo albums, anything like that?'

'It all looks so different. He kept everything beautifully here. There was no dust, it all shone. The lights reflected in the chairs and the stereo came on at a touch. Now it looks like the contents of an old garden shed.'

She walked across the carpet – I guess the idea of testing the music gave her courage to enter the room. With one finger she prodded a panel beside a bookcase where a red light was winking under a glaze of soot.

Trumpets and strings blasted out – 'Tarrah-tarrah, tirrah-tarrah, tarrah-tarrah, tirrah-tarrah, ta-ta-tarrah ta-ta-daaaaa . . .'

And Frank Sinatra opened up, 'I got the world on a string, sittin' on a rainbow . . .'

'Shit that's loud,' Louisa gasped.

She jabbed the panel again, and again.

The Voice got louder, and louder: 'I can make the rain go with my finger – Oh what a world, what a life . . .'

She scooped up a pair of remote zappers and tapped frantically on them.

The TV flicked on and off.

Frank blasted, 'This Is LOVE!'

And then he disappeared.

The silence was juddering. All over the room, ash was settling, stirred up by the speakers. I was expecting Flunkey to come scrambling up the stairs.

But nothing happened, except for a clacking as Louisa's shaking hands laid down the remotes. 'That gave me a fright.'

'We're jumpy. Your boss had taste in music. I like him better now.'

She went over to a drawer and hesitated before it. 'It sounded like Bing Crosby or something.'

144

Bing Crosby! My God, if I hadn't learned my lesson from Jane Lyons – you could never know a woman's worst faults just from first impressions. Bing Crosby!

With a decision and a tug, Louisa opened the drawer and plunged her hand in. Which took nerve. I still liked her a lot.

I started pulling books off the shelves, looking for a wedding album. Under the soot, everything was orderly. No stray pictures slid between volumes, no packets of photos, no love letters or souvenir wedding service. There would have been plenty of that stuff – I knew Jane. But maybe she'd kept everything, or he'd destroyed his stuff.

I had an idea there would be something, in its place, filed, labelled. I didn't think Ingman would trash old stuff. He wasn't scared of his possessions, so long as he controlled them. Everything in its own compartment, under control.

I wondered what he'd thought of Louisa's pile-'em-high approach to filing. Maybe he looked out of his tranquil office haven, into the heaving mess of papers where his researchers worked, and his innate, North European sense of superiority was reassured.

Maybe, so long as the chaos stayed away from him, he didn't give a damn. Ingman had been a totally self-contained man. Ice-cold.

Until someone with a blowtorch got to him.

I wandered through to the kitchen, which was mostly clean. The killer had taken the trouble to keep internal doors closed. I stared at my reflection in the gleaming sink unit. Where the drainer was ridged, my face rippled. I stood for a few seconds, rocking back on my heels, watching my features distort.

Not that I had time to kill. And Louisa was grimly squatting with the contents of one drawer, picking over it. But I just didn't know where to start looking.

I pulled open a cupboard. A rack of knives hung inside. They were bright and bloodless.

Maybe one of them was the murder weapon. The killer could have made an excuse, gone to the kitchen, selected the blade, done the deed, gone back to this shiny sink and washed the knife.

Or a meteorite could have hurtled in through an open window and frazzled him. That was about as likely.

So who could get into Ingman's apartment without any struggle? Someone who had taken the trouble to dodge Flunkey. Maybe someone dressed as a hobo. But that made no sense, because Ingman wouldn't open the door to a hobo. And if he hadn't opened the door, the killer must have had a key, because it sure as hell hadn't been kicked down.

I called out to Louisa, 'Did Ingman hand a lot of doorkeys around?'

'He claimed mine was the only one in existence. I was to treat it with the kind of religious awe my people once reserved for the Arc of the Covenant. Those were his words. And if he ever locked himself out, my orders were to drop whatever was on hand and take the first available taxi to Baker Street. Not the bus, not the Tube – taxi, chop-chop.'

'Did he get locked out often?'

'Never.'

'So why not leave a key behind the desk? And they must have one down there, anyhow.'

'Obviously not, or I wouldn't have been on twenty-four-hour call.'

'Maybe he just wanted you to know your life was never completely your own.'

'That's a point. Astute. Being around a scientist must be sharpening your brain up.'

'Are you making a joke?'

'Ye-es.' Like I was too dumb to know.

'Because,' I said, 'I think that's the first time I've heard you use humour.'

I walked through to the bedroom. One wall was sliding mirrors, with his coats and suits behind. There were tweeds, silks, pinstripes, a gabardine, and a varsity gown lined in orange and purple.

The bed was a double, with the blankets turned down. That gave me a chill. The bed was ready, and the sleeper would never get between the sheets.

And beside the bed, on a built-in table, next to the reading lamp, there were two pictures. A girl, in some kind of graduation kit-out, and a couple on their wedding day. Confetti on the shoulders on Ingman's suit. And a tiara in Jane Lyons's hair.

God knows why, but I picked up the girl's portrait first. She had shoulder-length blonde hair which could have been cut to length with a chisel. Her eyes were the same deep blue as Ingman's, and her nose and jaw followed the pattern. I tipped the print out of the brass frame. On the back, in felt-tip, was written, 'To Daddy. Solka. 97'. I shook my head. I'd been getting along OK, thinking of Ingman as

146

a non-human ego. It was depressing to realise someone had known that pile of ashes as 'Daddy'.

I picked up the second picture and turned that out of its frame too. A red felt pen had noted, '8.6.96.' That probably meant the wedding day, unless the prof had a warped sense of humour and had written the date of his decree nisi on his register-office snap. But it wouldn't be a good enough joke for the bedside. Divorce dates got scrawled over the bride's face, not neatly inscribed on the back.

Deduction: Jane married Ingman in either June or August 1996.

Mystery: Why keep the picture on show?

Inquiry: When did they split?

Quandary: How to find out who hated them enough to cremate them separately on the same night.

I took both photos to Louisa. She had a pile of papers by her foot, and nothing in her hands, but she brightened up when I produced the evidence.

'We can go now?'

'I don't figure there's more to find. Unless the murderer's name is scrawled in blood on the back of the door.'

I looked down at the papers, stacked in the middle of the blackened oval in the rug. And my fingers were shaking as I bent down to pick up the top sheet.

It wasn't the murderer's name, and it wasn't written in blood. But it might as well have been.

CHAPTER TWENTY-EIGHT

I want to be clear about this. I want every detail in sharp focus.
I always figured the reason Sinatra was the biggest idol of the radio age was his diction. Every syllable got the respect it was due. He monkeyed with the tunes, he made up fresh lyrics, but the words he sang were delivered with total clarity. Pre-video, pre-MTV, pre-promo candy bars and tubs of margarine, a singer had to use his voice if he wanted to get heard.

Sinatra used his voice. He was my ideal, my example, in everything, but most specially on radio. I worked to cut all the elisions and the slurrings out of my speech. I honed my accent till I could peel fruit with it. And when the going got weird, it was a point of pride with me – the listeners might not know what I was talking about, but they would know every word I said.

So it works on air, I want it to work on paper. I want you to experience this now, like it happened to you.

You can feel the toe of your trainers grinding the grit on the burnt floor. The thick, burnt smell is everywhere, but it gets rawer as you bend over to pick a leaflet off the pile of papers. A little stream of acid bubbles up from your stomach and burns the back of your throat. Your fingers scrape and fumble at the leaflet. When you try to hold it, the muscles in your hand are too feeble to grip.

I can replay those two or three seconds like my life is on CD. Logically, it was no more than the time it took to bend down and pick up the document. But memory isn't logical. I replay it, and everything around me slows. I can hear my heart, and the echoing lull between beats. I can hear my long intake of breath.

When you're in a car, and suddenly there's another car sliding towards you, and there's half a second to impact, that half a second passes slowly. You might live, you might not, but either way this is a defining instant. And that's how it was in Ingman's apartment when I saw that leaflet.

The cover was stamped with a black-and-white circle like a

medallion. The contrasting halves fitted together with a wavy line, and in the white area there was a little black circle and in the black area there was a little white circle. The yin-yang symbol. Denotes wholeness, oriental wisdom, balance. Also denotes bullshit.

Across the circle in grey lettering was 'ESP'. And under that in ornate script, the translation: Evangelists of Superhuman Perfection.

Louisa didn't comment. I turned it over – it was a piece of yellow A4, printed both sides and folded once.

If I waited for Flunkey to come and find us, he might take it off me. Maybe he'd only thought we wanted university papers. I wasn't going to waste time wondering. I stuffed the leaflet into my pocket, and took the photos from Louisa.

'Is there a cappuccino bar near here?' I asked.

'Burger King do coffee,' she said.

'So I'll buy you a burger,' I said. 'Flame-grilled.'

I swear this is true, and I'm not just telling it for poetic effect: when we slid onto the bucket seats at the burger bar, the muzak system was playing Sinatra and 'I've Got The World On A String'. I mean, synchronicity.

I didn't point it out to the psychical researcher. I would have had to explain the difference with Bing Crosby. And there was something more difficult to explain.

'These ESP people,' I said, fingering the leaflet and stirring two sachets of gummed-up sugar into my polystyrene beaker, 'they've been pestering me on the show. Was Ingman one of them?'

'One of who? What?'

So I took it she knew as much as I did, and started to read aloud: 'The universe is a place without limits, and the human mind is a power without limits – Madox Bligh.'

'I've heard him talk about Madox Bligh,' Louisa said immediately.

'In what context?'

'Keep reading, let me think about it.'

So I read on: 'As you scan these words, you are unaware of the perfectly evolved mechanism that is your brain. In your lifetime, your brain will process more pieces of information than there are atoms in the galaxy. Even though it is running at barely one-tenth of its potential, your brain is the most powerful tool in existence.

'Imagine what you can achieve when you access its deepest resources. Visualise the riches and happiness that will be yours when you unleash the dormant energies of your mind. Throughout history one secret above all others has been known to the enlightened sages of every culture – the secret of transforming dreams into reality through the power of thought alone.

'Now this limitless gift lies within your grasp. Have you the courage to seize it, the courage to transform your life and the lives of those you love?'

I looked at Louisa. She was staring into her coffee like the ghost of the professor was shaping up in the yellow froth.

'This is a helluva pitch,' I commented. 'Why do I get the feeling I'm about to be asked for my credit-card number?'

'What else does it say?'

'Your brain can read the thoughts of others,' it continued. 'Your brain can see objects on the other side of the world. Your brain can take flight from its corporeal form. Your brain can move objects with the sheer force of its thought-power. These are not rare talents given to the inexplicable few. They are normal human abilities, and they lie within your grasp. Your brain is supercharged with extra-sensory perception – the measureless power of ESP.'

I flicked over the leaflet. 'ESP – Evangelists of Superhuman Perfection. And Ingman picked on that phrase to me – he claimed he'd written a book about some Victorian who invented the term, extra-sensory perception. Am I right?'

'Richard Burton.'

'Yeah, I said Liz Taylor and we all died laughing. So was he dropping a hint with this ESP thing? Was he trying subliminal suggestion? Was this his bag, did he hang round Leicester Square handing this stuff out?'

'He's talked about it. Let me think. Read the rest.'

'It goes into quotes – "I was sleepwalking through life until Madox Bligh opened my eyes ... K.A." More like that. No names. just initials.'

'Anyone J.L.?'

'For Jane Lyons? Smart point – P.D.R., L.de V., B.M., all of them praising His Holiness Madox Bligh. So where's the sting?' I turned to the back. 'Ah, el stingeroo – Intrigued? Excited? Or just open-minded, willing to give anything a second look if it promises to make your dreams come alive?

'But maybe you're waiting for the catch. The request for payment. The Evangelists for Superhuman Perfection believe in keeping everything simple and open. Yes, there will be some financial cost if you decide to retrain your brain to its utmost capacity. But you'll never be

150

out of pocket – because one of the incredible abilities unleashed with your ESP powers will be the gift of making money. Wealth is the first and, incredibly, the least significant of the gifts that lie within your grasp. And when your brain is functioning beyond your imagination, you'll be delighted to donate just 10 per cent of your new-found riches to our non-profit organisation. Yes, all we expect is one-tenth of the money we'll teach you to attract – all by thought-power. And until you've acquired that skill, there's nothing to pay. NOTHING TO PAY!!!

'Small wonder that many of our students go on to become enthusiastic Evangelists, donating 20, 30, 40, even 50 per cent of their income – and still enjoying a lifestyle that was unthinkable . . . before they learned a new way of thinking.'

I stopped to sip my coffee. This spiel was leaving a foul taste in my mouth. The coffee made it worse.

'It's too long, there's no punch,' I said. 'What they want to state is, "Nothing to pay". End of story. Hit you with the 10 per cent when you sign up.'

'You're the expert,' agreed Louisa.

'And it's promising way too much. The normals aren't going to buy this. Do you buy it? I don't, and I'm a sucker for a good spiel, I'll buy anything if the window dressing is smart. But this is gaudy-gaudy. Full volume, world on a plate. This is bait for desperate types.'

'I get offered courses in telepathy and psychokinesis every week,' said Louisa. 'They don't normally promise you the earth, but the product is basically the same. Psi awareness for businessmen, psi for sportspeople.'

'Right, pitches for normals. Most people want normal clients. But this is pitching for freaks – turn dreams into reality, transform your life. Wealth beyond your wildest imagination, and that's just the soup course. Mr Madox Bligh wants to surround himself with crazies, this is how.'

'Where do you send the money?'

I looked. 'You don't. You go to the Madox Bligh Institute at 444 Southampton Row, any Wednesday, Friday or Sunday at three p.m., and marvel at the mysteries of the mind.'

'Ingman talked about Bligh with respect,' Louisa recalled.

'Which tells us good Captain Bligh is not Jewish, Mediterranean or black.'

'Also, it suggests to me that Bligh's not such a quack as you think.

151

Ingman could see through the shysters and the conmen in a trice.'
She suddenly clammed up.

'Go on,' I told her, 'say it. I'm hard to hurt.'

'The first time he heard your show, he talked me through what you were doing. One call was rigged in advance, in another one you were fishing for clues, on another you were so vague that what you said could apply to anyone anywhere.'

'I never rig callers.'

'Ingman said you did.'

'Then he was even dumber than I realised. Listen, every time I cheat I take a risk – I could get caught. But at least if I do my own cheating, I know one thing for sure – I'm not going to talk about it afterwards over cocktails.'

I pushed my coffee away. 'Whenever I call in outside help, the risk factor sky-rockets. Because my accomplice is bound to tell at least one other person. It's human nature. What's the point of working a hoax if no one ever knows? So that's three people who know I'm faking. And maybe the third person tells a fourth, and pretty soon there are deaf-and-dumb hermits on Easter Island who know how Mikki works his stuff. So I never rig callers.'

'I thought you weren't over-sensitive about this.'

'When you tuned in, did Ingman claim this was the first time he'd heard my show?'

'So he said.'

'But he pretended to spot all the business, right? He was lying. He wasn't that good. Even I can't tell you how I'm working sometimes. Cold reading is very subtle. You can't buy a handbook, you have to employ instinct. To understand what I do, Ingman would have to study me a long time. Like, months.'

'We're getting sidetracked.'

'We're not – Ingman was being used by Jane to discredit me, remember. They were married. We don't even know they were divorced. So how long had the professor been on my case? Since before I told Jane, "I do"? Since before she even met me? Were Jane and Ingman staking me out from right at the very start?'

'You're paranoid.'

'I'm entitled to be.'

'What you're saying is, he knew how you did your act, therefore he'd been taking an interest in you for a little while, therefore yesterday's test was the culmination of a long plot.'

'I'd say that's obvious. You knew he was fitting me up, Jane knew the results before I did, the £5,000 was never going to materialise, Ingman was in the pasta restaurant Thursday night . . . Nothing happens by accident.'

'And how does that conspiracy account for two horrible deaths?'

'The connection must be there. It's a chain reaction. Ingman is killed, then Jane. Same night, same method. It's a chain, and I'm one of the links. Because he was married to Jane, and so was I. Because I saw both of them yesterday. Because they must have discussed me yesterday. Have you got flip charts at the university?'

'What have flip charts got to do with murder?'

'We did flow diagrams in college – circles and lines everywhere, showing what caused which reaction. And mind maps, they're like spider webs with all your thoughts criss-crossing. And another one, force field analysis, which turns all your pros and cons into percentages.'

'I don't follow.'

'Me neither. I never understood flip charts, it's just if you do them right with lots of coloured markers and Day-Glo, you look like you've got all the connections worked out. I feel if we could lay out all these facts and connect them in felt-tip, the pattern would emerge.'

'All the intersecting lines might spell out the name of the murderer.'

Louisa wasn't taking the flip chart thing seriously.

'You British are so negative,' I complained.

'You Americans don't understand anything unless it's in jargon.'

'Listen, if you think it'll help find whoever killed my wife, why don't we sit here and bicker till one of us bursts into tears?'

She didn't answer back. I knew I was being cheap. If the grieving process for my dear departed spouse had started, I hadn't noticed yet. But sometimes cheap works.

'So,' I said, 'Ingman is killed, Jane is killed. I'm one link. Where are the others?'

'They were married.'

'OK, that's good, a direct connection. If we knew when they split up, why they split, who else was involved, whether they're divorced yet . . . all this would clear the picture. He ever drop any hints?'

'I had no idea he was anything but a bachelor.'

'So probably he and Jane were finished before you ever joined Ingman's department. And the only time Jane ever alluded to another marriage, aside from Ambrose, she was dismissive. Like, "Can't a girl be allowed to make one mistake?" So we can take it, this marriage was a disaster. I can buy that – I tried marrying Jane, it wasn't too great. Stand-out question: Why does Jane call on Husband No. 2 to stitch up Husband No. 3?'

'Would she know many other parapsychologists?'

'Maybe it's that simple.' I was doubtful.

'The private detective,' Louisa said, 'he's a link.'

I stared at her. 'Marsh!' She was right, and it was brutally obvious. 'He was working for Jane. He seems to be the last person who saw her. He must have seen Ingman at the pasta place, but he didn't comment. He's part of a three-way conspiracy. That's why he also claims he followed me to Ingman's apartment – when I didn't go there. And it was Marsh who called the police after I went to your room.'

'How did he know Ingman's body was in the office?'

'He must have looked. Maybe he was lurking in the corridor outside, heard the call. Maybe he came to have a look.'

'Maybe he put the remains there.'

That one was brutally obvious too, now that Louisa brought it up. Both these ideas had passed me right by. I was too focused on my place in the chain. She was right, I was perhaps a little over-concerned with myself.

Louisa's face was flushed red with thought, and her eyes were bright. This was a girl who liked using her brain. She was whispering, so the rest of the burger bar couldn't hear: 'He killed Ingman, moved the body, waited till he was sure you'd found it, called the police, went to kill Jane.'

'Why?'

She sat back, opened her mouth and raised her hands, and looked helpless. 'Because he's the killer.'

'So he's got the opportunity. I haven't, you haven't, because definitely we have alibis for when Jane died. Marsh made a police statement, but he must have been available for murder some time around four a.m. Opportunity, yes, but what's his motive?'

'Why did Jane hire him?' she countered.

'To monitor my movements.'

'So she used Ingman to catch you cheating professionally, and Marsh to catch you cheating sexually.'

'And £30,000 to catch me matrimonially. It's another pattern. And I'm right in the middle again.'

'Possibly,' she said gravely, 'science will eventually discover that the entire universe revolves around you.'

154

'Motive,' I repeated. 'If Marsh killed them, what for?'

'Money? A sex crime? Something from the past we don't know about? That's for the police to discover.'

'This faith in your national institution, it's very touching. Perhaps one day you'll be an innocent but obvious choice of suspect for Scotland Yard, and you'll suddenly understand why Mikki feels cynical about Great British Justice.'

'You'll have to be interviewed again.'

'Yeah? Am I under arrest? Is there a warrant? I have no intention to make a martyr of myself. If they want me, they can find me, and I won't be wearing a big badge saying, "Hi, I'm Mikki, please shine a lamp in my face and ask me trick questions".'

'Calm down.'

'Calm down already! There's a serial killer wants to keep a dinner date with me. Very possibly he's a licensed snooper named Marsh. I'd love to ask him but I don't know how. And he knows what I look like and who my friends are and he has a big pack of refills for his flamethrower.'

'You'll be safe in my apartment.'

'Right, the police will never think of looking for me there,' I said acidly. 'Listen, if I can figure out any kind of motive why Marsh would want Jane dead, or we turn up one piece of evidence, I dial my pals at Notting Hill Gate. Until then, I stay away from them. I know where we can go.'

'The Ritz?'

'A hotel if we have to, but a friend is better.'

'Who?'

'You don't know her. But she's nice. She'll look after your little boy and we can go out finding some answers.'

'I'm not leaving Dani with a stranger.'

'She's not a stranger. She's Mimi. You'll like her.'

'And where will we find your answers?'

'Marsh, for instance. I'm not scared to tackle him. If the light is good and there's a firehose nearby.'

'And if he doesn't prove helpful?'

'My neighbours. Your colleagues. We can start here, in Baker Street. Maybe someone got a better look at that bum your commissionaire kicked out.'

'That was just a homeless person. What's he got to do with anything?'

'Nothing, except one: he wanted in. Two: he probably got in.

Three: bums can walk in and out of your office building with their own latchkey, because of Professor Politically Correct upstairs. And four: a bum was watching me as I arrived in Queensberry Place last night.'

'Why would – I can't call them bums – why would a homeless person murder Ingman?'

Finally, I was ahead of her on brainwork.

'Maybe this was a homeless bum called Marsh.'

CHAPTER TWENTY-NINE

I gave Mimi the ESP leaflet and she gave me coffee. Real ground Java beans, no milk and she didn't have to ask if I wanted a cup or a mug. That girl knew how to look after me. Marrying someone older and richer had been a grievous mistake.

I did the introductions, explained we'd come to stay, and let Mimi relate her mother's latest atrocity while I concentrated on caffeine intake. It was nice to hear a story that didn't involve corpses or divorces, and Mimi was dying to get it off her chest. Her family was the kind which made murder by cremation look like a reasonable option. She didn't have any inhibitions about detailing her parental traumas in front of a woman she'd never met, but I did notice she talked to me the whole time and scarcely spared a glance for Louisa.

Basically, Mimi's older brothers were both dirty no-goodniks, with a busload of kids by enough women to overcrowd all the maternity wards of north London. They worked so hard at filling the streets of Stratford and Wanstead with tiny pattering feet, they didn't always have time to find different girls. So they swapped them back and forwards, with the result that Mimi had plenty of nephews and nieces who were half-brothers and half-sisters, with the same sets of grandparents.

When you need a slide rule to establish family relations, it's messy. Mimi's family defined messy.

I liked her brothers. They were always having fun. I didn't like her mother so much, going on what I'd heard, and I'd heard a lot. She came to Britain from Korea in 1959, when by all accounts she was pretty and fiery and the object of much attention. She refused to learn English then, and she still claimed to know nothing except, 'How much?' and 'Fucking crazy'.

Mimi's dad married her in March 1964, and had been regretting it since April 1964. This I could relate to.

You don't need to know all this about Mimi's relations. It has no relevance. But I figure it would make some light relief for you, same as it did for me.

'My brother brought two of his kids round for Mumma to look after.'

'Which brother?'

'The older one, Ken Lo. The other one's on remand in Pentonville.'

'I knew that.'

'Ken Lo thought it would be OK to dump the children on us – they're six and five, and by the standards of my nephews and nieces they're pretty well behaved.'

'They haven't been caught impaling cats on sticks and making their own petrol bombs yet?'

'They're nice children. Ken Lo knew I'd look after them. He's back with their mother this month, which is fun for the children. I should think he's a good daddy. Anyway, Friday night, why shouldn't he go out? Mumma and me were only going to be cooking and her nagging me about when I must get married. And Dad would just sit and drink himself to sleep in front of the TV. We'd be glad of the kids.'

'You're getting broody.'

'Cluck-cluck. Anyway, I thought at first Mumma was pleased to see him – gives him a kiss, gives him some food, takes the children in without a murmur. Then he left, and he hadn't been gone ten minutes when she suddenly went ballistic. I didn't even see what set her off. I think the older girl asked to watch TV late. Something and nothing. She threw them out.'

'Literally?'

'I don't mean she picked them up and threw them out – but she opened the door and pushed them out onto the walkway and slammed the door. This was nine thirty – two little kids not old enough to read yet. They don't know where they live, they don't know nothing.'

Mimi's parents lived in a council block with perspex-covered landings along the front of each row of apartments, like sidewalks in the air.

She was talking very fast and excited, in her sing-song way: 'And I started screaming at Mumma, and she screams back, and there were people hammering on the walls and the ceiling, and in the end I had to go chasing after these poor little brats and bring them home here. And they cried all night, because they thought their dad wouldn't know where to get them, and they didn't believe I was going to phone him. At five o'clock this morning I was sitting reading Fireman Sam stories to them. So if I look like I haven't slept since Thursday, that's why.'

'Are you sure we can stay?'

'It's open house. I'm putting a sign up under Westminster Bridge later, free beds for the winos.'

'No homeless, Mimi. I mean it – don't even look a bum in the face until I give the all-clear.'

'Explain?'

Louisa excused herself, saying she had to collect Dani and would be gone maybe an hour. I offered to go with her, but the suggestion didn't even get thought about. I guessed she didn't want Dani's dad seeing her with a man. I didn't argue. There was some stuff I needed to talk about.

It was almost worth living through the last forty-eight hours, just to tell it to Mimi. She stared at me like I was Humphrey Bogart, dropped by to run through the plot of *Casablanca* with her. She didn't ask any of the questions that Louisa kept irritating me with – like, Mikki, why don't you go to the police station, and was it you that killed Ingman, and who is this Sinatra person anyway?

Mimi was shocked when I found the prof's ashes, and outraged when I was arrested, and terrified when Jane got pipped. She held the ESP leaflet in her little trembling hand and declared it was plainly a clue and I was very clever to spot it. She kept saying, 'You poor thing!' and 'That's so unfair on you!' She was a great audience.

'Have you any ideas?' she asked at last. 'Ideas you're not telling her? The university girl?'

The thunder of the trains suddenly got louder – too loud to talk. It did that every ten minutes or so, and kept it up through the night. Dalston Junction was very near, almost in Mimi's window box. You noticed the shaking but you didn't notice the noise, unless you were trying to say something that mattered.

Before the noise died away, Louisa came in with Dani.

CHAPTER THIRTY

Dani was like his mother – all red curls and big bones, and a face you could read like headlines in the *National Enquirer*. His sleep had been invaded by police officers and his day had been spent with a father he didn't know and now he was being dragged to a two-room dive that was close enough to a railway that passengers generally mistook it for the waiting room. And he was under orders to be polite to the woman who owned it, and not to pay any attention to the American man, and to eat his tea and shut up and sleep in a chair.

He looked like a six-year-old was entitled to look in this situation.

I thought Mimi might burst into a fuss over him, but she barely glanced up. Not as broody as I guessed.

But she did say, 'You can have the bed. If you like. I don't mind sleeping on the floor.'

Louisa looked surprised and grateful. She managed to protest, but it was obvious she thought Dani deserved a bit of comfort.

Mimi said, 'It's not for long, is it? Mikki thinks the police will have a better idea after tomorrow, and he can go and answer their questions when he's done Monday's show.'

I nodded. This was a schedule for crime-solving I'd invented in Louisa's absence.

We ordered pizza, and I bought Dani his own cheese-and-onion even though he was never going to be capable of eating more than half, and that cheered him up. He had a woolly scarecrow with orange hair which he never let go, and this scarecrow sat on his lap to share the pizza. He watched an animal programme and we sat at the small table which marked where Mimi's sitting room became the kitchen. I didn't want to talk too much murder, because the boy was having a hard enough time already, but the conversation kept sliding back to the blowtorch and the bum. Louisa said she knew when Dani was listening and when he wasn't.

160

Mimi said: 'This needs organising. If you're going to do a proper investigation, it needs writing down.'

Louisa said: 'You know about these things?' She was being sarcastic but she asked the question like she wasn't, absolutely flat.

'I know about organising Mikki. He's got to have a clear direction in his mind.'

The look Louisa gave me said, 'Yeah? That'd be a first,' but she kept her mouth shut.

'So I think we should write down all the possible suspects and assign them percentages. Based on how likely it is they could have done it. Alibis and motive and all that.'

'Which detective series did you get that plan from? Not *Starsky and Hutch*, was it?'

'It's called force field analysis and Mikki taught me how to do it. He learned it at college.'

What a sweetheart. I bet she remembered every word I ever mumbled in my sleep too.

'Who's your prime suspect?'

'Marsh,' I said. 'He's got motive, opportunity, and the right character.'

'I thought you said you didn't know his motive,' countered Louisa.

'Well, OK. If he did it, he's got a motive. He's not a mad, meaningless killer. We've got to find it out. That's part of the detective work. But for opportunity, give him 100 per cent. And I get zero per cent. Put that, let's get it clear on paper. We all score zero for opportunity, so it can't be us. See, it helps to write these things down,' I told Louisa. I'd said this in Burger King and now Mimi's scrap of paper, a folded PrimeTime press release which she was decorating with her thick, dark doodles, was proving me right.

'You just want Marsh to be the killer because he made a fool of you,' said Louisa.

Mimi glared. 'If you don't take a positive attitude, we won't get very far.' She resumed doodling and asked me, without looking up, 'What did he do to . . . embarrass you?'

'Nothing. Why don't we . . .'

'You have to tell me all the facts. It might be a clue.'

'He was just snitching. You know – him and Jane laughing behind their hands at me.'

'Why did Jane hire a private detective in the first place?'

'Keep tabs on me. Louisa's right, I don't like Marsh, I just feel he invaded my space. But the fact remains . . .'

161

'How did he embarrass you?' Mimi repeated. She still wasn't looking up. Louisa on the other side of the table had frozen, and even the TV had dropped into silence. This was a different kind of Mimi, a brooder, suddenly sullen – I'd seen this unexpected shadow fall over her, a few times, when we were living together, or when I'd said something dumb after a show. But those times, I'd been able to dodge out. This time, I was stuck with her. Maybe there was an easy way to snap her out of it. I didn't know what it was.

'How did he embarrass you?' She said it again.

'OK, well . . .'

'The truth, Mikki.'

'Come on, would I lie to you? Listen, you know me. Occasionally I stray. I step off the straight and narrow. Maritally speaking. So Jane had her suspicions, and she got this shamus, and it turns out that maybe they ended up doing the things I was accused of.' I tried to look moderately sickened by my late wife's hypocrisy. It was the right approach, but Mimi was still staring down at the paper.

'You haven't told me. How did . . .'

'Yeah, I was embarrassed. In flagrante. Caught red-handed. Use your imagination. Am I the soul of discretion? No. So I don't have to go into details, especially with children present.' It was a last, desperate throw. It failed.

'Who was she, Mikki?'

Mimi must have known. Or at least have harboured serious suspicions. She wouldn't have dragged me down this way unless she'd been pretty certain. Still, it went against my code to give up without one last lie.

'No one you know,' I said.

'Who? – I want you to tell me who.'

'It was Kerry.' I almost added, 'Sorry,' but I stopped myself. Apologising could make this worse.

Mimi said nothing. She didn't even repeat Kerry's name. I waited for her to stand up and storm into her room. But she just kept scoring the ballpoint into the press release. The pen went back and forth, back and forth. She'd drawn a deep, dark triangle, and now she was blacking it out.

Louisa was hardly breathing. I swivelled my eyes sideways – I didn't want Mimi to know I was looking away from her. Louisa met my glance and there was real anxiety on her face.

Mimi jabbed the tip of her pen through the paper and said, 'That's important evidence. It's important, we both have to know all the

162

facts.' She clearly wasn't including Louisa here. 'Because the first time you spoke to Ingman, on the show, you were with Kerry.'

'Right, yes, that's right. You see, I hadn't thought of that.'

'In fact, we have to put Kerry down as a suspect. Kerry Allison,' she said aloud as she wrote it. 'Because we don't know – opportunity, 100 per cent, question mark. Alibi, zero per cent, question mark. And Jane,' she said.

'You can't put Jane . . .'

'She could have murdered Ingman.'

'How?'

'Zero per cent alibi unless you believe the private eye really was sleeping with her. And if he was helping her, she had 100 per cent opportunity. And if Jane and the professor were married, there's motive in there. 100 per cent.'

'Like what?' said Louisa.

Mimi stared at her pityingly. 'Like sex,' she said. 'They obviously had a sexual relationship. Who knows what that involved?'

'Nobody burns their partner to a crisp for kicks,' I said.

'What do you know? You're not exactly Mr Adventurous Sex. You just want to do the same thing with as many women as possible.'

OK, I could let that one pass.

Louisa said, 'Even supposing Jane killed Ingman in some strange sex ritual, she couldn't have killed herself that way. It's not possible.'

'Marsh,' said Mimi. 'It's a three-way thing. Marsh and Jane killed Ingman, maybe accidentally. A bondage session where the knots got too tight, or perhaps Ingman was their slave and they beat him too hard. He's dead, and his body shows he died in a sex game. So all the police have to do is find Ingman's lovers.'

'There's a doorman at Ingman's apartment,' said Louisa. 'He didn't show any visitors up.'

'He says he didn't,' Mimi answered, like her patience was close to snapping. 'But Jane had lots of money to spend. He's been paid off. Probably he's expecting to get paid off for the rest of his life. When he hears Jane is dead too, perhaps his story will change, and he'll remember Ingman's visitors.'

'And who killed Jane?'

'Marsh,' Mimi said simply.

'To cover his own tracks? But that doesn't make sense – he's made things worse for himself, in that case. Alive, Jane was his alibi, if anyone ever happened to ask him about the professor. But dead, she just makes him a suspect.'

'Why else is that suitcase at Jane's apartment? The one they dragged the corpse across town in? It was Jane's case.'

'There isn't time,' I said. 'They can't rendezvous with Ingman, get into some weird games, kill him by accident, zip back to collect a suitcase, return, torch the body, load it into plastic bags, take it to his office, lay it out and vanish before Louisa and Judith drop in at midnight.'

Mimi was shaking her head at me. Pityingly, like I was too dumb and naive to be mixed up in anything like this. Which I was.

'He died yesterday afternoon,' she said. 'Very soon after he got home. At least, that's my guess. Do you know what time he left the office?' she asked Louisa, sharply.

'After Mikki's tests. Maybe four fifteen?'

'So he could have been dead some time before you talked to Jane in her bath,' Mimi told me. 'She's washing the smell of death off her.'

'She must have got clean before I came home,' I said. I didn't like any of what was happening, but I particularly didn't like this version of events.

'Meanwhile,' Mimi said, 'Marsh is busy with his blowtorch. That could be giving him the biggest thrill of all. The power of destroying this brilliant, famous man completely, turning him into a bagful of charred dust. And the flames, fire can be very sensual. The heat could be erotic, even the smell. You can see that, can't you? What he was doing could really turn him on.'

'If,' I said, 'he was deeply, deeply sick.'

'Whoever killed Ingman and your wife was sick. Maybe Marsh got such a kick out of burning the body, he wanted to experience it again. That's why he called the police to get you arrested, to be sure you wouldn't go home to Jane, and then he went back to your apartment, had sex with her, killed her, and . . .'

'OK,' I said. 'I understand. I just don't think it's as plausible as you do.'

'And your theory is?'

'I don't have one. I agree, maybe Marsh is the killer. But that can't be the motive.'

'Why not?'

'Because I can't get my head round it.'

'It fits the facts. But all right, forget my ideas for a minute if you like.'

164

'Good,' Louisa cut in. 'Let's see what other theories can fit the facts.'

'There's the people at the university,' I tried. 'They all have 100 per cent access. To Ingman at least.'

Mimi glanced at Louisa coldly, then turned her paper over with a slap. 'OK, give me their names.'

'Laurel. Stanley. Wurt. They're the professors. Judith. Annette. Carla. They're admin, research, that kind of stuff. You can give them all a question mark for motive, except Carla, who hated Ingman's guts. And with Stanley there's the tramp connection – a tramp was hanging round outside when Mikki found Ingman's body, and there was a tramp seen near the Baker Street apartment, and Wurt's analysis subjects include a lot of tramps.'

Neat, I thought. Louisa had just summed up every unshakeable fact we'd been able to discover since the prof had been turned into a black mark on the university records.

So far as solid proof went to keep me safe from Detective Sergeant Bowen's steel-capped boots, it didn't seem much.

'That should be enough,' said Mimi.

'Enough what?'

'Suspects. When you've interviewed them all, and taken detailed notes, compare the stories and you'll see who's lying.'

'Suppose they don't want to be interviewed.'

'But that's where you're so lucky. Being a celebrity. It'll keep everybody off their guard. Plus, you can play on their sympathy, because you'll be searching for the man who killed your wife. You don't need to tell people that the police are stupid enough to suspect you.'

I didn't want to talk to all the suspects, or even any of them. I just wanted to guess who killed my wife, and go to sleep.

'Maybe,' said Louisa, 'that's what links Ingman and Jane. Not that they were married – but that you had a motive for killing them both.'

'You mean someone wants me framed?'

'It's a theory.'

'Then it's a stupid theory,' said Mimi. 'Because as my diagram shows, Mikki couldn't possibly have anything to do with Jane's death, and he doesn't have the personality to even dream of doing it. And, he doesn't have any enemies either.'

Not exactly true, but we could let it pass.

'You should go back to the police,' said Louisa. 'Otherwise,

165

what'll you do if they turn up while you're broadcasting on Monday?'

'You mustn't let the station know anything,' gasped Mimi, horrified. 'They hate scandal.'

'Even Dan Nally reads papers,' I pointed out.

'Yes, but you've got to solve it before Monday. You've got to prove that one of these tramps did it. Or something.' She was ashen, as though the thought I might lose my job had only just hit her.

'Listen, if I get sentenced to life in maximum security, followed by deporting my corpse, Dial-the-Psychic is a minor problem. It won't affect you. None of this connects with you and your job.'

'God! As if I'd think of that!'

'All Louisa is saying, the station will probably want me to keep a low profile till the killer's caught. None of that "show must go on" noble sentiment. Do they want listeners ringing up to say, "If he's so psychic why doesn't he learn the killer's identity in a mysterious dream?"'

'Perhaps you will.'

'And perhaps I'm on the first cheap flight to JFK either way. Because I bet I don't qualify for work-permit status now I'm single again.'

'I thought of that,' said Mimi. 'In fact, it was the first thing that occurred to me when you said Jane was dead. Am I awful? I was just so shocked. I thought, "Now Mikki's going to have to marry another Englishwoman".'

Louisa snorted. 'Don't be ridiculous.'

'It's been very difficult for him, these past few months,' Mimi said, controlling her anger. She was staring right at the other woman. 'What do you know about anything? He would never have had anything to do with Jane Lyons if he hadn't been desperate to stay with PrimeTime and keep from disappointing his fans. People love him. Lots of people really love him. I bet he's the most popular psychic on any radio show anywhere in the world.'

Her loyalty was very touching. I was a schmuck not to love her for ever for it. But then, being a schmuck was nothing so new.

Louisa had to back off. She managed not to do it too gracefully.

'I'm sure he's wonderful. But you know, in a world like yours, people can get permits. The employers apply for them. You'd only have to speak to the station manager. Where are they going to get another psychic from? The dole queue?'

166

Mimi goggled at me. 'You had to marry that Jane woman,' she insisted.

'I had to marry Jane,' I agreed. But maybe I was goggling too.

'It had nothing to do with her money or anything.'

'Definitely not.'

'And you weren't really attracted to her sexually.'

'As if.'

'It was the only way of keeping you in Britain,' she insisted.

'Exactly right.'

Louisa asked, 'You truly believed that? You never mentioned it to your boss, your producer, you never rang the immigrations people? You didn't see a lawyer? You just married this poor middle-aged woman who happened to be dripping with cash?'

'Yes!' Louisa was very honest, and the thing about honest people is they never know when to shut up.

Mimi stood up. 'Didn't you ask anyone's advice?'

'It was private, personal. You were just about the only one I told.'

'I thought you must have checked,' she said. She turned and walked to her bedroom door. Over her shoulder, she said sadly, 'I should have sorted it out for you. Like I sort out everything else of yours. Goodnight.'

Louisa started to say, 'Ah?' I think she was still under the impression she and Dani were getting the bed.

I cut her off. 'Something you've forgotten? Something else she might need to know? You've told her I was sleeping with Kerry, you've told her I didn't have to dump her and marry Jane – you've remembered now, you saw me coming out of the prof's office with my clothes on fire?'

'You dumped her?'

'Yes. So?'

'You were in a relationship?'

'I lived here.' I wanted to scream at her, but I kept it down to a strangled whisper. 'Have you really just worked that out? You're a worse fucking psychic than I am. Sorry,' I added, meaning my language, and looking at Dani.

'He's long gone,' Louisa replied. And the little fellow was all curled up in the light of the TV, with his head on his hands and pizza on his chin. His mother brushed his hair off his face. It was a warm, moist night, and the boy wouldn't need a blanket. Maybe he shouldn't have been sleeping in his day clothes, but moving him now would

167

risk waking him. I figured Mimi wouldn't want another night of small children wailing through the early hours. And avoiding any more upsets for Mimi was a big thing with me at that moment.

There was one small sofa and one carpet. I knew which I was getting. There was no hurry. I turned Mimi's press release over in my hands, and wrote a number beside each name – the order of interview, if anyone felt they'd like to answer my questions.

'You know who I think I still want to talk to? Madox Bligh. The ESP guru. There's something so weird about all that. They suddenly start buzzing me on the show, they want me to heal their great leader or some other voodoo, and your boss starts telling you about their boss. He's going on the list.'

'Good,' said Louisa.

She turned off the television and the light, and the room seemed to lurch into space. It was just my exhaustion, but we were drifting. I had no sensation that the sidewalk would be three storeys down, or that there were two floors above us occupied. The cramped little flat was suddenly flung out into a void. Maybe it was the cars rolling past, with their yellow lamps sweeping up the wall and over the ceiling as they rounded the corner.

Something screamed into Dalton Junction and thundered through, shaking the windows like a cat with a bird. When the noise cleared, I'd lost the sensation of being abandoned in space.

I sat at the table, listening to Dani and Louisa breathing, and wondering whether to try climbing into Mimi's bed. Was it better to beg her forgiveness, and present myself as the errant lover returned, or was it better to be honest and celibate and plead for a comfortable night's sleep?

In the end I stayed at the table. I slumped down with my face in the crook of my elbow.

I must have been asleep, and I must have been dreaming, because the reality of the voice woke me with a kick.

I was doing my show, and there were cans on my head, and the voice inside was a caller from the ESP people, the Madox Bligh weirdos, the Evangelists of Superhuman Perfection.

And what he said was exactly what one of them had said to me on my last programme.

'Our enemies will be consumed by the avenging flames.'

CHAPTER THIRTY-ONE

Marsh's office was above a video store on Kensington Park Road, about ten minutes walk from what was no longer my home. The shop was one of those blue-and-yellow family affairs, with the summer blockbusters posted over every foot of plate glass. Inside, last summer's blockbusters would be on sale for £5.99 and you'd have more chance of dating Sharon Stone than of getting a genuine dirty movie slipped to you under the counter.

If you wanted genuine dirty movies, upstairs would be the place. Marsh probably had shelves stacked high. Strictly records of investigations, naturally.

Louisa and I went through the flaking blue door marked Malcolm Marsh: 24-Hour Surveillance, and up the stairs with flaking walls, and pressed a buzzer in a door that had two of its panels patched with cardboard, like from time to time Mr M. Marsh's twenty-four-hour visitors were so anxious for some surveillance, they couldn't be bothered to use the handle.

I hung back from hammering on the door. He might open it.

'It's just possible,' I said, 'that I'm about to give a human arsonist the ideal opportunity of burning me up.'

Louisa said reassuringly: 'He can't attack both of us with flame guns.'

'I'll feel so glad about that, when the cleaners are sweeping me into a cigar-box.'

'If you weren't so paranoid about the police, you could just report your suspicions to them.'

'They aren't cops, they're Her Majesty's Loyal Anti-Yank Squad with a license to break my fingers off one by one. I show up at Notting Hill, first they'll cripple me for life. Then they'll ask about my suspicions.'

We were standing four steps down from the door, and talking in whispers. I hadn't imagined detective work would be like this. Louisa should have been clinging to my gun arm, clutching the bosom of her blue-silk evening dress. There should have been a half-pint of hooch in my jacket and a bullet-hole in my fedora – also, there should have been a gun for my gun arm. But I didn't have a weapon, or a hat, and drinking spirits always made me throw up. And Louisa was still wearing Friday night's jumper, a bag of knitting so shapeless that I still hadn't decided how much of a bosom was in there for clutching.

Mimi could have played the part. She would have worn a forties jacket with suggestive lapels, and a skirt that was tight but not long enough to make walking difficult. She'd have tied some imitation pearls round her neck, that would have turned out to be real pearls. Probably those pearls were the reason for all the killings. The Case Of The Radio Pearls. And at some point I'd have been obliged to light two cigarettes and hand Mimi one.

Lack of nicotine. It was making my mind wander. Mimi hadn't come with us, and I was sorry because she wouldn't have asked dumb-ass questions like, 'Why not go to the police?'

Mimi had woken up when Louisa and Dani were fixing breakfast and I was trying to straighten my back out at the kitchen table. She hadn't acted sore, but she was. I knew the gestation rate for Mimi's forgiveness. She always wiped my score clean, but I had to suffer unspoken disapproval and hurt first.

Minor offences, like forgetting to meet her when we were supposed to be seeing a movie or meeting friends: one day.

Serious offences, like using her credit card and signing her name (and this only happened once, and it was pretty much an accident): four days.

Unforgivable offences, like ditching her to marry a wealthy pensioner: three weeks.

Worse-than-that offences, like turning up at her home with another woman and her child, letting slip that I was screwing my presenter, then admitting I didn't just get married for the sake of my radio listeners – well, I was mortified myself. No knowing what view Mimi took of it.

She managed to be civil as she poured me coffee. She didn't even sound like she was gritting her words out through broken glass. But she declined to join our investigations. She had things to do. Nothing important, just family stuff.

She could look after Dani, if we liked.

Louisa accepted gratefully. There was nothing the kid's education could gain from schlepping round London on a sweaty Sunday, watching his mother and an interesting American talk tough to a bunch of suspected serial killers. Plus, Mimi seemed to be taking more interest now in the boy, who had a cute six-year-old way of talking even if his profile wasn't going to win any Delightful Juniors competition. He had ears like mug handles and hair you could scrub pots with, but he grinned a lot when Mimi told him funny stories. Women always like a guy with a sense of humour. He'll go far.

Where he got to go to this Sunday was the zoo. Mimi promised to take him for a gawk at the lions in Regent's Park after she'd run her errands. I gave them £30, because Jane's cash cards were burning a hole in my jeans, if that isn't an unfortunate metaphor under the circumstances. Louisa kissed him and promised to see him again at tea-time.

She didn't know how she'd be keeping her promise.

So we were on the stairs, over a video store, hissing at each other as we cooked up the courage to confront our Number One suspect.

I took three quick steps.

I slapped hard on the door.

He didn't answer.

Feeling braver, I kept knocking, and in the end I turned and started leading Louisa down the stairs. I said, 'He's out surveilling. We'll look up Laurel and Hardy, and if they're out too we'll ring the Marx Brothers. Mr Marsh will be around later.'

That's when he opened the door.

There's a psychological disadvantage, being six steps down from the guy you're wanting to surprise. Plus, if you've been outside his door for five minutes and he's a surveillance specialist, that element of surprise may have been lost.

Marsh wasn't looking like any sudden noises could bring on a heart attack. He said, 'Come to give yourself up? What's the matter, couldn't you find a nick?'

The with-respect-M'Lud manner was missing. I wasn't a client.

I started up towards him.

'Stay where you are!'

It was a commanding voice now, full of the arrogant tension you get from cops the world over when they're reining themselves back from blowing your head off.

I stayed.

'Hands out to the sides.'

'I don't have a gun.'

'Or a box of matches?'

171

'Now that's funny. Almost a coincidence. Because what I wanted to ask you . . .'

'Shut up. Come up the stairs, both of you, and keep your hands where I can see them.'

I edged past him. 'So which one are you?' I asked. 'Cagney or Lacey?'

The room was seedy. If you stayed standing in any one place too long, the carpet bugs would start to make nests in your socks. The window had a thick yellow grime smearing it. It could have been the residue of a cremation, though the stench of roasted shit was missing. The stench of Marsh's sweat made up for it.

'Why are you here?'

'The pleasure of your company,' I replied. I sat down, uninvited, on a worn typist's chair. It didn't even swivel.

'You've been photographed entering the building, and there's a tape running.'

'I wouldn't expect anything else of you. Will you dub the grunts and groans on later?'

'What I'm saying is, try anything now and you'll have a hard time proving your alibi.'

'I have an alibi,' I said. 'It's a pretty good one. At the time you were murdering my wife, I was helping the police with their investigation.'

'So you're telling everyone it was me, eh? Are you going on your big radio programme to make the announcement? Don't forget about our quaint English libel laws before you do. Or were you dropping round to extract a confession first?'

I didn't know what I was supposed to be extracting. When Sinatra was acting Tony Rome, his movie detective, extraction presented no problem. Frank would turn up, there'd be a soupçon of rough-house, and when the bad guy's face had been ground in the furnishings a little the confession came out. It wasn't hard, and I guess I'd been imagining something like this would occur. Only I was a poor choice for rough-house. Maybe I was hoping Louisa could handle that.

She was standing up. But I noticed she didn't grind his face any.

'Somebody killed my employer,' she said, 'and the police think it's Mikki.'

'So do I,' said Marsh, and he leaned back against his desk. He was wearing a loose, light brown jacket that must have been frightened by a dry-cleaner when it was little and been tortured by a phobia ever since. The phobia was contagious – his tie had it too. It was

172

head-achingly hot in the office, with the sun glaring on the street-side windows, and the clammy moons of sweat under Marsh's arms had spread almost to the buttons. His head was bare, and the sun was shining on it. There were pinpoint beads of sweat on the follicles of his thin hair.

'You told the police I'm the killer,' I accused him.

'What if I did?'

'You know I'm not.'

'Then you can explain that to them.'

'You told Tripp and Bowen you followed me to Ingman's apartment.'

'That's what they say, is it?'

'You never followed me anywhere.'

'No?'

'Not that night.'

He shrugged, like an adult brushing aside a child. 'You've got all the facts.'

The contempt in his manner was riling me. It was meant to, of course. He'd spent long hours practising in front of the mirror.

I hung on to my image of him fawning over Jane in the pasta parlour. If she'd snapped her fingers, he would have taken her order. Marsh wasn't going to get me off-balance. He was nobody. Except, he was probably the guy who torched my wife.

'Let me check my facts,' I said. I stretched my legs out and tried to look like I was at ease in the swivel seat that didn't swivel. No one could have been, which was why Marsh was standing.

'Go ahead. I don't have to call the cops till you've said your piece.'

'One,' I said, 'you must have known I was in Ingman's office, and you must have known there was something there to interest the police. Because I don't usually get arrested at three a.m. for being in the wrong apartment.'

'Assuming it was me that called them,' he said.

'Two, you were questioned, but Jane wasn't killed until after you were released.'

'Nobody released me. I was offering information, not under arrest.'

'Three, the police say you were the last lucky man to screw my wife.'

'I was doing you a favour,' said Marsh. He was looking at Louisa. 'Your new boyfriend wasn't giving enough satisfaction. Take this as a warning. I reckon he's a nancy-boy. Looks a bit of a nancy, yeah?'

173

Louisa stared flatly at him. The insult was aimed at her as well as me, and it was much too limp to sting.

One thing that never bothered me is sexual taunts. Plenty of women will be happy to tell you whether I'm up to the mark.

'Is it always something you include in the twenty-four-hour service?' I asked. 'Personal attention?'

'Your late wife got a bit turned on by that tape in the restaurant.'

'I noticed.'

'I took her home and she got very insistent.'

He still seemed to think this was getting under my skin. 'She wasn't fussy,' I said.

'Neither am I.'

'So you went back for more and that's your alibi for Ingman's murder, right? You were providing professional satisfaction to my wife.'

'That can be my statement. If it suits. It can't be an alibi without corroboration.' He was unwinding. I obviously hadn't come here to try to set fire to him. And he seemed totally confident I wasn't going to shake his story.

'Anyone see what time you arrived at the flat, my place? Conan Doyle House?'

'How should I know?'

'You didn't make certain you were seen? Careless.'

'At that point I didn't know murder was about to be committed. All I knew was I'd seen you leave with a face that didn't look like it was coming back.'

'And you went straight in.'

'Put it like that if you want.'

'You didn't follow me to Baker Street after all?'

'Listen, arsehole, I followed you if I want to say I followed you. I fucked your wife – excuse me, miss, but you're keeping bad company – I fucked your wife if I want to say that's what I did. If I want to say I saw you carry a body into Ingman's office, that's what I'll say. Frankly, I'm beginning to think you didn't kill the Kraut because I don't think you've got the guts. But if you want me to tell the police that, you can fuck off.'

Moral victory: he got riled first.

Like I should care. Marsh was nobody.

Maybe he wasn't even the guy who killed my wife.

CHAPTER THIRTY-TWO

An hour later we were sitting in the back row of a big hall with hard red seats and long red curtains. I couldn't remember when I'd been anywhere like this, but it seemed totally familiar. I was starting to convince myself I was undergoing some kind of past-life *déjà vu* phenomenon and revisiting a scene from another incarnation, which incidentally is a very popular explanation with my listeners for just about everything from recurring dreams to repeats on TV. Then I got what it was I was trying to remember. Prayers in the Big Hall in first grade. America the Beautiful. Mrs Codd the head teacher saluting the flag. Mrs Wilson playing 'This Train Is Bound For Glory' on the guitar.

Somehow I figured Glory was the destination for today's train too. This station, the Evangelists of Superhuman Perfection. Engine driver, ticket collector, guard and guru, Madox Bligh. All major credit cards accepted.

There were about eight rows between us and a semi-circle stage with a lectern, a mike and a bunch of weak footlights. There was no one in front of us till the first two rows, and the people settled in front of the stage were all bums. Or they looked like bums. Maybe they were a squadron of highly trained blowtorch killers.

This was the Madox Bligh Institute, 444 Southampton Row.

I'd walked out of Marsh's office feeling deflated. I was supposed to be solving a murder. I'd spent two hours searching out Marsh, I'd learned nothing, I'd been rubbed up the wrong way till my hair stood on end, and if I had to go back and do it again, I wouldn't have any idea how to do it better. So this was being a detective? No — Sam Spade, Phil Marlowe, Tony Rome, they were detectives. That was movies. This was life. Personally, I prefer movies.

We ate at Pizza Express because, what the hell, Sunday lunch was an important institution, and also I was hungry and there were seats, and also I'd just drawn another £250 on Jane's card. Louisa said, 'He didn't tell us much,' and there wasn't any good answer to that.

175

'Think he did it?' I said.

'No. He could have done. I don't know.'

'It wasn't that everything he said was a lie,' I told her. 'There's signals to look for – hands, that's the giveaway. People rub their noses with crooked fingers. They speak through their knuckles. They put their palms on their lips when they're listening. They don't look at you, or they don't stop looking at you.'

'You're a body-language linguist as well, are you?'

'Listen, you get cocky because you think your pack of kiddies' cards proved I'm a fake. But I'm not a fake. I'm just a fake psychic. What I don't fake is being a cold reader. This I'm good at. I'm not in the top rank, but I get a with-merit pass. I learn, and I think, and I make an OK living. Plenty of my listeners think I'm living proof that *The X Files* is all certified fact.'

'Mikki, for once I don't think you're bullshitting me. Are you feeling ill?'

'I don't want to bullshit you. I never bullshit my friends.'

'Bullshit.'

'OK, so maybe, but I don't bullshit you. And I don't want you to think there's no science behind anything I do. Just because you're a kosher scientist – there's other kinds too.'

'I know that.'

'I'll tell you, one kind of person I hate – I get them on my show once a month, once every six weeks. They call themselves skeptics. Spelled with a "K". They've got closed minds and are they ever proud about it. They know what I'm doing is fake, not because they got big evidence but because everything that's not science-proven already has to be fake. There's no new earth-shattering theories to be discovered. No human powers Darwin didn't know about. And they make you wild because they never give you a real argument. They just sneer. They don't have any facts to back up what they're saying, because they don't need any, it's enough that they say it's so. They act like, "Oh, I'm so brainy because I went to college and I've got these letters after my name, and that proves I know everything." I hate those schmucks.'

'I'm not one of the schmucks.'

'Sorry. I'm not calling you names. I'm not even particularly mad about skeptics. That's the way they want to live, closed minds, so who cares? Marsh is like them, that's all. So full of himself and, basically, so stupid. Real dumb ass. Either he knows he killed Jane, or he thinks he knows I did it. Whatever, he doesn't have to waste his time with details like evidence.'

'Do you usually get steamed up like this, or are you feeling the strain?'

' "No, I don't get *steamed up*. What is that – like a window?" '

'Like a train, I suppose. Full of energy and ready to burst.'

'Well, for your information, I am not steamed up now because I am never steamed up. I keep my cool at all times, and I've had worse days than this, OK? This is a walk in the park. This is a picnic. This is bonzer-no-worries and I am not steamed up. Only I feel the need to do the talking because it hasn't escaped my notice that you don't ever tell me anything unless I drag it out of you with fishing hooks.'

'Let me get a word in edgeways.'

'Fine. Go ahead. Talk. Tell me something. Fill in some blanks. I leave you to choose the topic. Maybe you'd like to explain exactly why it is that you're a scientist but you're not a schmuck skeptic? So feel free, start gabbing.'

'Mikki . . .'

'Great, we've known each other less than two days and already you know my name.'

'Shut the fuck up.'

She was right. I was blasting off steam like a pressure cooker.

'You know what?' she said. 'You ought to start smoking. Not only might it calm you down, but every two or three times a minute you'd have to stick something in your mouth, which would give the rest of the world a rest.'

'Thank you. I'm in the throes of nicotine addiction withdrawal . . .'

'I told you, shut up.'

'. . . and you want to taunt me with cigarettes already. Let's go find an AA meeting and pour them all a drink, that'd make you laugh, right?'

'I'm not rising to your bait. I'm going to do what I tried to do five minutes ago and answer your point about sceptical scientists.'

She pushed her plate away.

'What I do, my area of research, is very much despised among the academic community. I won't bore you with all the prejudice stories. But I think it's significant that everyone in my department is, or was, an outsider. I'm Jewish, Ingman and Carla aren't English. So we had a thicker skin and, believe me, we needed it.'

'Ingman was thick-skinned?'

'More than you'd think. He hated all the jokes, worse than I did, mind. A lot of jokes – you'd think certain professors had nothing to

177

do but think up sarcastic humour. "How many parapsychologists does it take to change a lightbulb?"'

'So tell me.'

'"None, because they live in the Dark Ages."'

'Is that a play on words – "Dark" Ages?'

'I'm sorry, you're American, I shouldn't tell you jokes. It's not fair. And then some of my colleagues hate paranormal investigative science much too much to make jokes about it. It scares them.'

'They think you're going to discover an ancient spell to turn them into frogs?'

'No one would notice the difference. No, they're scared because one day we'll prove something. And half the history of science will have to be crossed out. All these small-minded berks who can't bear to think that anything in the universe could exist which their pea-sized brains couldn't understand – they're all desperately trying to knit the universe into a simple pattern. Parapsychology has got hold of one of the threads and it's unravelling the pattern like crazy.'

'That's why you study it? You want to unravel everything?'

'I study it because . . . because . . . because I know it's real.'

'You know it or you just want to believe it?'

'I know it. All my life I've kind of felt things, telepathic impressions or second sight or whatever. Mostly it feels natural and it's very petty – you know, guessing what someone's about to say or who's on the phone when it rings.'

'That happens to everyone. Sometimes they guess wrong but those are the times they never remember.'

'Not true. I think it's harder to remember the times when you're right, because usually you're in that frame of mind, slightly tranced out, a bit spacey, almost dreamlike. And you tend to forget your dreams. It's the hard-fact reality state of mind where you remember. And that's not so conducive to telepathy.'

'OK, that's a bit convenient – "it happens all the time but we forget".'

'Not convenient really. Convenient would be if it happened in some recordable, measurable way. Also, telepathy is not socially acceptable. People feel threatened; at the very least they feel irritated. Many, many times as a girl, I was told off for finishing people's sentences for them. If they spoke slowly, or they were distracted for an instant, I'd leap in and complete what they were saying. It drove older people up the wall. My grandmother used to shout at me, "Do not butt in, Louisa," and I wasn't butting in,

178

I was just sharing her side of the conversation. But I learned not to do it.'

'Mimi does that,' I said. 'Finishes what you're saying.'

'With her, I can imagine it's irritating. Does she have a mobile phone? I want to know what Dani's doing.'

'She had a phone, we left it in a taxi. Dani's fine. She'll love him to pieces.'

'Dani's the reason I know telepathy is real.'

'What happened?'

'No one thing. Just everything, from about the time I was three months' pregnant. I knew he was a boy. I knew what kind of person he was, that he was sensitive, lots of physical energy, not very talkative, given to brooding and sulking.'

'You knew this before he was born?'

'Definitely.'

'But you were kind of guided by the characters of other men in your family?'

'There were no other men. Only my dad, and I was devoted to him, but he and Dani are chalk and cheese. You can see Dad in Dani's face, if you know where to look, but character-wise, you'd never guess they were related. His personality is all from his father's side, I should think, but I hardly know Dani's father now and I certainly didn't know him more than very superficially back then.'

'So how can an unborn child be telepathic?'

'You tell me.'

'It's got no language, the only concept it's got of anything is just instinct. Instinct that tells it there's an outside world maybe. But basically, to a foetus, its mother isn't a mother like we'd understand it – it's a whole life-support system. An entire planet.'

'That's nice, I like that image.'

'But we don't have telepathic connections with our planet.'

'Don't we? What about people whose moods change with the earth's magnetic currents or the moon's course? What about dowsers? Aren't they in mental communication with the earth?'

'Can I use all this stuff in my next show?'

'I'll ring up,' she promised, 'and we'll discuss all of it. I'll be the Featured Scientist.'

'That'll add class.' And in case she was starting to think that I liked her, I had to add, 'It's so good that it's radio, you've got a great face for radio.'

'I was going to tell you about the Thinking Game. I won't now.'

179

'Go on, what's the Thinking Game?'

'It only works when Dani's in the right mood. In fact, both of us have got to be, and if I want it to work too much, of course it won't. Wanting gets in the way. The first time, I tried it on a whim. He was about three, nearly four, and I think I'd just given him his bath. We were just sitting on the sofa, he had a towel round him and we were being very quiet. Sitting there, sharing a nice sensation of togetherness. And I thought, We're so in tune. I bet he could see whatever I'm thinking. I said, "Shut your eyes," and I thought very hard of an elephant, and I said, "What animal is in your head?" He said, "Effalunt!" That's how he said it. And I gave him masses of praise, obviously, and he loved that, so he was keen to do it again. Next time was a polar bear, he got that. Next time was a giraffe, he got that. Then we couldn't do any more. He tires of any game quickly, and with real telepathy like that, fatigue seems to set in very quickly. In anyone's case, even top subjects. No one can keep it up for long. But what are the mathematical chances of him seeing three animals in his head, that I'd picked completely at random? No visual cues, nothing we'd been talking about earlier. Just animals I plucked from the ether.'

'Why animals? Why not colours or numbers?'

'I wanted something very concrete. Something a three-year-old could grasp. He couldn't count at that age, remember. I don't know, animals was just instinctual.'

'Ever tried it again?'

'Dozens of times. Sometimes it doesn't work. Sometimes it blows my mind. Dani takes it totally in his stride, obviously.'

'What did Ingman think of it?'

'Impressed. He wanted us to demonstrate it, but you just can't. For the same reason, you could never try it on TV, even if someone bet you a million pounds – especially if you were doing it for money. Anything that creates any level of anxiety, the connection fizzles out. Also, I definitely didn't want to turn my son into a freak show for Ingman's benefit. He could be very weird. You know what he did when I first told him about the Thinking Game? Dug out some Soviet research, about rabbits. The KGB did a lot of parapsychology in the sixties, and there was a very low level of ethics involved. One of the tests, they took a litter of baby rabbits and handed them to a nuclear submarine crew. And the submarine sailed halfway round the world with these baby rabbits on board. They kept the mother in a lab in Moscow with electrodes stuck in her brain. And when

180

the crew were 4,000 miles away, they killed the babies. One a day, at different times, for a week. Every time one of her babies died, the mother registered sudden high levels of anxiety and stress. The litter was thousands of miles away, underwater, inside a massive steel tube, and she was only a rabbit, when all's said and done. But right across that distance, she heard them die.'

'I don't believe that.'

'Ostrander and Schroeder,' she said, quoting the report's authors at me. 'I can show you the book at home.'

'And that was Ingman's response when you told him about Dani? The guy was too weird to live.'

CHAPTER THIRTY-THREE

So we were in the Madox Bligh Institute, and I was thinking about school assemblies. I got off the point back there for a minute. I'm with you again now. Entrance had been free – two geeks on the door handed us a leaflet, like the one from Ingman's room, but they didn't attempt to take money off us. 'We pay to get out,' I told Louisa.

She was wishing she could check up on her son. 'I feel a bad mother, leaving him with a woman he's never met. She's not even someone I know.'

'I know her. Dani'll love her, and she'll love Dani. I told you, I'm vouching for her.'

'Yes, and I've known you for all of thirty-six hours.'

We tried ringing Mimi's flat from a payphone in a corner of the hall, but no one answered. So we sat down again at the back, and watched the bums who'd come in to find some shade out of the scorching sunshine. There were four or five of them, and I'd assumed they were regulars until a couple of Evangelists in suits and spray-on smiles walked out of the wings and shooed the bums out. They went without protest.

'Not very Christian,' I called out to one of the smiles.

'They're always in here. They're welcome at any time, unless Lord Bligh is addressing an audience.'

'So they're too dirty to be preached at? You need class to get the firm's message?'

'They say things,' said the smile, edging up the row of chairs towards us. 'Hi, I'm Lucas.'

'Hi, Lucas. If I say things, will that upset your boss?'

'I mean they heckle.'

'Jesus got heckled too.' It was the school hall feeling, it was making me religious. And sarcastic.

'We find it distracts. And this isn't a Christian mission, as you'll soon discover.'

'So your Lord Bligh, is he a real lord?'

'Much more real than any member of the self-styled aristocracy.'

'So that's a "no"?'

'I didn't catch your name.'

'That's because I didn't say it.'

'I hope we'll be able to talk further after the address,' he said sweetly. The smile had been glued on his face with industrial strength polymer. If I could have thought of anything to wipe it off, it would have been my pleasure, but he suddenly edged away. A red light had flicked on above the stage, like an On-Air signal outside a studio. A crowd of suits and sensible skirts, all with the superglue smile, came trotting out and spilling off the stage into the seats.

When they were all in place, there were still four blank rows between us and them. I felt like the naughty boy of the class with his girlfriend, who always got the back seat of the bus on outings. We couldn't move forwards now. That would be like admitting we were eager for the good Lord's message.

There were eight paid-up Evangelists and two of us. Badly outnumbered. Maybe it was a good thing I wasn't such a fists-first detective.

The doors onto the bright street were wide open, but no one else stepped into the gloom. So much for advertising by leaflets. This was why they'd been desperate for exposure on my show.

I was expecting maybe a fanfare, or a guy on stage giving us the Madox Bligh build-up: 'Ladies and gentlemen, for your enthrillment and delectation . . .'

Or maybe the front-row Evangelists would start stamping their feet and chanting his name, like the *Jerry Springer Show*. This guy had an ego to maintain.

So what I wasn't expecting was a guy in a wheelchair, leaning heavily on his left arm, with his face set rigid. The girl who was pushing him wore the regulation smile, but it was a reverential one. She positioned the chief in a beam of light, shuffled him back and forward to get him dead centre, and bowed out.

The only things moving under that light was Madox Bligh's left eye. Two bulging, watery globes, like searchlamps shining through ice, were directed on the audience. The left eye roamed. The right eye stared fixedly across the rows of seating.

Madox Bligh wore his white hair in waved locks to his shoulders, a monocle above the last button of his diamond-blue waistcoat and a mirror shine on his black boots. His long and bony left hand played

183

restlessly with the arm of his chair. The right lay like a stick along his thigh.

His left foot flexed and twisted at the ankle. The other one remained carved from stone.

The right side of Madox Bligh was paralysed.

'I should be dead,' he began. 'By rights, by everything the doctors and the medicine men and the quacks thought they knew, Madox Bligh should be damn well dead.'

His words were slurred from a half-open mouth. The left-hand corner was twitching exaggeratedly, to compensate for the rigidity of the right. Inside his motionless jaw, his half-alive tongue flopped like a fish. The voice was carried by a wheeze of air from one overworked lung.

It should have been a pathetic voice, a repulsive voice.

Nothing like.

Madox Bligh had the most arresting voice I ever heard. He looked to be at least seventy, probably eighty-plus, and how he'd lived through the Age of Communication without becoming a massive media star was an instant mystery to me. I would have done a lot to possess his voice – deep and hoarse and every word crackling with the desire to be heard. I would have sat in a wheelchair. I would have lost the use of one arm and a leg.

Almost. Not quite. I'm not wishing for it.

Maybe his voice got to be that way when the paralysis hit him. Maybe it was some sort of divine compensation. I simply could not understand what condemned a man with that way of speaking to preach in a dark, faded hall to eight of the converted and two no-hopers.

'I should be dead,' he said. 'And I am not. If you look at me with feeble pity in your heart and think, "Perhaps the old man would be better off in his grave" – I can assure you he would not.'

He slapped his hand down against his wheelchair. 'The body crumbles, like a statue from ancient days, like a decaying cliff-face. Disintegration of the material is an inevitable condition. But the mind is not a material thing. The mind is energy. The mind is pure atomic force. Inside this skull – behind this single seeing eye –' he pointed to the glistening, swollen eyeball – 'my mind is a nuclear reactor. A cauldron of atomic fission. It is the ultimate force in the universe. My mind is unquenchable. It is *ALIVE*.'

The Evangelists were bowed forward on their seats, staring up

184

at Madox Bligh like dogs waiting to be fed. They were hungry for his voice.

Suddenly I was conscious of my own posture. I was leaning into him too. I made an effort to sit back and cross my legs away from him, insouciant and rebellious. It was a tough pose to hold.

'The human body is the vessel of the human soul – but it is less than that. It exists merely because the mind wills it. The fabulous energy of the mind creates the body and maintains it and ultimately, when new challenges are required of this sublime, divine *weapon* – it discards it.'

He wielded the word 'weapon' like an avenging angel swinging his sword.

Jesus. That guy's charisma, his sheer breath-sucking presence, hit me so hard it knocked half my teeth out. I'm burbling like a sap with a faceful of knuckles and jewellery. What do you want, I should pretend the way he talked didn't leave any impression? I'm telling you, he said 'weapon' and the word came slicing through the air at me.

'When a human child is conceived, the mind rushes into its ever-splitting and dividing cells, like air into a vacuum. It is the force of the mind which shapes the burgeoning mass. The force of the mind which creates something unique and extraordinary – your body. Think – five thousand million people live today, perhaps ten thousand million have died before them. Not one identical to any other. Not one. In some, perhaps, the same-cell twins, the physical differences will be subtle. Fingerprints. Moles. But their minds are furiously unique. And most human faces, physiques, forms, are so utterly unalike, that one single mugshot photograph would be enough to tell any individual from any other.'

He'd lost me. I still have no idea what he was talking about. It didn't matter. I was drinking the voice in.

'The mind does this. It creates physical uniqueness. The scientists tell you DNA is the building block. They are infantile – like the peasants of prehistory who thought the world was carried on the shoulders of a giant. They never thought to ask, Where did the giant stand? And a scientist never stops to enquire of himself, What is the building block of DNA? A scientist is a man who has trimmed the raging inferno of his mind to fit a cracked lantern.'

I kind of liked that. I nudged Louisa. She ignored me.

'The nascent mind creates the body, and it sustains it. For disembodied, the mind cannot exist – in this dimension. But do not suppose the body to be indispensable. For after all, where was the

185

mind before the body had existence? On an earlier plane. And so where will the mind be when the body is crumbled to dust? On a different plane again.'

Madox Bligh's left hand grasped his right wrist, lifted it and let it fall like an empty sleeve.

'The body dies slowly. The slowness of death is controlled by the quickness of the mind. And my mind is not ready to depart for the next plane. It desires to blaze on this plane a while longer – not for its own glory but to light the way and kindle other, weaker, flickering minds. This mind is a beacon. Fix your sights on it, follow it and inevitably, as you approach, the brightness will increase and enlightenment will dawn in your own mind. Allow no distraction. Banish weakness. See how the mind can defy death itself. Allow your own, extraordinary mind to *LIVE!*'

Madox Bligh sank down. His whole posture had been elevated as he spoke. He was almost levitating in his chair. Now he clammed up, and it was like watching a hovercraft when you shut off the engine. Everything deflated. Just the one, bulging eye kept roving, searching the hall.

His good arm beckoned one of the skirts from the front row. He whispered to her, but he was still on mike – 'Where's our new friend from PrimeTime? Not here?'

I half-stood up. How in hell did he know I was here? Was he psychic?

But then I heard him murmuring, 'Such enthusiasm at our meetings recently – I do trust she has not been dissuaded from our path. And indeed, what an attractive young woman.'

186

CHAPTER THIRTY-FOUR

Attractive young woman – no way was that me. So who was the
Evangelist of Superhuman Perfection at PrimeTime?

It didn't have to be anyone I knew, of course. It could be a
coincidence. But so far this weekend all the many and unpleasant
coincidences had spun around to point at me.

Was it Mimi? Was that possible? In my wildest nightmares? Was
she the reason I'd been getting these weirdos on the phonelines,
morning after morning?

The one moving eye was glistening in my direction. This was my
opportunity. If I could find the right question, because 'Who do you
know at PrimeTime then?' wasn't going to cut it.

But the eye wasn't on me. The miked-up voice whispered, 'And
who is the redheaded young lady at the back?'

'My name is Louisa Simons, and I worked with Johannes-Kristian
Ingman.'

'Worked? Past tense, I note. Did the strain become too much?'

'He's dead.'

The left eye narrowed. The right gazed past us into the darkness.

'Why do you and your companion sit at the back?'

'Nearer the door,' I answered. 'Do you know how Ingman died?'

'Since the news was evidently unknown to me, and since in fact I
take pains to avoid all news broadcasting . . .'

'Consumed by flame,' I said.

The left fist clenched.

'I should appreciate an interview with you two young people. In
my chambers. At four o'clock.'

The skirt propelled him offstage. He didn't have to turn his back
on us like that. I wasn't going to argue with him.

'What do you think?' whispered Louisa.

'Hell of a personality.'

'Textbook,' she murmured.

The suit called Lucas came grinning over. It was hard to see his face, but his uptight swagger told me it wasn't a happy grin.

'I never got round to asking your name.'

'You asked. I didn't tell.'

'And are you going to tell me now?'

'What do you think, Lucas?'

'I don't understand. Why is it a secret?'

It was a secret because I didn't want anyone knowing who I was. They might have phoned me on the show already. I wasn't here to do an impromptu faith-healing, and I didn't want to be anybody's guru. No surprise Madox Bligh was having a tough time enlisting a successor, if this was the Sunday congregation.

This I didn't say. What I said was, 'Take me to your leader.'

'You can't be allowed to speak with Lord Bligh unless I know your name.'

'Fine. We're going. But you should hand round cups of coffee, maybe homemade muffins or something. It'd make all the difference to your box office. A busy day, you could get five, maybe six people in here.'

I'd stood up and was working my way to the end of the row, waiting for him to stop me. He did.

'Lord Bligh would be disappointed if you refused his audience.'

'That's sad. And he doesn't even know my name.'

'Don't bet on it. He has awesome mindpower. He is telepathic.'

'So I don't need to meet him. I'm walking down to the Tube, he can read my mind from there.'

'Please. Follow me.'

I turned to Louisa. 'Since he said please,' I told her, 'we should do what he's asking. So many brainwashed people these days have bad manners.'

'He seems very well brought up,' she agreed. We marched single-file up two flights of wooden stairs.

'Do you come from a nice family, Lucas?'

'This is . . .'

'Don't tell me all these friendly smiling people are your family?'

'This is the residential area. Lord Bligh's door is beyond that curtain. When he is ready to speak, his assistant will summon you. Please sit down and I shall bring a drink.'

'I told you, so nicely brainwashed.' I watched Lucas go. He walked stiffly, like a guy who wanted to have some dignity and didn't know how. 'I don't get this Lord Bligh. He was hypnotic just now. I'm

188

in awe. I don't know what the fuck he was saying, but that voice impressed me.'

I stopped. It wasn't adding up. 'Who is he preaching for? The smiley brigade? He acted surprised to see even us. Two extra faces – apparently that makes it a good day. What a waste of talent – it's like Art Bell decides to lock himself in his bedroom and only broadcast to the cat. Plus, how old is he? At least a hundred and ten, and he doesn't look good for making a hundred and eleven. So why make all this effort?'

'You can ask him in a moment.'

'You said he was "textbook" a minute ago – what does that mean?'

Louisa put her elbows on her knees. We were sitting in a leather sofa, with an abstract in oils behind us, the whole width of the wall. It looked like a Jackson Pollock, but I didn't like to think it was a real one. Just an imitation. A good, convincing imitation. Unless it was real. In which case it was worth more money than I could comfortably think about.

Hot sunshine was pouring through the high arched windows on one side, and the wall ahead of us was curtained in the same heavy red they used on stage. No one was walking around. The corridor led off someplace – I didn't want to investigate. A person could get lost.

The public area of 444 Southampton Row was a very small percentage of the building. It felt like a rabbit warren after an attack of myxomatosis – badly under-populated and not a healthy place to be.

'The Forgotten Emperor,' said Louisa. 'Textbook psychology.'

'I must have skipped that page – remind me.'

'He's like a very powerful ruler whose subjects have all defected. Until he's left with a hard core, and he's exhausted from fighting all his old allies.'

'How do you work that out?'

'This is the Madox Bligh Institute and clearly he didn't set it up for half a dozen dopey teenagers. I should think at one time he had a real community going here – lectures and courses and scores of people living and eating and working here. There were dozens of set-ups like that in London in the sixties. You'd be amazed how many are still around. And some of them have got a lot of money. I know of one that hires the Albert Hall every year for a mass meditation.'

'So what happened?'

'Classically, the Emperor – the charismatic at the centre of the

189

movement, the guru – gets old but doesn't die. He won't relinquish power, so his natural successors lead breakaway factions instead. That means divisiveness and infighting and loss of focus on the outward objects, like raising funds and winning fresh recruits. Everything collapses in recrimination. Most people around him quit, but the Emperor refuses to give up. It's a point of pride, central to his whole self-image. He has to hang on to prove that his enemies, the protégées who turned against him, didn't destroy him. He has to show them he's the ultimate survivor.'

'Like Howard Hughes.'

'Or Margaret Thatcher, up to a point. Too weak to carry on, too stubborn to quit.'

'You made a study of this?'

'Ingman lectured me on it. Another of his hobby horses.'

There was one of those silences, when you don't want to pursue the subject because it's getting forced, but nothing else pops into your head.

I asked – though I really didn't care about the answer – 'How do you think we should address him? As a lord?'

'According to my theory,' she said, 'as Your Imperial Highness.'

Silence again.

The curtain flapped back. A suit said, 'Lord Bligh will see you now.' We went in.

The room was square, with one wall loaded with books and another looking out towards the British Museum. The velvet in here was green, billiards-table green, and it hung down the long, torpedo-shaped windows and was stitched onto the cushions of a dozen high-backed chairs that looked like they might have been genuine Charles Rennie Mackintosh, all round the walls. There was a desk, with a brass-hooded reading lamp, and a library ladder on wheels with a book-rest at the top.

Madox Bligh was not there.

I looked around and a side door was opening. The same girl as before was backing into the room, dragging his wheelchair. The Forgotten Emperor was staring upwards with a mild smile on half his face. He was refusing to register our presence until he had been imperially installed at his desk.

His head tilted down as the nursemaid stepped back. The one good eye locked onto my face.

In a rich, deep, bubbling whisper he said: 'Do not attempt to question me on any subject. Being helpful is for morons.'

190

CHAPTER THIRTY-FIVE

Great trick. Say something so unexpected that the mug, the target, is struck dumb. Knock him silent. Then you can put your own arguments, lay down the law, without interruptions.

It worked. Madox Bligh said: 'You have come here with a battery of questions to fire at me. So much is obvious. You were not here to hear me speak because those days, when the young sought me out to sit at my feet, are gone. Nowadays I am attended by the damaged and the deficient. You appear to be neither.'

He pointed a long, white fingernail at each of us in turn. 'I am a very old man. I am also in ill health. Whatever your motive may be, I do not share it. I have nothing to gain by assisting you – and my time is too short.'

He looked half dead. I mean literally. The whole right side was rigid, and that portion of his face sagged lifelessly, and the skin over his paralysed muscles was brown and blistered, like rotting fruit.

He didn't act so dead.

'You will be sufficiently kind as to tell me the circumstances of Professor Ingman's death. I in turn will recount whatever reminiscences your explanations provoke. Then you will leave. If you attempt to cross-examine me, you will be evicted.'

'Fine. I can't order you to answer questions. I'm not a policeman.'

'Evidently.' He managed to make the word toll, like a bell. I was shaved, and I'd washed, but I probably looked like I'd slept in my shirt. 'And precisely who are you?'

'Moral and physical support.'

'I enquired as to your name, not your function.'

'This is Mrs Simons, the late professor's research assistant, who is unhappy about certain aspects of the death. My name is Panagiotis Michalakopoulos.' Which, even if Bligh knew about the calls to my show, was not a name he'd recognise.

'And which aspects distress you particularly, Mrs Simons?'

191

She waved a hand at me and I answered for her: 'Particularly she's distressed by the aspect that by the time the killer finished with Ingman's body, there wasn't enough left of him to grease a cake-tin.'

Bligh's gimmick played back at him – it worked. I didn't get interrupted.

Things I left out: our suspects, our clues, what the police thought, what Marsh thought, anything about Jane Lyons.

Things I said slowly and clearly and twice: Ingman's expressed interest in Madox Bligh, the leaflet in his apartment, the ritual overtones of the killing.

'You've used that word three times,' he commented at last. 'By ritual, do you suggest there was some kind of religious significance to this murder?'

'Could be. Does your cult make a big thing of cremation?'

'There are societies,' he answered, 'which advocate the cleansing force of death by fire. Think how we burned heretics and witches.'

'You did,' I said. 'I'm Greek.'

'Then you will know that the island of the fire god Hephaestus, or Vulcan, was the setting for two of mankind's most horrific slayings – the massacre of all the men by their wives, and the destruction of all the children born to the Athenian captives.'

'I'm Greek. Not Ancient Greek.'

'Doubtless even a modern Greek is aware of the Hindu taste for suttee – when the family and neighbours of a man urge his widow to immolate herself upon his funeral pyre. And perhaps you have read of the pre-Roman custom in this country, to bind a man inside a wicker idol and consign it to flame?'

'So you think this is nothing unusual. We're worrying over nothing?'

'Worry! Will that revive the man? When did worry do even one ounce of good? Worry is an impotent mind's effort at masturbation – ceaseless, chafing movement without relief.'

'OK, save the sermon.' This I didn't have time for. 'I've heard your power-of-the-mind line, it's good but I'm not buying today. I want to know if Ingman died in one of your rituals.'

He did the thing of holding up the dead arm and letting it drop. 'I could not have killed him.'

'No one imagines you did. But did you inspire it? Did you incite it?'

'That is possible.'

192

He said nothing for several seconds. Neither did I. He was dying to be asked. But if I did ask, his ego might be provoked. He'd already threatened to have me thrown out if I asked questions. So I didn't. I just sat and stared at the one good eye and waited for answers.

'I have said nothing to anyone directly. But I have preached. It is possible my sermons may be misinterpreted by the dull-witted. I would not advocate the actual destruction of my enemies. I like to compare the human mind to a devouring flame, which consumes the dead and useless elements to nourish the living. This metaphor is powerful, but somewhat esoteric. Applied literally, the result might be as horrific as the event you have described.'

'Your followers could run off with the notion that enemies of the ESP deserved to fry?' This tallied with the threat I remembered from Friday's caller. I didn't want to mention that. I had a big question about my radio station, and this wasn't it.

'I have enemies, indeed.'

'Tell me who your greatest enemy would be, the one who wishes you most harm.' Straight cold-reading technique – ask them the question they'll most enjoy answering. For extra points, turn it into an order.

The left eye glittered with hatred. 'Ingman was the one. He sought to obliterate me utterly. His death is mete, very mete.'

I was pressing my hand hard on Louisa's arm, to shut her up. She stifled a gasp.

'Kris.' He slurred the name, and fell into such a long contemplation that I began to think he'd clammed on us. Or croaked.

'Johannes-Kristian. I wonder how much you knew about your professor. Born Helsinki, 1943, during the Nazi presence. Claimed to have been kissed as a baby by Himmler. Make of that what you will. Regrettably it would be as truthful as the rest of his self-devised histories. But I imagine Ingman would have been the type of baby a Himmler would appreciate.'

'I knew he was a racist,' Louisa said.

'The personality invariably runs deeper than the politics. Ingman was racist because he was born to despise his fellows. His search for the *Übermensche*! The superman! My God, what kind of halfwit even reads Nietzsche nowadays, never mind bases an academic career on his ravings?'

I turned my head in a gesture of intelligent inquiry.

'My talk too rich for you? The modern Greeks have given up on philosophy, eh? Ingman's passion for the paranormal was driven by his desire to find a man with the strength of the gods. The power to read minds. The gift of speaking with the dead, of seeing through walls. A man to stand at the fore of a superior race.'

'Whites only need apply?'

'He would never have been interested in you,' said Bligh. 'Far too black! The idea of some creature like you, possessing powers! And it is typical that his researcher would be a Jew. He would enjoy using his greater intellect to torment a Jewish woman. I do you no injustice, I trust?'

'By calling me Jewish? You compliment me. Or by thinking Ingman had a "greater intellect"? You don't know me.'

'I knew Ingman. And I am sadly certain – sadly, because the man revolted me – certain that no woman alive was his intellectual equal.'

Louisa said nothing. The man was old. And nearly dead.

'He sewed my garments once. He washed my feet. He addressed me as Lord.'

'You were his superman?'

'Some little while ago. A little while to me. During the sixties. When LSD was legal, and so less abundant. Back then, when the whole of London was being born anew, the Madox Bligh Institute was a shop. An enlightenment shop. We sold open minds. Empowered minds. And everything we sold was on credit. Free acid for anyone who walked across the threshold – through the door of perception. In both theory and practise, all was beautifully simple. We revealed new ways of living and creativity to thousands. Tens of thousands. So many of them were inspired to greatness. The whole world was receptive to greatness, to great art, in those days. My pupils created. The world purchased. I collected my tithe. Ten per cent of what I enabled them to earn was due to me. Some of them paid. John Lennon gave us ten per cent of his royalties from *Sergeant Pepper*. Brian Jones gave us what he claimed was ten per cent of his portion from *Their Satanic Majesties*, though never for one moment did I believe him. Marc Bolan dropped acid for the first time in this room, and I never saw him again.'

'Free acid isn't popular anymore? Couldn't you give away free crack?'

'I deal in the most powerful drug of all – undiluted mindpower.'

'Not such a great loss-leader.'

'One must be true to one's intuitions. They are a mainspring of mental strength. The man who heeds the promptings of his

194

unconscious takes better advice than any committee of the wise can offer. My intuition was this – drugs are a detour. They take us through the doors of perception, but lead us also through the lanes and byways of deception. Dispense with the chemical crutches, and make the journey unaided. Perception is an unlocked door. Free your mind. Turn the handle.'

'You stopped handing out sugar cubes? So the crowds beat a hasty retreat. And young Ingman stopped sitting at your right hand.'

'Oh, I had long disappointed him. His sojourn was brief. He sought his superman, and for a few months supposed I was that hero. I demonstrated telepathy, I revealed to him some of the mind's simplest powers. He was awestruck. He asked me to submit to tests. I dallied. He insisted. I refused. We argued. He left. The academic scientist is a vulgarian – show him a Michelangelo marble and he wants to smash it with a hammer, to satisfy himself the work is not hollow at the centre.'

'That doesn't seem enough to make him your world's worst enemy.'

'I heard intermittently about Kris. Over the decades. Three or four years ago, I heard he visited Sri Bhasa and was not impressed.'

I'd heard of Sri Bhasa. I'd done a couple of programmes about him. Droplets of milk materialised in the air around him. Neat, but not as head-on capitalist as giving away free drugs.

Louisa said: 'He felt Sri Bhasa insulted him.'

'By not submitting to his tests? What fool would?'

Good question. I didn't volunteer the answer.

'Two years ago he returned. With a thirty-three and one-third stake in the Institute.'

'He held shares?'

'His wife held them. A woman whose husband had been intimately connected with the Evangelists from the beginning. A woman, indeed, with whom most of us had been intimate at one time or another. She had of course become Mrs Ingman. But she was known to me as Jane Lyons.'

CHAPTER THIRTY-SIX

M y turn to do the stifled gasp routine. Bligh was staring over my head, deep into the past, and whatever it was he was seeing I didn't want to look.

'She was a ravishing creature.' Bligh drooled the word. I mean a thread of clear saliva ran over his lip and swung as he said, 'Ravishing!'

'Night before last,' I said, 'someone scooped her into an ashcan too.'

'They both died? Jane is murdered?'

'Two different attacks. In different apartments. But one killer.'

'This is our crime.' He sank his forehead onto the points of his fingers. 'This is some horrific aberrance of our movement.'

'I'm beginning to think so.'

'Oh no, it is certain. You have no idea how interwoven their lives were with my mission. Though Ingman believed himself the harbinger of my destruction, my mission was yet rooted in his heart. It had become twisted there, for his heart was twisted. But Jane . . .'

'Mr Bligh,' I said, 'a guy once gave me some whacked-out seventies prophecies called the *Book of Angels' Song*. I didn't understand one damned word and you're making even less sense to me. Would it be too hard to spell this out in short sentences? For a dumb Greek from Brooklyn?'

He lifted his head. 'Ingman wanted me dead. Have I not made that plain? He desired my corpse, and he intended to take over my mission.'

'For God's sake, why?'

'He had searched thirty years for a superman and failed to find one. Gradually he had despaired of proving that paranormal powers existed. He had become a sceptic. I met him again four years ago and he declared to my face I was a charlatan.'

'So why hold shares?'

'To Kris Ingman's mind, I was a charlatan who lived as a superman.

196

I had been elevated to the mystical pantheon by my followers, people thought I was some kind of god. It did not matter whether I could truly move objects with the power of my mind. I cannot, incidentally. I tell you frankly. Once I could, but I was not old then, for psychokinesis is a young mind's gift.'

'He wanted people to treat him like a superman?' I asked.

Bligh twisted his monocle into his sunken eye-socket and stared at Louisa. 'Does that resonate with what you knew of his character?'

'One hundred per cent.'

'He had settled in his mind that I commanded awe because I claimed psychic powers. He ignored the simple verities, that I no longer held sway over aught but a rump, that my erstwhile popularity had been founded on a culture of mental stimulants and not mental strength, that the powers for which I was renowned had been genuine, and he had seen them enacted before him.'

'When people are skeptics,' I said, 'they don't believe what their own eyes see.'

'Quite so. It is a constant bewilderment to me, how ten thousand instances of telepathy can be witnessed and not one of them credited by a scientist . . . but a single sub-atomic particle, which cannot even be observed reliably, is alleged to defy the laws of physics, and the whole fellowship of science applauds. Why? Why are particles permitted to be psychic when men are not?'

I ignored the question. Either it was rhetorical or I didn't want to get into that debate. 'You're convinced,' I pressed him, 'Ingman got hold of shares so he'd become chief priest of this cult when you pegged? Right? To be a demigod like you? Are you sure you're not just focusing these murders on yourself? It's possible Ingman got croaked and it had zilch to do with you.'

'Impossible.'

'So according to you, Ingman married Jane, Jane Lyons, to get her shares. She had shares in this place?'

'It all returns to that woman,' Bligh mumbled. He started to sink back into his reverie. It had the look of a dirty daydream.

'Tell me about her.'

'I was in love with her. Of course. No longer – love is an emotion of the brain's left hemisphere, and mine was obliterated by a stroke. One half of the most extraordinary tool in creation, a human mind, wrecked in an explosion of self-destruction. My blood pressure, my own heart, is the weapon which slays me. But I survived, you see. Most remarkably, I can still speak. Some expert or other suggested

197

this means, most uncommonly, my speech centres are located in the right-hand hemisphere. It is quite possible. The right-brain governs psychic energy. Why should my eloquence be merely logical? Might it not always have been magical? A power of the right-brain? But the experts ignore the real miracle – that by strength of mind I can force the brain into action. My stroke should have killed me – if not stone dead, then spiritually dead. I should no longer be able to think. But my mind forces my brain to think. *Forces it.* Do you see? The mind must be something separate, something over and above the work-a-day neurons and synapses and cortexes. The mind is supernatural.'

'Jane? You wanted to tell me about Jane?'

'And instead I talked about myself. You are fortunate. Many people have waited years to learn what I have revealed to you in an afternoon.'

'And I am truly grateful.'

One of the great things about doing a lot of radio, it's so easy to sound sincere.

When what I meant was, tell me where Jane fits in – just tell me or have another stroke, I mean, for Christ's sake, do one or the other.

'Jane Lyons was a gift from the gods. A sign that my mission harmonised with the music of the spheres. For the universal good. I was a holy benefactor, and she was the benison of heaven.'

'That's from the *Book of Angels' Song*, right?'

'You are an unpleasantly conceited young man. If the truths of the Angels are too sublime for your apeish mind, am I to be impressed?'

'You have to forgive him,' Louisa put in quickly. 'The subject of Jane is very sensitive with Mikki.'

'So you are he!'

Boy, that girl knew how to let cats out of bags. She should have worked for the RSPCA.

'I am whom?'

'You? You? She thought *you* could be my successor?'

'Just tell me about Jane? Please?'

'Jane came here in the summer of 1965,' he said, and though his mouth moved on his monocled eye was riveted on me.

I obviously wasn't going to be handed the mantle of demigodness. He was very upset that anyone had ever applied in my name.

Not that I'd asked anyone.

Especially not anyone I worked with.

Mimi was the only one who believed I was truly more than human.

198

Wasn't she? And Mimi couldn't ever be dumb enough to think I'd want to inherit this dump. Could she?

'In 1965 we had "Help!" and "Sounds of Silence" and "Like a Rolling Stone" and "Satisfaction". A summer to be alive.'

'"It Was A Very Good Year".'

'You remember it, young man?'

'No. Sinatra recorded that in 1965.'

He was still staring at me like I'd landed from Planet Zog.

'Johnson pounded the National Liberation Front,' he slurred slowly, while I disliked him even more for swaggering because he lived through the sixties. People do that, and it's a giant bore. Was it cool in the sixties to go on about the Great Depression? No. So who wants to hear about the Viet-Cong and Bob Dylan now?

My God, at his age now, he must've been having a mid-life crisis in 1965. And he was talking about riots on campuses and Malcolm X getting iced.

'She made me feel like a teenager,' he drooled. 'Jane, Jane, not-at-all-plain. The mindblowingest fuck of my life.'

He kept that glassy eye boring into me. I was getting used to it, that and the sudden shockers. I just looked back.

'And you married her.' He said it like an idea that had just reached him. 'That's right, someone told me. The radio psychic married Jane. You did it for the shares too, I imagine?'

'I don't have a clue what you're mouthing about.'

'Jane. Your wife? Yes? So. I'll tell you what you don't know about her. She was sex mad.'

Like, this I didn't know.

'She came here that summer and we shared her. Ambrose Lyons and I, and how many others I have no idea, and later Ingman. Her body was a gift very widely bestowed. I don't doubt that in her later years she needed the energies of a young man. My only surprise is that, even now, one could be enough. Perhaps it wasn't. You would be the last to know.'

I would have said something back but my mother taught me to never speak ill to the half-dead.

'She had her vanities. Claiming to be twenty-one, when close acquaintance with her delicious charms made one suspect she must have concealed a decade.'

'She was knocking off ten years already?'

'Her insistence on sleeping alone. Quite peculiar. Even when she

199

shared herself with two – even, on one most memorable occasion, three – always afterwards, we were banished from the boudoir.'

'For Christ's sake, keep your pervert memories. You think we care?'

'She treated me imperiously. I found it amusing. I was at her command, even when she sat at my feet.'

'So she married Ambrose. Not you.'

'My mission was my marriage. She ached to marry me, of course. But as I gently opened the doors of her mind, she perceived that a woman's place, even such a creature of delight as she was, must be as a home-maker. She needed Ambrose because he needed to be cared for and fussed over and cosseted. Stupid soft Ambrose. Thinking was always too hard a task for him. He had the acumen, the business brain, but not the mind to command it. So he drifted into money-making, and capitalism, and commerce, forgetting all the lessons I had revealed to him – that the surest way to receive is first to give. Lavish your last possessions on the first humans who crave your boon. Wealth will return to you tenfold and a hundred times more.'

'So did Ambrose make money?'

'I believe he died a millionaire many times over. A million for every week of the year, he told me, and I have no reason to distrust his word.'

Fifty mill. And that was a few years back. Where was it? And was I getting any of it?

It wasn't possible I could have been written right out of all that. Surely.

'Ingman told me,' said Bligh, 'that her friends took most of it. What the government hadn't already taken, at any rate. But I'm sure you know what your wife is worth. Was worth. And now her shares must be yours. Ambrose Lyons devised the Institute as a private limited company, you understand. I held two-thirds. You are powerless while I live. Wait and see what happens when I die. Maybe you'll be able to seize power for yourself. Maybe not. You may have to endure a frustrating delay before you know. My mindpower is fresher than ever.'

'Who told you I wanted it?'

'Why else are you here?'

'You haven't got this yet? Somebody killed Jane. And Ingman.'

'Of course, and you imagined I could offer some clue. Perhaps you hoped I might shed psychic light upon the mystery. Demonstrate the complex art of psychometry – hold her glove, her bag, a scrap of her dress, and witness in my mind's eye the awful moments of her ultimate doom.'

'I don't know what I thought. Which is fine, because I also don't think you know what you're thinking most of the time.'

'I may do you an injustice. Maybe you will be my successor. Someone must, after all.'

'Too bad to let all this good work just stop,' I agreed.

'Perhaps you are the One. Jane, at least, had a deep regard for your mental abilities.'

'What?'

'It was she, after all, who suggested you possessed healing powers. It was she who urged Ingman to put my Evangelists in touch with Psychic Mikki of Radio PrimeTime. Ingman, however, was sceptical of all paranormality. He was convinced that your powers could do me no good and perhaps some harm. And so naturally, Ingman was only too glad to recommend you.'

'Maybe Jane knew I was fake,' I said dryly. 'Maybe she wanted you dead too.'

'It is possible. I treated the idea with some amusement. But when I met with your delicious colleague, she was so insistent about you, so fervent in your praise, so enraptured by everything that was Mikki . . .'

Mimi. It had to be Mimi. There was no one else who could fit that description.

'I might add I was charmed by her prettiness. She wore quite revolting tinted glasses, of course, but even then she contrived to be pretty. She has become quite a regular here. A most enchanting ambassador for Psychic Mikki. Mikki must heal me. Mikki must be my adopted son. Mikki must have all the shares. Mikki must be the anointed one. She was most enthusiastic about the idea of Demigod Mikki. Perhaps she will be your blonde Demigoddess.'

I doubted it.

Louisa said, 'Blonde?'

'She's dark-haired,' I said. 'Chinesey. Only she's Korean in fact.'

'I have one eye left. It sees. It is not colour-blind. Go now. I am depressed by you.'

'She isn't blonde.' But I could think of someone who was.

'When she comes to see me, your colleague Kerry – Kerry Allison, am I right? – Kerry Allison is blonde.'

201

CHAPTER THIRTY-SEVEN

'OK,' I said. The Sunday traffic on Southampton Row was light and fast, and we were trying to cross and failing. 'What for you was the weirdest part of that conversation?'

Louisa didn't answer. She was staring to the right, at a Merc a couple of hundred yards off that was aiming for the land-speed record. When it was halfway towards us, she yanked my arm. 'Now!' she demanded.

I yanked back. The Merc burned past. 'What is this, you can't wait for me to be murdered? You have to throw me under a sedan?'

'Sorry. I'm not very good at judging distances.'

'It's OK,' I said, 'I'm not so good at judging wives. Or any women. What the hell has Kerry Allison got to do with Lord Freakshow? Why in hell should she care if I use healing powers to save his life? And if that's what she wants, why not say something to me? She doesn't have to get the zombies to phone our show.'

'She must have her reasons. You know her – is it something to do with her parents, do you think? Were they members of this institute?'

'I have no idea. I only work with her.'

'And sleep with her.'

'That too.'

'So what do you know about her family?'

'Nothing.'

'What about all the cold reading? Do you ask all these nosy questions and then switch off? Don't you even listen?'

'Of course I listen, you think I'm shallow? She's very private. We talk work, politics, movies. We talk shop. She says the smart stuff, I do risqué jokes. Innuendo. She's very serious-minded, I'm not, that's why she likes me. Also for my looks.'

'Did she ever mention the ESP people?'

'To me, no, I don't think so. But once I heard her tell Mimi to keep the freaks off the lines. Listeners didn't like them. People would think we were handing over free publicity. Which doesn't figure to me. She wanted me to get involved with Bligh, right? She must have known I'd get shares through Jane, and she wanted me to use them. Become a great guru.'

'Would that be good for her show?'

'I don't see it like that. No one goes to these meetings. Why would I get better audiences, if I was some obscure cult guru?'

'But Kerry sincerely believes in your powers?'

'Not that I know. She loves the feature, Call Psychic Mikki – it was Kerry who insisted I should be on every morning, not just Monday-Wednesday-Friday. But that's a radio thing. She's a radio girl. Nuts about the wireless, she turned down two TV presenter jobs this year already. Would I turn down television?'

'I doubt it.'

'You bet you doubt it. Radio I love too, but on TV I'd get to show my face. You know they say your face is your fortune. On radio how can I cash in? Kerry could be such a TV star, but she doesn't want it. Very narrow interests. And if they include the Church of the Loony Tune – all I can say is, she never told me.'

'It seems she wasn't entirely frank with you, then.'

'Maybe Kerry asked me sometimes, "How do your powers work?" or "What does it feel like in a trance?" But these are standard no-brainer questions. Party talk.' We were still dawdling on the kerbside. 'Mimi, now she asks the hard questions. Because she truly believes, in everything paranormal. Aliens in your bedroom and spirit guides on the next plane and poltergeists and Ouija boards. I could pull my handkerchief out of my pocket and tell her, "This is ectoplasm," and she'd believe me. If it was Mimi selling my pitch to Madox Bligh, then I'd understand.'

'Go back a bit,' said Louisa. 'Why did Kerry Allison tell your assistant not to put Bligh's people on the show? If it was Kerry who roused their interest in the first place?'

'I get your point. It only makes sense if Mimi knew to ignore the instructions. That conversation was for my benefit, in my earshot. Which means Kerry and Mimi both are working to get me elected as God of the Weird Ones. So they both knew about Jane's shares in Bligh's Institute. So they both knew about Ingman. Which follows, Jane and Mimi and Kerry all fixed me up to take Ingman's tests. You did too. Am I paranoid or does this look like a conspiracy of every woman I know?'

'You're paranoid.'

'You'd have to say that, though.'

'Where are we trying to go now?'

'Across this road would be a start. I think I have to talk with Kerry. Even though she won't want to see me.'

'Even though she might be the murderer?'

'Come on, I'm the paranoid klutz here.'

'Your friend Mimi said, Kerry could have had opportunity. Now we know she had some kind of motive. You really want to confront her?'

'I confronted Bligh, didn't I? And Marsh. Can today get any stranger?'

Dumb question.

CHAPTER THIRTY-EIGHT

We were on Grafton Way now and the PrimeTime studios in New Cavendish Street were less than a five-minute walk. I told Louisa, 'This is a low trick, but Kerry's got desk space in the studio. Maybe there's something there, something to point our way. Documents, or a letter from Bligh or Ingman – something to connect the dots.'

'Or a blowtorch.'

'I honestly can't see that. She's a sweet girl.'

'So was Myra Hindley.'

'She was? The child killer? I thought she was a low-life sicko.'

'OK, I don't mean Hindley was a nice person, but she was under someone else's control. That's the point. Maybe a man is forcing her into certain actions. One of the ESP people. Maybe it was Ingman himself, and she turned on him. Or Ingman and Jane, acting together.'

'How would they get to Kerry?'

'That's what we have to ask. If we don't find the answers in your studio.'

'I still prefer the idea it was Marsh. Marsh dressed up as a hobo. That makes sense to me.'

'But where does he fit in? Motive? Connections?'

'OK,' I admitted. 'He doesn't fit. But as a suspect, I prefer him to Kerry.'

'For all you know she could have been one of these people for years. Bligh wasn't telling you the truth the whole time.'

'I know that.'

'How do you know she's not his daughter? The way they were all taking drugs and having sex with each other, there must be dozens of his illegitimate children all over London.'

'I think you're secretly kind of a prude.'

'No, I'm not. I just thought Madox Bligh was a glorified Dirty Old Man, that's all.'

'So Kerry is his lovechild, right?'

'What do you know about her? Nothing. It's a theory.'

'You got no evidence, but it's a theory. If she is involved, and I can't bring myself to believe this for one nanosecond, but here's my theory, and this is more likely: she could have found out about the cult in reverse. By which I mean, first they ring me, looking for a mindpower cure for their mindpower wizard. Then Kerry looks them up, discovers they've got a big townhouse and maybe a stash of money. She makes inquiries, and discovers that I'm a major shareholder without even knowing it. So she figures, I'll be rich if I can take over this cult. She's hopelessly and helplessly in love with me, but she doesn't want me to know. She tries to arrange for me to get to be the next holy man, without showing her hand. I get fabulously wealthy, she gets the satisfaction of a duty well served. Meanwhile, one of the Loopy Lous who live under Lord Bligh's bed snuck out with a few sticks of napalm. That makes sense.'

'You don't really live on planet Earth, do you? You're out there somewhere in the stars.'

'The view's better where I am,' I said.

'You couldn't really set yourself up like Madox Bligh. Pretending to have psychic superpowers.'

'Couldn't I?'

'Yes, but not to rip people off and take all their money and strut around like a maharaja, or mahasiddha, or maharishi, or whatever.'

'Couldn't I?'

She stopped and caught my arm, and stared into my face with her wide malachite orbs. With a deep breath she shook her head.

'You might think you'd like to. All that money, and the sex.'

'Sounds OK.'

'You're not ruthless enough. Nowhere near. You're all swagger. Black jeans, black leathers, black shades, like you're in the Mafia.'

'Of course,' I said, 'Brooklyn's never heard of the Mafia. We don't do that stuff.'

'In your imagination you're a big dangerous star, and you'd like to be surrounded by girls and bodyguards. I should think you imagine yourself sauntering into a crowded restaurant and pointing at your favourite table, and the manager has to pay the diners to leave just so you can eat there.'

'A guy can't have fantasies? How do you know about them? You daydream the same stuff?'

206

'Mikki, you couldn't scare a three-year-old. You'll never be a star, you don't have the aura. You're a big softie, who'll do anything to make anyone like him.'

'You think I'm a softie?'

I grabbed her arm and twisted her towards me, pulling her face into mine.

She stamped on my foot.

'Let me go or I'll hurt you.'

I let her go.

'Do that again, idiot, and you'll be seeing double all day.'

'Sorry.'

'Sorry! The great Latin lover says sorry-I-tried-to-kiss-you. You're a softie and that's why all the fluffy middle-aged ladies like your show. Get used to it, you're never going to be Humphrey Bogart.'

'I didn't want to be Bogart anyhow.'

I wanted to be Sinatra. But I guess I couldn't remember him apologising for trying to kiss the girl any time either.

'Some of those fluffy old ladies,' I said after a while, 'turn out to be rough stuff.' I didn't want her to think I was a softie who sulked, so I tried to give our conversation the kiss of life. She couldn't knee me in the crotch for that.

'You're thinking of the fluffy old lady you married?'

'She was sex crazy.'

'Where do you think that side of her character came from?'

'Old-lady hormones.'

'She hit the menopause and turned into a ravening nymphomaniac? Male myth, I'm afraid. Obviously she enjoyed sex when she was older because she'd enjoyed it when she was younger.'

'Enjoyed! The Great British understatement. You're right, she'd been hot for it since Marilyn Monroe was a virgin.'

'Here's another reason you're not Bogart. You couldn't use sex as a weapon. A woman like your wife exerts power through sex. Look how Bligh admitted she dominated him.'

'He loved it.'

'It wouldn't have mattered – that just made it easier for her. Jane used sex against men. She teased you with it, but she probably had Ingman on a short leash.'

'Literally.'

'It's not impossible to imagine.'

'With a strong stomach.'

'Sex is a toy to you, Mikki. You play at sex because it's fun.'

'So I don't have hang-ups. You need hang-ups to be Bogart?'

'For some people, sex is a very grown-up weapon. Men use it as a heavy blunt object. Women get battered with it. Jane used it as an instrument of torture. Lots of barbs and razor edges. Ingman probably liked it that way. But you, it scared the living daylights out of you. You like your sex warm and cuddly, like a soft toy. It helps you sleep soundly.'

'Excuse me, have we been to bed together?'

'Not yet.'

'Don't make yourself any promises – I don't like you so much anymore. You want to sleep with a teddy bear, don't pick me.'

'You're the kind of man who puts ads in the paper on Valentine's Day: Dearest darling, cuddle me for always, your adoring Mikki.'

'I'm just glad I didn't kiss you. Some escape.'

'Look how miserable you were to let your friend Mimi find out you were sleeping with Kerry. Someone with Jane's mentality, or Ingman, or Bligh, they would have loved to twist the knife. The point of going to bed with Kerry wouldn't have been for pleasure, or carving a big notch on the bedpost like a boy who collects number plates. You'd have seduced Kerry, just to torture the other girl. That's not your style.'

'OK, I'm not a bastard.'

'No. You're not. But somebody is. And ask yourself – what was Kerry Allison's motive in sleeping with you? Who was she trying to torture? Who was she sticking the knife into?'

'Mimi?' I asked, puzzled.

'Maybe. Or maybe Jane.'

CHAPTER THIRTY-NINE

Being independent with good advertisers means PrimeTime can afford two studios on a central London street, ground floor. The presenters and the producers are different people. There's even a receptionist and a security guard. Take away the advertisers, and everyone gets sacked, except the security guard, and now he has to be the broadcaster, answer the phones and work the desk. In independent radio, advertisers are the boss. They pay your wages.

Not mine, not for much longer. Advertisers are very nervous about associating their products with serial killers.

Raymond, the guard, reminded me about this as I pushed through the plate-glass entrance ahead of Louisa. He was a little guy with a moustache and goatee, with his uniform two sizes too big and his cap on the back of his head. He was also a karate black belt. So he said.

Raymond called out: 'Mikki! Collecting your stuff then? Brought a bag?'

'I'll be on air tomorrow, Raymond, same as ever. I've got to collect a script, that's all. This is Monica, my girl. She's coming in with me. Want me to sign her in.'

'No, that's all right,' said Raymond, like he was a billionaire inviting us to a barbecue on his private Hawaiian island. 'Does Mimi know about Monica?'

'Make sure you tell her, Raymond.'

'I will,' he promised, and I believed him. That was OK. Mimi would be glad just to think I was two-timing Louisa.

Raymond opened the black door to the producer's room without leaving his desk, flicking the buzzer behind him. I glanced back, at the semi-circular reception with its fake red leather and copper-coloured railings, and the windows onto New Cavendish Street, mostly blocked out by the huge red-and-blue PrimeTime logos. Then the door clicked behind us and I felt for the lights in the semi-darkness.

Louisa said, 'Isn't it small?'

'Now that's not a remark I hear much when the lights are out.'

'I meant your brain. And this studio.'

'This is just the production section. Producer sits here, Mimi sits there. Eight phonelines, see? Through this window, that's the studio. See how it's on a slightly lower level, so the producer can look down onto the presenter's desk and see what she's doing?'

'It's still small.'

'You imagine wide open spaces when you're listening, right? Not logical. Not scientific. How much room does a guy need for talking?'

'With you, I imagine you could talk inside a matchbox.'

'Not funny. Someone has ambitions to scrape me into one. Jackpot question, is that someone Kerry? And what can we find here to tell us?'

I turned up the spotlights over Dan Nally's desk. His ashtray was still full from Friday. Louisa put her fingertip on a fader switch.

'Can I slide this slider?'

'That one's just his cigarette lighter,' I said. 'Push this, it's the indicator. See here – gas, brakes, clutch. Want to try driving?'

'That's what I was going to ask you – you don't have a car. Can you drive, Mikki?'

'No, but I can hail a cab in seventeen languages.'

'I had to sell my car last year. Now Dani has to walk to school, even in the rain. It's roasting this week, but before the holidays it seemed to pour almost every morning. I'm a good driver, though. I passed my test first time. Couldn't you get one of those radio outside-broadcast cars? I'd be your chauffeur.'

She was sitting in Dan Nally's swivel seat, twisting round like a little girl. The little crystal at her throat was shining in the spotlamps.

'What do you do with Dani in the holidays? When you're working?'

'He goes to a minder, when he has to and if I can afford it. I prefer him to go to a friend's house, but that's not fair on the other mothers if I can't reciprocate. Which is difficult, working full-time and living in that little flat. Occasionally he had to come to work with me, but Ingman wouldn't allow him in the offices. He had to sit downstairs with Judith in reception.'

'You don't leave him at home ever?'

'Never. He's only six.' She stopped twisting. 'I wish there was some way I could telephone him. Suppose he doesn't like your friend?'

210

'He liked her this morning,' I reminded her. 'Mimi's great with kids.'

'And she's trustworthy?' She was so anxious for the answer to be 'Yes'.

'I'd trust her with my life. Anybody's life.'

'Where do you want to start looking?' she asked suddenly.

'Anywhere. You take Mimi's desk.'

'You think I should go through this drawer?'

'Sure. She'll never know. It's a mess. And if I say it's OK, it's OK with Mimi. Maybe we'll dig out details of Ingman's call or something. Anything is worth finding.' She still looked doubtful. 'Don't be so scrupled.'

'And you?'

'Kerry's desk is through there. Opposite mine. You want to come and sit in the chair I use when I'm broadcasting?'

'Don't you think we ought to hurry up a little?'

'Shout if you find something you're not sure about.' I sauntered into the studio. My own studio. I got such a big kick just walking into this place. I'd talked myself into the best job in the world. Londoners call it blagg. New Yorkers call it chutzpah. Sometime I'll tell you how I did it.

I sat in my chair, tucked my headphones over one ear and opened my mike. 'Can you hear me?' She nodded. 'Push the faders on your left – on the right of the mixing desk – all the way up. Say something. OK, I can hear you too. This is how it looks when I'm on air. Me in this chair, Kerry there – side-on to you. This black window facing me is the VIP lounge.'

'For the Queen when she comes calling?'

'We had the Duchess of Kent here once. On behalf of a charity. You don't look impressed, I thought you English were crazy about everything royal.'

'Are you just going to sit there pretending to be on the radio?'

'Found anything useful?' I answered. 'OK, so I guess I'll have to.'

I pulled open my desk drawer. It was a big wooden compartment on plastic runners, and it glided out silently. All the furniture in a radio studio has to work silently. I already knew what was in my drawer – a mess, a lot of bills and brown envelopes I hadn't opened and ought to have done, a lot of things that would cost me money if I followed the instructions, nothing that would show a profit whatever I did with it. This was my conscience drawer. I didn't have a conscience, so I had a drawer.

Still sitting in my chair, I wheeled myself around the desk, to where Kerry sat. She was the meticulous kind whose desk would always be locked at the weekend.

It wasn't.

There was something in the lower, larger drawer but it flew open. Mine was weighed down with papers. Kerry's wasn't. It was light. There was a bundle of clothes, more like rags. And a wig.

The wig was long and it stuck out from under the rags. I pulled it. It flopped out.

'Louisa,' I said, 'I want you to look at this.' The wig was soft in my hands. I flipped it over. There were no labels, and no bits of sticky tape, but I pricked a finger on a couple of pins stuck in the top. The hair felt real.

The hair was blonde.

I pulled out the rags. There was a pair of jeans, ripped and patched. A pair of trainers, with the soles ripped half away. Sunglasses, and a tunic with a hood and a dark stain sprayed across the chest.

I held up the tunic, pinching the shoulders with my fingertips. It looked like it should stink of urine and high-alcohol lager, but what it stank of was butane and sweet roast pork. The hood flopped back. Inside there were blonde hairs. That wig was shedding.

In the shining black glass opposite I saw my reflection. What I was holding looked like a ghost.

Louisa said: 'Is that blood?'

I stared at the tunic. Maybe it had been kind of fawn when it was new. Maybe it had been cream. What it was now was dark brown. The cloth was greasy with stains, but there was only one that mattered. Louisa was right – blood it had to be. So much blood, it had dried rigid in the fabric, and the body of the tunic hung like it was starched.

I was assuming whoever wore this top hadn't died in it. So to get hosed with this amount of blood, someone had been in close contact with a severed artery for a long time, long enough to get at least a pint squirted on them. Granted whoever was dressing like this didn't worry overmuch about unsightly spills and dry-clean bills. Still, it is human nature to get out the way when there's hot blood fountaining at a distance of three inches.

Unless getting out of the way could be fatal. To you.

To get this much blood on you, you had maybe to be kneeling on your victim's shoulders while you cut her throat.

'It doesn't make sense,' I said. 'Kerry isn't violent. It isn't her. She's

212

got that British cold inside her, kind of repressed, doesn't like to kid around. The whole country's full of people like her. It's normal. And this isn't a nation of mass murderers.'

'Why would she hide this evidence, in such an obvious place, if she didn't do it? And where's the flamethrower, or whatever she used? Why isn't that here?'

'Why has she got a blonde wig?' I countered. 'She's already blonde.'

'A different kind of blonde?' suggested Louisa.

'Yeah, and this wig looks shorter.' I held it up. The pins jabbed my hand again, and I dropped it, cursing.

'The owner isn't bald,' she said. 'Pins hold a wig onto your own hair. If you don't have hair, you use tape. My dad had a toupee.'

'So apart from your dad, do we know any bald people?'

'Marsh,' she said. She was right. This stuff had never been a private eye's disguise.

'I see why she dressed as a tramp,' Louisa went on, as I hunted in the pockets of the jeans for clues. 'She could hang around outside Ingman's apartment, and she could smuggle his body into the university, where they let tramps come and go. I don't see why that had to be done, though, unless it was part of the ritual. And I don't understand why a blonde woman hides her hair under a blonde wig.'

'I don't understand anything,' I answered. 'Except that this has to put me in the clear. The police can DNA test this blood and the fibres and everything. They can prove I never handled any of it.'

'Until now.'

There was a silence. Then I threw the clothes back into the drawer in disgust.

'Fuck it,' I said, 'I'm too stupid to be a serial killer.'

'There'll be other fingerprints than yours, there's bound to be,' Louisa tried to console me. 'Unless,' she added, 'Kerry was wearing gloves.'

'I just don't believe – it doesn't make sense. Why? Why get involved in this cult, why get obsessed with me, why do anything so awful? If we talk to her, there'll be an explanation. I know there will.'

'Mikki, you have to go to the police. Immediately. This is evidence. I know you want to stay away from them, but please, if they find out you knew about this, and they will find out because you've touched all of it, you could go to prison. Obstructing an investigation, or something. It might make them even more determined to blame you. And ignore the killer.' She was pleading now.

'I'm sorry,' I said. 'I have to talk to Kerry first. I know she'll have an explanation.'

'Mikki, that is so misguided! You think you're being loyal, but it's just stupidity. Protecting a killer because you slept with her.'

'It's not because I slept with her. It's not even because she got me my job. We work together, it's because of that. And because she's more serious about radio than anyone I've ever known.'

CHAPTER FORTY

We were too late. I knew it as we walked down the steps of Kerry's basement flat.

There had been another murder.

We could smell it. The stench hit you in the stomach and rose into your gorge like vomit.

But, Christ forgive me, I still thought Kerry was the killer until I saw her body.

The door was partway open and she was lying in the passageway. She was still burning.

The smoke was curling under the top of the doorframe and swaying as it floated up. I remember it looked like hair to me, strands of Kerry's hair, as if she was underwater.

Someone had killed her with a blowtorch and I had this macabre flash of how her body would look if she'd been drowned. There's no saying what weird ideas flare up in your brain at the moment you realise someone you love is dead. But I know this – if the thought is simply, 'Oh no, that's awful,' then it never really was love.

I loved Kerry a lot. I shouldn't have slept with her, because that wasn't the way I loved her. She was my friend, that's how I loved her. As a friend. But I persuaded her to sleep with me anyhow. Look what came of it.

Finding Ingman and seeing Jane was nothing like this. For one thing, the person inside this corpse was still recognisable. She lay on her back with her hands splayed at her sides and a big hole burned in the middle of her face.

Her hair had all been scorched off her scalp but the blonde tips were scattered like a halo, twelve inches from her head. The killer had left the eyes. The skin around them was bloody and wrinkled from the flames but the eyes were open and they were blue and they were staring at me as I pushed back the door.

It would have helped to scream but my throat was locked tight.

The air in my lungs was trapped. I lurched against the door, and the rancid smoke was making my eyeballs throb, and I realised I was not dizzy from nausea alone. It was lack of oxygen. All the blood had drained from my head and I wasn't breathing and if I didn't turn round I was going to collapse.

I turned my back on her. It was all I could do. But I can still see the way her jeans were burning with a low blue flame on her legs and her hips, soaking the fabric in her melting body fat. The candle effect. Turning her into a human wick.

I can still see how the blowtorch had carved a black chasm across her ribs, slicing her body in two. And I can see the middle of her face, where her lips used to be and where the murderer had blazed a big black 'O'.

I see that in my sleep, and when I forget to push the memory away, and even when I'm not thinking about it. Like when a blonde head goes by in a crowd, I see that carbon-black hole gaping in it.

Louisa had already retreated up the steps. She knew what was there and she didn't want to see it, but she was still staring down at the smoke-filled doorway. As I staggered up to the sidewalk Louisa held out a hand to me. Her face was white and her fingertips were chilled.

As I leant against the railings, my own flesh turned cold. The sunshine was hot enough to boil up beads of sweat on my scalp, but under my skin the blood was filtering through crushed ice.

I needed to breathe. I needed to get the sight of her burning corpse out of my head, and I needed to get some oxygen into me.

I tried focusing on something normal. Something safe. I tried to imagine I was back in my studio, and I wasn't hunting through drawers or holding bloodstained rags, I was just talking. Broadcasting. Staring up at the window where Mimi sat.

I had to think of something normal. I thought of Mimi.

The restricter on my throat loosened off, and I sucked in some air. That made everything easier, and the grip loosened some more. Then I was breathing.

Above me someone leant out of a window and yelled, 'Your dinner's burning! Turn the bloody gas off!'

That was what people were going to think. Someone in one of the flats had drunk a bottle of wine and fallen asleep while their Sunday roast got cremated. This was London. No one knew who lived upstairs, next door, in the basement. The nearest they got to being neighbourly was bellowing out of the window.

How long till someone else found Kerry? Tomorrow, when she didn't turn up for work? The next day? When?

Louisa was holding my arm. She said, 'Now will you call the police? Because you know it's Kerry now. And she's going to keep on killing people, until she kills you.'

I shook my head. 'That's her. In there. That's Kerry.'

Louisa stared at me, and kept staring at me until I had the strength to stand on my own again. I pushed her across the road, away from the stench.

'I'm going to have to phone the police. Anonymously.'

Louisa was still staring. She said, 'It's Dani.'

'It's not Dani. It's the girl we were looking for, the one I work with . . .'

'It's Dani. Oh God! It's going to be Dani next, it's going to be Dani now.'

'Listen to me, it's not your son in there.'

'Oh God, you don't understand. Dani, I have to find him. I have to be with him. He's not safe.'

'He *is* safe.'

'My God, he's going to be killed.'

'Louisa,' I screamed, 'he's safe. He's with Mimi.'

She seized the cuffs of my jacket and tugged at them in hysterical despair.

'Yes, it's her. Isn't it? She killed them. It's Mimi.'

CHAPTER FORTY-ONE

'What?' I pulled my jacket free and held Louisa's wrists. 'You're not being reasonable. You're upset. Try to be calm.'

'Mikki, please understand me. Please believe what I'm telling you. I know Dani needs me.' She was trying to keep the desperation out of her voice. 'He's yelling out to me.'

I looked at her. The cloudy green eyes were alive with red sparks. Her face was flushed and she was breathing rapidly through her nose.

'This isn't panic?'

'No!' There had been a wave of panic, but she had stood up to it, and now she was focusing all her distressed energy on my face. Forcing me to understand what she felt. Pushing the sensation into my brain.

I was convinced. 'This is some mother telepathy thing, right?'

'I just know Dani needs me. He's scared for his life.'

'And it's not only that it's tea-time and maybe he wants his mum back now?'

'Mikki. Oh God, Mikki, please.'

'OK, I believe you. Have you any idea where they've gone?'

'He's with Mimi.'

I just didn't want to believe Mimi could be a danger to Dani, that she had ever been dangerous to anyone. I guess part of me must have already suspected, but it wasn't a part I wanted to be in touch with. I said: 'If he's with Mimi, they're both in danger.'

'It's her. Don't you see?'

'No. No, I don't see.'

'It has to be her. That's why the clothes were in Kerry's drawer, and the wig. It was Mimi who went to Bligh, wearing the wig, pretending to be Kerry. And it was Mimi who kept putting those calls through to you, and Mimi . . .'

'It can't be,' I said.

218

I was lying, naturally. I knew now. Every question I'd been asking since midnight on Friday, the answer was 'Mimi'.

'Where would she go?'

'I don't know, she was taking him to the zoo.'

'But she didn't, did she? She came here.'

'How do you know?' And then I realised, and the full horror of the killings began to seep through. Mimi had come here to kill Kerry. She had not worn her disguise this time, because Kerry wouldn't have opened the door to a bum in rags.

And Dani must have been with her.

'Where would she go?' Louisa repeated.

'Who's she going to kill next?' I answered. 'That's where she'll go. Maybe Bligh's Institute. Or maybe back to her flat, to wait for us. If it's me she wants next.'

'You still don't understand. It's Dani she's going to kill.'

I made a despairing gesture.

'Where?' Louisa was demanding. 'Where? You know her, Mikki. Think like she's thinking.'

'I can't think that way.'

'All the people she's killed have been in their homes. Your wife, and now your presenter. And Ingman.'

'But she took Ingman to his office,' I said. 'Maybe because that was where I'd met him. But she doesn't know where I met Dani. She doesn't have your address. She must know it's around Ingman's offices somewhere, but even if she got Dani to tell her, she couldn't get in. You're on the third floor.'

'You and Dani were together in her flat.'

'She can't connect her home with Dani. He's been there once. Mimi and me lived together there for weeks – if anything connects, it's that. Not Dani.'

'You're making sense,' she encouraged me, trembling.

I was still standing with my back to Kerry's apartment, and the sickly smoke was in every breath.

Ingman had died at his apartment but his body was dumped in the office where he tricked me.

I ran a hand through my hair. It was wet with sweat. Thinking was hard.

Jane was killed in the apartment we shared. Kerry was murdered in the basement flat where we'd had sex. If none of these locations were chosen by chance, Mimi would take Dani somewhere that mattered very much to me.

'She's at the station,' I said. 'In the studio. Where we've come from.'

'Call the police,' she pleaded.

'If we call the police, we won't be believed. They'll want to know about, Kerry, not Dani. Kerry is dead. We can still save Dani.'

We'd ridden out to Fulham in a cab, and now there was no cab to be seen. We went running out to Fulham Palace Road, and waved uselessly at the cars until a black cab drove down and jinked into the kerb. I scrambled in first and told him, 'PrimeTime,' and when he said that's what he was listening to, I begged him to turn it up.

I looked at my watch. At six forty-five this would be Dan Nally's show. He hated doing it, and it showed – back-to-back playlist, no variation, and half the time he didn't bother to announce the songs. He played every second of intro and outro, because that meant he had to talk less.

No one was listening, he claimed, because at six forty-five on Sunday you could listen to the official Radio 1 Top Forty or the Independent Chart Countdown – so who would be tuning in to PrimeTime oldies?

Anyone who usually listened to PrimeTime, that was the answer. Anyone whose dial was set there and didn't like to move it. Anything up to 400,000 people. And Dan Nally couldn't be bothered to talk to them.

Usually.

Tonight, he was bothering.

'Turn it up, turn it up,' I was pleading.

'. . . so once again, this is a call for Mikki. PrimeTime's psychic Mikki. Mikki, if you're listening out there, give us a call. We need you here, so call in.'

He sounded deeply unhappy about something. It had to be more than the inconvenience of talking between records.

'Have you got a phone?'

'Yeah.' The cabbie took a few seconds to answer, and he didn't turn round.

'Can I borrow it?'

'No.'

'Please, I'll pay you.'

'Not for use of the customers.'

'Just one call.'

'Yeah, to Pakistan.'

'Why am I going to call Pakistan?'

'You're not. Not on my phone.'

'Please, that's me they're asking for on the radio.'

'Like shit it is.'

'I just have to make one call. I'll pay you £50.'

'I told you "No".'

I pulled what was left of my cash from my hip pocket. 'I've got £110. You can have all of it. That's for the fare, and the call, and keep the rest.' I had my hand thrust through the dividers.

The cabbie looked sideways at it. He had to take it. Anyone would have had to take it.

'Phone. Phone,' I urged him.

He handed it back. It was a little Nokia in a green case and the battery was flat.

'There's no power,' I yelled.

'Tough shit, pal.'

'You could have said something!'

'I did. I said "No". Didn't I? Over and over again, but you weren't taking "No" for an answer. Were you?' He shook his head like I'd learned a sad lesson. 'You want to get out here or go on? It's all the same to me. 'Cos you ain't getting your fuckin' money back.'

'Stick the money up your ass.'

'Oh, I don't think I'll be doing that with it.'

'Just get me to New Cavendish Street.'

'I could have done that for . . .' He flicked the meter and read the fare – '£7.80.'

I sat back. Killing the cabbie wouldn't speed anything up. Dan Nally's voice came back through. It was still thick with displeasure.

'I have to keep saying this, because we haven't heard anything yet. If PrimeTime's psychic Mikki is listening, call us now, Mikki.' I already knew it was serious, but what confirmed the status of this appeal was the lack of humour. No jokes about telepathy. No attempt to reach me with a Ouija board. Just, 'Mikki, call in. It's urgent.'

Dan Nally said, 'I can't keep saying this, so here's another song, and I hope if Mikki's anywhere near a radio this will make him prick up his ears. This is Frank Sinatra.'

And it was Sinatra, Sinatra singing, 'Something's Gotta Give'.

For the first time ever I hated that voice.

CHAPTER FORTY-TWO

The police were there. I didn't see Bowen and Tripp but it wasn't them I was looking for. I announced myself to the uniforms at the end of New Cavendish Street and they escorted me and Louisa past a line of cop cars to the studios. Back at the cordon, there were dozens of people staring at us.

They didn't know why they were rubber-necking, they just knew something was going on here. That was about all I knew too.

The officer in charge was a woman. She was carrying a gun, a Heckler and Koch sub-machine-gun slung across her chest. I stared at it. British police don't carry guns unless they're planning to shoot somebody specific very soon.

There was a squad more police in the foyer, and they were all armed. I was suddenly more scared of the police than I had been of confronting Mimi.

The sub-machine-gunner said she was Chief Inspector Elizabeth Gray and did I know a woman who gave only her first name and claimed to be my production assistant? And did I know the identity of her hostage, a redheaded child?

'It's Dani, it is Dani,' Louisa cried.

'That's her son. Can you explain to us what's happening exactly?'

From where we stood I couldn't see into Kerry's studio – only into Studio B, the single-operator set-up where Dan Nally was still broadcasting. He looked up and saw me through the smoked glass. I didn't see any expression on his face. He wasn't relieved to see me, he wasn't anxious, nothing. I stared back.

'At 18.30 hours the woman calling herself Mimi entered the building with the young boy,' Chief Inspector Gray informed us, 'and insisted on being given access to her work area. She achieved this by issuing threats against the child.'

'Is he all right? Has she hurt him?'

'At the present time he is unhurt but nevertheless a hostage.'

222

Again those irrelevant thoughts come crowding in, the thoughts which come with real emotional confusion. I was wondering: does this woman always talk so stilted? Even with her family? Does she talk this way in bed?

'Where is she now? Can we talk with her?'

'You should speak with a negotiator first.' She led us to the black door, the door to my studio. Two officers stood either side with their guns in both hands, like they were poised to burst in and shoot out the lights.

The door was open two inches. Gray pointed and I could see two dark outlines at Nally's desk. They were the negotiators. The studio below them was lit, but I didn't have the angle to see Mimi and Dani.

Gray spoke into the palm of her hand. She was holding a radio set the size of a silver dollar. I didn't see the earpiece till she lifted a finger to it.

'The men in there are Sergeant Powell and Inspector Dance. They will explain you are here, and one of them will come out to fetch you. In this situation we want to avoid any unannounced entrances or exits.'

One of the shadows lifted from the desk a few seconds later. Gray introduced us. He said, 'Call me Tony. Tony Dance.'

'Mimi knows we're here?'

'I've only told her about you, Mikki, at this stage.'

'Is Dani OK?' Louisa asked.

'Your son is fine. A bit scared, but bearing up well.'

'Will she let him go? Can I go in there? I can take his place.' Louisa was holding herself back from the door. She knew it would be dangerous, dangerous for Dani, if she pushed her way in. Knowing a thing doesn't make it easier to act on it.

'How long has she been here?'

'Less than thirty minutes. The security officer contacted us at 18.31. This woman works here and therefore has a front-door pass. There's a panic button, and he pushed it when she walked in with the child. Everything about her state alarmed him. If you're going to talk to her,' Dance told me, 'be prepared. She's probably different to usual. A bit scary.'

This was a woman holding a six-year-old hostage, and the police called it 'a bit scary'. But he was a negotiator, so maybe he was trained to downplay everything. He had to warn me without panicking me.

'She insisted on being given access to the studio, which I understand is where she'd normally be. The security man let her in because she

223

was threatening the child. Just threatening, not hurting. Very wisely he didn't want to push his luck.'

Dance glanced over his shoulder. Mimi was expecting me, and we were keeping her waiting.

'By the time the first police arrived, she'd already issued her basic demand, which was to see you. We arrived within five minutes. And she won't negotiate further. She says she'll only talk to you, Mikki. Which is why we asked your colleague to put out those appeals, since we didn't exactly know where to find you.'

I got the irony of that one. If I'd been good and stayed at the police station, all this might be over by now.

'Will she hand over Dani if she sees me?'

'She isn't saying. Sergeant Powell and I have tried drawing her out but she's locked into a very simple demand pattern.'

Dance talked clearly, in a flat voice. He could have been telling us the weather.

'It's essentially what we'd term a negative demand scenario. The captor wants to speak with you. She doesn't want to discuss anything with us, she doesn't have an alternative requirement, she doesn't believe you are unobtainable. She doesn't want to negotiate a safe passage, she doesn't respond to threats, she doesn't pay any attention to pleas for the child's welfare. Not that we have particular concerns, except obviously we want him out ASAP, but with her being a woman we had initial hopes of using her maternal instincts as a lever.'

'She isn't setting deadlines or anything?'

'Yes, but she seems to recognise they're impotent. We're saying, if we could find you, we'd produce you. First she said six forty-five, then seven. That deadline is about to elapse.'

'Then what?'

'She is issuing threats. Our response has been the boy has to be released. No joy there. Obviously she realises if she does that, there's nothing to stop us locking the doors, going away and leaving her to think things over for a couple of days.'

'Deadline is seven p.m.,' I said. 'And it is now—?'

'Six fifty-eight.'

'So do I go in or is it more English to have a cup of tea first?'

'Try not to let tension get the better of you,' Dance advised. He looked at Louisa. 'I'm sorry, but until we see how the land lies I think it's better you wait outside.'

'I'm going in.'

'No.'

224

I said: 'Can I explain to Dani his mother is here?'

'Not immediately. When I judge it's safe, I'll say so, or I'll signal you to say. OK? Now I want you to follow me in, say nothing unless I give you the nod, and keep your movements very low-key and relaxed.'

The production room was dark. In the studio, Mimi wouldn't see me till I got close to the glass.

She was sitting on my desk. She was wearing a red Hilfiger sports top and knee-length black cycling shorts and her legs didn't quite touch the floor. Her head was dipped and her shiny black hood of hair hung to her chin.

She looked just like Mimi. That was all. Just normal. Sitting on my studio desk, waiting for me.

Except her right hand was reached out, gripping a little redheaded boy by the wrist as he sat hunched in my swivel chair.

Across her lap a butcher's knife was balanced.

And by her left hand, against my monitor, there was a litre Coke bottle with some tubing and a Zippo at the top.

Dance pointed to the open microphone. I said, 'Hi, Mimms.'

Her face jerked up. Her hand stretched out to the Zippo.

The look in her face wasn't my Mimms. She looked sick to death and her eyes stared out of a swollen skull. She peered up into the dimness and fixed on me.

'You bastard,' she said.

'Come on, Mimi. Why don't I take you for dinner, you can insult me over pasta. Like we always do.'

'Were you sleeping with her, you bastard, when you were sleeping with me?'

I didn't look sideways at Dance. I didn't want to know what he thought I should do. I wanted Mimi to know she was talking with me, no one else. And I thought I knew best about negotiations with Mimi.

Her eyes were red-rimmed. On her red top there were dark stains. If it was Kerry's blood I wasn't going to let myself think about it now.

I said, and it was true: 'I swear to Christ, Kerry and I only started a few days ago. It was stupid, and I'm sorry. It's finished now.'

'Oh yeah,' she said grimly. 'That's right.'

Her left thumb flicked up the Zippo.

Flame spurted out, eighteen inches, pale at the base and orange at the tip. Its torpedo shape didn't flicker. Just a fat cigar of flame, burning sideways from a lighter clamped to a plastic bottle.

225

The noise was like soft blowing on a microphone.

Dani flung his arm over his eyes, though the torch was three feet from him. From his hand dangled his woolly scarecrow. He was shaking so much the chair was shivering. I was glad his mother couldn't see him. He looked so terrified it froze me.

What had he watched done with that bottle of fire? Had he stood and seen while she killed Kerry?

The flame flicked out.

'I killed her,' she said. She was staring right into my face.

'Mimi, I don't understand what's been happening, but we can get it sorted. You and me. As a team. But I need your help.'

'You understand,' she said.

'I don't, but I know you're going to help me.'

'Hasn't your college girlfriend worked it all out yet?'

'She's not my girlfriend. You're my girlfriend. That's the truth. Always in my heart, Mimms is my girlfriend. Would I lie?'

'Everything you do is a lie.'

'Not where you're concerned.'

'Mikki, I'm not going to sit and listen to your bullshit. I don't believe it anymore. Don't you understand?'

Her thumb flicked, and the flame shot out. I saw Dance gesturing minutely from the corner of my eye, but I ignored it.

I knew what I was doing. I was going to make Mimi forgive me. She liked forgiving me.

Then she'd trust me again, and she'd let Dani go.

I said, 'I don't understand yet, but I know you're going to help me.'

'It's like this,' she said, simply and tiredly. 'I killed the first two because I loved you. But I killed the last one because I hate your guts.'

CHAPTER FORTY-THREE

I repeated quietly, 'You hate my guts.' Basic cold-reading technique – play back the key phrases. It sounds like you're empathising. 'What can I do to change that?'

'Die slowly and painfully.'

'OK, maybe I deserve that, but you know, that little boy doesn't deserve to suffer.'

The flame flicked on. Off. On. Off.

'I want his mother to suffer too.'

'Mimi, I'm not sleeping with her, I'm not even trying to sleep with her. Believe me. I spin a few tales but I always tell you the truth. You know that.'

I was keeping my voice low and rhythmic. It's hard to hypnotise someone through glass, and harder if they're fiddling with a flamethrower. But I was trying.

'Everything you ever said to me was a lie. From the first day. Even before you knew who I was, you were making me believe your lies.'

'I don't understand.' I said it softly and respectfully, as an encouragement. Not a denial, not as an argument. She could say whatever she wanted, as long as it made her feel better. Until she felt well enough to let the boy free.

I saw Dani squint bewilderedly towards me, and hide his eyes again. He was looking for his mother.

'I don't hate you because you screwed Kerry. You'd sleep with a bag lady if she winked at you. That makes me pity you, it doesn't make me hate you.'

'Was it because I married Jane?'

'You're a fake. Everything you say is a lie. You tell me, "I swear to this" and "I promise that" and you don't know what it means to be honest. Even if you accidentally told the truth, you'd think you were lying.'

'But you know I really thought I had to marry Jane . . .'

'I don't give a fuck about Jane!' she screamed. 'It's nothing to do with her. You were the biggest two-faced scumbag in history, but by the time I worked out that you married her for the money, Jane was already dead. I killed her! For you!'

'That was . . .' What was I supposed to say? Thank you? 'That was incredible.'

'And then I watched you go into lying overdrive. You lie and lie and lie. And you do it so perfectly. And finally I've realised that it's what you always do. You're not psychic. You can't be. If you were psychic, you would have known last night, when we were pretending to be detectives – you would have known I killed Jane, and I killed Ingman. You're not psychic, you don't even have basic intuition.'

'You were always smart enough to catch me out,' I mumbled.

'Oh no. I fell for it. All the way. You said you were psychic, you said you could read minds, you said you could talk with the spirits . . . It was all bullshit, wasn't it, Mikki?'

'It's very complicated . . .'

'Don't keep lying, Mikki. Admit it. It's all fake.'

'Look, it's a sort of a mixture. When the little boy is out of here, I'll explain how I do most of them.'

'That's a trick too. It is. You just want me arrested.'

'I don't. But the police are here, you know that. They want to see me too. I'm in no hurry.'

'I am,' she said. She flicked off the flame. The plastic around my workstation screen was scarred and oozing. 'I won't have any fuel left soon. And then they'll come in and shoot me dead.'

'I won't let them, Mimi.'

'Lies, lies.'

'If they wanted to, they could come in and get you. That toy couldn't hurt them. They've got flameproof clothing. You know that.'

Mimi twisted Dani's arm up. He cried out.

'He hasn't,' she said.

'Come on, Mimms. You're not going to hurt a kid.'

Her hand clenched over the lighter. The flame must have seared her fingers but she didn't flinch as she lifted the bottle and turned it towards Dani.

I yelled, 'No.'

Dance's quiet voice on the studio com said, 'Put it down.'

She paused, the flame snapped off. She put the bottle down.

'Mimi,' I said, 'for Christ's sake, these guys are losing patience.

228

There's about eight people with big guns here. I can't stop them if they decide to kill you. I can't stand in front of them all.'

'Lies, lies.'

'Gospel truth, Mimi. If they think you're going to hurt the boy, they'll kill you. But if you let him out, they'll give us all the time in the world to talk things through and get them straight.'

'You can do the talking,' she said. 'As always.'

'OK. What do you want me to talk about?'

'I want you to tell everyone how you've lied to them.'

'I will,' I said glibly, because the inner meaning of her demand wasn't registering yet, 'I'll confess. I promised you that.'

'I want you to go on air and tell all the listeners you're a fake.'

OK, now I got the inner meaning.

'That's, umm. That's a big thing. That'll finish my career.' But hey, what career? I thought. And would it be so much fun without Kerry and Mimi? No, so tell Mimi 'Yes'. Then she'll let the boy go.

I said, 'Errr.'

Why? What was so hard about this? All she's asking is for me to open the microphones and tell the truth for once. She was right – even if I was totally honest it would still feel like I was lying. So what could be so hard?

What was difficult about abject humiliation?

After living with Jane Lyons, would I even notice?

'You're a coward,' she said. 'A liar and a fake and now I can see what you're really like, you're a coward too. And even when I hated you, the one thing that kept me going was thinking I could stand up to anything you could. I let you bring that woman to my flat, and I let you leave this with me –' she gestured at Dani – 'and I went and rang on Kerry's door. And all the time it would have been a lot easier to crumple.'

'I wish you had.'

I shouldn't have said it, I didn't say it loud, but I couldn't keep it in.

'Of course you wish I'd crumpled. Wouldn't that make everything easy for you now? It'll be easy soon enough again. All you've got to do is change yourself for one minute. Be everything I thought you were, just for one minute. Be brave, and be honest. Can you? Can you?'

'Sure.'

'Sure what?'

'Sure I'll go on air and tell the world I'm not a genuine psychic,

229

that it's an act, I just put it on. Who's going to be shocked? It's not such a big deal.'

'You're still lying to me.'

'This is official. This is part of your one minute of honesty. First, I've got to understand, though. What the hell was going through your head?'

'When I made this flame thing? When I killed that professor? And your women? You were. You were going through my head.'

'I never wanted you to do those things? Did I act like I did?'

'I thought at first you knew it was me, and you were pretending you didn't.'

'I don't get that. Sorry.'

'No. No, I always have to spell things out for you. Spoonfeed you.'

For a moment she sounded like my old Mimi.

'I always need you to look after me,' I said. 'Give it to me in easy soundbites.'

'You were married,' she said. 'Remember?'

'I'm not likely to forget.'

'And I took a call. After a show, when you'd been married about two weeks. The caller was very mysterious, and he wanted to speak to you and you only, but I thought he might be a crank and I didn't want to let him near you at first.'

My old guard-dog. It sounded like she'd forgotten to hate my guts for a minute.

'He said he had information about shares you didn't know you had. His name was Lucas, and I met him at a big hall on Southampton Row.'

'Where you met Madox Bligh, who told you about Jane's fabulous wealth, right?'

'They'd found out she was married to a psychic, and they all hated her last husband and they were scared he might close them down, so they wanted you to use your shares. I said I was Kerry.'

'And you wore a blonde wig. Why?'

'So they would trust me.'

'Because they'd heard her name on the radio but not yours? I don't imagine Madox Bligh was much fazed by media reputations. He didn't seem to like mine.'

'He was a pompous old idiot, and he couldn't keep his good hand to himself. But I had to be Kerry, don't you understand? Because you dumped me. If Madox Bligh knew that, he'd think I didn't have

230

any influence over you at all. If I was just the tarty little production assistant who got dumped.'

Whatever she said about believing in me or not believing in me, this was at the heart of it. I'd dumped her. And despite what I thought, she hadn't forgiven me.

Louisa would say this theory was just placing myself at the centre of the universe again.

'So I told them I was Kerry, I wore my wig, and I behaved myself properly because I had to keep up a good reputation for Miss Nice Knickers. Every morning, accidentally on purpose, I put through one call from one of Bligh's workers, trying to persuade you to go along. If you'd ever had the brains to do that, you'd have found out how much your shares were worth. But instead of that, you went for Ingman and his £5,000. Which was as fake as you are.'

'You helped set me up for that?'

'No! I wouldn't ever have done anything to trick you. I'd heard his name at the Institute, and I thought he was going to blurt out something about Jane. Or the shares.'

'Why didn't you just tell me about the money?'

'You'd have thought I was after some of it.'

'I'd never think anything like that of you, Mimms.'

'Lies, lies. I'd learned all sorts of things at the Institute. One was never to go straight after something you want. They wouldn't need to tell you that, of course. Your middle name is Devious. But I'd found out all about that particular mistake, wanting something and making it obvious what you want. If I'd been more devious with you, perhaps you'd never have dumped me. I just made it too easy for you.'

Was there some truth in that? Maybe.

'Whereas Jane, who was three times my age and ten times uglier, was also a hundred times more devious. So she had you nicely in her net.'

What was there to say? This was like radio – any silence was a bad thing. I said, 'Jane used to sleep with Madox Bligh. A long time ago.'

'Oh, I learned a lot of fascinating information from that man. He had repeated visions of fire. Especially when he was getting over his stroke. He saw his enemies being consumed by fire. What was really strange was his enemies were your enemies. Jane Lyons and Professor Ingman.'

'So you began to believe I might really be marked down by the angels to lead this cult of his?'

231

'You'd be a wonderful religious leader. Much better than Bligh. Better than Jesus . . . that's what I thought, until I hated you.'

'What else did they teach you? How to construct a flamethrower?'

'They were all making them, after Bligh got his visions.'

I remembered him saying, 'It is possible my sermons may be misinterpreted.'

'They downloaded plans off the Internet. It's perfectly simple – a few pints of lighter fuel in here, and this tube is kept pinched shut until you flick the Zippo.'

The flame sighed alive.

'We'd like you to put that out. For your own safety and the child's', said Dance. He sounded totally relaxed, totally calm.

Mimi gazed into the production area for the voice, but he had stepped back into darkness. I was the only one she could see. That must mean they trusted me. That must mean they thought I could get Mimi and Dani out safely.

She let the hood clip forward. The flame snuffed out.

'You couldn't kill anyone with this,' she said. 'It's not dangerous really.'

'Are you being serious?'

'I had to knife all of them first.'

'I'm glad to know that. I think.'

'Your wife was difficult. She was much bigger than me, and she put up a fight. Even though she was asleep when I stabbed her.'

'You killed her when she was asleep?'

'Do you want me to explain this properly? At the Institute they used to have all these tramps coming in, and we killed one of them. Lucas and me and a couple of the other boys there. I've been sleeping with Lucas. Does that make you jealous? No, you wouldn't understand jealousy, would you, Mikki? It's an emotion, it involves feeling something for another person.'

'You killed a bum?'

'To find out what it felt like. How it felt to kill him, and how it felt to fulfil Lord Bligh's prophecy.'

'The one about his enemies being consumed in flames? So how was this bum an enemy?'

'They were always hanging round. Leeching off the people there. He wasn't a real enemy. Lucas is into nasty sex – much nastier than anything you could think of. Nastier than I ever dreamed of, even. I've been doing some things that would shock you, Mikki.'

232

This much I had worked out already. But I didn't have to say anything. She was talking fast and loud.

'Burning the body turned Lucas on very much. I was sick at first, but after an hour or two I started to break down my prejudices. It's always like that. At first you can't see anything but sick sex. Then there's a lot of pain, or fear, and then your inhibitions start to go. I know I could have turned you on to a lot of things, Mikki, if you were only a tiny bit adventurous.'

'You enjoyed seeing this bum burn too?'

'We torched him till there wasn't a lump left the size of a penny. And yes, that was an amazing trip. Very liberating. There was something else I had to be grateful to the tramps for. I found out all the best places to go when you're down and out. So when Ingman rang up wanting you to go to Queensberry Place, it was very useful to know I could walk in any time I liked if I put rags on. Open house for tramps. That was useful. I spent a whole evening as a tramp.'

'This was Friday?'

'The day before yesterday. I wanted to steal your results. I wanted to make them look better, if I could.'

'I had the same great idea.'

'I didn't know Ingman was plotting against you then. I hung around for ages outside. You never saw me. Then I wandered in, pretending I was seeing Professor Stanley, and I passed Ingman and your girlfriend. She wasn't your girlfriend yet.'

'Still isn't. I told you that.'

'Lies. lies. And I heard them laughing about you. How badly you'd done. What a fake you were. And do you know what – I didn't believe it even then. But I did believe that Madox Bligh's enemies and your enemies were the same. And I saw it as one more proof that you were destined to lead the Institute. You would be Lord Bligh's chosen son. So I went home for a nice big knife, I went to the Institute for this apparatus –' she flicked the flame on, off – 'and I caught a cab to Baker Street. In my tramp's gear. I told the cabbie I was an actress.'

Dani moaned and struggled to free his legs, which were cramped under him.

Mimi, who was still holding his wrist, said, 'Shut up!' She didn't look at the boy. His little wool scarecrow was hanging in despair. He didn't even have the energy to hug it.

CHAPTER FORTY-FOUR

I said, 'Mimms, this is a very long one minute. Why don't I come in and we'll let the boy out?'

'Don't try and twist me. Not after everything you promised. Not when I've got my knife. And there's still a lot left in my big Coke bottle.'

'You keep talking,' urged Dance's voice from the darkness. 'No one's coming in till you're good and ready. Why not let the lad sit comfortably now?'

Mimi ignored him. She never let go of Dani's wrist.

'How did you find Ingman's apartment?'

'Bligh knew the address.'

'Did he know what you were intending to do?'

'Of course. He's a real mindreader. He can do everything you pretend. Even though he's a horrid, lecherous old cripple. At least he's not a liar.'

'Sure,' I said.

'Bligh understood. Your enemy was his enemy, and would be consumed in flames. Only I didn't have much idea how to go about it. I had to hang around ages before I could sneak past the doorman.'

'How did you kill him?'

'He was really helpful. I thought it would be pretty sickening, but it's so easy. A child could do it. And Ingman explained it all first.'

'He told you how to kill him?'

'He opened the door and I put the point of the blade straight under his chin and tried to stare at him with the most menacing face I could manage. I expect he was pretty frightened.'

'I expect he was.'

'And I waved the burner at him, and I said, "You're a professor. What's the most painless way to kill someone?"'

'Ingman said, "I am not a professor of medicine," and I tried to be all cool and smart like you are, so I said, "You'd better become

234

one, or I might kill you very painfully by accident." And he started gabbling about a knife thrust straight up through the jaw into the brain, which wasn't very clever of him, because if he'd told me to stab him through the heart I would have had to move the blade and then he might have overpowered me.

'Then I told him a lie. I said, "If you tell me what happens medically when a corpse burns, I won't kill you." My God, he did talk. He talked and talked, and there was sweat running down his face onto the knife. You cannot fantasize a feeling like it. Like an orgasm that goes on, and on, and on, growing and growing, filling out every inch of me. To have such power over this man, that I could make him tell me how to kill him and then describe to me how his corpse would be destroyed. It was like sex ripping apart every thought in my brain. Mind-fucking. He told me everything you could imagine about what happens to a body when you set fire to it. All of it accurate, I proved later. How the water in your body stops the flesh burning as soon as a direct flame is taken away. How the body fat melts, especially in women, as he said, and soaks into the clothes and creates a human candle. What the smell would be like and how there would be grease on the windows and how long before a body completely burned to ash.'

I was close to running out screaming. I had to keep talking with her, just to stabilise my fear. 'It was kind of his speciality,' I said.

'Funny, that,' said Mimi. 'Synchronicity, that's what you'd tell your listeners. Yes?'

'Yes.'

'And then, in the middle of a sentence, I killed him. Just stuck the knife straight up into his head. It was ever so easy, just like he described. Instant and painless. There he was, dead. That was the culmination. You think you know what it's like when I orgasm, right, Mikki? You have no idea. *No idea*. I know why serial killers go back and kill again, and again. It's sex. Sex and death – the same thing. And I sat down next to his body and burnt it to ash. It took about two hours, and there was a hell of a smell by the end. I was getting a bit careless and I set fire to some curtains, and I could hardly see through the smoke to wrap the embers up in some of his zipper-up suit covers and put them in a big suitcase I found in his bedroom. But there weren't any smoke alarms, and the moron in a uniform had long gone home by the time I walked out of the foyer, and I got straight into a taxi, said I was an actress again and went straight to Queensberry Place.'

'Why?'

'Because I was still in love with you then, stupid.'

'Tell me what you were thinking. Tell me why he had to be taken so carefully to the university.'

'Well, that's where he tricked you. His office. That's where he laughed about you. I expect that's where he phoned Jane to tell her about your tests and what a fake her new husband was. I couldn't kill him there, but I could at least make it look that way.'

'You really went to a lot of trouble.'

'As always. And then, when I'd laid all the bits out cleverly on the carpet and sneaked back outside – loads of people saw me but it's so totally normal for tramps to be wandering through that place on a Friday night – who did I almost bump into?'

'Me,' I guessed.

'You!' she said triumphantly. She was enjoying her story. Getting it off her chest. She'd probably find, by the end, that she'd forgotten why she was ever mad at me.

'I hid in a doorway, and I was sure you recognised me, because you stared, but I covered my face. And I thought, that's so typical. You're just getting round to doing something for yourself, and I've sorted everything out in advance. By the time you think it, I've done it. You just couldn't last a day without me. I watched you go in. Then I realised you were being followed. That horrid detective from the pasta restaurant. So I knew you'd find the body, and I thought you'd phone the police and be stuck for hours. And your follower would be stuck too. So it was a very good time to finish off the business and kill your other enemy.'

'You just decided on the spot? No plans?'

'I'd got all the stuff with me. The burner, a spare bottle of butane, the knife. There'd never be a better moment. And no one could accuse you, because I knew you'd be the natural suspect, being her husband, but you'd be with the police. Good alibi. So I let myself in with the spare key, which was exactly where you said you kept it.'

'I told you that?'

'When you first moved in with her. You said, "Remember where the spare key is, in case I forget."'

It occurred to me I'd treated Mimi a little like Ingman had treated Louisa.

'You remember everything,' I said.

'One of us has to. I opened the door. Jane was sleeping as I said. I stabbed her. Only her throat was rather fat and I didn't push hard enough, and she put up quite a fight. I was kneeling on her chest and there was blood going everywhere, but she wouldn't let me stab her again. She wouldn't.'

'She was very stubborn,' I said.

'Luckily she got weak from losing all that blood, and I got to finish her off. But it was much worse for both of us than it should have been. I didn't enjoy it nearly as much, and I was so angry with her when she was dead. I pulled off her ring and stuffed it in her mouth, and I set to burning her with a real vengeance. I spent hours at it. Then all of a sudden I panicked. Perhaps it was getting to first light, and I realised how long I'd been with the body. I'd almost finished, but not quite. It didn't look as good as Ingman's.'

'Up all night. So that story about your brother's children, that was all lies.'

'That happened, just as I told you. I never lie to you. It happened on a different night, that's all.'

'A white lie,' I said.

'I washed and washed to get the smell off me. I can still smell it now, or maybe that's the gas in this thing. Then I hid the clothes in Kerry's drawer, here.'

'I found them. Why her?'

'I was toying with the idea of making the police think she was the killer. After all, I'd used her name with Madox Bligh. And plenty of people had seen me dressed as a tramp, with a blonde wig and tinted sunglasses to hide my eyes. And I was sure she wouldn't have an alibi. Can you believe it, I decided that wouldn't be fair on her. If I'd known then . . . But I wasn't mad at her till you came round last night with your girlfriend and her son. This boy,' she said, jerking his wrist, as though she suddenly remembered his existence.

'Where was he when you killed Kerry?'

'That took a lot of courage. I had to work myself up for hours before I could knock on her door. I wanted to do it, and then I didn't want to. But it's like I said – you've got to push aside your prejudices and break down your inhibitions, and then you get the real experience. In the end it was possible because I hated you so much.'

'I never wanted you to be hurt,' I said lamely.

'Lies, lies. You dumped me, then you cheated on Jane with Kerry. *With Kerry*. And then, on her doorstep, she was so surprised to see me, and she was dead before her expression changed. I wasn't going to make the same mistake with her. I pushed the knife in very, very hard.'

'Where was Dani?' I repeated.

Mimi shrugged. 'Holding my hand. But I made him stay in the bathroom while I used the burner. We couldn't hang around long. I wanted to tell you what I'd done. But you didn't look surprised. Did you already know? Or was it psychic?'

'I found her body.'

'Was she still burning? That's Ingman's candle effect, it really works.'

I always thought madness was wild laughter and staring eyes and jerky movements. But Mimi's eyes, which had been glassy and bulging when she started to speak, were normal now. Her gestures were normal. She wasn't laughing, she was just Mimi. My good old Mimi. As if I could ever cope without her.

CHAPTER FORTY-FIVE

M imi said, 'Your turn.'
     'For what?'
'Your turn to talk.'
'I'm a bit – shocked. Shocked is the word.'
'We made a pact. It's your turn for talking now.'
'OK. But you've left me kind of speechless.'
'Don't twist me. I told you.' She was fidgeting with that Zippo.
'Mimi, I would never twist you.'
'You promised.'
'And I meant it. Listen, Mimms, we're still a team. We need each
other most now. Kind of. I mean, you were trying to do all that stuff
for me. Even though I think you know now I never wanted it.'
'If you were psychic, you would have known. You would have
read what was in my mind. And you always said you could.'
'That was a game. Fun.'
'You're going to go on the radio and tell the world what a lying
faking cheater you are.'
'We could get married. Mimi.' This was desperate, but give me
credit. I wanted the boy out of there. 'I'm a free man now.'
'If I stop hating you,' she said slowly, 'I'll marry you. But if you try
and twist out of admitting you're a fake, and you never were psychic
. . . I'm going to hate you for ever.'
'I'll confess,' I said. 'I promised, and I'll stick to it. That's my side
of the bargain. But we'll have to time it.'
'Do it now.'
'Come on, Mimms. You know radio. Can I just cut into whatever
Dan's playing now and say, "This is a public announcement"?'
'Yes.'
'No! It's got to be on my show. Grant me that privilege. Let me
tell it to my own listeners.'
'You're twisting me.'

'My listeners, I owe it to them.'

'Lies,' she shouted, 'lies!'

The flame flashed from the plastic bottle. She twisted it towards Dani.

I felt a lurch behind me. Men with guns. They were out of my vision, but I felt them like a dark, dead surge. Like the beating of the wings of the angel of death.

I flung my arms out and yelled, 'No!'

I really don't know who I was shouting to – the armed police or Mimi. I don't know. Maybe I was shouting out at God to stop this.

Mimi had pulled the woollen toy from Dani's hand and was playing a jet of flame into its head. When I screamed she cut the flame short. The scarecrow was a charred body in her hand, with a spray of bubbled black fibres where its orange head had been.

The boy was lying face down on the floor, wailing.

The angels of death were ranged either side of me with the Heckler and Kochs drawn up. It looked to me like the safeties were off. If they opened fire now there would be splinters of thick glass right across the studio, and who could say where the ricocheting bullets would hit? Surely to God they couldn't fire.

But if Mimi did that again, they were going to.

I said, 'Open the mikes. I'll say whatever you want me to. And then you and the boy are out of there. Deal? Mimi?'

She looked down at Dani and said, 'Shut up.' He knew what her voice meant, and the sobbing stopped.

The red lights over the desk snapped on. I took two steps left, telling Mimi as I did it: 'I'm fixing Dan's faders. OK? And we're on. Before I start talking, I want that boy out here now.'

'No twisting.'

I stared at her for a long moment. But any kind of silence is bad silence on radio. Even tension silence.

I said: 'Good evening, my name's Mikki and if you're a listener to PrimeTime on weekday mornings we'll have met before. I'm Kerry Allison's favourite psychic.'

I stopped. There was an unexpected thickness in my voice. What was I going to do, cry? Was crying a good way to avoid the discomfort of this broadcast? All that smoke in my eyes this weekend hadn't made me cry. If I started now, would Mimi believe me?

I glanced at the child on my studio floor. I wasn't going to crack up. Not yet.

I pretended to be studying the output meters.

'So a colleague has asked me to clear up a little point. About my powers. But before I do that, I should tell you how I got this job. I was in New York, which is such a great place if you've got dough in your wallet, and I didn't. I'd been trying various business ideas, which were based on the idea I liked to tell people I was psychic. I guess I'm not psychic. Not like you might imagine. I'm not magic. I don't talk to ghosts and if you've heard me do that, I'm pretending. It's a game. Fun. Not harmful. It helps people. But it's an illusion.'

I looked across at Mimi. She was staring at me like she couldn't believe I was saying it. I never could understand why she didn't see straight through me from day one. But now, it was plain, she couldn't see through me even when she was accusing me that every word I ever said was a lie. It was somehow that the logical part of her brain was on permanent holiday where my psychic powers were concerned. She could know one thing, and believe the opposite.

And now I was shattering the illusion. I could tell in her face she didn't like it. And it was too late to stop.

'So I had a good natal horoscope scam running, that's where you send me twenty bucks and your birthdate, and my computer does you a nice print-out of what the stars hold for you. Only the computer got a virus, which is to say a customer became deeply dissatisfied, and I decided personal readings were going to be much more lucrative.'

I wanted to smoke. I desperately wanted to. When I was in New York, I was smoking thirty, forty a day. Very rebellious, smoking, in America nowadays. Just the right dissipated image for a dangerously mysterious psychic.

No one can see you smoking on the radio. If there'd been a packet in reach, I would have opened it. There wasn't.

'I started charging for readings at parties, I organised psychic get-togethers, someone invited me on a Brooklyn radio station and pretty soon I was a fixture. I discovered I was good at radio, because I love it. I love the way my voice sounds to you now. If that sounds conceited, well, I'm not trying to make you like me today. This is supposed to be a confession.'

I looked at Mimi. She was still in shock. I could have walked in and prised that burner out of her hand, and I wish I had. But I was broadcasting now.

'I was a celebrity. This meant I could charge more. Suddenly I had dough in that wallet, and New York was the best place it had ever been. Obviously I blew it. It wouldn't be my style, to live happily ever after. What I did was, there were these brothers. The Benji brothers. They were my age, mid-twenties, but these boys were big successes.

241

Rode Porsches, rode BMWs, one of them rode a left-hand-drive Lotus Elan. Canary-yellow. Very cool boys. And what they did wasn't legal. I don't know what it was, exactly, because whenever I saw them it slipped my mind to ask, but it definitely was not painting and decorating for invalid old ladies.'

I was neck-deep in my story now. I can't recall if what I said was exactly the truth. Some of it may have been embellished. I definitely remember making up that fact about the canary-yellow Lotus. But the general feel was on target.

'One day, a car pulls up outside the station. I'm being summoned. Big black limo, two guys in reflector shades and midnight-black suits get out. They come to the desk. They want Mikki to go for a ride with them. Security tries to claim I'm not in the building, but these boys don't take No for an answer, ever. So I'm fetched, and I get taken for a trip, and where I end up is not the bottom of the Hudson but the top of a skyscraper. In the Benji brothers' executive suite.

'The oldest of them, Reuben, sits across a big, big desk from me, and he throws me a newspaper. There's a racing guide, and four names are ringed. And then he hands me a piece of paper with the four names and some dates. He says, "These are the horse's birthdates. Get me their full astrological readings by midnight, and tell me which one is going to win." He thinks if a guy is psychic enough, he can spot a horse by its starsign.

'What this was from the Benji brothers was not a request, it was an order. Bizarre, but so what? I told them it would be hard, without knowing exactly what time the horses were born, but I could do my best. So naturally I revived the computer programme and printed twenty pages of emotional analysis for these horses, and then I took a guess that the third one on the list was going to win. The bad thing was, it did.

'Not only that, but so did the next one and the next one. And the next one. And so on, for a week, and I couldn't get it wrong, even when I switched off the computer and just pointed at the racing page with my eyes shut. And it turned out that at first the Benji brothers had been having a joke on me, but when my horses kept winning, they started taking me seriously. No joke, predicting six winners in a row.

'On the seventh day, they gave me fifty thousand bucks. That was mine, I could put as much of it on a horse as I wanted. And they were going to bet everything, their grandmother's heirlooms and their sisters' trustfunds and everything they could hock, even the canary-yellow Lotus, it was all going on the next horse I predicted.

'I believed I couldn't fail. They believed I couldn't fail. I picked the horse. It was called Solomon's Child. It ran last.

'You'd think maybe the brothers would see the dumb side. No one can be right for ever. And after all, I'd lost everything they gave me. I bet the whole fifty Gs. But I didn't keep the betting slip, and do you know, they didn't completely believe me when I said the money was gone. They wanted it back. Said I shouldn't have spent it until I'd proved it was honestly earned. In other words, till my horse came home first.

'They were very unhappy about everything but especially they put some emphasis on getting that $50,000 back. They weren't going to ask where I raised it, they were just anxious to collect. So for six months I paid interest on it, very high interest, interest that made me understand how the Benji brothers got rich to begin with. And it got so I couldn't meet the payments. They wanted $5,000 from me, and I managed to scrape $199, which got me a bucket flight to London. And I hoped very much they wouldn't hear about me. But when the only way you can make a living is to talk on the radio, I guess it's hard to keep a low profile. They found me, they started phoning me with menaces. That was about the time I got married. But you don't need to hear the rest. You can read it in the papers.

'The point I want you to understand is, this is proof positive I am a fake. OK? I have been asked to say this, and I'm saying it. I'm a fraud, a cheat, I make it up. I am not psychic. I didn't used to think psychic even existed, but I'm not so sure now. Weird things happen. But I'm promising you this, I don't make them happen.'

I looked at Mimi. 'Is that OK? Plain enough?'

She shook her head.

I mean, Christ! What more could I tell the people?

'Finish your story,' she said.

'The voice you just heard,' I said, 'is my production assistant. She helped me seem psychic. And I don't think she knew I'd be a lost cause without her. My unwitting accomplice. And Kerry Allison, she never knew I was faking. I don't think she ever believed either way. She just knew good radio when she heard it.

'I listened to her programme when I first came to England and I rang her and persuaded her to let me try out on her show. It was a good phone call – I laid all the tricks on her. It's called cold reading, and I don't have time to explain it all to you now. Another time. I'll

243

write it down and all you at home listening, you can buy my book, OK? Because I'm going to need a job. Anyhow, after the first time I talked with her, Kerry thought either I was her long lost brother who grew up with her and knew every family secret, or I was the greatest psychic of the age. And whichever way, she wanted me on her show. She insisted, and she kept insisting till she got me five days a week. She was a great professional.'

So that was my tribute to Kerry. I didn't have the heart to tell the people listening she was dead.

I shut off the mike.

I didn't say anything to Mimi, I just looked at her. It was time to come out now.

She kept flicking that flame, little spurts, puff-puff-puff.

Then she opened her mouth, a big wide black 'O', and pointed the flame inside.

She screamed, and one of the police threw himself at the door, but she held the Zippo wide open, and that blue-and-orange flame was roaring into her mouth. It was a scream like a demon bursting out of the pit of her stomach, out of her soul, up through her lungs and her throat to be blazed into nothing by the flaming butane. A purging, purifying shriek, the sound of a damned spirit escaping into destruction. And she was still screaming as she fell sideways off the desk, and then the screaming stopped.

The bottle split and the butane came spilling out over the carpet tiles and ignited. The police officer scooped Dani off the floor as the flames rippled out, and hugged him to his chest as he carried him past me. I was pushing my way in, into the studio. Dani's face was white and his green eyes were the image of his mother's. That thought hit me even as I was stepping down onto the flaming studio floor. Another of those meaningless, trivial thoughts.

I scrambled over to Mimi, who was face down on the burning carpet. Dance was behind me and we dragged her to the door. The flames were only ankle high, and though later I saw my boots were mostly burned away, it was weird, because the fire didn't feel hot. It felt cold. Dead cold.

Chapter Forty-Six

Outside, Dani was in his mother's arms. She was sobbing into his shoulder, and he had his arms clutched round her head. I wanted to go and hold them, but I had the feeling that if I did that, I wouldn't ever be able to let them go.

The air in the foyer was thick with cigarette smoke. I waved aside Chief Inspector Gray as she came up. I didn't know if she wanted to arrest me, congratulate me, deport me. I didn't care a damn. There was a guy right by the door, and I said to him, 'Got a smoke?'

He must have been a newsman. He wanted to know, 'Mikki, what are your emotions right now?' and I was conscious of a TV camera crew closing in.

I said, 'I feel like a smoke.' And then, 'Got a light?'

What he pulled out was a Zippo light, and he flicked up the flame right there in my face.

It had an effect on me.

I took the cigarette in my fist and ground it into the wall behind me. Then I strode over to Louisa and Dani and I wrapped both my arms around them. She pressed her face into my neck, and she was shaking, but there was no sound of crying. Just trembling. I led the two of them towards the door. I've never felt that protective towards anyone. I haven't stopped feeling this way since. Maybe it's because no woman ever needed me in remotely this way before.

It must have made good television, the three of us, holding on like that. So what? I'm a radio man.

And I still am a radio man, though naturally the psychic shenanigans belong strictly to the past. I'm a producer now. More pay, better title, and I still get to do a show on Sunday nights. Dan Nally walked out of PrimeTime after that Sunday and didn't come back. I got his office. Suitable reward, said everyone, though I never figured for what.

The extra pay is useful, now I'm having to earn for Louisa and Dani. Louisa's going to turn up another researcher's job – they're

245

hard to come by, but that girl's got qualifications, and a brain. Two things no one is going to claim for me.

I got the £30,000 Jane had always promised me. She was very thorough with her lawyers. All the rest of her fortune, the apartment included, went to Ambrose Lyons's family. About £75 million. I had no idea there was that much in her purse, else I would have held out originally for a lot more than £30,000. But it translated nicely to $50,000, which meant I could send a money order to the Benji brothers and start saving for airline tickets to New York State. Return tickets. I'd just like to show Louisa what a real city looks like.

Mimi took a week to die. It was unpleasant. I made myself go and see her in hospital, but she wasn't conscious. Madox Bligh died before she did. I hope there's an afterlife, and I hope he's suffering in it. And the grinning weirdo, Lucas, the guy who twisted Mimi's mind with strange sex, he's in jail. Waiting to be tried for murder.

It's good to have my own show. Obviously I made it a phone-in. But not psychic. Strictly current affairs, which means whatever you want it to mean. Only not psychic. So don't ring me, asking for a consultation with the spirits, or some guidance with your lovelife, or a peek at your financial future.

Because you'll be wasting your call. I don't do that stuff anymore. As if.